THE BEST HORROR OF THE YEAR

VOLUME SEVEN

Also Edited by Ellen Datlow

A Whisper of Blood
A Wolf at the Door (with Terri Windling)
After (with Terri Windling)
Alien Sex
Black Heart, Ivory Bones (with Terri Windling)
Black Swan, White Raven (with Terri Windling)
Black Thorn, White Rose (with Terri Windling)
Blood Is Not Enough: 17 Stories of Vampirism
Blood and Other Cravings
Darkness: Two Decades of Modern Horror
Digital Domains: A Decade of Science Fiction and Fantasy
Fearful Symmetries
Haunted Legends (with Nick Mamatas)
Hauntings
Inferno: New Tales of Terror and the Supernatural
Lethal Kisses
Little Deaths
Lovecraft Unbound
Lovecraft's Monsters
Naked City: Tales of Urban Fantasy
Nebula Awards Showcase 2009
Nightmare Carnival
Off Limits: Tales of Alien Sex
Omni Best Science Fiction: Volumes One through Three
Omni Books of Science Fiction: Volumes One through Seven
OmniVisions One and Two
Poe: 19 New Tales Inspired by Edgar Allan Poe
Queen Victoria's Book of Spells (with Terri Windling)
Ruby Slippers, Golden Tears (with Terri Windling)
Salon Fantastique: Fifteen Original Tales of Fantasy (with Terri Windling)
Silver Birch, Blood Moon (with Terri Windling)
Sirens and Other Daemon Lovers (with Terri Windling)
Snow White, Blood Red (with Terri Windling)
Supernatural Noir
Swan Sister (with Terri Windling)
Tails of Wonder and Imagination: Cat Stories
Teeth: Vampire Tales (with Terri Windling)
Telling Tales: The Clarion West 30th Anniversary Anthology
The Beastly Bride: And Other Tales of the Animal People (with Terri Windling)
The Best Horror of the Year: Volumes One through Six
The Beastly Bride: Tales of the Animal People
The Coyote Road: Trickster Tales (with Terri Windling)
The Cutting Room: Dark Reflections of the Silver Screen
The Dark: New Ghost Stories
The Del Rey Book of Science Fiction and Fantasy
The Doll Collection
The Faery Reel: Tales from the Twilight Realm
The Green Man: Tales of the Mythic Forest (with Terri Windling)
Troll's Eye View: A Book of Villainous Tales (with Terri Windling)
Twists of the Tale
Vanishing Acts
The Year's Best Fantasy and Horror: First Annual Collection to Sixteenth Annual Collection (with Terri Windling)
The Year's Best Fantasy and Horror: Seventeenth Annual Collection to Twenty-First Annual Collection (with Gavin J. Grant and Kelly Link)

THE BEST HORROR OF THE YEAR

VOLUME SEVEN

EDITED BY ELLEN DATLOW

NIGHT SHADE BOOKS
NEW YORK

Night Shade books may be purchased in bulk at special discounts for sales promotion, corporate gifts, fund-raising, or educational purposes. Special editions can also be created to specifications. For details, contact the Special Sales Department, Night Shade Books, 307 West 36th Street, 11th Floor, New York, NY 10018 or info@skyhorsepublishing.com.

Night Shade Books™ is a trademark of Skyhorse Publishing, Inc. ®, a Delaware corporation.

Visit our website at www.nightshadebooks.com.

10 9 8 7 6 5 4 3 2 1

Library of Congress Cataloging-in-Publication Data is available on file.

Interior layout and design by Amy Popovich
Cover illustration by Noia Hokama

Print ISBN: 978-1-59780-829-3

Printed in the United States of America

ACKNOWLEDGMENTS

I'd like to thank Kristine Dikeman for being my first reader.

Also, thanks to Peter Tennant for being a careful reader and letting me know my slip was showing and to Dave Truesdale for his recommendation.

I'd like to acknowledge *Locus* and the *British Fantasy Society Journal* for their invaluable information and descriptions of material I was unable to obtain. Thanks to the editors who made sure I saw your magazines during the year, the webzine editors who provided printouts and efiles, and the book publishers who provided review copies in a timely manner. Also, the writers who sent me your stories when I was unable to acquire the magazine or book in which they appeared.

Thanks to Merrilee Heifetz and Sarah Nagel at Writers House.

And thank you to my in-house editor, Jason Katzman, for his patience.

Table of Contents

SUMMATION 2014

First, here are some numbers: There are twenty-two stories and novelettes in this year's volume. They were chosen from magazines, webzines, anthologies, single-author collections, and an author's monthly digest distributed by email. Four of the stories are by writers living in England, two are by writers living in Australia, two are by writers living in Canada, and fourteen are by writers living in the United States.

Four stories are over 9,500 words, the longest is 10,000 words. The shortest is 2,500 words.

The authors of nine stories have never appeared in previous volumes of my year's best. Thirteen stories are by men, nine stories are by women.

There are a few writers who seem to be on an especially consistent roll with regard to the amount of top-notch short fiction they've been producing in the last year or two: Caitlín R. Kiernan deservedly won two World Fantasy Awards for work published in 2013: short story and collection. Her dense, brilliant sf/horror novella "Black Helicopters" was also nominated. In 2014, in addition to the story reprinted herein, she had at least two other brilliant stories and a number of others that were really good. It was difficult to choose only one. John Langan is not prolific, but had exceptional work published in 2014. One, a novella, was too long for me to reprint. Other writers who had multiple important stories published during the year are Gemma Files, Carole Johnstone, Stephen Graham Jones, and Livia Llewellyn.

AWARDS

The Horror Writers Association announced the winners of the 2013 Bram Stoker Awards® on May 10, 2014, at the Doubletree Hotel in Portland, Oregon. The presentations were made at a banquet held as the highlight of the Bram Stoker Awards Weekend, which in 2013 incorporated the World Horror Convention. The winners:

Superior Achievement in a Novel: *Doctor Sleep* by Stephen King (Scribner); Superior Achievement in a First Novel: *The Evolutionist* by Rena Mason (Nightscape Press); Superior Achievement in a Young Adult Novel: *Dog Days* by Joe McKinney (JournalStone); Superior Achievement in a Graphic Novel: *Alabaster: Wolves* by Caitlín R. Kiernan (Dark Horse Comics); Superior Achievement in Long Fiction: "The Great Pity" by Gary Braunbeck (*Chiral Mad 2, Written Backwards*); Superior Achievement in Short Fiction: "Night Train to Paris" by David Gerrold (*The Magazine of Fantasy & Science Fiction*, Jan./Feb. 2013); Superior Achievement in a Screenplay: *The Walking Dead: Welcome to the Tombs* by Glen Mazzara (AMC-TV); Superior Achievement in an Anthology: *After Death . . .* edited by Eric J. Guignard (Dark Moon Books); Superior Achievement in a Fiction Collection: *The Beautiful Thing That Awaits Us All and Other Stories* by Laird Barron (Night Shade Books); Superior Achievement in Nonfiction: *Nolan on Bradbury: Sixty Years of Writing about the Master of Science Fiction* by William F. Nolan (Hippocampus Press); Superior Achievement in a Poetry Collection: *Four Elements* by Marge Simon, Rain Graves, Charlee Jacob, and Linda Addison (Bad Moon Books/ Evil Jester Press).

The Specialty Press Award: Gray Friar Press, Whitby, UK.

The Richard Layman President's Award: J. G. Faherty.

The Silver Hammer Award: Norman Rubenstein.

Life Achievement Awards: R. L. Stine and Stephen Jones.

The Shirley Jackson Award, recognizing the legacy of Jackson's writing and, with the permission of her estate, was established for outstanding achievement in the literature of psychological suspense, horror, and the dark fantastic. The awards were announced at Readercon 23, July 14, 2013, held in Burlington, Massachusetts. Jurors were Kelly Link, Jack Haringa, Chesya Burke, Paul Witcover, and Graham Sleight.

The winners for the best work in 2012: Novel: *American Elsewhere*, Robert Jackson Bennett (Orbit); Novella: "Burning Girls," Veronica Schanoes (Tor.com, June 2013); Novelette: "Cry Murder! In a Small Voice," Greer Gilman (Small Beer Press); Short Story: "57 Reasons for the Slate Quarry Suicides," Sam J. Miller (Nightmare Magazine, December 2013); Single-Author Collection: *Before and Afterlives*, Christopher Barzak (Lethe Press) and *North American Lake Monsters*, Nathan Ballingrud (Small Beer Press); Edited Anthology: *Grimscribe's Puppets*, edited by Joseph S. Pulver, Sr. (Miskatonic River Press).

The World Fantasy Awards were presented November 9, 2014, at a banquet held during the World Fantasy Convention in Arlington, Virginia. The Lifetime Achievement recipients, Ellen Datlow and Chelsea Quinn Yarbro, were previously announced.

The judges were Andy Duncan, Kij Johnson, Oliver Johnson, John Klima, and Liz Williams.

Winners for the best work in 2013: Novel: *A Stranger in Olondria* by Sofia Samatar (Small Beer Press); Novella: "Wakulla Springs," Andy Duncan and Ellen Klages (Tor.com); Short Fiction: "The Prayer of Ninety Cats," Caitlín R. Kiernan (*Subterranean Magazine*); Anthology: *Dangerous Women*, George R. R. Martin and Gardner Dozois, eds. (Tor Books/Voyager UK); Collection: *The Ape's Wife and Other Stories*, Caitlín R. Kiernan (Subterranean Press); Artist: Charles Vess; Special Award: Professional: Irene Gallo for art direction of Tor.com, William K. Schafer for Subterranean Press; Special Award: Non-Professional: Kate Baker, Neil Clarke, and Sean Wallace for *Clarkesworld*.

Notable Novels of 2014

The Enchanted by Rene Denfeld (HarperCollins) is a gorgeously written, exceedingly dark heartbreaker of a novel about an old, corrupt prison. A brilliant, dogged investigator takes on hopeless cases on death row, delving into childhood abuse and mistreatment for clues and mitigating circumstances to save the lives of men who have committed heinous crimes. One reclusive inmate believes that golden horses run free and wild under the prison, affecting the tides of violence that occasionally erupt behind the bars.

The Quick by Lauren Owen (Random House) is an absorbing, enjoyable historical vampire novel set in the Victorian period. A young man leaves his country home to make his way to London and is introduced to both the mysterious Aegolius Club and to previous unacknowledged desires. The club is composed of vampires who seek to increase their own "gentlemanly" numbers and eliminate all vampires created from the lower classes. The tension between classes and the necessity for homosexuals to disguise their sexuality creates a well-told multilayered story.

Blood Kin by Steve Rasnic Tem (Solaris) is about a young man's return to the family home in the southern Appalachia to care for his grandmother, who parcels out tantalizing glimpses of her childhood in the 1930s. The family, imbued with a preternatural empathy, is charged with keeping a mysterious iron box safe. Add a dash of snake handling and you've got a powerful southern gothic.

We Are All Completely Fine by Daryl Gregory (Tachyon Publications) is a brilliant short novel about a therapy group comprised of five men and women traumatized by violent supernatural events. As they learn to trust each other (slightly) they slowly realize that their experiences might be related and that their ordeals may not be over. Clever, and filled with the creeping dread of what's in the flickering shadow next to you and what's just around the corner that suffuses the best horror.

The Severed Streets by Paul Cornell (Tor) is the excellent follow-up to the author's *London Falling*. This is urban fantasy dark enough to entice readers not usually interested in the subgenre—grisly murders are being committed by an invisible person, inspired perhaps by Jack the Ripper. There's a lovely, very British scene with several ladies of the secret service taking tea during a cricket match and interviewing a London policewoman who is investigating occult events.

Bring Me Flesh, I'll Bring Hell by Martin Rose (Talos Press) is a hard-boiled zombie novel with some fascinating twists and turns. Vitus Adamson is a rare (albeit dead) survivor of a US government experiment gone wrong. As a zombie, he killed and ate his wife and young child and has lived with that guilt for ten years and counting. Although his body has been slowly deteriorating, he's been able to keep his hunger in check with special pills while earning a wage as a private investigator.

The Getaway God by Richard Kadrey (HarperVoyager) continues the author's popular series about the Nephilim named James Stark (aka Sandman Slim), a romantic despite himself who is determined to save the world from renegade angels, demons, and other assorted supernatural baddies.

The Southern Reach Trilogy: Annihilation; Authority; Acceptance by Jeff VanderMeer (Farrar, Straus & Giroux) is a compulsively readable, densely rendered, magnificently weird creation consisting of three connected novels. In the first, an expedition of four is sent into Area X—a section of the US that has been infected/colonized/altered by a possible alien visitation—to explore, survey, and perhaps find clues as to what happened to earlier expeditions and to measure changes to the terrain. The second and third volumes run in counterpoint, explicating, analyzing, and breaking down the elements of the first volume. In *Authority*, the reader meets Control, a conflicted former field operative put in charge of the expeditions into Area X presumably by the influence his mother wields in the organization.

The Girl with All the Gifts by M. R. Carey (Orbit/Grand Central) is an absorbing, fresh take on zombies by the pseudonymous Mike Carey. A young girl named Melanie, along with other children around her age, are kept shackled, muzzled, and imprisoned within a mysterious compound. They are also taught by an assemblage of teachers, only one of whom seems particularly compassionate. The children are zombies but zombies varying in intelligence, unlike the "hungries" outside the compound, who only need to consume. The compound is primarily a laboratory in which experiments are being done on the children in a desperate attempt to save the human race from extinction.

An English Ghost Story by Kim Newman (Titan Books) is about a dysfunctional family that attempts to escape the battering of outside forces by moving to a house in the country. Newman does a great job of working against expectations by taking the haunted house motif in a surprising direction.

Bird Box by Josh Malerman (Ecco) is a marvelous, suspenseful horror novel debut about the survivors of a mass extinction of humankind—resulting from madness induced by seeing . . . something. The two strands of the book follow Malorie and her two young children leaving the sanctuary they've lived in for several years, and the other backtracks up to how she came to live at the house with other survivors.

The Wolf in Winter by John Connolly (Emily Bestler Books) is about a small, insular town in rural Maine with secrets that draw private investigator Charlie Parker into its web. As usual in this series, the author provides a perfect blend of violence and the supernatural.

Butcher's Road by Lee Thomas (Lethe Press) is a fine novel about a too-honest wrestler done in by his inability to let things go in the brutal world of Depression-era Chicago. After being set up to take the fall for a murder he didn't commit, Butch Cardinal is on the run from the mob, crooked cops, a hired assassin, and two men with odd powers. The only thing he's got going for him is a seemingly worthless bauble he was supposed to pick up from the murdered man.

Also Noted

The Unquiet House by Alison Littlewood (Jo Fletcher Books) is about an unhappy young woman whose distant relative bequeaths her an abandoned house with an unfortunate history. *The Bird Eater* by Ania Ahlborn (Amazon/47North) is about a man who returns to his Arkansas hometown in order to find peace after family tragedy, but is instead faced with nightmares and mysterious happenings. *Horrorstör* by Grady Hendrix (Quirk) is a clever haunted house novel taking place in the IKEA-inspired Orsk superstore in Cleveland where strange things happen at night. *The Winter People* by Jennifer McMahon (Random House/Doubleday) is about the disappearance of a young woman's mother from the town where other, earlier disappearances took place. *The Troop* by Nick Cutter (Gallery Books) is about a Boy Scout troop camping on a wilderness island off Canada, and an intruder who brings a monstrous contagion. Gemma Files's *We Will All Go Down Together* (ChiZine Publications) is a novel made up of interlocking novellas recounting the history of five clans that make up the Five Family Coven in Ontario, Canada. *Broken Monsters* by Lauren Beukes (Mulholland Books) is a police procedural with supernatural aspects and a serial killer stalking the depressed city of Detroit. Stephen King had two new novels out from Scribner: *Mr. Mercedes* is about an ex-cop trying to stop a serial killer who uses cars to kill. *Revival* is about a young boy from a small New England town and his relationship with the local reverend who lost his faith spectacularly and was run out of town. *The Madman* by Mark Hansom (Dancing Tuatara Press) is a reissue of a rare, psychological terror novel written under a pseudonym in 1938. An added bonus is a short story by the author, originally published in 1937. *Zombie Apocalypse! Endgame* created by Stephen Jones (Robinson) is the ingenious third part of a trilogy assembled by Jones from multiple contributors whose entries include newspaper clippings, diaries, email messages, vlogs, and letters. *Coldbrook* by Tim Lebbon (Titan) is about scientists who create a portal to a parallel Earth that unleashes zombies. *Suffer the Children* by Craig DiLouie (Gallery Books) is about what happens when children become bloodsuckers. Sarah Pinborough has two novels out: *The Death House* (Gollancz) is a sf/horror novel about young people isolated from the rest of the world because of a mysterious genetic test they've taken and failed. *Murder* (Jo Fletcher Books), a sequel to the excellent novel *Mayhem*, is about the Victorian forensics expert who, after the horrific events of the first book (chasing down two serial killers in London), is hoping to return to normal life. *Consumed* by David Cronenberg (Scribner) is the first novel by the director. A famous couple—Marxist philosophers and libertines—makes headlines in Paris when one is found dead, her body mutilated and partially consumed, her partner missing. An American journalist and photographer couple are drawn into the mystery and chaos surrounding the murder. *Code Zero* by Jonathan Maberry (St. Martin's Press/Griffin) is the sequel to *Patient Zero*, and the sixth volume of the author's popular sf/horror series featuring Joe Ledger. *Seeders* by A. J. Colucci (St. Martin's Press/Thomas Dunne Books) is about plant-human communication and the consequences for a group of humans trapped on an island.

Hyde by Daniel Levine (Houghton Mifflin Harcourt) is a retelling of Robert Louis Stevenson's *The Strange Case of Dr. Jekyll and Mr. Hyde* told from Hyde's point of view. *Wakening the Crow* by Stephen Gregory (Solaris) has a plot set in motion by a man who opens a bookstore he names Poe's Tooth, after the gift made to him of what is supposedly Edgar Allan Poe's baby tooth. *December Park* by Ronald Malfi (Medallion) is about what happens when suburban children begin disappearing and showing up dead in 1993. *The Three* by Sarah Lotz (Little, Brown) is about three child survivors of four air crashes in one day and the belief by some people that they are harbingers of the apocalypse. *Bathing the Lion* by Jonathan Carroll (St. Martin's Press) is another magical novel by the author. This one begins with five residents in a small New England town sharing the same dream. Surreal, lyrical, mystical with dark undertones. *Nyctophobia* by Christopher Fowler (Solaris) is about a young Englishwoman—with a history of nyctophobia (fear of the dark)—who moves into a magnificent house in the Spanish countryside with her rich, older husband. Unfortunately, her past fears are revived when she begins to research her new home. *The Boy Who Drew Monsters* by Keith Donahue (Picador) is about a boy who has become agoraphobic after almost drowning three years earlier. His new-found obsession is with drawing monsters, which somehow become real. *No One Gets Out Alive* by Adam Nevill (Pan) is about a young woman at the end of her rope emotionally and financially, who moves into a house in Birmingham, England, in desperation, only to discover horrible things about it. *Think Yourself Lucky* by Ramsey Campbell (PS) is about a serial killer in Liverpool who blogs about his exploits and the ordinary man who somehow gets sucked into the whole mess. *The Vines* by Christopher Rice (47North) is about the sinister forces still alive beneath a newly restored plantation on the outskirts of New Orleans.

Magazines, Journals, and Webzines

I believe in recognizing the work of the talented artists working in the field of fantastic fiction, both dark and light. The following artists created art that I thought especially noteworthy during 2014: Santiago Caruso, Joachim Luetke, Richard Wagner, David Gentry, Anthony Pearse, Ben Baldwin, Daniele Serra, Kim Solomon, Danielle Tunstall, Peter Allert, Dave Senecal, Matt Bisett-Johnson, John Banitsiotis, Helbanim, Warwick Fraser, Luke Spooner, Anja Millen, Wednesday Wolf, Matt Edginton, Adam Domville, Kurt Huggins, MANDEM, Gregory St. John, Jim Burns, Joel Grunerud, Sebyth, Brom, Mikio Murakami, John Jude Palencar, John Stanton, David Verba, Sandro Castello, Shannon Legler, Stephen Archer, Santiago Caruso, and Ula Jemielniak.

The Ghosts & Scholars, M. R. James Newsletter, edited by Rosemary Pardoe, is published twice a year, and includes news, articles, reviews, a letter column, and some original fiction all relating to James and his work. Mark Nicholls had a notable story in Issue 25.

Fangoria, edited by Chris Alexander, and *Rue Morgue*, edited by David Alexander (no relation as far as I know), are different only in the fact that the former is published in the US, the latter, Canada. It's where the horror movie aficionado can find superficial but entertaining and up-to-date information on many of the horror films being produced. Both magazines include interviews, articles, and lots of gory photographs. They both focus on the bloodiest, goriest special effects they can for their features. But both also run regular columns on books and graphic novels.

Video Watchdog, edited by Tim Lucas, is a gem. It's erudite yet entertaining. In addition to movie reviews, the magazine runs a regular audio column by Douglas E. Winter, a book review column, and a regular column by Ramsey Campbell. There were two issues published in 2014.

The Green Book: Writings on Irish Gothic, Supernatural and Fantastic Literature, edited by Brian J. Showers, brought out two issues in 2014. Issue #3 celebrates the 200th birth anniversary of Joseph Sheridan Le Fanu, with three meaty articles on Le Fanu and two other pieces—one on Lovecraft's connection to Ireland and the other about Charles Robert Maturin. I have not seen Issue #4.

Dead Reckonings: A Review of Horror Literature, edited by June M. Pulliam and Tony Fonseca, has been doing a marvelous job covering horror and weird fiction and nonfiction in this twice-yearly journal.

Lovecraft Annual, edited by S. T. Joshi (Hippocampus Press), is an invaluable resource for Lovecraftian scholarship accessible to the layperson. It's published in the fall and the 2014 edition featured seven papers and essays plus reviews.

Weird Fiction Review is an annual fiction and nonfiction journal edited by S. T. Joshi (Centipede Press) devoted to weird/dark fiction. Included in Issue #5 is an art portfolio by Travis Louie, articles and essays by Dennis Etchison, Danel Olson, John Pelan, and others, plus original stories and poetry.

Black Static, edited by Andy Cox, continues to be the best horror magazine out there, with fine art illustrating each story, regular interviews, plus book and movie reviews in addition to the consistently interesting fiction. In 2014 there were notable stories by Usman T. Malik, Joel Arnold, Chris Barnham, Vajra Chandrasekera, Tim Casson, Ray Cluley, Matthew Cheney, Malcolm Devlin, Steven J. Dines, John Grant, Stephen Hargadon, Andrew Hook, Carole Johnstone, Tyler Keevil, David D. Levine, Thersa Matsuura, Maura McHugh, Paul Meloy, Ralph Robert Moore, Suzanne Palmer, Sarah Read,

Sarah Saab, Steve Rasnic Tem, Leah Thomas, Alyssa Wong, and Annie Neugebauer.

Mythic Delirium, edited by Mike Allen, evolved into a webzine in 2014 with one online issue dated January–March. It's also begun publishing more prose than it used to. During 2014, there was notable fiction and poetry by Kenneth Schneyer, Sandi Leibowitz, Valya Dudycz Lupescu, and Nicole Kornher-Stace.

Weird Tales' second issue under the editorship of Marvin Kaye is partially themed, with ten brief stories about different types of undead. There are also seven un-themed stories and five poems, plus an interview with Joyce Carol Oates. There are strong stories by Kurt Fawver, Helen Grant (completing an unfinished tale by M. R. James), Ramsey Campbell, Elizabeth Bear, Keris McDonald, and David C. Smith.

Supernatural Tales', edited by David Longhorn, brought out three issues in 2014, with notable stories by Tom Johnstone, Jane Jakeman, Sean Logan, Anthony Oldknow, David Surface, William H. Wandless, and John Greenwood. There are also reviews by the editor.

Nightmare Magazine, edited by John Joseph Adams, has been publishing consistently impressive fiction (and columns) monthly since its inception in 2012. In 2014 there were strong stories by Maria Dahvana Headley, Kat Howard, Genevieve Valentine, Marie Ness, Sera Nikita, Lane Robbins, Damien Angelica Walters, Martin Cahill, and Adam-Troy Castro. A special issue, *Women Destroy Horror*, was funded by Kickstarter and edited by me. The stories (five originals and three reprints) chosen were intended to focus on the variety of horror stories that women produce. The nonfiction focused on some of the problems women face as writers of horror. The original stories are by Katherine Crichton, Gemma Files, Pat Cadigan, Catherin MacLeod, and Livia Llewellyn. The Files story is reprinted herein.

Lovecraft eZine, edited by Mike Davis, is a good monthly print and webzine specializing in new Lovecraftian fiction and poetry. During 2014 there were notable stories by Harry Baker, K. G. Orphanides, Ann K. Schwader, Neil Murrell, and L. T. Patridge.

Cyäegha, edited by Graeme Phillips, is an irregularly produced fanzine devoted to Lovecraftian fiction that uses original and reprinted stories and poems. There were two issues in 2014, with notable work by David Barker.

Hellfire Crossroads, edited by Trevor Denyer, is a new magazine available only for the Kindle and launched in the UK in 2013. There were three issues in 2014, with strong stories by Ian Mullins and Ed Blundell.

Dark Discoveries, edited by James Beach, and beginning with Issue 27, by Aaron J. French. In addition to fiction, the magazine includes interviews, essays, and book reviews. There were notable horror stories by Gemma Files, Bentley Little, Brian Evenson, Tom Piccirilli, Laird Barron, Glen Hirshberg, Simon Strantzas, and Hank Schwaeble.

Shock Totem, edited by K. Allen Wood, had two issues in 2014 with notable stories and poetry by Harry Baker, John C. Foster, Michael Wehunt, Peter Gutiérrez, Tim Lieder, and Stephen Graham Jones. The magazine also runs book reviews, articles about horror, and interviews.

Disturbed Digest is a quarterly magazine of dark fantasy and horror edited by Terrie Leigh Relf. I saw three issues in 2014 and there were notable stories and poems by Adam Phillips, Stephanie Smith, and Alan Ira Gordon.

Mixed-Genre Magazines

The British Fantasy Society Journal is a quarterly perk of membership in the British Fantasy Society, and in 2014 was edited by Max Edwards, Sarah Newton, Stuart Douglas, and Ian Hunter. It contains poetry, prose, articles, and interviews. Four issues were published in 2014, and there were notable dark stories in them by Erik T. Johnson, Robin Hickson, S. Marcus Jones, and Al Kratz. Surprisingly, the fiction editor included her own story in one issue—setting an unfortunate precedent. I also note my disappointment that *Dark Horizons* seems to have been subsumed by its former sister publication *New Horizons* to the extent that there's only a minimal amount of horror in the journal these days. *Jamais Vu: Strange among the Familiar*, edited by Paul Allen, debuted in 2014 with a mixture of prose, poetry, and nonfiction. The fiction and poetry was a mixed bag of science fiction, the weird, and dark fantasy, and the first issue included an entertaining anecdote by Harlan Ellison about meeting the criminal James (Whitey) Bulger. There were notable stories by Gary A. Braunbeck, Sandra M. Odell, Jack Ketchum, and Stephanie M. Wytovich. *Lore*, edited by Sean O'Leary and Rod Heather, is a mixed-genre magazine that published some notable (mostly non-horror stories) in 2014 by Patricia Russo, Jacob A. Boyd, Sonia Orin Lyris, and Garrett Ashley. *Innsmouth Magazine*, edited by Paula R. Stiles and Silvia Moreno-Garcia, published its last issue in the fall of 2014. The strongest stories were by Ran Burgess, Chehelnabi Amin, and Ben Godby. *The Dark*, edited by Jack Fisher and Sean Wallace, features more weird fiction than dark, and rarely publishes horror. The best of the darker stories were by Helena Bell, Stephen Graham Jones, S. L. Gilbow, Eric Schaller, and Yukumi Ogawa. *Aurealis*, edited by Dirk Strasser, Stephen Higgins, and Michael Pryor, is one of only a few long-running Australian mixed-genre magazines. In 2014 there were strong dark stories by Emma Osborne, Leif Shallcross, Meryl Stenhouse, and Matthew J. Morrison. *Luna Station Quarterly*, edited by Jennifer Lyn Parsons, is a mixed-genre quarterly publishing only female writers. The best dark stories in 2014 were by Chikodil Emelumadu, Suzanne W. Willis, Jan Stinchcombe, Llinos Cathryn Thomas, and O. J. Cade. *Shimmer*, published by Beth Wodzinsky and edited by E. Catherine Tobler, published four issues of science fiction and horror during 2014. The strongest dark stories were by Seth Dickinson, Ben Peek, Ben Godby, Margaret Dunlap, K. M. Ferebee, Alix E. Harrow, and A. C. Wise. *Fantasy & Science Fiction*, edited by Gordon Van Gelder (with Charles Coleman Finlay guest editing the July/August issue), often has some dark fantasy and horror. In 2014 the strongest of those were by Michael Libling, Scott Baker, Albert E. Cowdrey, Paul M. Berger, Seth Chambers, Haddayr Copley-Woods, Dale Bailey, Tom Underberg, Cat Hellisen, Alaya Dawn Johnson, David Erik Nelson, Dinesh Rao, Jonathan Andrew Sheen, Andy Stewart, Ian Tregillis, and Alyssa Wong. The Bailey story is reprinted herein. *Bourbon Penn*, edited by Erik Secker, is an intriguing annual magazine that publishes weird, fantasy, and dark fantasy stories. In the 2014 issue, there were seven stories; the most notable of the dark ones were by Stephen Graham Jones and James L. Steele. *Postscripts to Darkness 5*, edited by Sean Moreland, seems to have become an annual, evolving slowly from magazine to anthology. It features weird fiction and horror prose and poetry. This issue had an interview with Michael Cisco and an excerpt from his work. There were notable horror stories by Mitchell Edgworth, Graham Tugwell, and Evelyn Deshane. Subterranean Press's fine online magazine published three final issues online in 2014. Two were edited by William Schafer, one was guest edited by Jonathan Strahan. The best of the dark stories were by Kat Howard, Caitlín R. Kiernan, Maria Dahvana Headley, Jeffrey Ford, and

Karen Joy Fowler. The webzine will be missed. *On Spec* is Canada's best-known mixed-genre magazine and has been published quarterly by the Copper Pig Writers' Society, a revolving committee of volunteers since 1989. There wasn't as much dark fiction as usual during 2014, but there were notable stories by Chris Tarry and Agnes Cadieux. (The fourth issue of the year arrived too late to cover.) *Three-Lobe Burning Eye Magazine*, edited by Andrew S. Fuller, is a mixed-genre webzine that publishes twice a year. In 2014 there were strong dark stories by Lauren Dixon, Lloyd Connor, and Bonnie Jo Stufflebeam. *Not One of Us*, edited by John Benson, is one of the longest-running small press magazines and continues to be published twice a year, containing weird and dark stories and poetry. In addition, Benson puts out an annual "one-off" on a specific theme. The theme for 2014 was *Coping*, and there was good fiction and poetry by Patricia Russo and J. C. Runofson. *Nightblade*, edited by Rhonda Parrish, is a quarterly webzine of fantasy and horror. There were notable stories and poems by Sandi Leibowitz, Megan Arkenberg, and Beth Cato. *Clarkesworld*, edited by Neil Clarke, is an important monthly venue for online sf/fantasy, dark fantasy, and some horror. Each issue includes reprints and original fiction, interviews, and essays. During 2014 there were notable dark stories by Helena Bell, E. Catherine Tobler, and Maria Dahvana Headley. *Lightspeed*, edited by John Joseph Adams, is an online magazine that specializes in sf/f but occasionally publishes dark fantasy and horror. In 2014 there were notable dark stories by Sunny Moraine, Damien Angelica Walters, and Sofia Samatar. Other magazines with some excellent dark fiction in 2014 were *Beneath Ceaseless Skies*, edited by Scott H. Andrews, *Space & Time*, edited by Hildy Silverman, Australia's *Andromeda Spaceways Inflight Magazine*, edited by Sue Bursztynski, *The Revelator*, edited by Matthew Cheney and Eric Schaller, and *Strange Horizons*, published by Niall Harrison, with fiction edited by Brit Mandelo, Julia Rios, and An Owomoyela. *McSweeny's*, edited by Dave Eggers, had two newly discovered Shirley Jackson stories in its forty-seventh issue and an original story by Kelly Link in its forty-eighth issue.

Anthologies

Sword and Mythos, edited by Silvia Moreno-Garcia and Paula R. Stiles (Innsmouth Free Press), presents fifteen original stories combining sword and sorcery tropes with the Lovecraftian mythos. Also included are five essays about the connections between Robert H. Howard's and H. P. Lovecraft's worlds. There are notable stories by E. Catherine Tobler, William Meikle, Edward M. Erdelac, Bogi Takács, and Nadia Bulkin.

The Children of Old Leech: A Tribute to the Carnivorous Cosmos of Laird Barron, edited by Ross E. Lockhart and Justin Steele (Word Horde), features seventeen new stories influenced by Laird Barron's work. While a bit premature for such a book to exist, many of the contributors do a good job of capturing the feeling of Barron's best work. Included are strong stories by Gemma Files, John Langan, Richard Gavin, Stephen Graham Jones, Jeffrey Thomas, and a collaboration by Scott Nicolay, Jesse James Douthit-Nicolay, and Paul Tremblay. The Langan story is reprinted herein.

The Spectral Book of Horror Stories, edited by Mark Morris (Spectral Press), is a strong non-theme anthology of nineteen original stories. The strongest were by Alison Moore, Brian Hodge, Stephen Volk, Angela Slatter, Robert Shearman, Rio Youers, Alison Littlewood, Ramsey Campbell, and Gary McMahon. The Littlewood and Youers stories are reprinted herein.

SNAFU: An Anthology of Military Horror, edited by Geoff Brown and Amanda J. Spedding (Cohesion Press), doesn't quite live up to the potential of its theme with too many similar tales. However, there are notable stories by Jonathan Maberry, James A. Moor, and Christine Morgan.

Shadows & Tall Trees 2014, edited by Michael Kelly (Undertow Publications), moved from being a magazine to an annual anthology showcasing seventeen new dark stories, mostly horror. The strongest horror stories were by Conrad Williams, David Surface, V. H. Leslie, Robert Shearman, Michael Wehunt, Charles Wilkinson, and a collaboration by Ralph Robert Moore and Ray Cluley. The Shearman story is reprinted herein.

Journeys into Darkness, edited by Trevor Denyer (Immediate Direction Publications), includes new and old stories put together by the former editor of several defunct small press magazines, the most recent being *Midnight Street*. The anthology is dedicated to the late Joel Lane and includes a reprint, an early interview with Lane, and a eulogy. The best of the five new stories are by Ralph Robert Moore and Maynard Sims.

Dark Duets, edited by Christopher Golden (Harper Voyager), revolves around the interesting idea of teaming up two writers who have never collaborated before. The result is decidedly mixed, with a few less-than-stellar stories going for shock and gross-out, but also has notable ones by the teams of Charlaine Harris and Rachel Caine, Robert Jackson Bennett and David Liss, Rhodi Hawks and F. Paul Wilson, and Kasey Lansdale and Joe R. Lansdale.

Fearful Symmetries, edited by Ellen Datlow (ChiZine Publications), is a crowdfunded, all original, non-theme anthology of twenty stories. The book is intended to showcase a wide variety of horror and darkly weird fiction. The Nix, Ballingrud, and Barron stories are reprinted herein.

Nightmare Carnival, edited by Ellen Datlow (Dark Horse), is an all-original anthology about carnivals and circuses. Most but not all of the fifteen stories are horror.

The Cutting Room, edited by Ellen Datlow (Tachyon Publications), features twenty-one stories and two poems about the dark side of movies and movie-making. All are reprints, except for one new story by Stephen Graham Jones.

Dead Funny: Horror Stories by Comedians, edited by Robin Ince and Johnny Mains (Salt Publishing), contains fifteen stories that mix horror and humor. I rarely find that humorous horror works so I'm not the audience for this anthology. The other problem is that all the contributors are British comedians so the humor might not work for US readers.

Lovecraft's Monsters, edited by Ellen Datlow (Tachyon Publications), is a reprint anthology in which each story has at least one of Lovecraft's creations in it. Every story is accompanied by an original illustration by John Coulthart, with a new novella by John Langan.

Hell Comes to Hollywood II: Twenty-Two More Tales of Tinseltown Horror, edited by Eric Miller (Big Time Books), has mostly new horror stories about Hollywood. The best are by William Lebeda, Hal Bodner, Eric Miller, and Brad C. Hodson.

American Nightmare, edited by George Cotronis (Kraken Press), is themed around the United States during the 1950s. There are fourteen stories, the strongest by Rachel Anding and Dino Parenti.

Mia Mojo, edited by Michael McBride and Nate Southard (Thunderstorm Books), is a limited edition of ten un-themed stories (two reprints) celebrating the hundredth publication since the press started up in 2008. There are notable stories by Mary SanGiovanni and Shane McKenzie.

A Mountain Walked: Great Tales of the Cthulhu Mythos, edited by S. T. Joshi (Centipede Press), is a big, beautiful, oversized anthology of new and reprinted stories, with illustrations by David Ho, John Kenn Mortensen,

Drazen Kozjan, Denis Tiani, and Thomas Ott. Among the usual suspects, there are a couple of unusual contributors: Patrick McGrath (with a new story) and T. Coraghessan Boyle with a reprint.

Dark Gates: Roads to Hell and Limbo by Alessandro Manzetti and Paolo Di Orazio (Kipple Officina Libraria) is a mini-anthology by two Italian horror writers, with two stories by each writer. Gene O'Neil contributes an introduction.

Searchers after Horror: New Tales of the Weird and Fantastic, edited by S. T. Joshi (Fedogan & Bremer), has twenty-one stories, all but one new, focusing on the "weird place." The best stories are by Michael Aronovitz, Caitlín R. Kiernan, Nick Mamatas, W. H. Pugmire, Ann K. Schwader, and Darrell Schweitzer.

The Madness of Cthulhu Volume 1, edited by S. T. Joshi (Titan Books), is a solid anthology with fourteen new stories and two reprints inspired by H. P. Lovecraft's novella set in Antarctica, "At the Mountains of Madness." The strongest new stories are by Caitlín R. Kiernan, Donald Tyson, Darrell Schweitzer, William Browning Spencer, Melanie Tem, K. M. Tonso, and Joseph S. Pulver, Sr.

Night Terrors III, edited by Theresa Dillon, G. Winston Hyatt, and Marc Ciccarone (Blood Bound Books), has twenty-two stories, with two reprints. There are notable originals by Jack Ketchum and Jay Caselberg.

Darkness Ad Infinitum, edited by Shawna L. Bernard, Matt Edginton, Alandice A. Anderson, and Michael Parker (Villipede Publications), is the publisher's first horror anthology and it's a nicely rounded mix of prose, poetry, and art. Darkness of various types seems to be the theme. The strongest stories and poems are by David Dunwoody, Kallirroe Angelopoulou, Pete Clark, Patrick O'Neill, Becky Regalado, and Dot Wickliff.

Hauntings: An Anthology, edited by Hannah Kate (Hic Dragones), is an all-original anthology of twenty-one ghost stories—sometimes uncanny, often quite dark. There are notable stories by James Everington, Jeanette Greaves, Rachel Halsall, Mere Joyce, Rue Karney, Keris McDonald, Sarah Peploe, Brandy Schillace, and David Webb.

Letters to Lovecraft, edited by Jesse Bullington (Stone Skin Press), is an all-original anthology of eighteen stories inspired by passages in H. P. Lovecraft's essay "Supernatural Horror in Literature." The best horror stories are by Livia Llewellyn, Brian Evenson, Jeffrey Ford, Stephen Graham Jones, Cameron

Pierce, Angela Slatter, Paul Tremblay, David Yale Ardanuy, and Gemma Files. The Llewellyn and Evenson stories are reprinted herein.

Cemetery Dance published two mini-anthologies: *Four Killers*, with serial killer stories by Peter Straub, Joe R. Lansdale, Brian Keene, and Ray Garton. The Keene and Garton stories are original for this anthology. *Four Zombies*, with zombie stories by Joe R. Lansdale, John Skipp, Norman Prentiss, and Norman Partridge. The Skipp and Prentiss stories are original for this anthology.

Of Devils and Deviants: An Anthology of Erotic Horror, edited by Adam Millard and Zoe-Ray Millard (Crowded Quarantine Publications), features twenty-three stories, eleven new. The reprints include stories by Lucy Taylor and Graham Masterton. The best of the originals are by C. W. LaSart and Bear Weiter.

In the Court of the Yellow King, edited by Glynn Owen Barrass (Celaeno Press), presents eighteen stories inspired by Robert W. Chambers's 1895 collection of ten stories about a play, *The King in Yellow*, which drives those who read it or see it performed insane. The more interesting stories avoid staying too close to the plot of the original. The strongest entries are by Cody Goodfellow, Glynn Owen Barrass, T. E. Grau, Laurel Halbany, Gary McMahon, William Meikle, Christine Morgan, and Peter Rawlik. The Goodfellow story is reprinted herein.

The Ghosts & Scholars Book of Shadows Volume 2, edited by Rosemary Pardoe (Sarob Press), features twelve stories inspired by eleven of M. R. James's ghost tales. It is overall very readable, although a few of the stories just seem to lose steam. Some of the strongest are by Helen Marshall, Rick Kennett, Christopher Harman, Reggie Oliver, V. H. Leslie, and Mark Nicholls.

Qualia Nous, edited by Michael Bailey (Written Backwards), is an anthology of twenty-eight science fiction/horror stories and two poems, all but five published for the first time. The best of the new ones are by Emily B. Cataneo, Usman T. Malik, and Elizabeth Massie.

Horror Uncut: Tales of Social Insecurity and Economic Unease, edited by Joel Lane and Tom Johnstone (Gray Friar Press), is a mostly original anthology of stories about the repercussions of permanent austerity measures on ordinary people living in the UK. Alas, the overall feel of the anthology is more monochromatic than I would have liked, but there are notable stories by Gary McMahon, Simon Bestwick, and John Howard.

Bugs: Tales That Slither, Creep, and Crawl, edited by Gregory L. Norris (Great Old Ones Publishing), has thirty-four mostly new stories about bugs. There are notable stories by Lawrence Santoro and Justin Hunter.

Black Wings III, edited by S. T. Joshi (PS Publishing), showcasing stories inspired by H. P. Lovecraft, appears to have become an annual publication (with IV scheduled for release in 2015). The most notable stories in Volume III are by Simon Strantzas, Brian Stableford, Mark Howard Jones, Caitlín R. Kiernan, Donald Tyson, and a collaboration by Jessica Amanda Salmonson and W. H. Pugmire.

Terror Tales of Wales continues this solid series of regional horror stories from around the United Kingdom, interspersed with true vignettes of local interest. This volume has fourteen stories, with notable ones by Stephen Volk, Steve Lockley, Ray Cluley, Steve Duffy, and Thana Niveau. *Terror Tales of Yorkshire* has fourteen stories (two reprints). The best are by Simon Avery, Mark Morris, Christopher Harman, Alison Littlewood, Keris McDonald, Stephan Bacon, and Simon Clark. Both volumes are edited by Paul Finch and published by Gray Friar Press. The McDonald story is reprinted herein.

Dangerous Games, edited by Jonathan Oliver (Solaris), is an all-original anthology of eighteen stories about people playing all kinds of games, some very dark indeed. The best are by Robert Shearman, Helen Marshall, Pat Cadigan, Gary McMahon, Nik Vincent, Tade Thompson, Hilary Monahan, and Lavie Tidhar.

For a snapshot of dark, weird fantasy, and horror published in 2013, you couldn't do better than check out the following Best of the Year anthologies:

The Year's Best Australian Fantasy & Horror 2013, edited by Liz Grzyb and Talie Helene (Ticonderoga Publications), is the fourth volume of this valuable overview of Australian and New Zealand fantasy and horror. Included are twenty-eight stories, with minimal overlap with the other Year's Bests. *The Year's Best Weird Fiction Volume One*, edited by Laird Barron (Undertow Publications), debuted with a strong lineup of stories that sometimes overlap with horror but sometimes do not. There will be a different guest editor each year. *The Mammoth Book of Best New Horror 25*, edited by Stephen Jones

(Robinson), contains twenty-one reprinted stories and novellas. There was only one overlap with my own *Best Horror of the Year Volume Six. Best British Horror 2014*, edited by Johnny Mains (Salt Publishing), is a new entry into the Best of the Year market. The first volume had twenty-one stories, one overlapping with my Best of, three overlapping with the Jones. *The Year's Best Dark Fantasy & Horror 2014*, edited by Paula Guran (Prime), reprinted thirty-two stories and novellas, two of which overlapped with my own Best of the Year. *The Best Horror of the Year Volume Six*, edited by Ellen Datlow (Night Shade Books), reprinted twenty-three stories and novelettes, and one poem.

Mixed-Genre Anthologies

Dead Man's Hand, edited by John Joseph Adams (Titan Books), presents twenty-three new weird westerns by a wide variety of contributors, with a handful of horror. Those I liked best were by Elizabeth Bear, Jeffrey Ford, and Ken Liu. *The New Black*, edited by Richard Thomas (Dark House Press), is an all-reprint anthology of twenty noir stories mixed with every other genre imaginable. Laird Barron provides the foreword. *Songs of the Satyrs*, edited by Aaron J. French (Angelic Knight Press), features twenty new stories about satyrs. Only a few are dark, but there's notable dark fiction by W. H. Pugmire, Josh Reynolds, and Mark Valentine. *Carnacki: The New Adventures*, edited by Sam Gafford (Ulthar Press), includes eleven new stories and a play about the titular "ghost-finder/detective" created in 1910 by William Hope Hodgson (published late 2013). Although the majority of the stories are pastiches, there are notable contributions by Amy K. Marshall, Buck Weiss, and William Meikle. *The End Is Nigh*, edited by John Joseph Adams and Hugh Howey (self-published), is the first in a triptych of apocalyptic anthologies. All the stories are dark, by nature of the theme, but a couple of them—by Matthew Mather and Seanan McGuire—are good horror stories. *Stamps, Vamps & Tramps*, edited by Shannon Robinson (Evil Girlfriend Media), is a dark fantasy and horror anthology combining three elements: tattoos, vampires, and tramps (hookers, homeless, etc). The best stories were by Daniels Parseliti, Megan Lee Beals, Adam Calloway, and Rachel Caine. *Noir*, edited by Ian Whates (Newcon Press), is a loosely themed mix of thirteen new science fiction, fantasy, and horror stories. The strongest stories are by

Alex Dally MacFarlane, Paul Graham Raven, Jay Caselberg, Simon Kurt Unsworth, and Donna Scott. *La Femme*, edited by Ian Whates (Newcon Press), themed vaguely around women, has less horror than *Noir*. There is one strong dark piece by Andrew Hook. *The Best of Electric Velocipede*, edited by John Klima (Fairwood Press), showcases thirty-four stories published during the lauded small press magazine's twelve-year run. Although not known for its horror, a handful of dark stories were published during its existence. *Dreams of Shadow and Smoke: Stories for J. S. Le Fanu*, edited by Jim Rockhill and Brian J. Showers (The Swan River Press), is an elegant-looking little book with nine original stories and a reprint of weird and/or dark fiction inspired by the Irish author's bicentennial, with a brief introduction by the co-editors. There are notable stories by Peter Bell, Emma Darwin, Martin Hayes, Sarah LeFanu, and Mark Valentine. *Streets of Shadows*, edited by Maurice Broaddus and Jerry Gordon (Alliteration Ink), bills itself as supernatural noir but is actually urban fantasy. Included are some very readable stories, but on the whole few that are dark enough to be characterized as horror. The best are by Tom Picirrilli, Gerard Brennan, Douglas F. Warrick, Laurie Tom, Jonathan Maberry, and Nick Mamatas. *The Monkey's Other Paw*, edited by Luis Ortiz (Nonstop Press), has thirteen retellings, sequels, and prequels to classic horror stories, including "The Monkey's Paw," *Dr. Jekyll and Mr. Hyde*, "The Sandman," and others. Oddly enough, only a few of the stories are horror but the best of those is by Alegría Luna Luz. *Burnt Tongues: An Anthology of Transgressive Stories*, edited by Chuck Palahniuk, Richard Thomas, and Dennis Widmyer (Medallion Press), has some really interesting stories bordering on horror. The most notable are by Fred Venturini, Richard Lemmer, Bryan Howle, Jason M. Fylan, Terence James Eeles, Keith Buie, Phil Jourdan, and Amanda Gowan. *Monstrous Affections: An Anthology of Beastly Tales*, edited by Kelly Link and Gavin J. Grant (Candlewick Press), is a young adult anthology with an interesting mix of fifteen stories, mostly dark fantasy. The best of the darker stories are by Nik Hauser, Nalo Hopkinson, Nathan Ballingrud, Alice Sola Kim, and M. T. Anderson. *Strange Tales IV*, edited by Rosalie Parker, presents fifteen original odd, dark, melancholy, and sometimes horrific, sometimes poignant stories. The notable dark stories are by Rebecca Lloyd, A. J. McIntosh, Angela Slatter, John Gaskin, and Richard Hill. *The Darke Phantastique: Encounters with the Uncanny and Other Magical Things*, edited by Jason V. Brock (Cicatryx Press), is big, almost

700 pages and with more than fifty stories and poems and one screenplay. I believe the intention of the anthology is to combine a magical realism sensibility with horror. It doesn't quite work, as very few of the stories feel like magical realism and many of the stories are not horror. Despite this, there are notable dark stories by Joe R. Lansdale, Mike Allen, Dennis Etchison, Andrew S. Fuller, Lois Gresh, D. T. Kastn, Lucy A. Snyder, Nickolas Furr, and Erinn L. Kemper. *Limbus, Inc. Book II*, edited by Brett J. Talley (JournalStone), is a loosely connected shared-world anthology about a mysterious company that recruits and retrains hopeless cases for jobs they're perfect for—usually odd, and always dangerous. The five novellas are strung together by interstitial material written by the editor. *Halloween Tales*, edited by Kate Jonez (Omnium Gatherum), is an anthology of eighteen new and reprinted stories taking place around Halloween and written by members of the HWA Los Angeles Chapter. There was a notable original by Michael Paul Gonzalez. *Tel Aviv Noir*, edited by Etgar Keret and Assaf Gavron (Akashic Books), continues the publisher's popular noir series of anthologies. The notable dark ones in this volume are by co-editor Etgar Keret and Alex Epstein. *Tehran Noir*, edited by Salar Abdoh (Akashic), contains powerful stories, some highlighting the harsh conditions for women in Iran. Two notable stories are by Mahsa Mohebali and Azardokht Bahrami. *Phantasm Japan*, edited by Nick Mamatas and Masumi Washington (Haikasori), features twenty fantasy and dark fantasy stories, vignettes, and a novella about Japan. All appear in English for the first time. The best of the darkest are by Gary Braunbeck, Yusaki Kitano (translation by Nathan Collins), James A. Moore, Lauren Naturale, Tim Pratt, and Sayuri Ueda (translation by Jim Hubbert). *Krampusnacht: Twelve Nights of Christmas*, edited by Kate Wolford (World Weaver Press), presents twelve stories featuring the anti-St. Nicholas. There's a notable non-horror story by Elise Forier Edie. *Far Voyager*, edited by Nick Gevers, is Postscripts #32/33 and, despite its title and jacket art, is neither a theme anthology nor one that focuses on science fiction. There are stories from all realms of the fantastic, including several striking dark fantasy and horror stories. The best of these dark tales are by Alan Baxter, Angela Slatter, Kurt Dinan, Thana Niveau, Suzanne Willis, and Alison Littlewood. The Slatter and Dinan stories are reprinted herein. *The Many Tortures of Anthony Cardno*, edited by Anthony R. Cardno (Talekyn Press), is a charity anthology intended to raise money for cancer research and support. There's a mixture of new

sf/f/h by twenty contributors, including Kaaron Warren, Mary Robinette Kowal, Jay Lake, and Steve Berman. *Long Hidden: Speculative Fiction from the Margins of History*, edited by Rose Fox and Daniel José Elder (Crossed Genres Publications), is an ambitious anthology of twenty-seven stories about the people who have traditionally been marginalized by history. There are notable dark stories by Victor LaValle and Sofia Samatar. *Phantazein*, edited by Tehani Wesseley (Fablecroft Publishing), contain thirteen stories inspired by myth and fairy tales. A mix of thirteen stories inspired by myth and fairy tales. The strongest dark ones are by Faith Mudge and Suzanne J. Willis. *Fractured: Tales of the Canadian Post-Apocalypse*, edited by Silvia Moreno-Garcia (Exile Editions), features twenty-three stories, the most notable by Orrin Grey, John Jantunen, Michael Matheson, and a three-way collaboration by GMB Chomichuk, Curtis Janzen, and Thomas Turner. The Grey story is reprinted herein. *Shock Totem: Holiday Tales of the Macabre and Twisted 2* (Valentine's Day), edited by K. Allen Wood (Shock Totem Publications), features nine stories (three of them reprints) and ten anecdotes about Valentine's Day. The best of the fiction is by Zachery C. Parker and Damien Walters Grintalis. *Shock Totem: Holiday Tales of the Macabre and Twisted (*Halloween), edited by K. Allen Wood, features seven short stories, a poem, and five anecdotes (two of the stories are reprints). The best piece was by John Langan. *Dead Water*, edited by Maynard Sims (Hersham Horror), is a mini-horror and sf anthology made up of five stories using the theme of water as a negative force. The strongest horror story is by Simon Bestwick. *Beast Within 4: Gears and Growls*, edited by Jennifer Brozek (Graveside Tales), does better than it has any right to with the unlikely theme of clockwork beasts. There are notable stories by Ken Liu, Caren Gussoff, and Chadwick Ginther. *Widowmakers: A Benefit Anthology of Dark Fiction*, edited by Pete Kahle, is a hefty self-published anthology of reprints and originals benefiting writer James Newman, the victim of a freak accident. Among the new stories there are notable pieces by MacLeod Bracken and Charles R. Rutledge. *Twisted Boulevard: Tales of Urban Fantasy*, edited by Angela Charmaine Craig (Elektrik Milk Bath Press), has twenty-seven stories (one reprint), a few dark, and the strongest by Gregory L. Norris. *Black Apples*, edited by Camilla Bruce and Liv Lingborn (Belladonna Publishing), is an all-original anthology of retold fairy and folk tales, a few of them horror. The best of the darker tales were by Elin Olausson and Alison Littlewood. *Smoke and Mirrors*, edited by

Richard Chizmar (Cemetery Dance), not only mixes genres but also mixes forms, including original screenplays, teleplays, stage plays, comic scripts, and treatments by thirteen writers including Neil Gaiman, William Peter Blatty, Poppy Z. Brite, Stewart O'Nan, Joe R. Lansdale, and others. This is only for die-hard fans of the contributors and possibly film students. But with no introduction or context for any of the work, the volume is of limited use as a teaching text. *Poor Souls' Light: Seven Curious Tales for Robert Aickman 1914–1981*, published by the Curious Tales collective, contains seven ghost stories, with two especially strong tales by Emma Jane Unsworth and Tom Fletcher. *Tales of Terror and Torment: Stories from the Pulps Volume 2*, edited by John Pelan (Dancing Tuatara Press), has thirteen stores, mostly reprinted from *Dime Mystery Magazine*, with an introduction by John Pelan. *The Very Best of Fantasy and Science Fiction Volume Two*, edited by Gordon Van Gelder (Tachyon Publications), includes science fiction, fantasy, and horror as the magazine regularly does. There are twenty-seven stories by Stephen King, Harlan Ellison, Elizabeth Hand, Jack Vance Lucius Shepard, Jane Yolen, and others, with a foreword by Van Gelder and introduction by Michael Dirda. *Philippine Speculative Fiction Volume 9*, edited by Andrew Drilon and Charles Tan (Kestrel DDM/Flipside Publishing), has been showcasing the range of speculative fiction being written by Filipinos for several years. For the 2014 volume of twenty stories (all but one being new), the contributors were asked to include a strong Filipino element in their sf/f/dark fantasy stories. *Out of Tune*, edited by Jonathan Maberry (JournalStone), is an anthology of all-original dark fantasy and horror stories based on ballads and folk songs. With notable stories by Nancy Holder, Christopher Golden, and a collaboration by Marsheila Rockwell and Jeffrey J. Mariotte. *The Baen Big Book of Monsters*, edited by Hank Davis (Baen Books), is an anthology of twenty-five stories, five original, about giant monsters.

Collections

Fatal Journeys by Lucy Taylor (Overlook Connection Press) features nine dark stories taking place on journeys, with an introduction by Jack Ketchum. Four are new, with one extra original published only in the limited edition of the book. This latter, "Wingless Beasts," is especially good and is reprinted herein.

After the People Lights Have Gone Off by Stephen Graham Jones (Dark House Press) is this prolific writer's fifth collection and features fifteen stories, two appearing for the first time. Jones's fiction is dark, quirky, and versatile.

The Lord Came at Twilight by Daniel Mills (Dark Renaissance Books) is an excellent debut collection of fourteen stories (two published for the first time) of dark fantasy, weird fiction, and horror, with an introduction by Simon Strantzas, interior illustrations by M. Wayne Miller, and an endpaper painting by Daniele Serra.

The Bright Day Is Done by Carole Johnstone (Gray Friar Press) is a terrific debut collection of seventeen stories by a British writer whose work has been published in *Black Static*, *Interzone*, and a host of anthologies including *The Best Horror of the Year* and *The Best British Fantasy*. Five of the stories and novelettes are new. A must-read. One story is reprinted herein.

Unseaming by Mike Allen (Antimatter Press) is a strong debut collection with fourteen stories published between 1998 and 2014 (three original), with an introduction by Laird Barron. Allen is better known as a poet and editor but his prose is also quite good.

Burnt Black Suns by Simon Strantzas (Hippocampus Press) is the author's fourth collection of stories. Four of the nine stories and novellas appear for the first time, with another originally published in the 2014 anthology *Black Wings III*. Strantzas has the chops and I usually like his stories, but this time I was occasionally disappointed by a schematic feel to some of his longer pieces.

Through Dark Angles: Works Inspired by H. P. Lovecraft by Don Webb (Hippocampus Press) brings together twenty-four stories and poems written over a thirty-year period. Eight of them appear for the first time.

The Shaman and Other Shadows by Alessandro Manzetti (self-published) is a strong mini-collection of six horror stories and one poem, translated and published in English for the first time. The translations are by the author and Sanda Jelcic, except for "Nature's Oddities," translated by Sergio Altieri and edited by Benjamin Kane Ethridge. Manzetti is a writer to watch.

Dreamlike States and *Weak and Wounded* are two mini-collections by Brian James Freeman (Cemetery Dance). The first features six stories (one new) with an introduction by Edward Gorman. The second features five reprints with an introduction by Ron McLarty.

Sirenia Digest is a long-running monthly email subscription-based project by Caitlín R. Kiernan. Some of her best stories are only published in the Digest. Each issue features two pieces of fiction—sometimes vignettes or stories, or excerpts from novels, or works in progress. The story "Interstate Love Song (Murder Ballad No. 8)" reprinted herein was originally published in Sirenia Digest 100.

Professor Challenger: The Kew Growths and Other Stories by Edward Malone by William Meikle (Dark Renaissance Books) is a charming collection of twelve pastiches featuring Professor Challenger, a character created by Sir Arthur Conan Doyle, who was a Scot scientist who became embroiled in adventures often involving monstrous creatures. All but three are original to the collection, which includes an introduction by the author. The book's frontispiece, endpapers, and interior illustrations are by M. Wayne Miller.

Summonings by Ron Weighell (Sarob Press) features ten supernatural stories (three new) in the author's first collection since 1997. The production is beautiful with great-looking jacket and signature page art by Santiago Caruso. Black endpapers and a ribbon bookmark complete the package.

Knife Fight and Other Struggles by David Nickle (ChiZine Publications) is the Canadian author's second collection. It includes twelve stories, mostly dark. Two are new, and one is an excerpt from a forthcoming novel.

Darkness by Mark Samuels (Egaeus Press) is another beautifully produced book by Mark Beech, the publisher. The book has nine stories, five of them new. Reggie Oliver provides an introduction. The endpaper uses artwork by Josef Váchel (c. 1900) and details of that art are repeated throughout the volume.

Strange Gateways by Simon Kurt Unsworth (PS) is the author's third collection of horror, and contains eleven stories, four new. I gather that the stories in this book were actually written before those in *Quiet Houses*, Unsworth's second collection of stories.

Dreams of Thanatos by William Cook (King Billy Publications) presents fifteen reprinted and new stories by this New Zealander.

The Master of the House: Tales of Twilight and Borderlands by John Gaskin (Tartarus Press), the author's third collection of stories, features twelve traditional ghost stories and strange tales, eight new.

Queen and Other Stories by Lincoln Crisler (Apokrupha) has fifteen horror and sf/horror tales, two new.

Aberrations of Reality by Aaron J. French (Crowded Quarantine Publications) features twenty-two stories, five new. With an introduction by Mark Valentine.

Little by Little by John R. Little (Bad Moon Books) features nine stories and the award-winning novella "Miranda." With an introduction by Lisa Morton.

Ana Kai Tangata: Tales of the Outer the Other the Damned and the Doomed by Scott Nicolay (Fedogan & Bremer) is a strong debut collection of eight novelettes and novellas, four of them new. Nicolay is a writer to watch. Laird Barron supplies an introduction, John Pelan, an afterword.

Leaping at Thorns by L. Andrew Cooper (Black Wyrm Publishing) has fifteen new horror stories.

Inflictions by John McIlveen (Macabre Ink) features twenty-four horror stories, eight published for the first time in 2014.

The End in All Beginnings by John F. D. Taff (Grey Matter Press) features five novellas about death, three of them new.

Hideous Faces, Beautiful Skulls by Mark McLaughlin (Wildside) features thirty stories of horror and the bizarre, spanning the author's thirty-year career.

Ghouljaw and Other Stories by Clint Smith (Hippocampus Press) is a debut collection of fourteen stories, six original. With an introduction by S. T. Joshi.

Dying Embers by M. R. Cosby (Satalyte) has ten dark stories, seven published for the first time in this Aickmanesque debut collection by a native Briton living in Australia.

Mixed-Genre Collections

Death and the Flower by Koji Suzuki, translated by Maya Robinson and Cemellia Nieh (Vertical), presents six stories translated into English for the first time. All six are thematically related to family and were originally published in Japan before Suzuki's horror collection, *Dark Water*. Readers hooked on the author's Ring Trilogy and the aforementioned *Dark Water* (made into both Japanese and American movies) might be disappointed, as none of the stories in this collection are horror and only a couple are dark at all. *Last Year, When We Were Young* by Andrew J. McKiernan (Satalyte

Publishing) features sixteen mixed-genre stories, two of them new, by this Australian writer. With an introduction by Will Elliott. *Here with the Shadows* by Steve Rasnic Tem (The Swan River Press) is a wonderfully evocative collection of twelve ghost stories, four of them published for the first time. Only some are dark, but all are haunting. *The Phantasmagorical Imperative and Other Fabrications* by D. P. Watt (Egaeus Press) is a gorgeously produced hardcover of ten absorbing darkly weird tales, two published for the first time. Some of the tales are like nesting boxes; others are transformative for the narrator or other characters. Illustrated throughout are photographic bits in black and white. *The Bitterwood Bible and Other Recountings* by Angela Slatter (Tartarus Press) is the author's third solo collection (one was co-written with Lisa L. Hannett) and it's another beauty, with thirteen stories, loosely connected (but perfectly readable on their own), eight published for the first time. Each story is graced with black-and-white spot illustrations by Kathleen Jennings, with an introduction by Stephen Jones and an afterword by Lisa L. Hannett. Slatter writes dark, sometimes dreamy fairy tale-like fantasies. She had a second collection out from Ticonderoga Publications: *Black-Winged Angels*, ten contemporary, retold fairy tales. With an introduction by Juliet Marillier. *The Female Factory* by Lisa L. Hannett and Angela Slatter (Twelfth Planet Press) is an excellent three-story mini-collection of sf/f and dark fantasy. *Death at the Blue Elephant* by Janeen Webb (Ticonderoga Publications) is the Australian author's first collection, and includes eighteen stories of science fiction, fantasy, and horror published between 1997 and 2014, six stories published for the first time. Pamela Sargent provides an introduction. For the past few years, Dancing Tuatara Press has been publishing a series of collections by forgotten writers who had been productive in the "weird menace genre." In 2014, the press brought out *Mistress of Terror and Other Stories: The Weird Tales of Wyatt Blassingame Volume Four*. In it are ten stories originally published between 1935 and 1939. *Death Rocks the Cradle and Other Stories: The Weird Tales of Wayne Rogers Volume Two* features eleven stories published under the author's own name and two pseudonyms between 1934 and 1937. *My Touch Brings Death and Other Stories: The Selected Stories of Russell Gray, Volume Two* features ten stories originally published between 1937 and 1940. *The Corpse Factory & Other Stories Volume Two: The Weird Tales of Arthur Leo Zagat* features eight stories originally published between 1934 and 1937. *Satan's Secret and Selected Stories* by Bernard Stacey includes the short novel of that title plus seven stories. With an introduction by Gavin O'Keefe and an appendix with an earlier version of one of the stories. *The Place of Hairy Death and Other Stories* by Anthony M. Rud contains five stories, all but one having appeared in the original *Weird Tales* Magazine. *Food for the Fungus Lady and Other Stories* by Ralston Shields, the pseudonym for John Baxter, presents ten stories published between 1937 and 1940. *Cathedral of Horror and Other Stories: The Weird Tales of Arthur J. Burks Volume 1* presents eleven supernatural tales and "weird menace" stories originally published between 1926 and 1950. All of the above have introductions by John Pelan unless otherwise noted. *Angel Dust* by Ian McHugh (Ticonderoga Publications) is the award-winning Australian author's impressive debut collection, with fifteen science fiction, dark fantasy, and occasional horror stories (five published for the first time in 2014). *Mercy and Other Stories* by Rebecca Lloyd (Tartarus Press) is a collection of sixteen weird stories (nine original). Most are very fine, although only some are dark enough to be considered horror. *Gifts for the One Who Comes After* by Helen Marshall (ChiZine Publications) is an excellent second collection filled with seventeen remarkable weird, creepy, dark stories. Six appear for the first time. *Merry-Go-Round and Other Words* by Bryn Fortey (The Alchemy Press) is a first collection, with stories and poems published between 1971 and 2014. Twelve pieces appear for the first time. Introduction by Johnny Mains. *Strings* by Darren Gallagher (Nocturnal Press) is this Irish writer's debut featuring thirty-three mostly dark tales. *The Wilds* by Julia Elliott (Tin House Books) is this cross-genre writer's debut collection. Her work, some of it darkly tinged, has mostly been published in literary magazines. Three of the eleven stories appear for the first time. *Unknown Causes* by Frank Duffy (Gallows Press) features eighteen quiet stories, more than half published for the first time. Only a few are horrific. *Songs for the Lost* by Alexander Zelanyj (Eibonvale) collects thirty-four well-written mixed-genre stories, very few horror. *Love & Other Poisons* by Silvia Moreno-Garcia (Innsmouth Free Press) includes eighteen stories and vignettes, three never before published. Rhys Hughes, more a talented writer of the weird with a dark tinge than horror, had two books out in 2014: *Bone Idle in the Charnel House: A Collection of Weird Stories* (Hippocampus Press) features twenty stories, more than half of them new. *Orpheus on the Underground and Other Stories* (Tartarus Press) contains fifteen previously unpublished stories and one reprint, with illustrations by Chris Harrendence. *Ghosts of Punktown* by Jeffrey Thomas (Dark Regions Press) is a collection of nine sf/dark fantasy stories, four new, about the author's futuristic city of Punktown. *Black Gods Kiss* by Lavie Tidhar (PS) contains five darkly fantastic adventure stories, novelettes, and one novella. Two stories and the novella are new. *Prophecies, Libels & Dreams: Stories* by Ysabeau Wilce (Small Beer Press) is a brilliant debut collection, with seven fantasy/dark fantasy stories and novellas taking place in the odd, sometimes dangerous kingdom of the Republic of Califia. *Other Stories and Other Stories* by Adam Browne (Satalyte Books) includes twenty-one stories in several genres. *They Do the Same Things Different There* by Robert Shearman (ChiZine Publications) is this talented writer's fifth collection and, as usual, is filled with a dazzling array of dark fantasy, weird, and horror fiction. One of the best collections of the year. *Gravity Box and Other Spaces* by Mark W. Tiedemann (Walrus Publishing) has eleven sf/f/dark stories, seven new. *Skin Deep Magic* by Craig Laurance Gidney (Rebel Satori Press) has ten stories, eight new. Most are fantasy and dark fantasy, with some horrific elements. *Escape Plans* by David Sakmyster (WordFire Press) has nineteen fantasy and dark suspense stories, one new. *The Nickronomicon* by Nick Mamatas (Innsmouth Free Press) collects thirteen of the author's Lovecraftian stories, all but one reprints. Sly, weird, charming, satirical—but above all, entertaining. *Soft Apocalypses* by Lucy A. Snyder (Raw Dog Screaming Press) has fifteen sf/f and horror stories, five first published in 2014. *William Hope Hodgson* is from the Centipede Press Library of Weird Fiction. It includes twenty-one stories, plus two short novels. With an introduction by S. T. Joshi. *Edgar Allan Poe* is also part of the Centipede Press Library of Weird Fiction. It include thirty-eight stories, twenty poems, and the *Narrative of Arthur Gordon Pym*. With an introduction by S. T. Joshi. *Like a Dead Man Walking and Other Shadow Tales* by William F. Nolan (Centipede Press) is a lovely mixture of stories, poems, excerpts, and reminiscences about old friends and colleagues. Eleven of the stories and poems are new (four with Jason V. Brock), others are previously uncollected. Introduction by Jason V. Brock. *Stone Mattress* by Margaret Atwood (Nan A. Talese) is a collection of nine sf/f/h stories (three reprints). *Lady in the Garden* by Delia Sherman (Small Beer Press) is the author's first collection, and although most of her work is fantasy, among the fourteen gems are a few darker works. *Things We Found During the Autopsy* by Kuzhali Manickavel (Blaft Publications) is the Indian writer's second collection and contains forty-five darkly weird stories, pieces of flash fiction, and vignettes. *Under Stars* by KJ Kabza (self-published) collects over twenty sf/f/h stories, including one reprinted in *The Best Horror of the Year Volume Six. The Fabulous Beast* by Garry Kilworth (Infinity Plus Books) has nineteen stories of sf/f and horror published between 2005 and 2012—a few of the stories are new. *Last Stories and Other Stories* by William T. Vollman (Viking) is purportedly a collection of thirty-two supernatural ghost stories but very few are dark.

Chapbooks

A Double Monster Feature: *Wait Your Turn* and *The Stability of Large Systems* by Peter Grandbois is the first in the new Wordcraft of Oregon series of fabulist novellas. The first is a reprint about the domestic life of the Creature of the Black Lagoon. The original is a retelling of *The Fly. Holiday Horrors* (no editor) (CD Publications) is a chapbook of four Christmas horror stories. The best is by Kealan Patrick Burke. "The Box" by Richard Chizmar (CD) is a short story about suburban life. *Dream Houses* by Genevieve Valentine was published by WSFA Press in honor of her Guest of Honor appearance at Capclave. It's a suspenseful, dark science fiction novella about a space journey gone bad, during which the sole surviving crewmember has only the ship's AI for company during the six years it takes to reach their destination. *The Spectral Link* by Thomas Ligotti (Subterranean Press) is a two-story hardcover limited edition by one of the weirdest (in a good way) writers around. If you're a fan of his work, you'll want this book. *The Night Just Got Darker* by Gary McMahon (Nightwatch Press) is about an insomniac in a failing relationship who becomes curious when he notices a man typing every night in a house across the way. JournalStone debuted a series of novellas dubbed the "double down" series in 2013 (two novellas in one book). In 2014 the following came out: *Outcast* by Mark Alan Gunnells and *Secrets* by John R. Little; and *Biters* by Harry Shannon and *Reborn* by Brett J. Talley. *By Insanity of Reason* by Lisa Morton and John R. Little (Bad Moon Books) is about a woman whose life has been destroyed and the mysterious circumstances leading up to her incarceration in a mental institution. *The Revenant of Rebecca Pascal* by David Barker and W. H. Pugmire (Dark Renaissance Books) is a limited edition, illustrated novella about possession, taking place in Arkham. With an introduction by Joseph S. Pulver, Sr. The cover art and illustrations are by Erin Wells. *The Dark Return of Time* by R. B. Russell (The Swan River Press) is a novella about a young British man who witnesses an abduction while visiting his father, who owns a secondhand bookstore in Paris. *This Is Horror* published two chapbooks in 2014: Stephen Graham Jones's "The Elvis Room," a wonderfully creepy and disturbing novella about a scientist forced against his better instincts to accept that the supernatural might be real. Ray Cluley's "Water for Drowning" is a moving (rather than dark) novella about a young woman who believes she's a mermaid and the musician who falls for her. Borderlands Press has started up a second series of Little Books. This one will have fifteen volumes. The first three to come out in 2014 were: *A Little Aqua Book of Creature Tales* by David J. Schow with six stories (one new) and an afterword by the author about each story. *A Little Orange Book of Ornery Stories* by Ed Gorman with four novelettes and stories. *A Little Black Book of Horror Tales* by Dennis Etchison with seven stories. *The End of the Sentence* by Maria Dahvana Headley and Kat Howard (Subterranean) is a novella about a man who finds letters from the previous owner of his house, an entity who claims he's been unjustly imprisoned for 117 years and demands that the new occupant perform a gory task for him.

Poetry Journals, Webzines, and Chapbooks

Dwarf Stars 2014, edited by Sandra J. Lindow (Science Fiction Poetry Association), is a selection of the best speculative poems of ten lines or fewer from the previous year. The SFPA members vote for the Dwarf Stars Award, from the works in this anthology. In this volume there are poems from more than a dozen venues. *The 2014 Rhysling Anthology: The Best Science Fiction, Fantasy, and Horror Poetry of 2013*, selected by the Science Fiction Poetry Association, edited by Elizabeth R. McClennan and Ashley Brown (Science Fiction Poetry Association/Hadrosaur Productions), is used by members to vote for the best short poem and the best long poem of the year. *Spectral Realms*, edited by S. T. Joshi, is a new journal being published twice a year. In addition to being a venue for dark and weird poetry—new and classic—the journal includes reviews and essays. The first year had good dark poetry by

Ian Futter, Ashley Dioses, and Ann K. Schwader. *Goblin Fruit*, a regularly published webzine edited by Amal El-Mohtar and Caitlyn Paxson, remains the best publisher of fantasy and dark fantasy poetry, consistently publishing varied, quality material. Some of the darkest poems in 2014 were by Megan Arkenberg, Sally Rosen Kindred, Seanan McGuire, Lynette Mejía, Shweta Narayan, Sonya Taaffe, and Lindsey Walker.

Mourning Jewelry by Stephanie M. Wytovich (Raw Dog Screaming Press) has more then one hundred short poems, most new, about death, desire, mourning, and pining away for love. *Sweet Poison* by Marge Simon and Mary Turzillo (Dark Renaissance Books) collects almost sixty poems written solo and together by Simon and Turzillo. They're a mix of sf/f/dark fantasy, and almost half are new. *Dreams from a Black Nebula* by Wade German (Hippocampus Press) is the debut collection of a powerful poet of dark fantasy. About half of the hundred poems are new. *Embrace the Hideous Immaculate* by Chad Hensley (Raw Dog Screaming Press) is a fine collection of about sixty-five dark poems. With an introduction by W. H. Pugmire. *Fearworms* by Robert Payne Cabeen (Fanboy Comics) has twelve dark poems, each illustrated by the poet. Cardinal Cox has been producing pamphlets of dark poetry for many years. His poetry is always worth a look. In 2014 he published *Codex Yuggoth* and *Codex Lilith*, the latter in collaboration with T. Kelly Lee. *The Madness of Empty Spaces: The Dark Poetry of David E. Cowen* (Weasel Press) is a fine collection of twenty-five poems, mostly dark and most published for the first time, with an introduction by Danel Olson. *Prophets* by Peter Adam Salomon (Eldritch Press) is a first collection, with forty-six dark poems. In *Venus Intervention* by Alessandro Manzetti and Corinne De Winter (Kipple Officina Libraria), each contributes fine poems to this dark collection.

Nonfiction Books

The Poisoner: The Life and Crimes of Victorian England's Most Notorious Doctor by Stephen Bates (Gerald Duckworth & Co. Ltd.) reexamines the case of Dr. William Palmer, accused and convicted of murdering dozens of people. *The Ashgate Encyclopedia of Literary and Cinematic Monsters*, edited by Jeffrey Andrew Weinstock (Ashgate), is over 600 pages with about 200 monsters covered, from Lovecraftian through myth, extraterrestrial, and demons from around the world. *Phantasm Exhumed: The Unauthorized Companion* by Dustin McNeill (Harker Press) is an in-depth exploration of the movie franchise with hundreds of photos, many never before published. *Found Footage Horror Films: Fear and the Appearance of Reality* by Alexandra Heller-Nicholas (McFarland) is a survey of such films by an Australian academic and focuses on *The Blair Witch Project* and *Paranormal Activity. Mrs. Wakeman vs. the Anti-Christ* by Robert Damon Schneck (Tarcher/Penguin) catalogs some of the weirdest happenings in US history such as the Ouija board craze, the origin of the fear of evil clowns in vans, a ten-year-old Californian who developed stigmata in fifth grade, and more. *Studies in the Horror Film Tobe Hooper's Salem's Lot*, edited by Tony Earnshaw (Centipede Press), is the sixth volume in this excellent series. It's generously illustrated in four colors throughout, includes interviews about the movie with Stephen King, Tobe Hooper, Richard Kobritz (producer), and several of the actors. *American Monsters: A History of Monster Lore, Legends, and Sightings in America* by Linda S. Godfrey (Tarcher/Penguin) is organized into three sections: Monsters of the Air; Monsters of the Sea; and Monsters of the Land. While I'm no expert, Godfrey seems to have found at least several monsters not widely known. *Sex and the Cthulhu Mythos* by Bobby Derie (Hippocampus Press) is an engrossing book that begins by using letters written by Lovecraft about sex, love, and marriage. The second section analyzes the impact of these beliefs on Lovecraft's fiction. The third section discusses writers and artists whose work has been influenced by him from after his death to the last few years. *Horror 101: The Way Forward*, edited by Joe Mynhardt and co-edited by Emma Audsley (Crystal Lake Publishing), is a straightforward and useful guide for anyone looking to work in the horror field, with advice from professionals including writers, publishers, and editors. *Poe and the Subversion of American Literature* by Robert T. Talley, Jr. (Bloomsbury USA), challenges the perception of Poe as a gothic writer and instead classifies him as a satirical fantasist. *Under the Bed, Creeping: Psychoanalyzing the Gothic in Children's Literature* by Michael Howarth (McFarland) explores how Gothicism is crucial in helping children progress through different stages of growth and development using five famous texts including Christina Rossetti's *Goblin Market*, Carlo Collodi's *Pinocchio*, Neil Gaiman's *Coraline*, three versions of "Little Red Riding Hood," and J. M. Barrie's play and then novel *Peter and Wendy. The Vampire in Science Fiction Film and Literature* by Paul Meehan (McFarland) considers the evolution of the vampire in literature and film. *Born to Fear: Interviews with Thomas Ligotti*, edited by Matt Cardin (Subterranean), includes seventeen interviews with the writer of weird, dark fiction. *The Gothic Fairy Tale in Young Adult Literature: Essays on Stories from Grimm to Gaiman*, edited by Joseph Abbruscato and Tanya Jones (McFarland), is a selection of essays on the topic. *Disorders of Magnitude: A Survey of Dark Fantasy* by Jason V. Brock (Rowman & Littlefield) is part of the Studies in Supernatural Literature series curated by S. T. Joshi. Brock analyzes the intersection of literature, media, and genre fiction with forty-nine essays, articles, and interviews (fifteen new). *Monstrous Bodies: Feminine Power in Young Adult Horror* by June Pulliam (McFarland) examines what each of three types of female monstrous Others in young adult fiction—the haunted girl, the female werewolf, and the witch—has to tell us about feminine subordination in a supposedly post-feminist world. *Lovecraft and a World in Transition: Collected Essays on H. P. Lovecraft* by S. T. Joshi (Hippocampus Press) is a monumental work that reflects Joshi's more than thirty-five years of study and analysis of Lovecraft's writing and life. The volume includes all of Joshi's critical essays since 1979. *The Zombie Book: The Encyclopedia of the Living Dead* by Nick Redfern with Brad Steiger (Visible Ink) has more than 250 entries ranging from the history of the zombie to conspiracy theories (the supposedly mysterious death of dozens of microbiologists). *The Curious Case of H. P. Lovecraft* by Paul Roland (Plexus) is a new, non-academic biography of Lovecraft. *The New Annotated H. P. Lovecraft*, edited and with a foreword by Leslie S. Klinger (Liveright Publishing Corporation), is a hefty 850-page book including its appendix, bibliography, and other back matter, with an introduction by Alan Moore. Entertaining, useful, beautiful, with almost 300 illustrations and photographs throughout. *Severed: A History of Heads Lost and Heads Found* by Frances Larson (Liveright) delves into the morbid fascination we westerners seem to have with the idea of decapitation. Anthropologist Larson entertains while explaining the history and uses of, and the experimentation with, decapitated heads.

Odds and Ends

Simon & Kirby Library Series—HORROR! (Titan) is the third volume in the Simon & Kirby series featuring the groundbreaking collected comic works of Joe Simon and Jack Kirby. *When the Stars Are Right: Towards an Authentic R'lyehian Spirituality* by Scott R. Jones (Martian Migraine Press) is a tongue-in-cheek collection of nonfiction essays and commentary on H. P. Lovecraft's mythos. *The Art of Ian Miller* written by Ian Miller and Tom Whyte (Titan) is a nicely produced coffee-table book loaded with over 300 distinctive pen-and-ink images created by a master of the grotesque. Miller has illustrated Lovecraft, Tolkien, and Peake as well as Warhammer. A must-have for aficionados of his art. *American Grotesque: The Life and Art of William Mortensen*, edited by Larry Lytle and Michael Moynihan (Feral House), is about an important figure in photography whose innovative techniques of photographic manipulation and penchant for the grotesque combined to bring him to prominence in the 1920s and '30s, and seems to have contributed to the erasure of his reputation for years afterward. His subject matter was racy and often considered blasphemous. He manipulated his photos to look like illustrations and prints, angering not only prudes, but those who believed that the purity of photographic technique itself must not be corrupted. The book is a large coffee-table-style volume with a gallery of Mortensen's work. Prominent photography critic A. D. Coleman argues persuasively that Anselm Adams, who hated Mortensen's work, helped obliterate it from photographic history until recently. *The Starry Wisdom Library: The Catalog of the Greatest Occult Book Auction of All Time*, edited by Nate Pedersen (Drugstore Indian Press), is a lovingly produced fake catalog with entries by newcomers and stars of dark and weird fiction such as Gemma Files, R. Paul Wilson, Jesse Bullington, Kaaron Warren, Karin Tidback, Ramsey Campbell, Livia Llewellyn, John Langan, and a host of others. *Through the Woods* by Emily Carroll (Margaret K. McElderry Books) is a wonderful collection of five new darkly disturbing illustrated tales influenced by fairy tales.

THE ATLAS OF HELL

NATHAN BALLINGRUD

"He didn't even know he was dead. I had just shot this guy in the head and he's still standing there giving me shit. Telling me what a big badass he works for, telling me I'm going to be sorry I was born. You know. Blood pouring down his face. He can't even see anymore, it's in his goddamn eyes. So I look down at the gun in my hand and I'm like, what the fuck, you know? Is this thing working or what? And I'm starting to think maybe this asshole is right, maybe I just stepped into something over my head. I mean, I feel a twinge of real fear. My hair is standing up like a cartoon. So I look at the dude and I say, 'Lay down! You're dead! I shot you!'"

There's a bourbon and ice sitting on the end-table next to him. He takes a sip from it and puts it back down, placing it in its own wet ring. He's very precise about it.

"I guess he just had to be told, because as soon as I say it? Boom. Drops like a fucking tree."

I don't know what he's expecting from me here. My leg is jumping up and down with nerves. I can't make it stop. I open my mouth to say something but a nervous laugh spills out instead.

He looks at me incredulously, and cocks his head. Patrick is a big guy; but not doughy, like me. There's muscle packed beneath all that flesh. He looks like fists of meat sewn together and given a suit of clothes. "Why are you laughing?"

"I don't know, man. I don't know. I thought it was supposed to be a funny story."

"No, you demented fuck. That's not a funny story. What's the matter with you?"

It's pushing midnight, and we're sitting on a coffee-stained couch in a darkened corner of the grubby little bookstore I own in New Orleans, about a block off Magazine Street. My name is Jack Oleander. I keep a small studio apartment overhead, but when Patrick started banging on my door half an hour ago I took him down here instead. I don't want him in my home. That he's here at all is a very bad sign.

The bookstore is called Oleander. I sell used books, for the most part, and I serve a very sparse clientele: mostly students and disaffected youth, their little hearts love-drunk on Kierkegaard or Salinger. That suits me just fine. Most of the books have been sitting on their shelves for years, and I feel like I've fostered a kind of relationship with them. A part of me is sorry whenever one of them leaves the nest.

The bookstore doesn't pay the bills, of course. The books and documents I sell in the back room take care of that. Few people know about the back room, but those that do pay very well indeed. Patrick's boss is one of those people. We parted under strained circumstances a year or so ago. I was never supposed to see him again. His presence here makes me afraid, and fear makes me reckless.

"Well if it's not a funny story, then what kind of story is it? Because we've been drinking here for twenty minutes and you haven't mentioned business even once. If you want to trade war stories it's going to have to wait for another time."

He gives me a sour look and picks up his glass, peering into it as he swirls the ice around. He'd always hated me, and I knew that his presence here pleased him no more than it did me.

"You don't make it easy to be your friend," he says.

"I didn't know we were friends."

The muscles in his jaw clench.

"You're wasting my time, Patrick. I know you're just the muscle, so maybe you don't understand this, but the work I do in the back room takes up a lot of energy. So sleep is valuable to me. You've sat on my couch and drunk my whiskey and burned away almost half an hour beating around the bush. I don't know how much more of this I can take."

He looks at me. He has his work face on now, the one a lot of guys see just before the lights go out. That's good; I want him in work mode. It makes him focus. The trick now, though, is to keep him on the shy side of violence. You have to play these guys like marionettes. I got pretty good at it back in the day.

"You want to watch that," he says. "You want to watch that attitude."

I put my hands out, palms forward. "Hey," I say.

"I come to you in friendship. I come to you in respect."

This is bullshit, but whatever. It's time to settle him down. These guys are such fragile little flowers. "Hey. I'm sorry. Really. I haven't been sleeping much. I'm tired, and it makes me stupid."

"That's a bad trait. So wake up and listen to me. I told you that story for two reasons. One, to stop you from saying dumb shit like you just did. Make you remember who you're dealing with. I can see it didn't work. I can see maybe I was being too subtle."

"Patrick, really. I—"

"If you interrupt me again I will break your right hand. The second reason I told you that story is to let you know that I've seen some crazy things in my life, so when I tell you this new thing scares the shit out of me, maybe you'll listen to what the fuck I'm saying."

He stops there, staring hard at me. After a couple seconds of this, I figure it's okay to talk.

"You have my full attention. This is from Eugene?"

"You know this is from Eugene. Why else would I drag myself over here?"

"Patrick, I wish you'd relax. I'm sorry I made you mad. You want another drink? Let me pour you another drink."

I can see the rage still coiling in his eyes, and I'm starting to think I pushed him too hard. I'm starting to wonder how fast I can run. But then he settles back onto the couch and a smile settles over his face. It doesn't look natural there. "Jesus, you have a mouth. How does a guy like you get away with having a mouth like that?" He shakes the ice in his glass. "Yeah, go ahead. Pour me another one. Let's smoke a peace pipe."

I pour us both some more. He slugs it back in one deep swallow and holds his glass out for more. I give it to him. He seems to be relaxing.

"All right, okay. There's this guy. Creepy little grifter named Tobias George. He's one of those little vermin always crawling through the city, getting into shit, fucking up his own life, you don't even notice these guys. You know how it is."

"I do." I also know the name, but I don't tell him that.

"Only reason we know about him at all is because sometimes he'll run a little scheme of his own, kick a percentage back to Eugene, it's all good. Well one day this prick catches a case of ambition. He robs one of Eugene's poker games, makes off with a lot of money. Suicidal. Who knows what got into the guy. Some big dream climbed up his butt and opened him like an umbrella. We go hunting for him but he disappears. We get word he went farther south, disappeared into the bayou. Like, not to Port Fourchon or some shit, but literally on a goddamn boat into the swamp. Eugene is pissed, and you know how he is, he jumps and shouts for a few days, but eventually he says fuck it. We're not gonna go wrestle alligators for him. After a while we just figured he died out there. You know."

"But he didn't."

"That he did not. We catch wind of him a few months later. He's in a whole new ballgame. He's selling artifacts pulled from Hell. And he's making a lot of money doing it."

"It's another scam," I say, knowing full well it isn't.

"It's not."

"How do you know?"

"Don't worry about it. We know."

"A guy owes money and won't pay. That sounds more like your thing than mine, Patrick."

"Yeah, don't worry about that either. I got it covered when the time comes. I won't go into the details, 'cause they don't matter, but what it comes down to is Eugene wants his own way into the game. Once this punk is put in the ground, he wants to keep this market alive. We happen to know Tobias has a book that he uses for this set-up. An atlas that tells him how to access this shit. We want it, and we want to know how it works. And that's *your* thing, Jack."

I feel something cold spill through my guts. "That's not the deal we had."

"What can I tell you."

"No. I told . . ." My throat is dry. My leg is bouncing again. "Eugene told me we were through. He told me that. He's breaking his promise."

"That mouth again." Patrick finishes his drink and stands. "Come on. You can tell him that yourself, see how it goes over."

"Now? It's the middle of the night!"

"Don't worry, you won't be disturbing him. He don't sleep too well lately either."

⟜

I've lived here my whole life. Grew up just a regular fat-white-kid schlub, decent parents, a ready-made path to the gray fields of middle-class servitude. But I went off the rails at some point. I was seduced by old books. I wanted to live out my life in a fog of parchment dust and old glue. I apprenticed myself to a bookbinder, a gnarled old Cajun named Rene Aucoin, who turned out to be a fading necromancer with a nice side business refurbishing old grimoires. He found in me an eager student, which eventually led to my tenure as a librarian at the Camouflaged Library at the Ursulines Academy. It was when Eugene and his crew got involved, leading to a bloody confrontation with a death cult obsessed with the Damocles Scroll, that I left the Academy and began my career as a book thief. I worked for Eugene for five years before we had our falling out. When I left, we both knew it was for good.

Eugene has a bar up in Midcity, far away from the t-shirt shops, the fetish dens and goth hangouts of the French Quarter, far away too from the more respectable veneer of the Central Business and the Garden Districts. Midcity is a place where you can do what you want. Patrick drives me up Canal and parks out front. He leads me up the stairs and inside, where the blast of cold air is a relief from a heat which does not relent even at night. A jukebox is playing something stale, and four or five ghostlike figures nest at the bar. They do not turn around as we pass through. Patrick guides me downstairs, to Eugene's office.

Before I even reach the bottom of the stairs, Eugene starts talking to me.

"Hey fat boy! Here comes the fat boy!"

No cover model himself, he comes around his desk with his arms outstretched, what's left of his gray hair combed in long, spindly fingers over the expanse of his scalp. Drink has made a red, doughy wreckage of his face. His chest is sunken in, like something inside has collapsed and he's falling inward. He puts his hands on me in greeting, and I try not to flinch.

"Look at you. Look at you. You look good, Jack."

"So do you, Eugene."

The office is clean, uncluttered. There's a desk and a few padded chairs, a couch on the far wall underneath a huge Michalopoulos painting. Across from the desk is a minibar and a door which leads to the back alley. Mardi Gras masks are arranged behind his desk like a congress of spirits. Eugene is a New Orleans boy right down to his tapping toes, and he buys into every shabby lie the city ever told about itself.

"I hear you got a girl now. What's her name, Locky? Lick-me?"

"Lakshmi." This is already going badly. "Come on, Eugene. Let's not go there."

"Listen to him now. Calling the shots. All independent, all grown up now. Patrick give you any trouble? Sometimes he gets carried away."

Patrick doesn't blink. His role fulfilled, he's become a tree.

"No. No trouble at all. It was like old times."

"Hopefully not too much like old times, huh?" He sits behind his desk, gestures for me to take a seat. Patrick pours a couple of drinks and hands one to each of us, then retreats behind me.

"I guess I'm just trying to figure out what I'm doing here, Eugene. Someone's not paying you. Isn't that what you have guys like him for?"

Eugene settles back, sips from his drink, and studies me. "Let's not play coy, Jack. Okay? Don't pretend you don't already know about Tobias. Don't insult my intelligence."

"I know about Tobias," I say.

"Tell me what you know."

I can't get comfortable in my chair. I feel like there are chains around my chest. I make one last effort. "Eugene. We had a deal."

"Are you having trouble hearing me? Should I raise my voice?"

"He started selling two months ago. He had a rock. It was about the size of a tennis ball but it was heavy as a television set. Everybody thought he was full of shit. They were laughing at him. It sold for a little bit of money. Not much. But somebody out there liked what they saw. Word got around. He sold a two-inch piece of charred bone next. That went for a lot more."

"I bought that bone."

"Oh," I say. "Shit."

"Do you know why?"

"No, Eugene, of course I don't."

"Don't 'of course' me. I don't know what you know and what you don't. You're a slimy piece of filth, Jack. You're a human cockroach. I can't trust you. So don't get smart."

"I'm sorry. I didn't mean it like that."

"He had the nerve to contact me directly. He wanted me to know what he was offering before he put it on the market. Give me first chance. Jack, it's from my son. It's part of a thigh bone from my son."

I can't seem to see straight. The blood has rushed to my head, and I feel dizzy. I clamp my hands on the armrests of the chair so I can feel something solid. "How…how do you know?"

"There's people for that. Don't ask dumb questions. I am very much not in the mood for dumb questions."

"Okay."

"Your thing is books, so that's why you're here. We tracked him to this old shack in the bayou. You're going to get the book."

I feel panic skitter through me. "You want me to go there?"

"Patrick's going with you."

"That's not what I do, Eugene!"

"Bullshit! You're a thief. You do this all the time. Patrick there can barely read a *People* Magazine without breaking a sweat. You're going."

"Just have Patrick bring it back! You don't need me for this."

Eugene stares at me.

"Come on," I say. "You gave me your word."

I don't even see Patrick coming. His hand is on the back of my neck and he slams my face onto the desk hard enough to crack an ashtray underneath my cheekbone. My glass falls out of my hand and I hear the ice thump onto the carpet. He keeps me pinned to the desk. He wraps his free hand around my throat. I can't catch my breath.

Eugene leans in, his hands behind his back, like he's examining something curious and mildly revolting. "Would you like to see him? Would you like to see my son?"

I pat Patrick's hand; it's weirdly intimate. I shake my head. I try to make words. My vision is starting to fry around the edges. Dark loops spool into the world.

Finally, Eugene says, "Let him go."

Patrick releases me. I slide off the desk and land hard, dragging the broken ashtray with me, covering myself in ash and spent cigarette butts. I roll onto my side, choking.

Eugene puts his hand on my shoulder. "Hey, Jack, you okay? You all right down there? Get up. God damn you're a drama queen. Get the fuck up already."

It takes a few minutes. When I'm sitting up again, Patrick hands me a napkin to clean the blood off my face. I don't look at him. There's nothing I can do. No point in feeling a goddamn thing about it.

"When do I leave?" I say.

"What the hell," Eugene says. "How about right now?"

⊸○⊷

We experience dawn as a rising heat and a slow bleed of light through the cypress and the Spanish moss, riding in an airboat through the swamp a good thirty miles south of New Orleans. Patrick and I are riding up front while an old man more leather than flesh guides along some unseeable path. Our progress stirs movement from the local fauna—snakes, turtles, muskrats—and I'm constantly jumping at some heavy splash. I imagine a score of alligators gliding through the water beneath us, tracking our movement with yellow, saurian eyes. The airboat wheels around a copse of trees into a watery clearing, and I half expect to see a brontosaurus wading in the shallows.

Instead I see a row of huge, bobbing purple flowers, each with a bleached human face in the center, mouths gaping and eyes palely blind. The sight of them shocks me into silence; our guide fixes his stare on the horizon, refusing even to acknowledge anything out of the ordinary. Eyes perch along the tops of reeds; great kites of flesh stretch between tree limbs; one catches a mild breeze from our passage and skates serenely through the air, coming at last to a gentle landing on the water, where it folds in on itself and sinks into the murk.

Our guide points, and I see a shack: a small, single-room architectural catastrophe, perched on the dubious shore and extending over the water on short stilts. A skiff is tied to a front porch which doubles as a small dock. It seems to be the only method of travel to or from the place. A filthy Rebel flag hangs over the entrance in lieu of a door. At the moment, it's pulled to the side and a man I assume is Tobias George is standing there, naked but for a pair of shorts that hang precariously from his narrow hips. He's all bone and gristle. His face tells me nothing as we glide in toward the dock.

Patrick stands before we connect, despite a word of caution from our guide. He has some tough-guy greeting halfway out of his mouth when the airboat's edge lightly taps the dock, nearly spilling him into the swamp, arms pinwheeling.

Tobias is unaffected by the display, but our guide is easy with a laugh and chooses not to hold back.

Patrick recovers himself and puts both hands on the dock, proceeding to crawl out of the boat like a child learning to walk. I'm grateful to God for the sight of it.

Tobias makes no move to help.

I take my time climbing out. "You wait right here," I tell the guide.

"Oh, *wye*," he says, shutting down the engine and fishing a pack of smokes from his shirt.

"What're you guys doing here?" Tobias says. He hasn't looked at me once but he can't peel his gaze from Patrick. He knows what Patrick's all about.

"Tobias, you crazy bastard. What the hell do you think you're doing?"

Tobias turns around and goes back inside, the Rebel flag falling closed behind him. "Come on in I guess."

We follow him inside, where it's even hotter. The air doesn't move in here, probably hasn't moved in twenty years, and it carries the sharp tang of marijuana. Dust motes hang suspended in spears of light, coming in through a window covered over in ratty, bug-smeared plastic. The room is barely furnished: there's a single mattress pushed against the wall to our left, a cheap collapsible table with a plastic folding chair, and a chest of drawers. Next to the bed is a camping cooker with a little sauce pot and some cans of Sterno. On the table is a small pile of dull green buds, with some rolling papers and a Zippo.

There's a door flush against the back wall. I take a few steps in the direction and I can tell right away that there's some bad news behind it. The air spoils when I get close, coating the back of my throat with a greasy, evil film that feels like it seeps right into the meat. Violent fantasies sprout along my cortex like a little vine of tumors. I try to keep my face still, as I imagine coring the eyeballs out of both these guys with a grapefruit spoon.

"Stay on that side of the room, Patrick," I say. I don't need him feeling this.

"What? Why?"

"Trust me. This is why you brought me."

Tobias casts a glance at me now, finally sensing some purpose behind my presence. He's good, though: I still can't figure his reaction.

"Y'all here to kill me?" he says.

Patrick already has his gun in hand. It's pointed at the floor. His eyes are fixed on Tobias and he seems to be weighing something in his mind. I can tell that whatever is behind that door is already working its influence on him. It has its grubby little fingers in his brain and it's pulling dark things out of it. "That depends on you," he says. "Eugene wants to talk to you."

"Yeah, that's not going to happen."

The violence in this room is alive and crawling. I realize, suddenly, why he stays stoned. I figure it's time we get to the point. "We want the book, Tobias."

"What? Who are you?" He looks at Patrick. "What's he talking about?"

"You know what he's talking about. Go get the book."

"There is no book!"

He looks genuinely bewildered, and that worries me. I don't know if I can go back to Eugene without a book. I'm about to ask him what's in the back room when I hear a creak in the wood beyond the hanging flag and someone pulls it aside, flooding the shack with light. I spin around and Patrick already has his gun raised, looking spooked.

The man standing in the doorway is framed by the sun: a black shape against the sun, a negative space. He's tall and slender, his hair like a spray of light around his head. I think for a moment that I can smell it burning. He steps into the shack and you can tell there's something wrong with him, though it's hard to figure just what. Some malformation of the aura, telegraphing a warning blast straight to the root of my brain. To look at him, as he steps into the shack and trades direct sunlight for the filtered illumination shared by the rest of us, he seems tired and gaunt but ultimately not unlike any other poverty-wracked country boy, and yet my skin ripples at his approach. I feel my lip curl and I have to concentrate to keep the revulsion from my face.

"Toby?" he says. His voice is young and uninflected. Normal. "I think my brother's on his way back. Who are these guys?"

"Hey, Johnny," Tobias says, looking at him over my shoulder. He's plainly nervous now, and although his focus stays on Johnny, his attention seems to radiate in all directions, like a man wondering where the next hit is coming from.

I could have told him that.

Fear turns to meanness in a guy like Patrick, and he reacts according to the dictates of his kind: he shoots.

It's one shot, quick and clean. Patrick is a professional. The sound of the gun concusses the air in the little shack and the bullet passes through Johnny's skull before I even have time to wince at the noise.

I blink. I can't hear anything beyond a high-pitched whine. I see Patrick standing still, looking down the length of his raised arm with a flat, dead expression. It's his true face. I see Tobias drop to one knee, his hands over his ears and his mouth working as though he's shouting something; and I see Johnny, too, still standing in the doorway, as unmoved by the bullet's passage through his skull as though it had been nothing more than a disappointing argument. Dark clots of brain meat are splashed across the flag behind him.

He looks from Patrick to Tobias and when he speaks I can barely hear him above the ringing in my head. "What should I do?" he says.

I step forward and gently push Patrick's arm down.

"Are you shitting me?" he says, staring at Johnny.

"Patrick," I say.

"Am I fucking cursed? Is that it? I shot you in the face!"

The bullet hole is a dime-sized wound in Johnny's right cheekbone. It leaks a single thread of blood. "Asshole," he says.

Tobias gets back to his feet, his arms stretched out to either side like he's trying to separate two imaginary boxers. "Will you just relax? Jesus Christ!" He guides Johnny to the little bed and sits him down, where he brushes the blond hair out of his face and inspects the bullet hole. Then he cranes his head around to examine the damage of the exit wound. "God damn it!" he says.

Johnny puts his own hand back there. "Oh man," he says.

I take a look. The whole back of his head is gone; now it's just a red bowl of spilled gore. What look like little blowing cinders are embedded in the mess, sending up coils of smoke. Most of Johnny's brains are splashed across the wall behind him.

"Patrick," I say. "Just be cool."

He's still in a fog. You can see him trying to arrange things in his head. "I need to kill them, Jack. I need to. I never felt it like this before. What's happening here?"

Tobias pipes up. "I had a job for this guy all lined up at The Fry Pit! Now what!"

"Tobias, I need you to shut up," I say, keeping my eyes on Patrick. "Patrick, are you hearing me?" It's taking a huge effort to maintain my own composure. I have an image of wresting the gun from his hand and hitting him with it until his skull breaks. Only the absolute impossibility of it keeps me from trying.

My question causes the shutters to close in his eyes. Whatever tatter of human impulse stirred him to try to explain himself to me, to grope for reason amidst the bloody carnage boiling in his head, is subsumed again in a dull professional menace. "Don't talk to me like that. I'm not a goddamn kid."

I turn to the others. The bed is now awash in blood. Tobias is working earnestly to mitigate the damage back there, but I can't imagine what it is he thinks he can do. Brain matter is gathered in a clump behind them; he seems to be scooping everything out. Johnny sits there forlornly, shoulders slumped. "I thought it would be better out here," he said. "Shit never ends."

"The atlas," I say.

"Fuck yourself," Tobias says.

I stride toward the closed door. If there's anything I need to know before I open it, I guess I'll just find out the hard way. A hot pulse of emotion blasts out at me as I touch the handle: fear, rage, a lust for carnage. It's overriding any sense of self-preservation I might have had. I wonder if a fire will pour through the door when it's opened, a furnace exhalation, and engulf us all. I find myself hoping for it.

Tobias shouts at me: "Don't!"

I pull it open.

A charred skull, oily smoke coiling from its fissures, is propped on a stool in an otherwise bare room no bigger than a closet. Black mold has grown over the stool, and is creeping up the walls. A live current jolts my brain. Time dislocates, jumping seconds like an old record, and the world moves in jerky, stop-motion lurches. A language is seeping from the skull—a viscous, cracked sound like breaking bones and molten rock. My eyes sting and I squeeze them shut. The skin on my face blisters.

"Shut it! Shut the door!"

Tobias is screaming, but whatever he's saying has no relation to me. It's as though I'm watching a play. Blood is leaking from his eyes. Patrick is grinning widely, his own eyes like bloody headlamps. He's violently twisting his right ear, working it like an apple stem. Johnny is sitting quietly, holding his gathered brains in his hands, rocking back and forth like an unhappy child. My upper arms are hurting, and it takes me a minute to realize that I'm gouging them with my own fingernails. I can't make myself stop.

Outside a sound rolls across the swamp like a foghorn: a deep, answering bellow to the language of Hell spilling from the closet.

Tobias lunges past me and slams the door shut, immediately muffling the skull's effect. I stagger toward the chair but fall down hard before I make it, banging my shoulder against the table and knocking Tobias's drug paraphernalia all over the floor. Patrick makes a sound, half gasp and half sob, and leans back against the wall, cradling his savaged ear. The left side of his face is painted in blood. He's digging the heel of his hand into his right eye, like he's trying to rub something out of it.

"What the fuck was that!"

I think it's me who says that. Right now I can't be sure.

"That's your goddamn 'atlas,' you prick," Tobias says. He comes over to where I am and drops to the floor, scooping up the scattered buds and some papers. He begins to assemble a joint; his hands are shaking badly, so this takes some doing.

"A skull? The book is a skull?"

"No. It's a tongue inside the skull. Technically."

"What the Christ?"

"Just shut up a minute." He finishes the joint, lights it, and takes a long, deep pull. He passes it over to me.

For one surreal moment I feel like we're college buddies sitting in a dorm. It's like there's not a scorched, muttering skull in the next room, corroding the air around it. It's like there's not a man with a blown-out skull moping quietly on the bed. I start to laugh, and I haven't even had a toke.

He exhales explosively, the sweet smoke filling the air between us. "Take it, man. I'm serious. Trust me."

So I do. Almost immediately I feel an easing of the pressure in the room. The crackle of violent impulse, which I had ceased to even recognize, abated to a low thrum. My internal gauge ticked back down to highly frightened, which, in comparison to a moment before, felt like a monastic peace.

I gesture for Patrick to do the same.

"No. I don't pollute my body with that shit." He's touching his ear gingerly, trying to assess the damage.

"Patrick, last night you single-handedly killed half a bottle of ninety-proof bourbon. Let's have some perspective here."

He snatches it from me and drags hard on it, coughing it all back out so violently I think he might throw up.

Johnny laughs from his position on the bed. It's the first bright note he's sounded since his head came apart. "Amateur!"

I notice that Johnny's head seems to be changing shape. The shattered bone around the exit wound has smoothed over and extended upward an inch or so, like something growing. A tiny twig of bone has likewise extended from the bullet wound beneath his eye.

"We need to get out of here," I say. "That thing is pretty much a live feed to Hell. We can't handle it. It's time to go."

"We're taking it with us," Patrick says.

"No. No we're not."

"Not up for debate, Jack."

"I'm not riding with that thing. If you take it you're going back alone."

Patrick nods and takes another pull from the joint, handling it much better this time. He passes it back to me. "Okay, but you gotta know that I'm leaving this place empty. You understand me, right?"

I don't, at first. It takes me a second. "You can't be serious. You're going to kill me?"

"Make up your mind."

For the first time since his arrival at my shop last night, I feel genuine despair. Everything to this point has had some precedence in my life. Even this brush with Hell isn't my first, though it's the most direct so far. But I've never seen my own death staring back at me quite so frankly. I always thought I'd confront this moment with a little poise, or at least a kind of stoic resignation. But I'm angry, and I'm afraid, and I feel tears gathering in my eyes.

"God damn it, Patrick. That doesn't make any sense."

"Look, Jack. I like you. You're weak and you're a coward, but you can't help those things. I would rather you come with me. We take this skull back to

Eugene, like he wanted. We deliver Tobias to his just reward. You go back to your little bookstore and all is right with the world. But I can't leave this place with anybody in it."

Tobias doesn't seem to be paying attention. He's leaning back against the bed, a new joint rolled up and kept all to himself. I can't tell if he's resigned to his own death or if he's so far away he doesn't even know it's being discussed.

I can't think of anything to say. Maybe there isn't anything more to be said. Maybe language is over. Maybe everything is, at last, emptied out. I still feel the skull's muted influence crawling through my brain. It craves the bullet. I anticipate the explosion of the gun with a terrible relish. I wonder, idly, if I'll hold onto myself long enough to feel myself flying.

The bellow from the swamp sounds again. It's huge and deep, like the ululating call of a mountain. It just keeps on going.

Johnny smiles. "Brother's home," he says.

Patrick looks toward the flag-covered doorway. "What?"

Tobias holds his hand aloft, finger extended, announcing his intention to orate. His eyelids are heavy. The joint he'd made for himself is spent. "There's a Hell monster. Did I forget to tell you?"

I start to laugh. I can't stop myself. It doesn't feel good.

Johnny smiles at me, mistaking my laughter for something else. "It appeared the same time I did. Toby calls it my brother." He sounds wistful.

Patrick uses the gun barrel to open the flag a few inches. He peers outside for a few moments, then lets it fall closed again. He looks at me. "We're stuck. The boat's gone."

"What? He left us?"

"Well . . . it's mostly gone."

I take a look for myself.

The airboat is a listing heap of bent scrap metal, the cage around its huge propeller a tangled bird's nest. Our guide's arm, still connected to a hunk of his torso, rests on the deck in a black puddle. The thing that did this is swimming in a lazy arc some distance away, trackable by the rolling surge of water it creates as it trawls along. Judging by the size of its wake, it's at least as big as a city bus. It breaches the surface once, exposing a mottled gray hide and an anemone-like thistle of eye stalks lifting skyward. The thing barrel-rolls until a deep black fissure emerges, and from this suppurated tear comes that stone-cracking bellow, the language of deep earth that curdles something inside me, springs tears to my eyes, brings me hard to my knees.

I scramble weakly away from the door. Patrick is watching me with a sad, desperate hope, his intent to murder momentarily forgotten, as though by some trick known only to me this thing might be banished back to its home, as though I might fix this scar that Tobias George, that mewling, incompetent little thief, has cut into the world.

I cannot fix this. There is no fixing this.

Behind us both, locked in its little room, the skull cooks the air.

⤚o⤙

It's the language that hurts. The awful speech. While that thing languishes in the waters out front, we're trapped inside. It seems to stay quiet unless it's provoked by some outrage to its senses: an appearance by one of us, or—we believe, since none of us heard the attack on the airboat and our guide—the effects of the skull in the room. As long as we're quiet and hidden, we seem to be safe.

"Why would you do that to a man?" Patrick says. We're all sitting in a little huddled circle, passing the joint around. We might have been friends, to someone who didn't know us. "Why would you send him a piece of his own dead son?"

"Are you serious? No one deserves it more than Eugene. He humiliated me. He made me feel small. All those years sending him a cut from money I earned, or doing errands for him, or tipping him off when I hear shit I think he should know. Never a 'thank you.' Never a 'good job.' Just grief. Just mockery. And his son was even worse. He would lay hands on me. Slap the back of my head. Slap my face, even. What am I going to do, challenge Eugene's son? So I became everybody's bitch. The laughing stock."

Patrick shakes his head. "You didn't, though. Truth is we barely ever thought about you. I didn't even know your name until you knocked over that poker game. Eugene had to remind me."

This is hard for Tobias to hear. He stares hard at the floor, the muscles in his jaw working. He looks at me. "See what I mean? Nothing. You just have to take it from these guys, you know? Just take it and take it and take it. It was one of the happiest days of my life when that kid finally got wasted."

He goes on. We have nothing but time. He robbed the poker game in a fit of deranged anger and then fled south, hoping to disappear into the bayou. The reality of what he'd just done was starting to sink in. He's of the vermin class in criminal society, and vermin come in multitudes. One of his vermin friends told him about this shack where his old granddaddy used to live. He gets a boat and comes out here, only to find a surprise waiting for him.

"The skull was in a black, iron box," he says, "sitting on its side in the corner. There's a hole in the bottom of the box, like the whole thing was meant to fit around someone's head. It had a big gouge in the side of it, like someone had chopped it with something. I don't know what cuts through metal like that though. And inside, this skull... talking."

"It's one of the astronauts," Johnny says.

I rub my fingers in my eyes. "Astronauts? What?"

Johnny leans in, grateful for his moment. He tells us that there are occasionally men and women who wander through Hell in thin processions, wearing heavy gray robes and bearing lanterns to light their way. They are invariably chained together, and led through the burning canyons by a loping demon: some malformed, tooth-spangled pinwheel of limbs and claws. They tour safely because they are shuttered against the sights and sounds of Hell by the iron boxes around their heads, which give them the appearance of strange, prison-skulled astronauts on a pilgrimage through fire.

"I recognized the box," Johnny says. "This is one of those guys. The box was broken, so I guess something bad happened to him."

"Where is it?"

Tobias shrugs. "I threw it out in the bayou. What do I need a broken box for? I started asking for things, and it sent them. The rock, the shard of bone."

"Hold on. How did you know to ask it for things? You're leaving something out."

Tobias and Johnny exchange a look. The burning embers in the back of Johnny's head seem to have gathered more life: little tongues of flame spit into the air from time to time, as though a small fire has kindled. The extending bone around his head has grown further, opening out as though a careful hand has begun to fashion a wide, smooth bowl. The bone growing from his face has grown little offshoots, like a delicate branch.

Patrick picks up on their glance, and retrieves his gun from the floor, holding it casually in his lap.

"Everything that's brought here has a courier," Tobias says. "That's how Johnny got here. He brought the bone. And there was one already here when I found the skull. It told me."

"It?"

"Well... it was a person at first. Then it changed. They change over time. Evolve."

Patrick gets it before I do. "The thing in the water."

"Holy Christ. You mean Johnny's going to turn into something like *that*?" I look again at the fiery bowl his head is turning into.

"No no no!" Tobias holds out his hands, as if he could ward off the very idea of it. "I mean, I don't know. I'm pretty sure that's only because the other one never went away. I think it's the proximity of the skull that does it. There was one other courier, the girl who brought me the rock. I sent her away."

"Jesus. Where?"

"Just... " He waves, vaguely. "Away. Into the bayou."

"You're a real sweetheart, Tobias."

"Well come on, I didn't know what to do! She was just—there! I didn't know anybody was going to be coming with it! I freaked out and told her to get out! But the important thing is I never saw any sign that she changed into anything. I haven't seen or heard anything from her since. You notice how the plants get weird as you get close to this place? It's gotta be the skull's influence."

"That's not exactly airtight logic, Tobias," I say. "What if it's not just from the skull? What if it comes from them too? I could tell something was fucked up about Johnny as soon as I saw him."

"Well I'm taking the fucking chance! If there are going to be people coming out, they need to have a chance at a better life. That's why I got Johnny here a job. He'll be far away from that skull, so maybe he won't change into anything." He looks at his friend and at the lively fire that's crackling inside his head. "Well, he wouldn't have if you guys hadn't fucked it all up. I've got this all worked out. I'm going to find them jobs in little places, in little towns. I got money now, so I can afford to get them set up. Buy them some clothes, rent them out a place until they can start earning some money of their own. A second chance, you know? They deserve a second chance."

He's getting all worked up again, like he's going to break down into tears, and I'm struck with a revelation: Tobias is using this skull as a chance to redeem himself. He's going to funnel people out of Hell and back into the world of sunlight and cheeseburgers.

Tobias George may be the only good man in a fifty-mile radius. Too bad it's the most doomed idea I've ever heard in a life rich with them. But there are several possibilities for salvaging this situation. One thing is clear: Eugene cannot have the atlas. The level of catastrophe he might cause is incalculable. I need to get it back to my bookstore and to the back room. There are books there that will provide protections; at least I hope so.

All I need is something to carry it in.

I know just where to get it.

"Patrick. You still want to bring this thing to Eugene?"

"He's the boss. You change your mind about coming?"

"I think so, yeah. Tobias, we're going into the room."

⊸⊷

He goes in gratefully. I think he feels in control in this room in a way that he doesn't out there with Patrick. It's almost funny.

The skull sits on the moss-blackened stool, greasy smoke seeping from its fissures and polluting the air. The broken language of Hell is a physical pressure. A blood vessel ruptures in my right eye and my vision goes cloudy and pink. Time fractures again. Tobias moves next to me, approaching the skull, but I can't tell what it's doing to him: he skips in time like I'm watching him through strobe lights, even though the light in here remains a constant, sizzling glare. I try not to vomit. Things are moving around in my brain like maggots in old meat.

The air seems to bend into the skull. I see it on the stool, blackening the world around it, and I try to imagine who it once belonged to: the chained Black Iron Monk, shielded by a metal box from the burning horrors of the world he moved through. Until something came along and opened the box like a tin can, and Hell poured inside.

Who was it? What order would undertake such a pilgrimage? And to what end?

Tobias is saying something to me. I have to study him to figure out what.

The poor scrawny bastard is blistering all over his body. His lips peel back from his bloody teeth.

"Tell it what you want," he says.

So I do.

⤙o⤚

The boy is streaked with mud and gore. He is twelve, maybe thirteen. Steam rises from his body like wind-struck flags. I don't know where he appears from, or how; he's just there, two iron boxes dangling like huge lanterns from a chain in his hand. I wonder, briefly, what a child his age had done to be consigned to Hell. But then, it doesn't really matter.

I open one of the boxes and tell the boy to put the skull inside. He does. The skin bubbles on his hands where he touches it, but he makes no sign of pain.

I close the door on it, and it's like a light going out. Time slips back into its groove. The light recedes to a natural level. My skin stops burning, the desire to commit violence dissipates like smoke. I can feel where I've been scratching my own arms again. My eye is gummed shut with blood.

When we stumble back into the main room, Patrick is on his feet with the gun in his hand. Johnny is sitting on the bed, the bony rim of his open skull grown further upward, elongating his head and giving him an alien grace. The fire in the bowl of his head burns briskly, crackling and shedding a warm light. Patrick looks at me, then at the boy with the iron boxes. "You got them," he says. "Where's the skull?"

I take the chain from the boy. The boxes are heavy together; the boy must be stronger than he looks. Something to remember. "In one of these. If it can keep that shit out, I'm betting it can keep it locked in, too. I think it's safe to move."

"And those'll get us past the thing outside?"

"If what Johnny said is true."

"It is," Johnny says. "But now there's only one extra box."

"That's right," I say, and swing them with every vestige of my failing strength at Patrick's head, where they land with a wet crunch. He staggers to his right a few steps, the left side of his face broken like crockery, and he puts a hand into the rancid scramble of his own brain. "I'll go get it," he says, "I'll go."

"You're dead," I tell him gently. "You stupid bastard."

He accepts this gracefully and collapses to his knees, and then onto his face. Dark blood pours from his head as though from a spilled glass. I scoop up the gun, which feels clumsy in my hand. I never got the hang of guns.

Tobias stands in shock. "I can't believe you did that," he says.

"Shut up. Are there any clothes in that dresser? Put something on the kid. We're going back to the city." While he's doing that, I look at Johnny. "I'm not going to be able to see. Will you be able to guide me out?"

"Yes."

"Good," I say, and shoot Tobias in the back of the head.

For once, somebody dies without an argument.

⟜

I don't know much about the trip back. I open a slot on the base of the box and fit it over my head. I am consumed in darkness. I'm led out to the skiff by Johnny and the boy. The boy rides with me, and Johnny gets into the water, dragging us behind him. Fire unfurls from his head, the sides of which are developing baroque flourishes. His personality is diminished, and I can't tell if it's because he mourns Tobias, or because that is changing too, developing into something cold and barren.

The journey takes several hours. I know we pass the corpse flowers, the staring eyes and bloodless faces pressing from the foliage. I am sure that the creature unleashes its earth-breaking cry, and that any living thing that hears it hemorrhages its life away, into the still waters. I know that night falls. I know the flame of our new guide lights the undersides of the cypress, runs out before us across the water, fills the dark like the final lantern in a fallen world.

I make a quiet and steady passage there.

⟜

Eugene is in his office. The bar is closed upstairs and the man at the door lets us in without a word. He makes no comment about my companions, or the iron boxes hanging from a chain. The world he lives in is already breaking from its old shape. The new one has space for wonders.

Eugene is sitting behind his desk in his dark. I can tell he's drunk. It smells like he's been here since we left, almost twenty-four hours ago now. The only light comes from the fire rising from Johnny's empty skull. It illuminates a pale structure on Eugene's desk: a huge antler, or a tree made of bone. There are human teeth protruding along some of its tines, and a long crack near the wider base of it reveals a raw, red meat, where a mouth opens and closes.

"Where's Patrick?" he says.

"Dead," I say. "Tobias, too."

"And the atlas?"

"I burned it."

He nods, as though he'd been expecting that very thing. After a moment he gestures at the bone tree. "This is my son," he says. "Say hi, Max."

The mouth shrieks. It stops to draw in a gasping breath, then repeats the sound. The cry is sustained for several seconds before stuttering into a sob, and then going silent again.

"He keeps growing. He's going to be a big boy before it's all over."

"Yeah. I can see that."

"Who're your friends, Jack?"

I have to think about that before I answer. "I really don't know," I say, finally.

"So what do you want? You want me to tell you you're off the hook? You want me to tell you you're free to go?"

"You told me that before. It turned out to be bullshit."

"Yeah, well. That's the world we live in, right?"

"You're on notice, Eugene. Leave me alone. Don't come to my door anymore. I'm sorry things didn't work out here. I'm sorry about your son. But you have to stay away. I'm only going to say it once."

He smiles at me. He must have to summon it from far away, but he smiles at me. "I'll take that under advisement, Jack. Now get the fuck out of here."

We turn and walk back up the stairs. It's a long walk back to my bookstore, where I'm anxious to get to work on the atlas. But I have a light to guide me, and I know this place well.

WINTER CHILDREN

ANGELA SLATTER

Grandma Jo's eyes light up when she sees me.

"You! You there, girl . . . boy. Girl?"

Oh, she recognises me, she just doesn't *know* me.

I pin on a smile and approach, tiptoeing through the minefield of rockers, wheelchairs, discarded knee rugs, drooled-upon dolls, magazines opened at half-done crosswords, all manner of old-age home sadnesses scattered across the floor. A sea of faces look up at me expectantly, all of them the same, the rigours of age rendering them alike.

Gypsy, the home's resident dog—in actual fact she belongs to Mrs. Buddenbaum, but a lot of days Mrs. B forgets she owns a dog, so the shih-tzu shares her love around to anyone who'll give her a pat—barks loudly. She's outside in the yard for her morning ramble, which generally consists of crapping on the most-likely-to-be-walked-on piece of grass and trying desperately to get back inside where there are tummy scratches, old people to feed her pieces of chocolate, cardigan-pocket-softened caramels, occasional meds, and a lot of other things not meant to be consumed by animals. Gypsy, it must be said, is basically a junkie with an accompanying sugar dependency.

She also has an unhealthy fondness for me.

I have to time my visits to make sure she's outside or she will not leave me alone, demanding attention and never-ending pats. Six months of pretending I like dogs is almost over. I move past the nursing staff, exchange frozen grins. Once, I worried someone might recognise me, but no. It's been too long.

"Don't know why that animal likes you so much, missy," Grandma Jo says, sure now that I'm a girl, although she eyes my very-short-hair in a disapproving manner.

"Guess I'm just special," I say and lean down to give her a peck on the cheek. "It's Kirsty, by the way."

"I know," she snaps, but I can see the relief in her face that she doesn't have to *remember*. She smells like talcum powder and lily of the valley eau de cologne. They've set her hair today or yesterday and the curls are still tight and white. You know the urge you get to write in wet cement? Well, I get the same kind of urge when I see curls like these—except I want to touch them and feel the springiness. Past experience has shown she gets cranky when I do that, so I don't. "How are you going, Grandma Jo?"

"Not going anywhere, obviously," she says waspishly. She puts a hand against her cheek, letting her fingers catch in each furrow, as if wondering where the lines came from. I saw the photo she keeps in her room, of when she got married; she was so beautiful she looked like a work of art. Who'd have thought it would fade away, that beauty? Not her. I think about this every time *I* look in the mirror and remind myself, *Nothing's permanent, certainly not life.*

"Well, I thought, maybe we could."

"What?" she asks. "What do you mean? You're not making sense and what's with that stupid haircut? Do you want to look like some kind of lesbian?"

She's not actually *my* grandmother, so I don't have to take this kind of shit.

"You old bat. Who do you think you are?" I take a breath, trying be *nice*, patient with an old woman's foibles. "I'll thank you to shut it or I won't be taking you on any excursions."

She shrinks, curls up like a spider for a moment, then turns on the biggest of smiles and her hair seems to positively *glow* and fluff before my very eyes. Some animals make themselves bigger to intimidate predators. Grandma Jo makes herself cuter. I sit next to her, giving her a sideways glance. Her face is a picture of expectation.

"What kind of excursion, Kirsty?" she almost trills and I nod approval; *Good girl.*

"Oh, just a drive, I thought. Maybe go into town for coffee and cake, maybe drive to a park and sit on the swings for a while?"

Her smile widens. "Can we have ice cream?"

"If you behave."

Her face clouds over. "But you'll bring me back here."

I lean in close and say very quietly, "No, Josephine. Tonight I won't bring you back here."

And her expression is a sunburst, the brightest thing I've seen in a long dark time. "Shall I pack a bag?"

I shake my head. "Nope. We'll get everything you need later. Nothing for you to worry about."

She settles in her chair, wiggles into the depths of the sheepskin rug and looks contented as a cat.

I stand and touch her shoulder. "I'll be back later this afternoon, okay? Can you be waiting outside at 5:30? Just after you have dinner?"

"Where are you going?" she demands.

"I've got some things to do. So, after your dinner, wait for me on the ring road around the back, okay? And be subtle."

"I *know* how to sneak out, young lady."

We nod at each other, satisfied, each thinking ourselves smarter than the other. There's a commotion at the door to the garden—Gypsy is throwing herself at the thick glass and one of the attendants is making her way over to let the thing in. Mrs. Buddenbaum is glaring at the dog as if she doesn't recognise it at all.

Exit, Kirsty, stage right.

⊸⊷

Grandma Jo doesn't believe in *in cognito.*

She's standing beside the bay where the ambulance parks, wearing Greta Garbo sunglasses that cover half of her face, a floppy straw hat, a scarf long enough to give Isadora Duncan nightmares, and some kind of drapey lounging outfit which may, in fact, be pink chiffon pyjamas. Her handbag, in conjunction with gravity, is working to overbalance her. I pull up and lean over to open the door before they win.

She gets into the car in a manner that can be described as either stately or god-awful slow, depending on your upbringing.

I'm calm; just a granddaughter collecting her nanna for a bit of a drive. Doesn't matter if anyone sees me, after this trip I'll be gone, no more than the dust of a memory. Grandma Jo has no family, no one to go looking for her. The home will put in the required paperwork, but they've got enough living ghosts to take care of, haven't they?

"Ice cream," she says first off.

I raise my eyebrows and she remembers to add, "Please?"

She's like an excited pup, head turning this way and that, trying to drink in all the sights before the sun goes down and her eyes can't quite function as they need to, as they used to. Grandma Jo is happy, all white teeth, not denture-y at all. The sun drops below the horizon and the last burst of golden-orange fire makes her eyes light up red and huge.

Then the afternoon flame is gone and she's ordinary again, a little old lady with eccentric taste in escape attire.

I remember these streets. Nothing seems to have changed; when I turn left, I don't find a new cul de sac, or street pacifiers; no new housing developments.

When I first came back, I found the outskirts of town existing in the same strange limbo world, part rural, part suburban: farm houses with wide porches at the front and designer barns out back, tidy white fences bordering big lots; each property not too close and not too far away from the next one over. When I'd put the key into the door of my parents' empty house, it still turned in the lock. They travel a lot nowadays—I get postcards, picking them up from a variety of PO boxes around the country—but they can't seem to get rid of the place. The furniture was all where it had been, the smell was different, though, dead air and dust. A lot of the houses around it were empty, too, victims of the economic downturn—when I'd walked around in the dusk I could see how dilapidated some had become. That and the distance between farm houses meant I didn't have to worry too much about being spotted.

"So," I say, trying not to act as though I'd forgotten she was there, "the park and ice cream? Dessert first, hey?"

"Delightful. All those years of having to eat my mains first and now I can please myself for a change. When I was a child, it was always no pudding if you don't eat your vegetables... or was it?" Her voice quavers with uncertainty. "Was there food? Enough food?"

I wonder what else she might remember, away from the atmosphere of the home, away from the regimen of pills, the cocktail of things to calm you down, pick you up, make you sleep, wake you up, keep your bowels regular, lower your blood pressure, thin your blood.

But her smile is sweet and has no depths, nothing hidden, nothing remembered.

All kinds of things can forget what they were; what they are.

I pull up near the cafe, the overpriced one with the bored teenager serving a limited night menu for the next couple of hours. *Brit'nee*, her badge insists, as she turns her listless attention from the young couple ahead of us (he overweight and spotty and she really quite lush) and takes our order, scrupulously not making eye contact.

Grandma Jo is distracted by the ice cream cone *Brit'nee* hands over—bubblegum flavour—and gives it a tentative lick. Her mouth twists askew and *this doesn't taste quite right* is written all over her face. She frowns at the treat then is diverted by something else—the girl is flipping raw, compacted, circular meat onto the grill.

Red seeps up and out, turns brown on the hot metal plate. She uses an ancient wooden-handled meat cleaver to hack at an onion, and thin translucent slices of white join the sizzling circles, sending out mouth-watering fumes. Grandma Jo's eyes light up.

"Burger!" she says.

Brit'nee gives me a flat look and I nod. "You want fries with that?"

"I want the lot!"

"Make it two," I tell Brit'nee and hand over more money. My wallet is feeling thin, a little anorexic. About time for an injection, I'd say. Grandma Jo's earrings would go for a pretty penny and her pearl necklace, if I'm not mistaken.

We take up metal seats that are cold without the sun. The table between us is rickety, designed that way, I'm sure, by someone with a grudge against public eateries. I stuff a handful of paper napkins under one leg—which stops the wobbling from east to west but causes more wobbling north to south. I give up.

The dusk-dimmed lawn rolls gently down a slope in front of us, to a play area dotted with swings and seesaws, plastic-and-metal spring animals, contraptions that go round and round really fast and make you want to vomit. And there are the cages—aviaries, koala, possum and wallaby habitats, petting zoos for goats, sheep, and calves—and koi ponds, shallow and murky with the occasional bright orange flash among the water plants, here and gone so quickly you doubt you saw it. A gentle breeze lifts the old lady's curls and then moves onto the leaves and branches of the trees.

"This is nice," Grandma Jo says. "Oh, so nice. I haven't been out in a very long time."

"Glad you like it," I reply, thinking that everyone deserves a last day out.

"You're not my granddaughter," she confides as if she's just letting me in on a secret.

I nod. "I know. Never said I was."

"Fibber. You told the nurses at the home you were."

"I may have been careless with the truth," I agree.

"I don't mind. It's just so nice to be out."

I don't say anything because Brit'nee brings over our burgers and bangs the plates down hard on the table top so the fries do a little dance as if they're making a break for freedom. Grandma Jo makes a grab for her burger, bites down through the inflated bun, tearing through tomato, onion, lettuce, an egg and into the meat pattie, which is burnt on the outside and pink on the inside. Crimson-brown juice spurts—or maybe that's beetroot?—and the white teeth turn an arresting shade of pink.

My appetite deserts me faster than a dead-beat dad on child support day. I eat half a chip, push the plate away. The old lady helps herself to my food when hers is gone without so much as a by-your-leave. I look away, down towards the swings where two small kids are still playing, seemingly unattended by any adults. I think of my sister on the swing that hung from the tree marking the boundary between two properties. It makes me nervous and angry, that people are so careless with their kids, so ignorant of what lives in the dark. Wilfully ignorant.

"Aleksandr loved burgers," she says, pushing her dead husband's name out around the last mouthful. Little shreds of lettuce fly across the table. "He was a meat man."

"I bet. Where did you meet?"

"He was so handsome, he was a Russian soldier and I was a Red Cross nurse." She frowns. "Wasn't I?"

"Your story."

"I remember cold. I remember snow." The trace of an accent creeps in and I don't suppose I expected that. I've looked for her for so long, but I can't remember if she had one before.

"Grandma Jo, where were you born?"

"Me? Why here, of course. But I travelled. Yes, I went so many places." The accent is stronger. "Didn't I?"

I watch her talk almost to herself, picking through lies and memories and trying to knit them together. "I had a family, so many brothers and sisters, all of us fighting for food, fighting so hard..."

Then it fades. I can see it in her face, remembrances dissolving one by one like candles blown out at bedtime. Around us, the night is suddenly heavy and empty and she's a sweet old lady with pale blue eyes and a gentle, lost sort of smile.

"I need to powder my nose," she announces. The sign for the toilets indicates they are attached to the cafe, the entrance just along the side wall, and I point. She makes her way with a tottering elegance, clutching her handbag, towards the bathrooms. The door closes behind her with a whisper.

I lean forward, rubbing my eyes until I see stars against the black of my lids. Am I right? Is this a mistake? Have I been tracking so long that I no longer see the signs? Have I gone blind to what's in front of me? Do I now imagine danger in every shadow, see a monster in every pensioner I meet? All those times I've never doubted. How many have there been before this one? *The* one that started everything?

The night is so quiet, just the distant rumble of cars and the last creaks of the now-deserted swing set. I feel as if my sister sits at my shoulder, but when I open my eyes there's nothing, no one.

I look about—the young couple moved off long ago and *Brit'nee* is applying a premature end-of-night enthusiasm to cleaning the grill.

Making my way to the toilets, I push the door open. Grandma Jo is washing her hands, handbag pooled on the slightly grubby floor at her feet. The light from the naked bulbs on the ceiling makes her hair shine silvery-purple. She looks up and sees me in the mirror.

I stand behind her and smile, finding the hanging ends of her long silky scarf and entwining them in my fingers. "What a lovely scarf, Grandma Jo."

She smiles back until she feels the silk tightening.

But she doesn't raise her hands, doesn't struggle. Doesn't do anything while her eyes start to bulge, tongue protrudes, lips go a little bluer in the bathroom lights. She's not heavy as I let her slowly slip to the ground. Grandma Jo makes a very small pile in the corner of the stall. I close the door, lock it, then stand on the toilet lid and heave myself over the top.

The handbag is on the tiles, soaked in a combination of water and urine. I open it and dig carefully around inside. Three rolls of peppermints, a can of mace, a variety of keys, a coin purse, a pair of support hose all wrapped up, and then the book. A diary, with a battered cover.

But it doesn't look the way my memory says it should. It's blue, not brown. There's no gold on the edges of the paper. No leather ties to hold the thing together. Maybe I mis-remember. It's been a long time.

I flip the book open.

Notes in a blue pen, sometimes a red pen, the handwriting grows worse, more spidery as the dates progress, the notes less comprehensible. And no photos. Not a one.

Nothing that's supposed to be there.

A weight that might be Grandma Jo presses on my chest, surprisingly heavy for a little old lady.

Back at the home: it must be there, in a drawer, under neatly folded clothes or in the top of a wardrobe. It has to be there.

⊸⊷

In the east wing there are rooms that are dark because their inhabitants are asleep, others because they're simply empty. In fact, the east wing is the least populated part of the home—only for the moment, a brief ebb tide in the population. Grandma Jo's door is closed, but not locked. No one, it seems, has realised she's missing yet. There are no police cars out the front of the building, no rushing panicking staff, no administrator racing around like a bureaucratic chicken trying to cover up the careless loss of an *inmate*.

I close the door behind me and flick the switch. The space is bathed in yellow light. There's a thin bed with a pastel pink doona and a crocheted rug at the foot, a brown rocker-recliner, a bank of photos cover one wall—all Grandma Jo and Aleksandr—a leadlight cabinet filled with crystal, commemorative spoons, and porcelain dolls. A tall stack of drawers stands next to the long glass window. I pull open the top one and start going through the neat shirts and light cardigans. In between the folds of fabric are necklaces, rings, and bracelets and earrings, all of which would pay my way for long months. But I don't stop to pocket them, I keep digging, one drawer after the next.

In the last one there's still nothing. I turn towards the cupboard and the weight on my chest is getting heavier, growing like a stain on a carpet.

"'I had a family, so many brothers and sisters, all of us fighting for food, fighting so hard, so hungry and so cold. We walked the white and so few of us came out. I was strong...' Did she say that?"

I didn't even hear the door. A woman's voice, and old; she's only a silhouette against the open doorway.

I nod. "Some of it."

"I taught her. So many times, I made her say it over and over and she cried, but I promised her, I promised if she did it someone would rescue her. Someone would take her away." Laughter lifts the voice and Mrs. Buddenbaum steps into the dim room. "You took her away, didn't you, Kirsty?"

I feel a chill limbo its way down my spine.

"I find it useful to have some camouflage." She sniggers. "I remember frozen meat and red on white..." she says and I feel myself fall out of time. I remember my sister there one day, gone the next. I remember red on the white of the snow, and limbs frozen in place.

She goes on, "Your sister was *sweet*." She steps back out and I follow her, slowly, along the quiet corridor.

In her room, she takes up residence in a rocking chair. "How did you find me?"

"Cold trails. Reports of missing children. Nothing that got me here very fast."

"Oh, but you were only—what, eight when we met? You couldn't have done much for years after that."

"I watched a lot of news. A lot of crime alert shows. I kept scrapbooks."

"Like this?" The tiny little octagonal coffee table beside her has a drawer in the front. She reaches in and pulls out a heavy leather-bound book.

This is exactly as I remember.

She opens the cover and leafs through thoughtfully, each page covered with children's photographs, some family snapshots stolen from grieving homes, some neatly clipped from newspapers. It looks like a diary, but I know it for what it was: a menu.

"Ah, yes." She gently peels out a photo, smaller than it should be, one half torn away, and holds it up. My sister, aged nine, smiles back at me. Her arms lead to the ragged edge of the paper, cut off at the forearm. In the space that's gone is where I once was.

"It was so good of you to give me this. I do like to have my memories all in the one place."

She'd said, back in the old days when her name was, however briefly, Lily Powers—Aunty Lil to the neighbourhood—that she wanted photos of her special friends. I gave it to her three days before my sister disappeared. If I let my eyes lose focus a little, let things blur the wrinkles on her face, let this little deception strip away the last twenty years, I can see it. I can see the nice lady who rented the house next door at the end of summer, baked cookies for us and made real lemonade, then one day took my sister's life and disappeared just as quickly in the night before anyone knew.

When my sister was seen again, it was in small pieces, in patches of red on white.

I swallow. All these memories, coming back here—it's made me stupid. I'm unarmed, all my lovely sharp things left in the boot of the car because I was sure I'd taken out the monster.

"How many?" We ask the question at the same time.

"Age before beauty," I say and she grins.

"That's the spirit! Ever wonder why I took her and not you? Why I took little Sally?" She waves the photo, makes it look as though it's walking in the air. "Because she was sweet and you were not. Even then, you were a sour little troll."

"Takes one to know one," I tell her, but my heart twists. I *had* wondered for so long and with so much guilt and with that tiny, stupid, insane little echo of *why not me?* "How many?"

"Hundreds. Thousands? So many years, so many meals." She shrugs, gestures at the diary. "And you?"

"A lot," I say. A lot of strange blood between then and now. "A lot of your kind out there, more than people might think."

"And how many mistakes? How many Grandma Jo's?"

I ignore that. "Why come back here? Didn't you worry someone might recognise you?"

"Did you? But I recognised you," she singsongs as if she's caught me out. "That bitter little mouth, those dark angry eyes. Never fear, no one else would know you, no one else watches like me."

My hands are shaking.

"I have so enjoyed our chat. Nothing lasts forever, though, does it?" She stands and offers me the photo. "I suppose I knew my run would come to an end some day."

Disarmed, I step across the room and reach for the photo. My fingers touch the torn edge and Mrs. B grabs my wrist. I find myself on my back, the photo fluttering away on the air. My head rests against Mrs. B's surprisingly hard thigh and her stringy arm is wrapped around my throat. A cold hard sharpness presses against the flesh. "But not today."

The blade bites and my blood trickles warmly.

"Pity you're too old for me now, I do so hate waste."

More pressure for a second and then it's gone and a smelly, silky mass bounds up my body and sinks its teeth into Mrs. B's wrist. The dog hangs on for dear life until the Swiss Army knife goes flying and the old lady manages to dislodge the animal. Gypsy hits the wall with the same noise as a squeaky toy and lies still.

I roll over, gasping for breath.

Outside there are sounds of stirring. I struggle to my feet. The room is empty. On the floor lies the photo of my sister and, not far from it, the pocket knife, its blade slick and dark. I pocket them both and fly out the door.

Blood tracks along the white corridor, through the day room and out the patio doors. The gate meant to keep the inhabitants in is hanging off its hinges. How fast is she? How strong?

Out the gate and left, past my car. Ahead of me I can see a white blur in the darkness moving into the stretch of nature reserve on the other side of the road. I follow.

Deep in the trees, with beams of moonlight streaking through the branches, I can't make out much, but I can hear her, crashing ahead of me. Then, quiet. I keep moving. Branches reach out and scratch at my face. Somewhere close by an animal has died and is busy rotting.

A snapping sound, then heavy breathing and the sensation of being hit from the side, knocking the air from my lungs. I fall, my nose and mouth filling with a combination of dirt and grass. I roll over as quickly as I can, spitting and coughing, but she's on my chest in a flash.

The old bitch leans in, eyes bulging and lined with darkest red, face smoothed of all wrinkles, and mouth opened wide as wide can be, lined with two rows of teeth, shiny-sharp.

I wonder if this was the last thing my sister saw, all those years ago, when the snow came and something walked through the white and turned her into a red smear on the pristine ground. Something that transformed them into winter children and left ragged remnants behind to mark their passing.

Long-fingered hands press at my throat, tightening, the nails sawing into my flesh. Little explosions are happening at the edges of my vision and I can feel the blood flowing from the gashes in my throat. In my pocket is the weight of the knife, painfully imprinting its shape into my skin, impossible to get to with Mrs. B on top of me.

My left hand is trying to pry her fingers away from my throat, the right is scratching around in the dirt, desperately seeking, finding a large stick, a small branch. Sharp enough, sturdy enough, I hope—I pull it back, trying to get as much force behind it as I can and then jam it into her side. For a few seconds, the flesh resists, then the pointy end pushes in, makes a sound and *she* makes a sound. I twist the stick, getting it farther and farther in. I angle it upwards and her grip loosens. I imagine I hear a *pop* somewhere in her chest and her mouth opens to emit a sigh, laden with nothing so much as disappointment.

Mrs. B slumps on top of me.

I slide her to the side and claw my way upwards, standing, swaying, staring down at her vacant eyes, at the two rows of teeth still gleaming in the moonlight. I look down at my boots with their steel caps.

At first I kick and feel the side of the head cave in. I switch to stomping and watch her face dissolve into a mess of crushed flesh and fractured bones. The blood looks black in the moonlight.

I limp back to my car, open the door and sit, half-in, half-out, gingerly breathing as my ribs protest. The trickle of blood around my throat is already slowing, going from slick to sticky. I lean my head back, close my eyes.

Time to get out of town. Time to leave. No time to go back to my parents' and pick up the few pieces of clothing I left. No one will look there. My parents won't be home any year soon.

In the darkness, something licks my shin and I just about piss my pants. I kick out and connect with a furry softness, but all I hear is an apologetic whimper. Gypsy limps into the splash of light thrown from the car's interior and licks at me again. It's her mistress's blood, I guess.

I have no choice but to pick her up.

She curls on the passenger seat and goes to sleep, the scent of slightly damp dog filling the vehicle. I'll get her to a vet as soon as I can; between me and Mrs. B, she'll need some attention.

I turn the key in the ignition and listen for a moment to the rumble of the engine. It's the sort of sound to keep monsters at bay. I peel off into the night, unsure if I feel lighter or lost.

There are always places to get lost.

A DWELLER IN AMENTY

GENEVIEVE VALENTINE

The Pernille's housekeeper shows me into the music room, where they've shoved the piano to the wall to make room for the coffin and the table and my seat.

You can always tell serious clients. They lower the lights.

The tablecloth has to be white, and linen, anywhere I go; it's in the contract. Natural fibers only, I explain if they ask. "The old ways," I say sometimes, pitched a tone lower than usual. It usually ends the discussion.

People like the old ways. The old ways sound like money. The old ways, they assume, must work—none of the dead have complained.

I need the tablecloth, and a dinner service, with utensils all in silver. Silver covers on the dishes, and a silver vase, with clippings of herbs and flowers that I tell them will keep evil out. (The list is several dozen long, and some of them aren't easy finds—verbascum, coriander, peony, rosemary, hawthorn, black mustard, all in flower, with larch bark as a wrapping—but I've never sat down to dinner and had any missing.)

The herbs cover the smell. After you've touched the plate to the corpse, you don't want whatever they've used on the body to linger.

When I first started, I did the ascetic routine with bread and wine straight out of a wooden bowl, because it looked suitably staged and it was faster to choke down, but people who are paying you the cost of a house for your services will still serve you stale grocery store bread as their final transubstantiation on this earth, and eventually my patience ran out.

You need to eat—that's an old way there's no getting out of—but I have standards. Now I ask for the deceased's favorite food.

It was a good idea; I deal in five-star dead.

It's sweetbreads this time, which always seems like a fuck-you from the grave. People claim them as a favorite food just to seem urbane and at peace with the transience of the flesh, when really all they want is the noodle soup from around the corner when they were drunk or the peanut butter and jelly sandwich their mom made for them once back when she had yet to be disappointed in them, which means I'm left eating fried throats and staring at the deceased across the table while we both know better.

I don't know why they bother to hide it. They can't hide anything. It's why I'm there.

There aren't many of us—you have to be born with the accidental hunger and the endless appetite. Rare gift, say some people who have no idea what they're talking about.

Most of the people who can do it just think they've lost their minds, unless someone recognizes them, taps them on the shoulder before the worst happens.

The appetite still drives you to the brink, sometimes. But sin eaters need money like anyone else, and sins are easier to swallow than poverty is.

Asking for us by naming what we do won't get you anywhere. Most people won't believe you; the ones who do will think you're gauche.

You find me by mentioning Ammut, the beast who stalks the kingdom of the dead to the west of the Nile: rough-fleshed and lion-footed, a crocodile's head with impassive eyes. She sat at the weighing of the soul, reptile teeth gleaming, to consume the hearts of the sinful. (The Old Ways. Best marketing tools you can come by.)

And it's the heavy-hearted who come looking for us. Someone who's done a lot of terrible things and has the money to turn back the clock will realize the shadow's beginning to fall, and they'll start going to invite-only gallery afterparties, hosting private dinners, asking quietly about who knows anything of use.

Those types always know something, if they're rich enough, and they love nothing better than a secret code; sooner or later, when they say, "I'm looking to live to the west of the Nile," someone will write down a number, say in flat English, "I know a dweller in Amenty."

That will be my number. I'll take care of it all.

⊸⊷

Riders on my contract:

1. No one in the room with me. I'm a professional; I demand the courtesy. (It's not hard to enforce. The people who need this service don't tend to have over-devoted families, and by the time they read my contract to the bottom they don't much feel like arguing this one.)
2. Client confidentiality goes both ways. I don't go to the press about what I discover—the Old Ways demand my silence, even from you—and your family never mentions my name. (This one they always break; if they didn't, I'd never get business.)
3. The table, the white cloth, the silver, the herbs. Trappings of the trade. (This is where they get to enjoy paying through the nose for a premium service, and start to feel like they've gotten the best in the business. It's why I wear seven-hundred dollar heels to our meetings. It was the same among my ancestors, I assure them, and explain canopic jars as if they're the same thing. No one's ever questioned it.)
4. Do not open the door, no matter what you hear.

(This is where they go quiet, for a long time, before they sign their name.)

⊸⊷

First sins I ever ate were my grandmother's.

She sat me down in the kitchen one day (there was a copper chicken mold hanging on the wall like a talisman in case you wanted to make chicken cake) and handed me a cookie still tacky from the tray.

"You're getting so tall," she said, like it was my fault, and told me stories about going to school in her village, and I gnawed my way through an almond cookie that was sweet and chewy and burnt just at the edges.

She'd wasted her life. She hated her husband for taking her from her home country; she'd resented my father for pinning her there and couldn't forgive his white English wife; she'd envied every woman with a byline she ever came across. Her faith was gone. Half a dozen times she'd sat at her dressing table and wondered how hard you'd have to drive your head into the wall to kill yourself.

She was going to die any day—she knew it, she knew it for sure—and she just wanted it all to be over.

"There were cats everywhere, back home," she told me. "When you walked alone at night, it was a sea of tails and eyes."

She was praying all the while, *If you're there, call my name, I'm so ready to be gone.*

I didn't know what was happening. I thought I was killing her.

I ate three cookies, one at a time.

⤙

Englishmen used to eat the sins right off the body—a plate of bread and a cup of wine rising slowly as the corpse bloat set in, and sometimes a little meat if any could be spared and you could manage to finish before the flies reached it.

You always could manage; you ate it all, because there was no telling where your next meal was coming from, if everyone else was healthy and young.

The stories mark out where a sin eater lived—on the edge of the wilderness in some half-home, with the trees or the open sky ready to swallow him—but never how they were summoned. Was there someone assigned to the job, or did some mourner have to break first, someone who left the body and staggered over the ground beyond the safety of the town, screaming for the sin eater to hurry?

They would have had to run as soon as the death rattle came, that poor soft-heart with tears in their eyes; sins have to be eaten before the body goes cold, and on a diet of true believers, a sin eater is so full he can barely lift his head. He'd have had to drag himself most of the way on all fours, as fast as he could—wolves were everywhere, back then—until he was close enough that he had to stand and look like he could do the job, to comfort the people who paid him to be outcast and hated for eating the worst of whatever they'd done.

(Strange where some stories wander from home. You begin with the outcast beast in the forest who consumes the dying obligingly and whole; when he's found and cut open and filled up again with stones, all anyone remembers is a messenger in red.)

Was that first mourner also the one who cut the bread and poured the wine for the sin eater? Was that the understood office of the first person to beg mercy for the dead?

Was it their wooden bowl and cup given up to the stranger, across the body of the one they'd loved?

I hope it was. You could pretend that was kindness.

(The Middle Kingdom knew better how to prepare a body with some circumspection; still, they left the heart in. Our kind is doomed to press food to the flesh.)

There are rumors I've never really wanted to track down, about sin eaters who were made to drink the blood of the dead as a proof of their work—from the palm or the skull or the stomach. Corpse bowls. You'd have had to suck at the wound—blood congeals so fast, you'd have had to work for every sludgy mouthful.

They're probably just stories. Anyone who knows what happens when a body dies hopes they're just stories.

I don't think about it. It has nothing to do with me, now, with half a dozen pieces of silver in a line between me and the dead.

Of course they're serving red.

⊸o⊷

A sin eater has to separate the taste of the sin from the food, or they'll never eat another easy meal.

I won't anyway—for the rest of my life I'll be accidentally confessing short-order cooks who are two days shy of a heart attack—but it can be managed, if you work at it. You have to work at it. You don't want to taste any more than you have to.

It's tempting to eat the sins of everyone I love. It's tempting to eat the sins of everyone good. We can ease suffering; it's easy to mistake that for a calling.

Every so often you give in. I carry something in my bag for emergencies: a granola bar I can lay against the heart of a friend gone too soon, or of a stranger shot down in the street—someone who won't have time to make peace. You shove it into your mouth all at once, press both hands tight to your mouth to stop the burst of screaming. Bystanders assume you're the next of kin; you looked so upset, they'll explain later.

You shouldn't do that—sins regretted are worse than stones—but mistakes happen.

You can, if you want, touch an almond cookie to the still-warm body of your grandmother, staring at her closed eyes as you eat as fast as you can manage through a dry throat, scrambling to be gone before anyone comes in and sees you.

It won't work. When your parents find you, too late, you'll be sobbing against the rug because you got so heavy you couldn't stand any more. When your father tries to lift you, he won't be able.

You'll learn to stand up under it, eventually. Trick of the trade.

You'd think some sins would taste heady, forbidden. Worth it. An affair would be sharply sweet, a murder would taste of panic and lurching triumph, a lie would taste like escape, or spring.

If it did, there would be more of us.

A love affair is stale breath. A murder is sweat. A lie is a fingernail of dirt.

Just as well I'm choking down sweetmeats. After a while it tastes of salt, no matter what you do.

I live in a small house way out from the center of the city, at the edge of the wild. It's far enough away from people that when the sun sets, all I hear are the insects buzzing, and the edges of the hunger like a wolf pacing always just shy of the trees.

When I eat, I have the sluggish rumble of the crocodile whose mouth is open wide. When I'm hungry, wolves.

I've known one sin eater who lived in the middle of the city. He called himself an afterlife consultant, to be funny; he got a lot of business. His line, when clients asked where the sins went or why he did it, was, "Damned if you do, damned if you don't."

He shot himself, eventually.

No one would touch the body. One of his clients finally called me in, and the funeral home director stood at a safe distance as I touched my friend's chest with a doughnut (only thing he had in the house, it soaked up a little blood), forced myself through it one bite at a time, trying not to look at anything above his sternum.

It took twenty bites. By the end, I couldn't breathe; I could see stars every time my teeth came together.

There was nothing to eat.

You owned all the sins you ate. I'd always wondered.

He was teeming, and the doughnut was gone, and not one sin of it was mine.

"He's clean," I said finally, had to clear my throat and try again before it sounded like words.

At home, I sat at my kitchen table and tried not to look up where the copper chicken had been in a kitchen a long time ago. I smelled almonds everywhere.

⊸⊷

Your clients will always ask you, "Where do the sins *go*?" as if you're a pâtissier who's managed to keep the weight off.

For them, it's a fair question. Keeping things in their proper places is a life's pursuit for the kind of people who want to outsource their sins.

When they see my skin is brown, when they hear my pronunciation of "Amenti," they get a look of relief you can't imagine.

(Once, someone's personal secretary asked me, "What's the loss rate in your profession," so flat it took me a second to realize she was asking about suicides.

"Lower than yours," I said, because I had some numbers for both—my clients drive a lot of people to the grave—and just before she opened the door she'd said tightly, "If you have apprenticeships, I'm all yours."

If there was one, I'd have let her. She'd been in training to eat someone else's wrongs for long enough.)

You'd think clients would ask what will happen to you, too, just to make sure their vessel's in good shape, but they never do; what happens to you isn't their concern. They just ask where their sins go, to make sure they won't be pressed cheek by jowl with a stranger's. Real estate considerations.

Every sin eater has a different line for this question. Inside joke. Mine's always been, "Sin is a renewable resource."

They usually laugh; eco-marketing terms are more familiar than death, and slightly less frightening, and they can be fond of renewable resources now after making a living off building stock markets otherwise. Every so often, you get one who actually regrets that, and you have five bites in a row that taste like wet money before they taste like salt.

They'll stop asking questions about it after that—deep down they're desperate, they know they can't ask too much of you—which is the point.

(You keep them in the part of you that has no choice, that was born to be forced into, to hold the suffering of others whether you want it or not; the part that waits with parted teeth for anything it can consume, the part you can't touch or reach, that deep open darkness along your spine that you can never, never fill.

For fuck's sake, don't listen, if anyone tells you what you are. Don't listen to the hunger. Run until there's no one left. Starve to death, if you have to, before you do any of this.

If you so much as breathe of Amenty, you're doomed.)

⊸⊷

Mr. Pernille and I sit in the room a while, quietly. I touch the bouquet, move the peony facing out, move my chair back from the table.

The sweetmeats are battered and swimming in a butter sauce, with a side of baguette. No wonder he died so young. At least there are no almonds in it; I send back anything with almonds.

When I have my nerve, I touch the end of the baguette to the body above the heart, arm out like I'm knighting it, alerting the departed to what will happen now. I come back to the table.

I take a bite.

Mr. Pernille feeds me his sins.

The repenting comes after, that list of sorrows isn't in the meat; you get everything first, everything they've ever done, long before the weighing happens, when the black-eyed beast ever opens her jaws to swallow diseased hearts whole.

Sometimes a wound's so great that the body goes into shock to protect itself, instantly—the body knows better than you do. You only realize you've been sliced open when you look down and see the blood. I had one, once, a bicycle accident when I was a teen, nearly lost the leg. My knee and shin are made of metal; I still have gravel embedded there. (I could probably get it taken out. I don't ask.)

But once you see the wound you can't lie to yourself any more, and you feel every vein and artery swinging gently as your brain tries furiously to process the white noise, the ground turning to sand, the strange deflating feeling that's all the support in your body giving out. It's more than pain. It's too great for pain. It's a total system failure you can never process. The pain is what happens when you live with it; the rest, your body can't understand.

That's the beginning of what it feels like to eat sins. A rabbit being blown up by buckshot is what it feels like to eat sins. Lighting a hill of ants on fire is what it feels like.

I make it through half a plate of sweetmeats before the sounds start.

The solitude rider's in my contract not because I'll scream (I probably will, eventually, I've turned my throat so raw I cough up blood after), but because before that it's utterly silent except for silver on the plate and the sounds of someone eating. There are little taps of the knife against the table, slow and dampened like a bad dream, and the sound of reptile teeth snapping shut. Nothing else.

It's not a silence people hear much anymore; it's not a sound that's easy to take, when you're waiting for something to happen.

The screams are welcome. The silence almost got them thinking.

⤙⤚

You come into this world screaming. You go out in tears.

There's no word yet invented for what happens when you and I are in a room alone.

There, it's the old ways and no mistake; there it's only a corpse gone purple at the bottom and two coins no one will ever take back and the bread soaked through with sweat and your sins gleaming in every maggot, and sand under my eyelids and the wrappings still waiting and four jars lined up neatly with the faces watching, and my feet aching and my body going heavy everywhere and my throat too dry to swallow but my teeth gleaming wide, and the dark night all around us and a long walk home, and far off, silent, coming closer: wolves.

The sounds for that, they've never put a name to.

⤙⤚

In the Middle Kingdom, you gave your symbols to the dead, but somehow Europe spreads out and out, and someone a thousand years ago comes across a sin eater dragged across the sea to absolve the sinful dying, and things become tangled.

Those sin eaters give two calls at the graveside.

The first is made to the assembled company, to assure the living that the sins of the dead have been consumed, that they got their money's worth—a few coins, thrown from a distance. Sin eaters shouldn't be encouraged to mingle with the population.

The sin eater reassures everyone they've forfeited their soul for the privilege. It's good for business. You don't want them worrying about how they're treating you. They're grieving.

When the sin eater goes, they burn the bowl and the cup and anything he touched, until nothing's left but the splinters he carries back in his fingertips.

The second call the sin eater makes to the dead, to keep them where they are. He sings out, "Come not down the lanes or in our meadows."

Nobody's looking for the dearly departed. They want their dead swallowed and gone.

I've seen wolves eat. They pull their lips back from their teeth, scrape the meat from the bone, peel it neatly out from the casing of skin.

A crocodile opens its mouth, and the animal vanishes.

When I stand up from the table, there's no sign of my being there.

There's no sign anyone's eaten at all. I lick the plate clean; not a drop of wine left over, not a crumb on the cloth. The utensils are perfectly aligned. I drank all the water that the herbs were standing in.

This is a religion of its own. You treat it seriously.

Europeans of our kind got in trouble in some places, back when, from priests who didn't like freelance transubstantiation. Poaching in the fields of the Lord.

We aren't. If there's a Lord, he doesn't have much use for the dear departed.

Pernille's son is waiting at the far end of the hall, holding a sealed envelope embossed with his monogram.

"You must feel terrible," he says. His eyes are filled with tears. They glitter underneath.

I fold my hands around the bouquet of herbs and nod once, slowly. They love this part. They're making a story, for later.

"It is done," I say, dropping the contractions so I sound like a seer in a play.

Mr. Pernille the Younger tries hard not to look thrilled as he hands me the envelope with the very tips of his fingers.

Once I was dealing with a widower who wasn't going to rest until he knew his wife's transgressions were awful enough to justify my price. He kept me twenty minutes, asking. He'd have demanded a list—he was one of those—except that I reminded him the Old Ways bound me to silence and he'd signed his name to it.

"It must be a terrible curse," he told me. I'd told him, "Like a bad marriage."

It's better business to nod and look heavy. Someone will come looking soon for a house to the west of the Nile, and the new Mr. Pernille should write down my number, and mention a dweller in Amenty.

For people who can afford to have their chefs impress you, my clients provide the lightest meals I've ever had.

You have to breathe through all of it, you have to sit through it all until your throat shreds, but you can only eat what the dead considered sins.

You can leave a four-course dinner still hungry, in this line of work.

Mr. Pernille's memorial service was busy—he was a powerful man—but night in a cemetery levels everything. Bodies all liquefy the same.

I've walked here, barely able to lift my feet, because it's important that only my own two legs have brought me. (old ways.)

I lay the bundle of herbs against the headstone. They're a risk—not all the old ways work the same, mix traditions at your peril—but none of the dead have complained.

The rosemary goes straight to the back of my throat.

It's been nearly thirty hours, but when vomited back up on the grave, the food becomes whole, exactly as it was when I sat down, unknifed, undisturbed; all that's missing is the plate.

The ground trembles underneath me, just enough to send up a layer of dust, but my hands are steady as I stick the herbs into the ground like the blade of a sword, and the dirt there trembles and falls away until the meal sinks into the grave and vanishes.

I feel lighter—the walk home will be faster than the walk here—but the hunger is already stalking the edges of the vast darkness, an animal prowling for sins, impassive eyes, a jaw crammed with teeth, one paw in front of the other.

I let it. I'll take plenty of transgressions to the grave with me, but with some people, however light their conscience is, I know what they've really done, and it's a sin even to ask someone else to carry that.

A sin eater has to stand trial for everything he eats. My heart will be devoured someday, when I go to the west of the Nile, but not for these.

Sin is a renewable resource, I tell them when they ask.

Sleep well, Mr. Pernille. See you soon.

The bouquet blooms from the hole in the dirt, a last gift for the dead that should keep him right where he is.

"Come not down the lanes or in our meadows," I say.

The sounds that will soon be coming from the grave aren't for human ears, and I turn my back. I've paid my respects.

I start the long walk home to the edge of the wild, soft as lion's paws, feeling light and ravenous.

Far off, silent, coming closer: wolves.

OUTSIDE HEAVENLY

RIO YOUERS

The pillar of black smoke could be seen from Heavenly. The townsfolk looked from their windows and gathered on sidewalks. They knew it was the Roth place burning, and they prayed for the girls but not the man.

⁂

Police Chief John Peck sat on the hood of his cruiser and watched the volunteer fire department hush the flames. It took all of the one thousand gallons carried in the engine and most of the two thousand carried in the tanker, but they got it down and when the smoke cleared the remains stood like an incomplete sketch. Ashes swirled and clung to the tall grass. Sassafras and oak at the edges of the lot creaked disagreeably. Some leaves were blackened. Beyond, the sky paled to iris-blue and a murmuration of starlings made a shape in the air and disappeared.

Calloway's voice crackled over the radio. Peck had posted Calloway on Dogwood Road to turn away the curious, and with the Roth place in flames they could be many. Calloway told him that a truckful of menfolk had turned up to help, but Peck knew what they really wanted was to witness, up close, Roth struck low.

"It's under control," Peck said. Through haze and dancing ash he saw the fire chief approaching. "You thank them boys and send them on their way."

He slid off the hood and met the fire chief in the climbing sunlight, away from the smoke and ash.

"She's out, but we'll keep a close eye." Joe Neath had headed Heavenly's fire department for seven years. In his other life, he was the foreman at Gator Steel and a father of five. "Out doesn't mean dead, 'specially in this heat."

"Any idea what started it?"

"No obvious point of origin, but Perry Horne will be out later and he can tell us more." Joe unzipped his jacket a little way and palmed sweat from his throat. "I don't need a fire marshal to tell you it wasn't an accident, though."

Peck sighed and stiffened his jaw. The fire chief nodded, started toward the ruin. Peck followed. They skirted the yard where dry grass ticked, then crossed to the house's eastern face, intact but damaged. The ground was soupy from the hoses' spray. Peck stepped around the deeper puddles where the sky was reflected dull. A child's soft toy stared at him with stitches for eyes.

"You might want to ready yourself," Joe said.

Heat drove off the building and kinked the air and Peck felt his shirt latch to his back. The smell was char and smoke but something else, too. A sharp scent that kicked like ammonia. Peck cupped a hand over his nose and mouth. Ashes brushed his cheeks. They neared a window black as a box of soot with the glass broken and faux wooden blinds part-melted to the frame. Within, the carbonized remains of the living room. Most everything was stripped to whatever wouldn't burn. Peck noted the steel frame of a bed that had collapsed from the room above and what remained of the armchair where Beau Roth no doubt watched TV and sank beer and contemplated wrongs. Peck would study the scene later, when it was safer, but for now he couldn't see much beyond the savagery.

The corpse hung by its arms from a support beam. It was headless and naked. The stomach was open from sternum to groin and the entrails strung around the room. They—like the rest of the body—were red and blistered but not burned through.

"Jesus Christ." Peck turned away and tried to breathe deeply but the air was too choked. He spluttered and spat in the dirt.

"No accident," Joe said.

"Well, Christ." Peck looked again and turned away quicker than before. His nostrils flared. "That Beau, you think?"

"I'd say." Joe wiped more sweat from his throat. "Torso's about the right size."

"Yeah." Peck nodded. "Why didn't he burn up?"

"Makes no sense."

"The girls?"

"No sign."

The two men looked at each other. They were the same age and height—forty-three, a little under six feet—and shared a similar build, once muscular but starting to soften. It was as if growing up in Heavenly had shaped them similarly, like two dunes sculpted by the same winds. They said nothing but much passed between them. Peck sleeved gray sweat from his brow and shook his head.

A small section of the back wall crumbled and fell. Embers lifted and died in the air. Peck's radio squawked and he grabbed it, thankful for the diversion. He started to speak but got a chestful of that bad air and coughed. He strode clear of the house and tried again.

"What you got, Ty?"

Tyler Bray was a part-time cop and most-time grease monkey at Go Auto, which made him useful when it came to maintaining the department's two vehicles. He was young and enthusiastic, but better with a wrench than he was with a badge. Peck had him skirting Roth's two acres for signs of anything untoward, mainly to keep him out of the way.

"I found Mary Roth, Chief."

"What's your twenty?"

"A short sprint northerly." Ty's voice was tight with nervous excitement; he wasn't rotating tires now. "A hundred yards, I'd say. There's an old pickup sitting on blocks, but I doubt you'll see it with the grass being—"

"Step on the roof a moment, Ty. Flap those long arms."

Peck looked north where grass moved like a great hand brushing over it, and after a moment Ty's head poked up and he waved his arms. Peck started briskly toward him, cutting a trail through grass that started at his knees, then climbed to his chest and beyond. Rat snakes whipped out of sight and some tightened as he stepped over them, tongues at the air. Peck kept the mast of dark smoke at his back and turned often to keep his bearing.

Mary Roth knelt head down, arms crossed over her face. Her dress was faded, dirty, and had rucked up to her pale stomach. Her thighs were smeared with soot and grime.

"She say anything?" Peck asked Ty, stepping abreast of him.

"Not a word, Chief."

"Mary? Mary... it's Chief Peck."

The sun had risen fast and seemed dedicated to this thin clearing behind the abandoned pickup. Peck felt sweat trickle to his beltline and the heat at the back of his neck was heavy as a metal bar. He blew over his upper lip and crouched beside the woman. He could smell the smoke in her hair.

"Mary?"

Peck had known her all her life—Beau's only child, and to look at her was to cry, imagining what she might have been under kinder circumstances. But Beau was a fiercely wicked man who crushed all that could be loved. Mary—like all—was born beautiful. Thirty-two now with ghosts on her shoulders, her spirit withered like some sweet fruit dried in the heat.

"Talk to me, Mary."

He crouched lower and saw her mouth through her crossed arms. Teeth clenched.

"Are you hurt?"

A beat, and then she shook her head and uncrossed her arms. She used the hem of her dress to mop wet eyes. Soot beneath her fingernails. Smudged across her brow. She breathed and her upper body trembled, as if the world's hard edges had been packed into her lungs.

"This all..." Mary gestured at the truck and the clearing, then wider: at the trees, sky, and everything. "This all seems lesser now, like something that can be opened and poured out."

Peck wiped his eyes and saw Beau Roth disemboweled and headless. Crows bristled suddenly from the grass and made south, calling.

"You need to tell me what happened, Mary."

She almost smiled. There was red in her eyes. "Nothing but the devil's doing." Her hands trembled, curled to fists. "That son of a bitch got what he deserved."

⊸

Mary Roth weighed all of one hundred and twenty pounds and her fifteen-year-old daughter—Cindy: missing—was yet smaller. There was no way that, even working together, they could have strung up Beau's corpse. He was a truck of a man, loaded with old muscle. Peck knew he had some work to do.

The interview room was small and cool and—until about an hour ago—used mainly for storage. Interrogation was not one of Peck's regular duties. His days were spent on admin, general upkeep, and—when there was time—patrolling. Every now and then he'd be called to settle a dust-up, or would ticket speeders on the open stretch of blacktop between Heavenly and Gray Point. It was an unremarkable department, comprised of three full-time cops, one part-timer, and one volunteer. Enough for a two-stoplight town. Even so, Peck rarely worked fewer than sixty hours a week.

He and Ty cleared the interview room while Mary Roth got cleaned up and checked by paramedics. Calloway led her in just a little shy of noon. Her chestnut hair had been brushed and clasped back from her face, which was pale and sad, and her eyes had the look of cold water. She wore clothes salvaged from the town hall's lost and found. A Nike sweatshirt and a pair of basketball shorts almost as long on her as pants. She took a seat and placed her trembling hands flat on the table. Her fingernails had been scrubbed.

"Am I under arrest?"

"No, Mary."

"I may as well be; I got nowhere else to go."

She closed her eyes and a tear slipped fast onto her cheek. Peck nodded at Calloway and he left the room. For a moment the only sound was electricity in the walls and the sigh of the A/C. Peck set the audio recorder running. Tape spooled with a hiss.

"Tell me what happened, Mary. Leave nothing out."

She looked at him. "I tell you a lie and you'll think I'm guilty." She looked away. "I tell you the truth and you'll think I'm insane."

"Let's go with the truth."

"I already told you." Another tear, quick as the first. "It was the devil's doing."

Peck looked at the running tape and knew that the clock was ticking. County forensic units were already on the scene. If he didn't get answers soon, Pine County or state police investigators would take the reins. They'd be direct, insensitive. Peck didn't want them in his town.

"Your father's dead," he said. "Your daughter's missing. No doubt the devil played his part."

Mary wiped her eyes and they flickered and she stared for a long moment at the blank wall. There was a depth to her expression that made him turn away. He'd learned to study aspect and body language, where the truths were often clearer than anything spoken. The weight of her eyelids, the set of her mouth, her hands palm-down on the table, illustrated a single truth that unnerved him: Mary was haunted.

"I want to help you," Peck said.

"I'm beyond that."

"And I want to find Cindy."

"She's been gone a long time."

"Talk to me, Mary."

A mile out of town the Roth place—what remained—stood black and wet. The air still smelled of smoke and that other thing, sharp like ammonia. The vehicles plugging the yard belonged to the fire marshal and the county forensics unit, each working to assemble pieces that might make something like a picture. In Heavenly proper, tongues ran like a new fire and the devil was mentioned more than once, always in regard to Beau himself. In the interview room, the tape ran and the A/C purred. John Peck said little. Mary Roth blinked tears that flashed and unbridled her ghosts.

⊸⊷

"Momma died. Some brain thing, so they say. Thirty and dead, and I think God walked out on us the day we parked her box in the ground. Daddy got closer. First in a way that was affectionate, and then overly familiar. He raped me on my eleventh birthday. I felt afterward like a dress that had been left out in the wind and sun, all colorless and tattered. Something that could never be worn pretty. At fourteen I was pregnant with his child. You didn't know about that. The child was born—a boy—and at five months he fell off the bed and knocked his head good. He cried a lot and died in the night. Daddy buried him in the garden, like a dog with a bone. This all has nothing to do with the fire, except it does: when God is so missing from your life, the devil has more room to move."

Peck inhaled through his nose, his teeth locked and lightly grinding. He showed no emotion, but felt inside as though a match had been struck close to his heart.

"Daddy lost his job when Gator Steel cut loose a lot of manpower, and life moved from bad to worse in a hurry. I thought about running away. Even killing myself. I don't know if it's courage or stupidity that keeps a person from doing those things, but whatever it is, I got plenty of it. Daddy found work after a time. Nothing solid. Just here-and-there jobs. Cutting wood. Raking leaves. That kind of thing. I started waitressing at Captain Griddle. Daddy didn't like me leaving the house, but I brought in as much money as him and he found no room to argue. Anyway, that's where I met Gordy Lee. Short-order cook. Some sweet, but not exactly busy between the ears."

Peck nodded. He remembered Gordy. Cleft lip and a stutter. Gordy got knocked around by his older brothers. Peck would often see him cooking eggs with bruises about his face and then one day he wasn't cooking eggs any more. Rumor was he'd made tracks to Canada, but nobody knew for sure.

"We fooled around," Mary said, "but it was nothing much. Then one night when we were alone, cleaning up, he lifted my skirt and pumped himself into me, and I didn't stop him. Boy came like a horse and we made more than eggs in that kitchen. I told him a couple months later and he ripped quick out of town. Guess he wasn't ready to be a daddy—or to deal with *my* daddy. Chicken-livered, harelipped ol' son of a whore, either way you cut it."

"And Gordy is Cindy's father?"

"Yes, sir. She got his brown eyes and that's all."

"You ever hear from him?"

"No, sir."

"You don't know where he is?"

"No, sir."

Peck let his mind run an unlikely track: Gordy Lee—nearly sixteen years tougher and uglier—shooting south to claim his little girl, and taking care of Beau Roth in the bargain. Again Peck saw Beau hanging by his wrists, headless, guts strung about the blackened room. He remembered the bruised, skinny kid cooking eggs at Captain Griddle and couldn't get the pieces to fit, no matter which way he turned them.

Still, he asked, "You think Gordy may have tried to get in touch with Cindy?"

"No, sir." Mary shook her head. "Boy was a coward. A stupid one, at that. He could cook eggs and fuck like a bug, but that's about it."

Peck nodded and made a gesture for her to continue.

"I'm telling you what happened, for better or worse. You don't need your police hat right now. You need your *believing* hat. This little slice of family history shows that I'm done hiding, and I got no interest in lies. You might want to bear that in mind as we move along."

Peck nodded again.

"I kept being pregnant from Daddy for as long as I could. But a woman will usually show sooner with her second child, and by four months not even the biggest of my dresses could hide the bump. Daddy didn't take it well. I never told him that Gordy was the father—never told nobody, until now—but he wanted blood, just the same. He got into a lot of fistfights around town, and I guess he spent a few nights in those cells you have downstairs. I tried to stay out of his way. There's a clearing in Brack Wood where the sun shines in and the flowers grow long and pretty, and I'd go there all the time—just sit and daydream with my hands curled around my belly. I wouldn't go home 'til after dark when I knew Daddy would be passed out drunk. But I couldn't avoid him all the time and he found ways to hurt me. One time he suffocated me with a pillow. Held it over my face until the whole world faded, then took it away at the last moment. Another time he pinned me to the kitchen floor and shouted hateful things at my belly—shouted until his throat split like old wood. I've never hated him more."

Mary took one hand from the table and stroked her stomach. A soothing, circular motion. She looked at Peck and then away. The tears came again. These bigger, slower. She let them run down her face and drop from her chin.

"Ain't life a string of woe?" she said.

"It can get better," Peck said.

She shook her head as if she didn't believe that, and Peck could hardly blame her. She could live until everything about her withered, but might always feel that contentment was like the clothes they'd appropriated from the lost and found: not hers by right, something she'd never grow in to.

"If the best God can do for me is a few tall flowers in the wood, I fear He may be outgunned." A stiff, bitter smile. Her yellow teeth gleamed. "The devil has cast a wider net, and left a deeper mark."

Peck bridged his fingers. He still smelled smoke when he inhaled.

"Heavenly is a small town and people talk. I could hear the whispers from my house. A sound like bugs in the grass. And the way you all looked at me. Part wonder. Part sympathy. The way you'd look at someone born with a deformity. It's no wonder I didn't come looking for help." She uttered a brittle laugh. "But for all the talk, you got no clue how bad it was. I spent my days in fear and always crying. Then Cindy came along and I feared for her, too. But abuse isn't like an uncomfortable pair of boots you can just kick off. It's like being the passenger in a car speeding the wrong way down the highway. You know there's hurt ahead, but you're too scared to jump out. All you can do is hope it slows down, or better still, that it stops completely. Maybe it's different for other victims, who have more family and friends, or who live in a bigger town. But I don't know of much beyond Heavenly and Daddy. This is all I got. This is my life."

Mary drew a long breath. Spittle glimmered on her lips and she wiped her face with baggy sleeves. A little time passed. Peck thought about his wife and boys, relieved to erase—if only for a moment—Beau Roth from his mind. He'd take the boys fishing this weekend, he decided. And tonight, instead of sitting on the porch with a beer or two, he'd hold Gracie. Hold her tight. Grateful that he could.

"Seeing Daddy with Cindy, the way he treated her—the way he *mis*treated her—was bad. Feeling that I couldn't protect her was worse. And knowing that *I* brought her into this . . . " She trailed off, wet eyes rolling to the ceiling. "She used to beg me to run away with her. She had it all planned out. We'd leave while Daddy was at work. Hitchhike to Carver, then catch a bus to New York City. We'd be dancers, she said. Pretty as flowers, she said. I recall a time when she took her makeup box and made us both up, and we sat for a long time looking at one another in the mirror. Painted like dolls. It was like looking through a window into what *could* be. Then we turned the radio on and danced until we were short of breath. I've never known such joy. Couple nights later, Daddy rolled in drunk and took to us both. He knocked me out cold and when I came to, I saw his ugly bull of a body atop Cindy, pounding into her while she cried and bled. Her eyes met mine and I remembered how we'd looked in the mirror, and I knew then that I had to do something. But Cindy beat me to it. She was gone two days later. Up and left—jumped out of that speeding car. I found a note in her makeup box and it read GONE DANCING with a little X for a kiss. Fourteen years old. I thought the world would tear her to pieces and my heart just broke for her. For *me*, too. I was alone with the monster again. I didn't think life could get any worse. But I was wrong about that."

Mary placed her damp hands on the table and they left prints that glimmered in the light. Her breath hitched twice in her chest like a cold engine starting. Tears, still, running from some deep reservoir.

"Cindy came home a few months later."

⊸○⊷

Flowers with petals like lace, their stems withered, placed in a bunch on the ground. Peck thought: *He cried a lot and died in the night. Daddy buried him in the garden, like a dog with a bone.* Had a feeling that if he dug down just a little way, he'd find a tiny human skeleton. He shook his head and made a note to get on that. Give the boy a decent burial, stone and all, even if he had to pay for it himself.

A pale morning after a night of stripped sleep and Peck was at the Roth place early. Beau's body had been removed and now all that remained was the burned shell surrounded by yellow tape. It rippled with a sound almost lonesome. There was more at the head of the driveway, tied between trees, where officers had been posted in shifts to keep away prying townsfolk. Peck received the call last night that state police were taking over the investigation, which meant that he could go back to pushing his pen around and attending fundraisers. He turned from the little grave marked only with dry flowers and approached the blackened house. That ammonia smell still touched the air. He looked through the charred window where he had seen Beau's body hanging. Reddened and blistered but not burned through. *Makes no sense,* Joe Neath had said. Peck looked at his watch. Five of eight. State police would roll in at noon, suited and clean. Until then, this was his.

Perry Horne, the county fire marshal, had called him last night, too. His investigation was hindered by anomalies, 'cause of the blaze chief among them. "This'll take some time," he said. "I've known you twenty-some years, Peck, friend and colleague, and I don't mind telling you I'm at a loss. There's no obvious origin point, direction of melt is not consistent, and the char patterns—normally clear as footprints—have got me in circles. There's no evidence of an electrical fault or accelerants, and every room is evenly damaged. If I didn't know better, I'd say the entire house spontaneously ripped into flames."

"Can that happen?"

"Well shit, no." Perry had made an exasperated sound. "Every fire has cause and origin, Peck. But not this one. Not that I can see."

Peck had asked about Beau's corpse.

"I've got no answer for that, either," Perry replied. "Second-degree burns are not consistent with the damage to the house. Temperature in there would have been over a thousand degrees Fahrenheit. He should have been barbecue."

"That's what I thought."

"The way I see it, the house was deep in flames—the fire department likely rolling into the yard—before Beau was strung up."

"That's impossible."

"Yeah, it is." And Perry had barked a short, humourless laugh. "This whole thing is one big question mark."

"There has to be an explanation."

"When you find it, you let me know."

Peck walked away from the house and the hard thoughts associated with it, but couldn't get distance from the latter. They followed him like hungry children. The sun lifted from behind a shelf of cloud on the horizon and his shadow sprang ahead of him. He skirted the infant's grave and made through the high grass toward a cluster of trees—Brack Wood—with leaves catching the morning light. A vague trail linked the edge of Beau's lot to the trees, marking Mary's frequent passage. Peck followed it. The woods smelled of pine and turned earth and the light was a cool, watery green. After a time he came to the clearing Mary spoke of and the flowers were tall. Snakeroot and bellwort and Carolina lily. They nodded their bright, pretty heads. The only sounds were birdsong and the branches whickering.

This was where Mary—and perhaps Cindy, too—had come to escape the monster. A shallow scoop of serenity within their troubled lives. And the earth was fuller, the needles greener, for having absorbed so many daydreams. Peck sat with his back propped against a yellow pine and gathered his knees to his chest. Eyes closed, he sought patience and open-mindedness. Guidance, too. He inhaled the forest smells and they were kind. After a long moment, he opened his eyes and tears spilled onto his cheeks. It occurred to him—and not for the first time—that he could have helped those girls a long time ago. *Should* have.

Peck linked his hands and brought his knuckles to his forehead.

"God hear me . . . "

He'd tried praying last night. He'd prayed with his wife, their hands joined, but he hadn't sensed God and it was the same now.

The sun rode higher as he walked back to the house. The day's heat was already hard. Peck rounded the field and approached from a different direction, more northeasterly. Here the ground was patchy, long grass in places but mostly bare earth cracked and polished by the sun. Peck kept an eye out for carelessly discarded evidence—anything Tyler may have missed. They still hadn't found Beau's severed head. The thinking was that—unlike the rest of Beau—it had burned up in the blaze, and that Perry Horne would find his blackened teeth, or the tough knots of his skull, while sifting through the ashes.

Closer to the house, Peck discovered several black tracks in the dry grass. He squatted to his haunches to examine them in more detail. They were each about ten inches long, as wide as his hand and arched on the inside. Eleven in total, tracking away from the Roth place. Peck measured them against his own stride. He touched the scorched grass and smelled his fingers.

Yes, they were burn marks, but they were also footprints.

⟜

She wore the same clothes as the day before and the same haunted expression. Her hair wasn't clasped but looped onto her shoulders. It looked a shade lighter.

Peck's finger paused over the red button on the audio recorder.

"Listen, Mary, the state police will be here this afternoon and they'll want to question you. They don't know Heavenly, and they have little patience for small-town ways. They'll be stiff-necked and businesslike. That's the way they work. The more you tell me now—the more we get on tape—the less you'll have to tell them. Do you understand?"

Her eyes were heavy and dark. Peck thought she might be the only person in all of Heavenly who'd had less sleep than him.

"You don't live with Daddy for thirty-two years," she began with a dry smile, "only to be intimidated by a couple of suit-and-tie cops from the city. They can ask their damn questions, and they can be as businesslike as they please. I'll tell them everything I know, just like I'm telling you. This investigation won't depend on my cooperation, but on how quickly you can explain the unexplainable."

Peck recalled Perry Horne declaring this whole thing one big question mark. He felt something like a knot in his chest.

"Just thought you should know," he said.

She nodded.

Peck pushed the red button. The tape rolled.

"Do you know how your father died, Mary?"

Her hands were clasped in her lap and she looked at them and when she looked up her eyes fixed on Peck and did not waver. She shook her head once and then, realizing this wouldn't come across on tape, said, "No. I was in the yard at the time."

"Do you know who killed him?"

"The devil," she said, still looking at him straight.

"You get a good look at him?" Peck asked. "The devil?"

"*Her.*"

"I'm sorry?"

"Devil's a she," Mary said. Another dry smile. "And yeah, I got a good look. She slept under the same roof as me. Baked bread with me. I cooked her meals and washed her clothes."

"You're talking about Cindy?"

"I'm talking about the devil," Mary said. "She just *looked* like Cindy. Same hair, same eyes, same skin. But inside . . . not my little girl. No, sir."

Peck took a calming breath. Any other time he would have applied a little pressure—let Mary know that neighborly indulgence only carried so far. This was not a game, and he was not going to be played with. The mystery of this all stood before him, though, and he could not as yet see around it. He remembered the clearing with its tall flowers, and how he'd prayed for open-mindedness.

"Help me out, Mary," he said.

Mary sat back in her seat. She still looked at Peck but didn't really see him. Her expression glazed as her mind drifted elsewhere. Peck sat back in his own seat and it creaked and he waited. Mary shook her head. The tears came again and she didn't try to wipe them away. It looked like she had her face turned up to the rain. Just her face. She started to speak, but then stopped and broke down. "Not my little girl," she managed between sobs, and didn't say anything else for a long time.

Peck fetched her Kleenex and hot coffee in a paper cup and gave her a moment. The clock inched toward noon.

She said once her eyes were damp but not dry, "Cindy came home, but she wasn't the same. Something had happened to her out there. Wherever she went. She'd moved from being a young girl to a young woman, but it was more than that. A mother knows."

Peck felt like saying that years of abuse will wilt even the prettiest flower, but he bit his lip. He encouraged Mary with warm eyes and she kept talking.

"There was an edge to her. She was always fine with me, but with Daddy, the way she looked at him sometimes... she could drive nails with a stare like that. And Daddy felt it, too, because he didn't take to her the way he used to. Oh, he was still heavy-handed, and plenty so, but he kindly backed away afterward. I'd never seen him like that. Not scared but... *uncertain.* And that scared *me.*"

Another long silence and she looked away again, remembering. Peck counted time in his head. Only his chest moved as he breathed.

"But it wasn't only this edge," she continued. "No, sir, there was an outright wrongness about her. She was still some sweet but it felt like thin ice—like something that could crack at any time. I thought it was depression. I made an appointment to see Doctor Everett but Daddy stopped us from going. He said Cindy would snap out of it—that Everett would only go poking where he had no business, and no good would come of that."

Peck felt the anger and guilt tick inside him again.

"You surprised she was acting that way?" he asked. "Given everything that went on in that house?"

"It wasn't depression."

"She needed help, Mary."

"Don't we all?" Mary fixed him with the same unwavering glare and color rose from inside her collar, touched her jaw. "Judge me all you like, Chief, for something I did or didn't do, but save a few stones for yourself, for this whole shitheel town. And remember this: casting judgment on someone who's seen hell is just about the same as whipping the dead."

She and Peck took long breaths and something in the air realigned itself.

"Okay, Mary." He nodded. "Continue."

"Cindy said that the only reason she came home was to get me. Said she'd found a place where I'd be made stronger, and where I'd never be hurt again.

She begged me to go back with her but I didn't, for all the reasons I said before. I told her to go alone, to be happy and strong, but she said she wasn't leaving without me. I guess that's when all the strange things started happening."

"Strange?"

"Growling in the walls. The trees moving closer to the house. Two moons appearing in the sky, one as red as a drop of blood. Crows crowding the roof and windows. Rats and snakes pouring from the well." Mary counted off on her fingers but now she spread her hands wide. "Lots of things. Strange."

Peck nodded. He'd seen his share of strange just lately, but still believed he'd find the truth. Nothing real was truly unexplainable.

"One night—Daddy was mean-drunk and had just taken to me with his belt—I looked out the windows, front and back, and saw at least a hundred coyotes sitting in a circle around the house. They didn't howl or fuss. They just sat there, like they were waiting for something. Cindy asked me again to leave with her. I told her no. Then she stepped onto the porch, spoke some language I didn't understand, and those coyotes turned tail and slipped into the dark. Let me tell you, Chief, I've never been so scared. Not even when Daddy was at his worst."

Peck opened his mouth but found he had nothing to say.

"Clocks running backward. Windows and doors blowing open. Rain falling hard on the house and not a cloud in the sky. Flies everywhere, inside the house and out—so many damn flies. And don't get me started on the smell."

"Like ammonia?" Peck shifted in his seat.

"I guess," Mary said. "Sharp and bitter. Back of the throat."

Peck knew the smell, and this at least rang true, but he let everything else sit for now. Very little about this whole mess was normal, but a picture had started to form in his mind. He saw Cindy leaving home, getting in with some vigilante group—strong boys and arsonists among them—who decided to take the law into their own hands. It didn't come close to explaining everything, but Peck felt he was on the right track.

"This place," he said, studying Mary's dark-ringed eyes. "Where Cindy went. Where she wanted to take you. She ever tell you where it is?"

"No, sir."

"You don't know anything about it?"

"I tried asking, but she wouldn't say much. Got all tight-lipped and sullen."

"Tell me whatever you remember, Mary."

She thought a while, sitting back in her chair with her brow knitted, picking at her fingernails. Peck, for his part, worked to push away the unexplainable, and concentrate on solid facts. He figured everything else would slide into place once he had a strong foundation.

"Outside Heavenly," Mary said. She frowned a little deeper, then nodded. "She went on foot. That I know. Must've gone east because she said she passed the old water tower—said its shadow was like a big ol' spider. All them legs, you know?"

Peck nodded.

"She walked, but I don't know how far. All she said about the place was that the raptors circle clockwise there, except for one—him bigger—going aboutways."

Peck pulled a notebook from his pocket and wrote this down. "Anything else? Landmarks? Or distinct sounds—you know, like a river, or a train? Anything?"

"No, sir."

"How about the people she was with? Shc givc you any names? Descriptions?"

Mary stopped picking her fingernails and linked her hands much as Peck had in the clearing. "For what it's worth." And here the frown was replaced with a cold little smile. "She called them the boys with the black feet."

Peck pulled over at the side of Cotton Road. Sun on the windshield like a branding iron. To his left, beyond a rusted chain-link fence, Ring Field and the old water tower which had stood dry for more than ten years. Faded letters across the tank once read HEAVENLY. In a certain light you could see the ghosts of those letters, but not now. Peck stepped out of the cruiser and Tyler Bray followed. They scaled the fence like children. Ty tore his pants and swore.

East the way was flat and hard. Rocky ground and dust devils with the sun always like a hammer thrashing. A mile beyond, Forney Creek marked the town limits. They stopped to douse their hats in water, to fill their hands and drink. They crossed where it was shallowest but still got wet to the thighs, even Ty with his crane-fly legs. Here Peck had no jurisdiction. Here he turned from a lawmaker to a citizen with a gun.

"How far we walking, Chief?"

"Until I say."

"This ain't even Heavenly."

Across the cracked grassland to the southwest of Gray Point, through a sparse forest where the boughs rattled dryly, skirting marshland where bullfrogs croaked and a fetid mist rose from between the reeds. Beyond this the flies grew fat and many. The men slapped at them with their hats. Peck looked at the sky but it was bare and blue. They walked another twenty minutes then rested a while. Peck checked the time but his watch had stopped.

"Got the time there, Ty?"

Ty checked. "I got two-twenty."

"Well, shit. That can't be right."

"That's what I got."

They carried on but with languor, following no course other than Peck's instinct. Across barren fields and through a narrow valley of mostly shale, where the sun was reflected in bullets and horned lizards blinked at them sleepily. They emerged into a field where grass swayed chest-high. The flies grew in number but were slower, fatter. Ty wheezed and wanted to rest but Peck spurred him on. He was tired, too, and the heat had placed a fierce ache across the inside of his skull. Whenever he felt like stopping, he remembered Mary Roth in her borrowed, too-big clothes. So many tears, like a face in the rain.

Tell me about the night of the fire, Mary.

She'd be with the state police now. They'd lean hard on her. Cross-examine her. They'd listen to the tape and believe not a word.

Daddy saw all the strange happenings, too. He was stupid and angry, but not blind. It all got too much for him. He felt threatened, I guess. So he took me aside and told me that Cindy had been chained by the devil, and that it was our duty to set her free. I'd had the same thoughts—had even contemplated calling Reverend Mathis. I told Daddy this, but he wouldn't let me bring an outsider into the house. Not even a man of the cloth. He said he had his own way of handling it, and just as Christian.

Their hats dried in the heat and felt stiff on their heads, and Ty peeled his off and fanned his face with it. His shirt was black with sweat.

"You notice anything strange?" he gasped.

Peck searched the sky and the long grass and it *all* felt strange. *Thin,* almost, like a bleached and moistureless backdrop with something darker behind. He thought Ty was referring to the smell, though. It rose from the earth here. Caustic and foul. Back of the throat, Mary had said.

"That smell," Peck said, nodding. "Same as at the Roth place. Maybe we're getting close."

"Smell's bad, but that ain't it." Ty knuckled sweat from his eyes. Foamy spittle nestled at the corners of his mouth. "We're walking east, right?"

"More or less."

"Then why is the sun setting ahead of us?" Ty pointed at the fried bullet hole in the sky, and even *it* appeared to be sweating. "Should be behind us, this time of day."

Peck pulled up and frowned and turned a loose circle. He took off his hat and scratched his head. "Must've got turned around somehow."

"We walked a straight line and you know it."

"Just keep going." Peck put on his hat and sniffed the air, following his nose now. "East or west, don't matter. We're close."

Ty used his hat to shade the sun. "And don't it look like a drop of blood?"

It was the early hours. I was sleeping. Not deeply. I'm always aware of the sounds around me. It's like sleeping with one eye open, I guess. I heard a commotion and stirred, but then the screaming started and I jumped out of bed like there was a rattler between the sheets. I ran downstairs and saw Daddy stepping outside, Cindy slung over one shoulder like a sack of firewood. He'd tied her wrists and ankles with rope. I screamed and followed, and he shouted back at me to stay in the house, that I didn't need to see any of this. Normally I do what Daddy says, but not this time. No, sir. I staggered outside and saw Daddy drop Cindy next to the woodpile. He grabbed her hair and dragged her head-down across the chopping block. Then he took up his axe.

They kept walking and Peck felt blisters growing inside his boots and it wasn't long after that he noticed the sleek shapes in the grass. They flowed alongside and the grass rippled. Peck tried to get a sense of their number. He knew what they were long before Ty drew his sidearm.

"Coyotes," Ty said.

"They won't hurt you." But Peck wasn't sure about that. He placed a hand on the grip of his own Glock and walked wary.

"This is crazy, Chief."

"Keep walking."

"We shouldn't be doing this." Ty stopped suddenly and the shapes in the grass stopped, too. "We got no business out here."

"We got every business."

"You're chasing shadows." Ty holstered his weapon. Flies crawled across his face. Some were so big they dragged. "This is a state police matter. Let *them* trek through hell and back." He flapped at the flies but only some buzzed away.

"You listen to me, Ty Bray, and you listen good. We—that's you, me, the whole damn town—we spent too many years ignoring what was happening at the Roth place. Hid inside our comfortable little lives and didn't do a goddamn thing to help those girls. It's time to put that right. There's a truth out here somewhere and we're going to find it."

Ty wiped his eyes. "Let the state cops find it."

"They won't believe a word Mary tells them." Peck's face was a shade of red and his headache almost blinding. "They'll think she's hiding something and tear her to pieces. She may wind up confessing to something she didn't do, and I can't let that happen. She's been through enough."

Daddy raised his axe and I ran at him—bounced off him, more than anything. I clawed at his legs and he kicked me away. I would have gone at him again, of course, but then Cindy started talking in that weird language, same as when she spoke to the coyotes. I saw a glow beneath her skin, deep and orange, and the ropes binding her turned to ash. She got to her feet as Daddy was raising the axe again, and he just about fell over backward. Her eyes... they were like burning coals, pouring smoke. The axe toppled from his hands and she pushed him. It was like she was pushing a door open—that easy—and he flew halfway across the yard like a leaf in the wind. He got to his feet and reeled into the house. Cindy picked up the axe and followed.

Ty was now fifteen feet behind and staggering. Teeth clamped, shaking his head. He'd given up on swatting away the flies and they droned around him and settled and drank the sweat from his open pink pores. Peck flapped his own hat and saw ahead a scratch of forest. He sniffed at the bitter air and walked that way.

Cooler beneath the canopy, but darker. Here the coyotes were shadows and some howled in the gloom. Something else ticked among the branches. Peck waited for Ty, resting his hand on a gnarled trunk that twisted beneath him and when he looked he saw no trunk, no tree. Evening light spilled through the canopy, like wine through a cracked glass.

"Let's stop awhile," Ty panted.

"I don't want to stop here."

They trudged on with Peck barely looking, his dread tamped down by determination. The thunder in his head was his heartbeat—a reckless, spirited thing. They made it through the forest and the light now was burned purple. Across a wide, dry riverbed and into a field marked by the outlines of trees and rocks. The grass here was knee-high and the coyotes' backs showed like otters in water.

"There's a hill ahead," Peck said, pointing to where the ground rose. "We can maybe get a bearing from there."

Ty nodded but he looked close to tears, no doubt wishing he was changing oil at Go Auto or hanging out with his girl. They struggled up the hill, which wasn't steep, but both men fairly crawled. At the summit, Peck looked around but saw nothing he recognized. The sky had grown pale. He'd swear it was getting light again. They caught their breaths and pushed on. Midway down the hill, Peck noticed—not a mile away—a small settlement. Glass and aluminum winked in the sunlight. It was definitely getting lighter. Hotter, too.

"This is some kind of nightmare," Ty said.

Peck's gaze drifted upward, and he saw several birds in the sky above the settlement. Red-tailed hawks, he thought, judging from the size. They circled clockwise, all but one—a raptor Peck had no name for, with a broader, crooked span—looping the other way.

He moved on. His stride was long.

"We're here," he said.

I can't tell you what happened in the house because I stayed in the yard. And I wasn't alone. The coyotes were back, sitting in the long grass with their ears high and their eyes shining. Seemed the devil was all ways and if there was any heaven to be found, I didn't know where. So I stayed put. And how I screamed, but not as loud as Daddy, and not for as long. Then the house went up. You know when you set fire to a book of matches and it flares in your hand all at once? It was like that. I thought for sure they were both dead, then Cindy stepped out of the flames. She was on fire, but she wasn't burning. I know how that sounds, but I swear it's true. It's like she controlled those flames; like the coyotes, they did whatever she told them to, and ain't that the devil's way? I watched her walk across the grass and away, all those coyotes by her side, and for a while I followed her flame and then she was gone. Then I took to my heels. I wanted to find my clearing but got lost in the dark. I wound up by that old truck in the field, and there I hid, and there you found me.

Peck thought "settlement" too grand a word for what amounted to a few tumble-down shacks and trailers. Some were painted faded colors, their windows either blacked-out or boarded over. There were no satellite dishes or barbecues. No washing strung to dry. Peck would think it abandoned but for the feeling they were being watched—and not only by the coyotes, mostly gathered in the grass around the site. Others sat on the tall rocks with their backs straight.

"What is this place?" Ty asked. He was a step or two behind Peck.

"I'm not sure."

Cogongrass sprung from the baked earth, strewn with trash. A dusty flag Peck didn't recognize rippled softly. They advanced cautiously and came across four listless hogs tied to a stake in the earth. The smell in the air was that same bitter ammonia, hard to breathe. The sun rode directly overhead and the heat was thick as tar.

"*Anybody home?*" Ty screamed. He brushed at the flies on his face. "*Anybody? I figured hell would be busier.*"

"Hush." Peck placed a hand on Ty's chest and he knocked it away.

"Don't touch me."

Sound of a door opening, closing with a snap. They turned and saw a boy walking toward them, bare-chested, eating something from a bowl. Five years old, Peck figured, having a boy of his own that age.

"Keep it together," Peck whispered to Ty. "Remember, we got no jurisdiction here, but these people don't know that. Keep your weapon holstered. Pull that trigger and you'll have a lot of questions to answer."

The boy wore faded blue jeans turned up at the ankles. His feet were soot-black. The bowl was filled with dry corn. It rattled between his teeth when he spoke.

"You probably shouldn't be here."

"We're looking for somebody," Peck said. He turned on his friendly police officer smile, perhaps to make up for his shapeless hat and the flies on his throat. "Maybe you can help me. Girl. Fifteen years old. Brown hair. Goes by the name of Cindy."

"She's with us now," the little boy said. He took a mouthful of corn that rattled. "And she ain't Cindy no more."

Even in the heat, these words sent a chill motoring up Peck's spine. They mirrored what Mary had said. Not that he needed more convincing. As a lawman he'd always favored a logical line, but after everything he'd seen and heard, that line wasn't nearly as solid.

"Where is she?" Ty asked.

The boy softened corn in his mouth. He spat yellow in the dirt, then turned around and walked away.

"Hey!"

"Rubin's trailer." He flicked a finger to his left.

The men—bone-weary but still upright—moved in that direction, beyond a screen of raggedy shrubs and toward a trailer the color of an old dime. It sat on its underbelly, wheels and jack long gone. Dry weed snaked through holes in the paneling and the windows were marked with red Xs. There were two coyotes perched on the roof, coats clotted with dirt and teeth showing. Somebody had buried an axe in the trunk of a nearby tree. A tin bucket hung from a branch by a length of twine.

Peck looked over his shoulder and saw the little boy watching and grinning. In the heat it looked like his black feet were smoking.

"We find her and go," Peck said. "We'll send the big boys back here to ask questions."

"Amen," Ty said.

Peck turned back toward the trailer and in so doing walked clumsily into the tin bucket hanging from the branch. A drove of flies were disturbed but didn't go far. The bucket swung and the branch creaked. Peck looked inside and saw Beau Roth's head, parched and blistered. One eye was filled with flies.

"Christ and Jesus." He staggered backward and drew his gun and Ty drew his, too. Peck flapped a hand at him that didn't make any sense and Ty hunkered, confused, and the barrel of his weapon moved unsurely. The flies settled again on the bucket. The coyotes on the roof howled. Peck looked the way they had come and saw the little boy laughing. He imagined the corn rattling between his teeth and had an urge to run a bullet through his narrow chest, then a door squeaked open and he turned to see Cindy Roth standing outside the trailer. Not the same girl who sat quietly at the back of the class while Peck gave one of his school talks, or the girl he often saw walking the mile from Sunshine Shopper to her house, weighed down with groceries, and who wouldn't accept a ride when he offered it. Cindy Roth now was fierce-eyed, closer to a woman, and with a charge about her—some deep thing desperate to break out. She smiled and stepped toward Peck. Her feet were black.

"Hello, Chief," she said.

⊸

All Peck wanted was a shred of solid evidence, something to lend credence to Mary Roth's story, enough for the state police to investigate further. He'd brought Ty along because he didn't want to be alone, but also because Ty—unlike Calloway—was green enough to follow, even when they went beyond the town limits.

He hoped he'd live to regret his decisions.

It all happened quickly.

There came a whirl of heat and dust and suddenly they were surrounded by black-footed boys, including two atop Rubin's trailer—thin and naked both—in place of the coyotes. Peck backed away and raised his gun in warning. Ty showed no such restraint. He fired two shots at the boys on the trailer and missed them both. Peck screamed at him to cease fire but he didn't listen. He turned and shot the little boy dead. Blew him backward, black feet smoking. His bowl of corn spilled everywhere.

Peck recalled Mary gesturing at the sky—at everything—and saying that it all seemed lesser, like something that could be opened and poured out, and now he knew exactly what she meant. He did then the one thing he thought would save his hide: turned his gun on Ty and shot him in the throat. Ty went down, dead as stone before he hit the ground.

Still the fire came.

The crooked raptor landed in a flurry of thick black feathers, squawking as flames ripped suddenly, viciously, around the site. Peck shielded his eyes and when he looked again, the bird was gone. A man strode toward him—black-footed, like the boys—over eight feet tall and narrow-faced. Smoke rippled from his eyes and he spat coal and bones. Peck was lifted into the air without being touched, fully ten feet above the ground, and then dropped. The boys howled and Peck tried to reel away but was lifted again. He saw the site burning and the fields beyond. He saw Cindy Roth twisting in the flames and laughing. Embers burst from her mouth and spiraled around her. Again Peck was dropped and he landed hard, breaking both legs. Still he tried to crawl.

Fire surrounded him. It sucked the oxygen from the air and he wheezed and reached for help that would never come. His skin bubbled in the heat but did not blacken.

The man stood over him. Flames crackled from the tips of his fingers.

Peck lifted his gun and pulled the trigger desperately. The first and second shots hit the tall man square in the chest. Fire and feathers flew. The third hit Cindy Roth and threw her thin, fifteen-year-old body back through the door of the trailer. Eleven rounds left in the mag and Peck spent them all. Some of those shots went astray but most found a home. Bodies and fire all around.

Peck tried to scream but there wasn't the air. He wished he'd kept a bullet for himself. He crawled a little way and then fell chest-down in the dirt. The cogongrass crackled as it burned and he heard the hogs squealing.

The last thing he saw before passing out was the little boy Ty had shot, back on his feet and scooping corn—popped now—off the ground and into his mouth. His smile was almost beautiful.

⊸

He came around with the fires still burning and the skin on his face and hands blistered. All the shacks and trailers were gone. The boys with the black feet were gone. Not a body in the dirt, nor a drop of blood. Not even Ty's.

Just him and that bucket twisting in the heat.

Peck dragged his broken legs and screamed. The fire raged around him, branding a shape on the land he felt but could not see: a five-pointed star enclosed in a perfect circle, burning hungrily and—from point to point—many miles wide.

SHAY CORSHAM WORSTED

GARTH NIX

The young man came in one of the windows, because the back door had proved surprisingly tough. He'd kicked it a few times, without effect, before looking for an easier way to get in. The windows were barred, but the bars were rusted almost through, so he had no difficulty pulling them away. The window was locked as well, but he just smashed the glass with a half brick pried out of the garden wall. He didn't care about the noise. He knew there was only the old man in the house, the garden was large and screened by trees, and the evening traffic was streaming past on the road out front. That was plenty loud enough to cloak any noise he might make.

Or any quavering cries for help from the old man, thought the intruder, as he climbed through. He went to the back door first, intending to open it for a quick getaway, but it was deadlocked. More afraid of getting robbed than dying in a fire, thought the young man. That made it easier. He liked the frightened old people, the power he had over them with his youth and strength and anger.

When he turned around, the old man was standing behind him. Just standing there, not doing a thing. It was dim in the corridor, the only light a weak bulb hanging from the ceiling, its pallid glow falling on the bald head of the little man, the ancient slight figure in his brown cardigan and brown corduroy trousers and brown slippers, just a little old man that could be picked up and broken like a stick and then whatever pathetic treasures were in the house could be—

A little old man whose eyes were silver.

And what was in his hands?

Those gnarled hands had been empty, the intruder was sure of it, but now the old bloke held long blades, though he wasn't exactly holding the blades . . . they were growing, growing from his fingers, the flesh fusing together and turning silver . . . silver as those eyes!

The young man had turned half an inch towards the window and escape when the first of those silvery blades penetrated his throat, destroying his voice box, changing the scream that rose there to a dull, choking cough. The second blade went straight through his heart, back out, and through again.

Pock! Pock!

Blood geysered, but not on the old man's brown cardigan. He had moved back almost in the same instant as he struck and was now ten feet away, watching with those silver eyes as the young man fell writhing on the floor, his feet drumming for eighteen seconds before he became still.

The blades retreated, became fingers once again. The old man considered the body, the pooling blood, the mess.

"Shay Marazion Velvet," he said to himself, and walked to the spray of blood farthest from the body, head-high on the peeling wallpaper of green lilies. He poked out his tongue, which grew longer and became as silver as the blades.

He began to lick, tongue moving rhythmically, head tilted as required. There was no expression on his face, no sign of physical excitement. This was not some fetish.

He was simply cleaning up.

⸺

"You'll never guess who I saw walking up and down outside, Father," said Mary Shires, as she bustled in with her ludicrously enormous basket filled with the weekly tribute of home-made foods and little luxuries that were generally unwanted and wholly unappreciated by her father, Sir David Shires.

"Who?" grunted Sir David. He was sitting at his kitchen table, scrawling notes on the front page of the *Times*, below the big headlines with the latest from the war with Argentina over the Falklands, and enjoying the sun that was briefly flooding the whole room through the open doors to the garden.

"That funny little Mister Shea," said Mary, putting the basket down on the table.

Sir David's pencil broke. He let it fall and concentrated on keeping his hand still, on making his voice sound normal. He shouldn't be surprised, he told himself. It was why he was here, after all. But after so many years, even though every day he told himself this could be *the* day, it was a terrible, shocking surprise.

"Really, dear?" he said. He thought his voice sounded mild enough. "Going down to the supermarket like he normally does, I suppose? Getting his bread and milk?"

"No, that's just the thing," said Mary. She took out a packet of some kind of biscuit and put it in front of her father. "These are very good. Oatmeal and some kind of North African citrus. You'll like them."

"Mister Shea," prompted Sir David.

"Oh, yes. He's just walking backwards and forwards along the footpath from his house to the corner. Backwards and forwards! I suppose he's gone ga-ga. He's old enough. He must be ninety if he's a day, surely?"

She looked at him, without guile, both of them knowing he was eighty himself. But not going ga-ga, thank god, even if his knees were weak reeds and he couldn't sleep at night, remembering things that he had forced himself to forget in his younger days.

But Shay was much older than ninety, thought Sir David. Shay was much, much older than that.

He pushed his chair back and stood up.

"I might go and . . . and have a word with the old chap," he said carefully. "You stay here, Mary."

"Perhaps I should come—"

"No!"

He grimaced, acknowledging he had spoken with too much emphasis. He didn't want to alarm Mary. But then again, in the worst case . . . no, not the worst case, but in a quite plausible minor escalation . . .

"In fact, I think you should go out the back way and get home," said Sir David.

"Really, Father, why on—"

"Because I am ordering you to," snapped Sir David. He still had the voice, the tone that expected to be obeyed, deployed very rarely with the family, but quite often to the many who had served under him, first in the Navy and then for considerably longer in the Department, where he had ended up as the Deputy Chief. Almost fifteen years gone, but it wasn't the sort of job where you ever completely left, and the command voice was the least of the things that had stayed with him.

Mary sniffed, but she obeyed, slamming the garden gate on her way out. It would be a few years yet, he thought, before she began to question everything he did, perhaps start bringing brochures for retirement homes along with her special biscuits and herbal teas she believed to be good for reducing the chance of dementia.

Dementia. There was an apposite word. He'd spent some time thinking he might be suffering from dementia or some close cousin of it, thirty years ago, in direct connection to "funny old Mister Shea." Who was not at all funny, not in any sense of the word. They had all wondered if they were demented, for a time.

He paused near his front door, wondering for a moment if he should make the call first, or even press his hand against the wood paneling just so, and flip it open to take out the .38 Colt Police revolver cached there. He had a 9mm Browning automatic upstairs, but a revolver was better for a cached weapon. You wouldn't want to bet your life on magazine springs in a weapon that had sat too long. He checked all his armament every month, but still . . . a revolver was more certain.

But automatic or revolver, neither would be any use. He'd learned that before, from direct observation, and had been lucky to survive. Very lucky, because the other two members of the team hadn't had the fortune to slip in the mud and hit themselves on the head and be forced to lie still. They'd gone in shooting, and kept shooting, unable to believe the evidence of their eyes, until it was too late . . .

Sir David grimaced. This was one of the memories he'd managed to push aside for a long, long time. But like all the others, it wasn't far below the surface. It didn't take much to bring it up, that afternoon in 1953, the Department's secure storage on the fringe of RAF Bicester . . .

He did take a walking stick out of the stand. A solid bog oak stick, with a pommel of bronze worked in the shape of a spaniel's head. Not for use as a weapon, but simply because he didn't walk as well as he once did. He couldn't afford a fall now. Or at any time really, but particularly not now.

The sun was still shining outside. It was a beautiful day, the sky as blue as a bird's egg, with hardly a cloud in sight. It was the kind of day you only saw in films, evoking some fabulous summer time that never really existed, or not for more than half an hour at a time.

It was a good day to die, if it came to that, if you were eighty and getting tired of the necessary props to a continued existence. The medicines and interventions, the careful calculation of probabilities before anything resembling activity, calculations that Sir David would never have undertaken at a younger age.

He swung out on to the footpath, a military stride, necessarily adjusted by age and a back that would no longer entirely straighten. He paused by the kerb and looked left and right, surveying the street, head back, shoulders close to straight, sandy eyebrows raised, hair no longer quite so regulation short, catching a little of the breeze, the soft breeze that added to the day's delights.

Shay was there, as Mary had said. It was wearing the same clothes as always, the brown cardigan and corduroy. They'd put fifty pairs in the safe house, at the beginning, uncertain whether Shay would buy more or not, though its daily purchase of bread, milk, and other basics was well established. It could mimic human behavior very well.

It looked like a little old man, a bald little man of some great age. Wrinkled skin, hooded eyes, head bent as if the neck could no longer entirely support the weight of years. But Sir David knew it didn't always move like an old man. It could move fluidly, like an insect, faster than you ever thought at first sighting.

Right now Shay was walking along the footpath, away from Sir David. Halfway to the corner, it turned back. It must have seen him, but as usual, it gave no outward sign of recognition or reception. There would be no such sign, until it decided to do whatever it was going to do next.

Sir David shuffled forward. Best to get it over with. His hand was already sweating, slippery on the bronze dog handle of his stick, his heart hammering in a fashion bound to be at odds with a cardio-pulmonary system past its best. He knew the feeling well, though it had been an age since he'd felt it more than fleetingly.

Fear. Unalloyed fear, that must be conquered, or he could do nothing, and that was not an option. Shay had broken free of its programming. It could be about to do anything, anything at all, perhaps reliving some of its more minor exploits like the Whitechapel murders of 1888, or a major one like the massacre at Slapton Sands in 1944.

Or something greater still.

Not that Sir David was sure he *could* do anything. He'd only ever been told two of the command phrases, and lesser ones at that, a pair of two word groups. They were embossed on his mind, bright as new brass. But it was never known exactly what they meant, or how Shay understood them.

There was also the question of which command to use. Or to try and use both command phrases, though that might somehow have the effect of one of the four word command groups. An unknown effect, very likely fatal to Sir David and everyone for miles, perhaps more.

It was not inconceivable that whatever he said in the next two minutes might doom everyone in London, or even the United Kingdom.

Perhaps even the world.

The first command would be best, Sir David thought, watching Shay approach. They were out in public, the second would attract attention, besides its other significant drawback. Public attention was anathema to Sir David, even in such dire circumstances. He straightened his tie unconsciously as he thought about publicity. It was a plain green tie, as his suit was an inconspicuous grey flannel, off the rack. No club or regimental ties for Sir David, no identifying signet rings, no ring, no earring, no tattoos, no unusual facial hair. He worked to look a type that had once been excellent camouflage, the retired military officer. It still worked, though less well, there being fewer of the type to hide amongst. Perhaps the Falklands War would help in this regard.

Shay was drawing nearer, walking steadily, perfectly straight. Sir David peered at it. Were its eyes silver? If they were, it would be too late. All bets off, end of story. But the sun was too bright, Sir David's own sight was not what it once was. He couldn't tell if Shay's eyes were silver.

"Shay Risborough Gabardine," whispered Sir David. Ludicrous words, but proven by trial and error, trial by combat, death by error. The name it apparently gave itself, a station on the Great Western Line, and a type of fabric. Not words you'd ever expect to find together, there was its safety, the cleverness of Isambard Kingdom Brunel showing through. Though not as clever as how IKB had got Shay to respond to the words in the first place. So clever that no one else had worked out how it had been done, not in the three different attempts over more than a hundred years. Attempts to try to change or expand the creature's lexicon, each attempt another litany of mistakes and many deaths. And after each such trial, the fear that had led to it being shut away. Locked underground the last time, and then the chance rediscovery in 1953 and the foolishness that had led it to being put away here, parked and forgotten.

Except by Sir David.

Shay was getting very close now. Its face looked innocuous enough. A little vacant, a man not too bright perhaps, or very short of sleep. Its skin was pale today, matching Sir David's own, but he knew it could change that in an instant. Skin colour, height, apparent age, gender... all of these could be changed by Shay, though it mostly appeared as it was right now.

Small and innocuous, old and tired. Excellent camouflage among humans.

Ten paces, nine paces, eight paces... the timing had to be right. The command had to be said in front of its face, without error, clear and precise—

"Shay Risborough Gabardine," barked Sir David, shivering in place, his whole body tensed to receive a killing blow.

Shay's eyes flashed silver. He took half a step forward, putting him inches away from Sir David, and stopped. There was a terrible stillness, the world perched on the brink. Then it turned on its heel, crossed the road and went back into its house. The old house, opposite Sir David's, that no one but Shay had set foot in for thirty years.

Sir David stood where he was for several minutes, shaking. Finally he quelled his shivering enough to march back inside his own house, where he ignored the phone on the hall table, choosing instead to open a drawer in his study to lift out a chunkier, older thing that had no dial of any kind, push-button or rotary. He held the handset to his head and waited.

There were a series of clicks and whines and beeps, the sound of disparate connections working out how they might after all get together. Finally a sharp, quick male voice answered on the other end.

"Yes."

"Case Shay Zulu," said Sir David. There was a pause. He could hear the flipping of pages, as the operator searched through the ready book.

"Is there more?" asked the operator.

"What!" exploded Sir David. "Case Shay Zulu!"

"How do you spell it?"

Sir David's lip curled almost up to his nose, but he pulled it back.

"S-H-A-Y," he spelled out. "Z-U-L-U."

"I can spell Zulu," said the operator, affronted. "There's still nothing."

"Look up my workname," said Sir David. "Arthur Brooks."

There was tapping now, the sound of a keyboard. He'd heard they were using computers more and more throughout the Department, not just for the boffins in the back rooms.

"Ah, I see... I've got you now, sir," said the operator. At least there was a "sir," now.

"Get someone competent to look up Shay Zulu and report my communication at once to the duty officer with instruction to relay it to the Chief," ordered Sir David. "I want a call back in five minutes."

The call came in ten minutes, ten minutes Sir David spent looking out his study window, watching the house across the road. It was eleven a.m., too late for Shay to go to the supermarket like it had done every day for the last thirty years. Sir David wouldn't know if it had returned to its previous safe routine until 10:30 a.m. tomorrow. Or earlier, if Shay was departing on some different course...

The insistent ringing recalled him to the phone.

"Yes."

"Sir David? My name is Angela Terris, I'm the duty officer at present. We're a bit at sea here. We can't find Shay Zulu in the system at all— what was that?"

Sir David had let out a muffled cry, his knuckles jammed against his mouth.

"Nothing, nothing," he said, trying to think. "The paper files, the old records to 1977, you can look there. But the important thing is the book, we... I must have the notebook from the Chief's safe, a small green leather book embossed on the cover with the gold initials IKB."

"The Chief's not here right now," said Angela brightly. "This Falklands thing, you know. He's briefing the cabinet. Is it urgent?"

"Of course it's urgent!" barked Sir David, regretting it even as he spoke, remembering when old Admiral Fuller had called up long after retirement, concerned about a suspicious new postman, and how they had laughed on the Seventh Floor. "Look, find Case Shay Zulu and you'll see what I mean."

"Is it something to do with the Soviets, Sir David? Because we're really getting on reasonably well with them at the moment—"

"No, no, it's nothing to do with the Soviets," said Sir David. He could hear the tone in her voice, he remembered using it himself when he had taken Admiral Fuller's call. It was the calming voice that meant no immediate action, a routine request to some functionary to investigate further in days, or even weeks, purely as a courtesy to the old man. He had to do something that would make her act, there had to be some lever.

"I'm afraid it's something to do with the Service itself," he said. "Could be very, very embarrassing. Even now. I need that book to deal with it."

"Embarrassing as in likely to be of media interest, Sir David?" asked Angela.

"Very much so," said Sir David heavily.

"I'll see what I can do," said Angela.

⊸

"We were really rather surprised to find the Department owns a safe house that isn't on the register," said the young, nattily dressed and borderline rude young man who came that afternoon. His name, or at least the one he had supplied, was Redmond. "Finance were absolutely delighted, it must be worth close to half a million pounds now, a huge place like that. Fill a few black holes with that once we sell it. On the quiet, of course, as you say it would be very embarrassing if the media got hold of this little real estate venture."

"Sell it?" asked Sir David. "Sell it! Did you only find the imprest accounts, not the actual file? Don't you understand? The only thing that stops Shay from running amok is routine, a routine that is firmly embedded in and around that house! Sell the house and you unleash the . . . the beast!"

"Beast, Sir David?" asked Redmond. He suppressed a yawn and added, "Sounds rather Biblical. I expect we can find a place for this Shea up at Exile House. I daresay they'll dig his file up eventually, qualify him as a former employee."

They could find a place for Sir David too, were the unspoken words. Exile House, last stop for those with total disability suffered on active service, crippled by torture, driven insane from stress, shot through both knees and elbows. There were many ways to arrive at Exile House.

"Did you talk to the Chief?" asked Sir David. "Did you ask about the book marked 'IKB'?"

"Chief's very busy," said Redmond. "There's a war on, you know. Even if it is only a little one. Look, why don't I go over and have a chat to old Shea, get a feel for the place, see if there's anything else that might need sorting?"

"If you go over there you introduce another variable," said Sir David, as patiently as he could. "Right now, I've got Shay to return to its last state, which may or may not last until ten-thirty tomorrow morning, when it goes and gets its bread and milk, as it has done for the last thirty years. But if you disrupt it again, then who knows what will happen."

"I see, I see," said Redmond. He nodded as if he had completely understood. "Bit of a mental case, hey? Well, I did bring a couple of the boys in blue along just in case."

"Boys in blue!"

Sir David was almost apoplectic. He clutched at Redmond's sleeve, but the young man effortlessly withdrew himself and sauntered away.

"Back in half a 'mo," he called out cheerfully.

Sir David tried to chase him down, but by the time he got to the front door it was shut in his face. He scrabbled at the weapon cache, pushing hard on a panel till he realized it was the wrong one. By the time he had the revolver in his hand and had wrestled the door open, Redmond was already across the road, waving to the two policemen in the panda car to follow him. They got out quickly, large men in blue, putting their hats on as they strode after the young agent.

"Not even Special Branch," muttered Sir David. He let the revolver hang by his side. What could he do with it anyway? He couldn't shoot Redmond, or the policemen.

Perhaps, he thought bleakly, he could shoot himself. That would bring them back, delay the knock on the door opposite... but it would only be a delay. And if he was killed, and if they couldn't find Brunel's book, then the other command words would be lost.

Redmond went up the front steps two at a time, past the faded sign that said, "Hawkers and Salesmen Not Welcome. Beware of the Vicious Dog" and the one underneath it that had been added a year after the first, "No Liability for Injury or Death, You Have Been Warned."

Sir David blinked, narrowing his eyes against the sunshine that was still streaming down, flooding the street. It was just like the afternoon, that afternoon in '43 when the sun had broken through after days of fog and ice, but even though it washed across him on the bridge of his frigate he couldn't feel it, he could only see the light, he was so frozen from the cold Atlantic days the sunshine couldn't touch him, there was no warmth that could reach him...

He felt colder now. Redmond was knocking on the door. Hammering on the door. Sir David choked a little on his own spit, apprehension rising. There was a chance Shay wouldn't answer, and the door was very heavy, those two policemen couldn't kick it down, there would be more delay—

The door opened. There was the flash of silver, and Redmond fell down the steps, blood geysering from his neck as if some newfangled watering system had suddenly switched on beside him, drawing water from a rusted tank.

A blur of movement followed. The closer policeman spun about, as if suddenly inspired to dance, only his head was tumbling from his shoulders to dance apart from him. The surviving policeman, that is, the policeman who had survived the first three seconds of contact with Shay, staggered backwards and started to turn around to run.

He took one step before he too was pierced through with a silver spike, his feet taking him only to the gutter where he lay down to die.

Sir David went back inside, leaving the door open. He went to his phone in the hall and called his daughter. She answered on the fourth ring. Sir David's hand was so sweaty he had to grip the plastic tightly, so the phone didn't slip from his grip.

"Mary? I want you to call Peter and your girls and tell them to get across the Channel now. France, Belgium, doesn't matter. No, wait, Terence is in Newcastle, isn't he? Tell him... listen to me... he can get the ferry to Stavanger. Listen! There is going to be a disaster here. It doesn't matter what kind! I haven't gone crazy, you know who I know. They have to get out of the country and across the water! Just go!"

Sir David hung up. He wasn't sure Mary would do as he said. He wasn't even sure that the sea would stop Shay. That was one of the theories, never tested, that it wouldn't or couldn't cross a large body of water. Brunel almost certainly knew, but his more detailed papers had been lost. Only the code book had survived. At least until recently.

He went to the picture window in his study. It had been installed on his retirement, when he'd moved here to keep an eye on Shay. It was a big window, taking up the place of two old Georgian multi-paned affairs, and it had an excellent view of the street.

There were four bodies in full view now. The latest addition was a very young man. Had been a young man. The proverbial innocent bystander, in the wrong place at the wrong time. A car sped by, jerking suddenly into the other lane as the driver saw the corpses and the blood.

Shay walked into the street and looked up at Sir David's window.

Its eyes were silver.

The secure phone behind Sir David rang. He retreated, still watching Shay, and picked it up.

"Yes."

"Sir David? Angela Terris here. The police are reporting multiple 999 calls, apparently there are people—"

"Yes. Redmond and the two officers are dead. I told him not to go, but he did. Shay is active now. I tried to tell you."

Shay was moving, crossing the road.

"Sir David!"

"Find the book," said Sir David wearily. "That's the only thing that can help you now. Find the leather book marked 'IKB.' It's in the Chief's safe."

Shay was on Sir David's side of the street, moving left, out of sight.

"The Chief's office was remodeled last year," said Angela Terris. "The old safe . . . I don't know—"

Sir David laughed bitter laughter and dropped the phone.

There was the sound of footsteps in the hall.

Footsteps that didn't sound quite right.

Sir David stood at attention and straightened his tie. Time to find out if the other command did what it was supposed to do. It would be out of his hands then. If it worked, Shay would kill him and then await further instructions for twenty-four hours. Either they'd find the book or they wouldn't, but he would have done his best.

As always.

Shay came into the room. It didn't look much like an old man now. It was taller, and straighter, and its head was bigger. So was its mouth.

"Shay Corsham Worsted," said Sir David.

ALLOCHTON

LIVIA LLEWELLYN

> "Taking definite form toward the middle of the century, comes the revival of romantic feeling—the era of new joy in Nature, and in the radiance of past times, strange scenes, bold deeds, and incredible marvels. We feel it first in the poets, whose utterances take on new qualities of wonder, strangeness, and shuddering."
>
> —H. P. Lovecraft, *Supernatural Horror in Literature*

On this planet, in this universe, geology is geology—the land simply *is*, and it is nothing else. Mountain ranges and forests and "Nature" in its entirety are not sentient, they have no wisdom or knowledge to impart upon the world, and whatever emotional expectations each individual traveler draws from their journeys into the wild is of their making alone—the landscape "speaks" to us, but it's only we who are doing the talking. Or so we say we believe—I myself am not quite as certain, and I suspect many of us feel the same. Lovecraft certainly didn't believe this to be the truth of our world. "There was a . . . cosmic beauty in the hypnotic landscape through which we climbed and plunged fantastically," Lovecraft wrote in "The Whisperer in the Darkness," "and I seemed to find in its necromancy a thing I had innately known or inherited and for which I had always been vainly searching." Time and time again, he wrote of the land around us as alive in ways we barely comprehend, watching us, calling out to us, drawing us in. How, then, can we really know for certain that the conversation is so one-sided, that those resplendent and horrifying feelings of *mysterium tremendum et fascinans* that the supernal wilderness of the world draws from us aren't the cosmic answers to questions we instinctively ask? Living as we do today, in cities and suburbs subtly crafted as if to seem once removed from unstoppable Nature, we forget that we came from the land; we are wet mortal ghost-slivers of the geologic forces out of which every living thing evolved. The land is always with us, because it *is* us. And when, in ways wondrous and strange, we are called home, we have no choice but to go.

North Bonneville, 1934

Ruth sits in the kitchen of her company-built house, slowly turning the pages of her scrapbook. The clock on the bookcase chimes ten. In the next room, the only other room, she hears her husband getting dressed. He's deliberately slow on Sundays, but he's earned the right. Something about work, he's saying from behind the door. Something about the men. Ruth can't be bothered to listen. She stares at the torn magazine clipping taped to a page. It's a photo of an East Coast socialite vacationing somewhere in the southern tropics: a pretty young woman in immaculate white linens, lounging on a bench that encircles the impossibly thick trunk of a palm tree. All around the woman and the tree, a soft manicured lawn flows like a velvet sea, and the skies above are clear and dry. Ruth runs her free hand across the back of her neck, imagining the heat in the photo, the lovely bite and sear of an unfiltered sun. Her gaze wanders up to the ceiling. Not even a year old, and already rain and mold have seeped through the shingled roof, staining the cream surface with hideous blossoms. It's supposed to be summer, yet always the overcast skies in this part of the country, always the clouds and the rain. She turns the page. More photos and ephemera, all the things that over the years have caught her eye. But all she sees is the massive palm, lush and hard and tall, the woman's back curved into it like a drowsy lover, the empty space around them, above and below, as if they are the only objects that have ever existed in the history of time.

Henry walks into the room and grabs his coat, motioning for her to do the same. Ruth clenches her jaw and closes the scrapbook. Once again, she's made a promise she doesn't want to keep. But she doesn't care enough to speak her mind, and, anyway, it's time to go.

Their next-door neighbor steers his rusting car down the dirt road, past the edges of the town and onto the makeshift highway. His car is one of many, a caravan of beat-up trucks and buggies and jalopies. Ruth sits in the back seat with a basket of rolls on her lap, next to the other wife. It started earlier in the week as an informal suggestion over a session of grocery shopping and gossip by some of the women, and now almost forty people are going. A weekend escape from the routine of their dreary lives to a small park farther down the Columbia River, far from the massive construction site for the largest dam in the world, which within the decade will throttle the river's power into useful submission. The wives will set up the picnic, a potluck of whatever they can afford to offer, while they gossip and look after the children. The men will eat and drink, complain about their women and their jobs and the general rotten state of affairs across the land, and then they'll climb a trail over eight hundred feet high, to the top of an ancient volcanic core known as Beacon Rock.

The company wife speaks in an endless paragraph, animate and excited. Billie or Betty or Becky, some childish, interchangeable name. She's four months pregnant and endlessly, vocally grateful that her husband found work on a WPA project when so many in the country are doing without. Something about the Depression. Something about the town. Something about schools. Ruth can't be bothered. She bares her teeth, nods her head, makes those ridiculous clucking sounds like the other wives would, all those bitches with airs. Two hours of this passes, the unnatural rattle and groan of the engines, the monotonous roll of pine-covered hills. The image of the palm tree has fled her mind. It's only her on the lawn, alone, under the unhinged jaw of the sky. Something about dresses. Something about the picnic. Something about a cave—

Ruth snaps to attention. There is a map in her hands, a crude drawing of what looks like a jagged-topped egg covered in zigzagging lines. This is the trail the men are going to take, the wife is explaining. Over fifty switchbacks. A labyrinth, a maze. The caravan has stopped. Ruth rubs her eyes. She's used to this, these hitches of lost time. Monotonous life, gloriously washed away in the backwater tides of her waking dreams. She stumbles out of the car, swaying as she clutches the door. The world has been reduced to an iron gray bowl of silence and vertigo, contained yet infinite. Mountains and space and sky, all around, with the river diminished to a soft mosquito's whine. Nausea swells at the back of her throat, and a faint, pain-tinged ringing floods her ears. She feels drunk, unmoored. Somewhere, Henry is telling her to turn, to look. There it is, he's saying, as he tugs her sleeve like a child. Ruth spirals around, her tearing eyes searching, searching the horizon, until finally she—

Something about—

—the rock.

Ruth lifts her head. She's sitting at her kitchen table, a cup of lukewarm coffee at her hand. The scrapbook is before her, open, expectant, and her other hand has a page raised, halfway through the turn. On the right side of the book, the woman in the southern tropics reclines at her palm in the endless grass sea, waiting.

Henry stands before her, hat on head, speaking.

—Ruthie, quit yer dreamin' and get your coat on. Time to go.

—Go where.

—Like we planned. To Beacon Rock.

The clock on the bookcase chimes ten.

Outside, a plane flies overhead, the sonorous engine drone rising and falling as it passes. Ruth rubs her eyes, concentrating. Every day in this colorless town at the edge of this colorless land is like the one before, indistinguishable and unchanging. She doesn't remember waking up, getting dressed, making coffee. And there's something outside, a presence, an all-consuming black static wave of sound, building up just beyond the wall of morning's silence, behind the plane's mournful song. She furrows her brow, straining to hear.

Henry speaks, and the words sound like the low rumble of avalanching rock as they fall away from his face. It's language, but Ruth doesn't know what it means.

—Gimme a moment, I'm gonna be sick, Ruth says to no one in particular as she pushes away from the table. She doesn't bother to close the front door as she walks down the rickety step into warm air and a hard gray sun. Ruth stumbles around the house to the back, where she stops, placing both hands against the wooden walls as she bends down, breathing hard, willing the vomit to stay down. Gradually, the thick sticky feeling recedes, and the tiny spots of black that dance around the corners of her vision fade and disappear. She stands, and starts down the dusty alley between the rows of houses and shacks.

Mountains, slung low against the far horizon of the earth, shimmering green and gray in the clear quiet light. Ruth stops at the edge of the alley, licking her lips as she stands and stares. Her back aches. Beyond the wave and curve of land, there is . . . Ruth bends over again, then squats, cupping her head in her hands, elbows on knees. This day, this day already happened. She's certain of it. They drove, they drove along the dirt highway, the woman beside her, mouth running like a hurricane. They hung to the edges of the wide river, and then they rounded the last curve and stopped, and Ruth pooled out of the car like saliva around the heavy shaft of a cock, and she looked up, and, and, and.

And now some company brat is asking her if she's ok, hey lady are you sick or just taking a crap, giggling as he speaks. Ruth stands up, and slaps him, crisp and hard. The boy gasps, then disappears between the houses. Ruth clenches her jaw, trying not to cry as she heads back around the house. Henry stands beside the open car door, ruin and rage dancing over his face. Her coat and purse and the basket of rolls have been tossed in the back seat, next to the wife. She's already talking up a storm, rubbing her belly while she stares at Ruth's, her eyes and mouth all smug and smarmy in that oily sisterly way, as if she knows. As if she could know anything at all.

The sky above is molten lead, bank after bank of roiling dark clouds vomiting out of celestial foundries. Ruth cranks the window lever, presses her nose against the crack. The air smells vast and earthen. The low mountains flow past in frozen antediluvian waves. Something about casseroles, the company bitch says. Something about gelatin and babies. Something about low tides. Ruth touches her forehead, frowns. There's a hole in her memory, borderless and black, and she feels fragile and small. Not that she hates the feeling. Not entirely. Her hand rises up to the window's edge, fingers splayed wide, as if clawing the land aside to reveal its piston-shaped core. The distant horizon undulates against the dull light, against her flesh, but fails to yield. It's not its place to. She knows she's already been to Beacon Rock. Lost deep inside, a trace remains. She got out of the car and she turned, and the mountains and the evergreens and thrusting up from the middle, a geologic eruption, a disruption hard and wide and high and then: nothing. Something was there, some thing was there, she knows she saw it, but the sinkhole in her mind has swallowed all but the slippery edges.

Her mouth twists, silent, trying to form words that would describe what lies beyond that absence of sound and silence and darkness and light, outside and in her head. As if words like that could exist. And now they are there, the car is rounding the highway's final curves before the park. She rolls down the window all the way, and sticks her head and right arm out. A continent behind, her body is following her arm, like a larva wriggling and popping out of desiccated flesh, out of the car, away from the shouting, the ugly engine sounds, into the great shuddering static storm breaking all around. She saw Beacon Rock, then and now. The rest, they all saw the rock, but she saw beyond it, under the volcanic layers she saw *it*, and now she feels it, now she hears, and it hears her, too.

Falling, she looks up as she reaches out, and—

⟜

The clock on the bookcase chimes ten. Her fingers, cramping, slowly uncurl from a cold coffee cup. Henry is in the other room, getting dressed. Ruth hears him speaking to her, his voice tired water dribbling over worn gravel. Something about the company picnic. Something about malformed, moldering backwaters of trapped space and geologic time. Something about the rock.

Tiny spattering sounds against paper make her stare up to the ceiling, then down at the table. Droplets of blood splash against the open page in her scrapbook. Ruth raises her hand to her nose, pinching the nostrils as she raises her face again. Blood slides against the back of her throat, and she swallows. On the clipping, the young socialite's face disappears in a sudden crimson burst, like a miniature solar flare erupting around her head, enveloping her white-teethed smile. Red coronas everywhere, on her linen-draped limbs, on the thick bark of the palm, on the phosphorus-bright velvet lawn. Somewhere outside, a plane drones overhead, or so it sounds like a plane. No, a plain, a wide expanse of plain, a moorless prairie of static and sound, all the leftover birth and battle and death cries of the planet, jumbled into one relentless wave streaming forth from some lost and wayward protrusion at the earth's end. Ruth pushes the scrapbook away and wipes her drying nose with the edges of her cardigan and the backs of her hands. Her lips open and close in silence as she tries to visualize, to speak the words that would describe what it is that's out there, what waits for her, high as a mountain and cold and alone. What is it that breathes her name into the wind like a mindless burst of radio static, what pulses and booms against each rushing thrust of the wide river, drawing her body near and her mind away? She saw and she wants to see it again and she wants to remember, she wants to feel the ancient granite against her tongue, she wants to rub open-legged against it until it enters and hollows her out like a mindless pink shell. She wants to fall into it, and never return here again.

—Not again, she says to the ceiling, to the walls, as Henry opens the door.

—Not again, not again, not again.

He stares at her briefly, noting the red flecks crusting her nostrils and upper lip.

—Take care of that, he says; grabbing his coat, he motions at the kitchen sink. Always the same journey, and the destination never any closer. Ruth quickly washes her face, then slips out the door behind him into the hot, sunless morning. The company wife is in the back, patting the seat next to her. Something about the weather, she says, her mouth spitting out the words in little squirts of smirk while her eyes dart over Ruth's wet red face. She thinks she knows what that's all about. Lots of company wives walk into doors. Something about the end of Prohibition. Something about the ghosts of a long-ago war. Ruth sits with her head against the window, eyes closed, letting the one-sided conversation flow out of the woman like vomit. Her hand slips under the blue-checked dish towel covering the rolls, and she runs her fingers over the flour-dusted tops. Like cobblestones. River stones, soft water-licked pebbles, thick gravel crunching under her feet. She pushes a finger through the soft crust of a roll, digging down deep into its soft middle. That's what it's doing to her, out there, punching through her head and thrusting its basalt self all through her, pulverizing her organs and liquefying her heart. The car whines and rattles as it slams in and out of potholes, gears grinding as the company man navigates the curves. Eyes still shut, Ruth runs a fingertip over each lid, pressing in firm circles against the skin, feeling the hard jelly mounds roll back and forth at her touch until they ache. The landscape outside reforms itself as a negative against her lids, gnarled and blasted mountains rimmed in small explosions of sulfur-yellow light. She can see it, almost the tip of it, pulsating with a monstrous beauty in the distance, past the last high ridges of land. Someone else must have known, and that's why they named it so. A wild perversion of nature, calling out through the everlasting sepulcher of night, seeking out and casting its blind gaze only upon her—

The company wife is grabbing her arm. The car has stopped. Henry and the man are outside, fumbling with the smoking engine hood. Ruth wrests her arm away from the woman's touch, and opens the door. The rest of the caravan has passed them by, rounded the corner into the park. Ruth starts down the side of the road, slow, nonchalant, as if taking in a bit of air. As if she could. The air has bled out, and only the pounding static silence remains, filling her throat and lungs with its hadal-deep song.

—I'm coming, she says to it.

—I'm almost here. She hears the wife behind her, and picks up her pace.

—You gals don't wander too far, she hears the company man call out.

—We should have this fixed in a jiffy.

Ruth kicks her shoes off and runs. Behind her, the woman is calling out to the men. Ruth drops her purse. She runs like she used to when she was a kid, a freckled tomboy racing through the wheat fields of her father's farm in North Dakota. She runs like an animal, and now the land and the trees and the banks of the river are moving fast, slipping past her piston legs along with the long bend of the road. Her lungs are on fire and her heart is all crazy and jumpy against her breasts and tears streak into her mouth and nose and it doesn't matter because she is so close and it's calling her with the hook of its song and pulling her reeling her in and Henry's hand is at the back of her neck and there's gravel and the road smashing against her mouth and blood and she's grinding away and kicking and clawing forward and all she has to do is lift up her head just a little bit and keep her eyes shut and she will finally see—

Ruth's hands are clasped tight in her lap. Scum floats across the surface of an almost empty cup of coffee. A sob escapes her mouth, and she claps her hand over it, hitching as she pushes it back down. This small house. This small life. This cage. She can't do it anymore. The clock on the bookcase chimes ten.

—I swear, this is the last time, Ruth says, wiping the tears from her cheeks. The room is empty, but she knows who she's speaking to. It knows, too.

—I know how to git to you. I know how to see you. This is the last goddamn day.

On the kitchen table before her is the scrapbook, open to her favorite clipping. Ruth peels it carefully from the yellowing page and holds it up to the light. Somewhere in the southern tropics: a pretty young woman in stained white linens, lounging on a bench that encircles the impossibly thick trunk of a tree that has no beginning or end, whose roots plunge so far beyond the ends of earth and time that, somewhere in the vast cosmic oceans above, they loop and descend and transform into the thick fronds and leaves that crown the woman's head with dappled shadow. All around the woman and the tree, drops of dried blood are spattered across the paper like the tears of a dying sun. The woman's face lies behind one circle of deep brown, earth brown, wood brown, corpse brown. She is smiling, open-eyed, breathing it all in. Ruth balls the clipping up tight, then places it in her mouth, chewing just a bit before she swallows. There is no other place the woman and the palm have been, that they will ever be. Alone, apart, removed, untouched. All life here flows around them, utterly repelled. They cannot be bothered. It is of no concern to them. What cycle of life they are one with was not born in this universe.

In the other room, Henry is getting dressed. If he's talking, she can't hear. Everywhere, black static rushes through the air, strange equations and latitudes and lost languages and wondrous geometries crammed into a silence so old and deep that all other sounds are made void. Ruth closes the scrapbook and stands, wiping the sweat from her palms on her Sunday dress. There is a large knife in the kitchen drawers, and a small axe by the fireplace. She chooses the knife. She knows it better, she knows the heft of it in her hand when slicing into meat and bone. When he finally opens the door and steps into the small room, she's separating the rolls, the blade slipping back and forth through the powdery grooves. Ruth lifts one up to Henry, and he takes it. It barely touches his mouth before she stabs him in the stomach, just above the belt, where nothing hard can halt its descent. He collapses, and she falls with him, pulling the knife out and sitting on his chest as she plunges it into the center of his chest, twice because she isn't quite sure where his heart is, then once at the base of his throat. Blood, like water gurgling over river stones, trickling away to a distant, invisible sea. That, she can hear. Ruth wipes the blade on her dress as she rises, then places it on the table, picks up the basket and walks to the front door. She opens it a crack.

—Henry's real sick, she says to the company man. We're gonna stay home today. She gives him the rolls, staring hard at the company wife in the back seat as he walks back to his car. The wife looks her over, confused. Ruth smiles and shuts the door. That bitch doesn't know a single thing.

Ruth slips out the back, through the window of their small bedroom. The caravan of cars is already headed toward the highway, following the Columbia downstream toward Beacon Rock. They'll never make it to their picnic. They'll never see it. They never do. She moves through the alley, past the last sad row of company houses and into the tall evergreens that mark the end of North Bonneville. With each step into the forest, she feels the weight of the town fall away a little, and something vast and leviathan burrows deeper within, filling up the unoccupied space. When she's gone far and long enough that she no longer remembers her name, she stops, and presses her fingers deep into her sockets, scooping her eyes out and pinching off the long ropes of flesh that follow them out of her body like sticky yarn. What rushes from her mouth might be screaming or might be her soul, and it is smothered in the indifferent silence of the wild world.

And now it sees, and it moves in the way it sees, floating and darting back and forth through the hidden phosphorescent folds of the lands within the land, darkness punctured and coruscant with unnamable colors and light, its dying flesh creeping and hitching through forests petrified by the absence of time, past impenetrable ridges of mountains whose needle-sharp peaks cut whorls in the passing rivers of stars. A veil of flies hovers about the caves of its eyes and mouth, rising and falling with every rotting step, and bits of flesh scatter and sink to the earth like barren seeds next to its pomegranate blood. If there is pain, it is beyond such narrow knowledge acknowledgement of its body. There is only the bright beacon of light and thunderous song, the sonorous ringing of towering monolithic basalt breathing in and out, pushing the darkness away. There is, finally, past the curvature of the overgrown wild, a lush grass plain of emerald green, ripe and plump under a fat hot sun, a wide bench of polished wood, and a palm tree pressing in a perfect arc against its small back, warm and worn and hard like ancient stone. When it looks up, it cannot see the tree's end. Its vision rises blank and wondrous with branches as limitless as its both their dreams, past all the edges of all time, and this is the way it should be.

CHAPTER SIX

STEPHEN GRAHAM JONES

They were eighty miles from campus, if miles still mattered.

It had been Dr. Ormon's idea.

Dr. Ormon was Crain's dissertation director. If dissertations still mattered.

They probably didn't.

Zombies. Zombies were the main thing that mattered these days.

Crain lowered his binoculars and turned to Dr. Ormon. "They're still following Ninety-Five," he said.

"Path of least resistance," Dr. Ormon said back.

The clothes Crain and Dr. Ormon were wearing, they'd scavenged from a home that had had the door flapping, the owners surely scavenged on themselves, by now.

Dr. Ormon's hair was everywhere. The mad professor.

Crain was wearing a paisley skirt as a cape. His idea was to break up the human form, present a less enticing silhouette. Dr. Ormon said that was useless, that the zombies were obviously keying on vibrations in the ground; that was part of why they preferred the cities, and probably had a lot to do with why they were sticking mostly to the asphalt, now: they could hear better through it.

Crain respectfully disagreed. They didn't prefer the cities, it was just that the zombie population was mimicking preplague concentrations. Whether walking or just lying there, you would expect the dead to be pretty much where they died, wouldn't you?

Instead of entertaining the argument, Dr. Ormon ended it by studying the horde through their one pair of binoculars, and noting how, on asphalt, there was no cloud of dust to announce the zombies' presence.

Sophisticated hunting techniques? A rudimentary sense of self and other?

"Do *horde* and *herd* share a root?" Crain asked.

He'd been tossing it back and forth in his head since the last exit.

"We use *horde* for invaders," Dr. Ormon said, in his thinking-out-loud voice. "Mongols, for example."

"While *herd* is for ungulates, generally."

"Herd mentality," Dr. Ormon said, handing the binoculars back. "*Herd* suggests a lack of intelligence, of conscious thought, while *horde* brings with it aggressiveness. Or, at the very least, a danger to the society naming those invaders."

Then no, the two words only sounded similar.

Crain could accept this. Less because he had little invested in a shared etymology, more because the old patterns felt good, felt right: teacher, student, each working toward a common goal.

It was why they were here, eighty miles from campus.

There had been families to return to, of course, but, each being a commuter, their only course of action had been to hole up in the long basement under the anthropology building. The break-room refrigerator could only sustain two people for so long, though.

Crain tried to frame their situation as a return to more primitive times. What the plague was doing, it was resetting humanity. Hunting and gathering were the order of the day, now, not books or degrees on the wall. Survival had become hand-to-mouth again. There was to be no luxury time for a generation or two, there would be no specializing, no social stratification. The idea of a barter economy springing up anytime soon was a lark; tooth and nail was going to be the dominant mode for a while, and only the especially strong would make it through to breed, keep the species going.

Dr. Ormon had taken Crain's musings in as if they were idle ramblings, his eyes cast to the far wall, but then he had emerged from their latrine (the main office, ha) two days later with a decidedly intense cast to his features, his eyes nearly flashing with discovery.

"What?" Crain had said, suddenly sure a window had been breached.

"It does still matter," he said. "All our—this. Our work, our studies, the graduate degrees. It's been a manual, a guide, don't you see?"

Crain studied the map of Paleo-America tacked on the wall and waited.

This was Dr. Ormon's style.

"Your chapter two," Dr. Ormon went on. "That one footnote... it was in the formative part, the foundational prologue. The part I may have said felt straw-mannish."

"The name dropping," Crain filled in.

Now that it was the postapocalypse, they could call things what they were.

"About the available sources of protein."

Crain narrowed his eyes, tried to feel back through his dissertation.

Chapter two had been a textual wrestling match, no doubt.

It was where he had to address all the mutually exclusive claims for why the various and competing contenders for the title of *man* on the African savanna had stood up, gone bipedal.

Crain's thesis was that a lack of body hair, due to the forest's retreat, meant that the mothers were having to carry their infants now, instead of letting them hang on. They had no choice but to stand up.

Part and parcel with this was the supposition that early man—a grand word for a curious ape with new wrist and pelvis morphology—was a persistence hunter, running its prey down over miles and days. Running it to death.

A lifestyle like this would require the whole troop—the proper word for a group of apes was a *shrewdness*, but Crain had always thought that a poor association for gamblers and inventors—to be on the move. No posted guards, no beds to return to, thus no babysitters like jackals had, like meerkats had, like nearly all the other mammalian societies had.

This meant these early would-be humans had to take their babies with them, each chase. They had to hold them close as they ran. Hold them with hands they could no longer devote to running.

It was elegant.

As for how these mutant bipeds were able to persistence hunt so effectively, it was those unheralded, never-seen-before sweat glands, those cavernous lungs, the wide nostrils. What was nice for Crain's argument was that this was all work others had already done. All he had to do was, in chapter two, organize and cite, bow and nod.

But, this being anthropology, and the fossil record being not just sparse but cruelly random, alternate theories of course abounded.

One was the water-ape hypothesis: we got the protein to nourish our growing brains and lengthen our bones from shellfish. Droughts drove us to the shores of Africa, and what initially presented itself as a hurdle became a stepping stone.

Another theory was that our brains grew as self-defense mechanisms against the up-and-down climate. Instead of being allowed to specialize, we had to become generalists, opportunists, our brains having to constantly improvise and consider options, and, in doing so, that accidentally give birth to conceptual thought.

Another theory was that that source of brain-growing protein had been on the savanna all along.

Two days after Dr. Ormon's eureka moment, Crain shouldered open the door to their basement for the last time, and they went in search of a horde.

It didn't take long. As Crain had noted, the preapocalypse population of their part of New Hampshire had already been dense; it stood to reason that it still would be.

Dr. Ormon shrugged it off in that way he had that meant their sample was too limited in scope, that further studies would prove him out.

To his more immediate academic satisfaction, though—Crain could feel it wafting off him—when a horde presented itself on the second day (the smell), the two of them were able to hide not in a closet (vibration-conducting concrete foundation) or under a car (asphalt . . .), but in a shrub.

The comparatively loose soil saved them, evidently. Hid the pounding of their hearts.

Maybe.

The horde had definitely shuffled past, anyway, unaware of the meal waiting just within arm's reach.

Once it had been gone half a day, Crain and Dr. Ormon rose, scavenged the necessary clothes, and followed.

As Crain had footnoted in chapter two of his dissertation, and as Dr. Ormon had predicted in a way that brooked no objection, the top predators in any ecosystem, they pull all the meat from their prey and move on. Leaving niches to be filled by the more opportunistic.

In Africa, now, that was hyenas, using their powerful jaws to crack into gazelle bones for the marrow locked inside.

Six million years ago, man had been that hyena.

"Skulking at the fringes has its benefits," Dr. Ormon had said.

In this case, those fringes were just far enough behind the horde that the corpses it left behind wouldn't be too far into decay yet.

I-95 was littered with the dead. The dead-dead, Crain christened them. As opposed to the other kind. A field of skeletons scummed with meat and flies, the bones scraped by hundreds of teeth, then discarded.

Crain and Dr. Ormon had stood over corpse after corpse.

Theory was one thing. Practice was definitely another.

And—they talked about it, keeping their voices low—even the ones with enough meat hidden on a buttocks or calf to provide a meal of sorts, still, that meat was more than likely infected, wasn't it?

Their job as survivors, now, it was to go deeper than that infection.

This is how you prove a thesis.

Once it was dark enough that they could pretend not to see, not to know, they used a rock to crack open the tibia of what had once been a healthy man, by all indications. They covered his face with Crain's cape, and then covered it again, with a stray jacket.

"Modern sensibilities," Dr. Ormon narrated. "Our ancestors would have had no such qualms."

"If they were our ancestors," Crain said, something dark rising in his throat.

He tamped it down, just.

The marrow had the consistency of bubble gum meant for blowing bubbles, after you've chewed it through half the movie. There was a granular quality, a warmth, but no real cohesion anymore. Not quite a slurry or a paste. More like an oyster just starting to decompose.

Instead of plundering the bone for every thick, willing drop, they each took a meager mouthful, closed their eyes to swallow.

Neither threw it back up.

Late into the night, then, they talked about how, when man had been living on marrow like this—if he had been, Dr. Ormon allowed, as one meal doesn't an argument prove—this had of course been well before the discovery and implementation of fire. And fire of course was what made the meat they ate easier to digest. Thus their guts had been able to shrink.

"That's what I'm saying," Crain said, piggybacking on what was becoming Dr. Ormon's research. "Persistence hunters."

"You're still attached to the romantic image of them," Dr. Ormon said, studying something under his fingernail, the moonlight not quite playing along. "You have this image of a Zulu warrior, I think. Tall, lean. No, he's Ethiopian, isn't he? What was that Olympic runner's name, who ran barefoot?"

"A lot of them do," Crain said, staring off into the trees. "But can we digest this, do you think?" he said, touching his stomach to show.

"We have to," Dr. Ormon said.

And so they did. Always staying a half day behind the horde, tipping the leg bones up for longer and longer draughts. Drinking from the tanks of toilets they found along the way. Fashioning turbans from scraps.

The smarter among the crows began to follow them, to pick at these splintered-open bones.

"Niches and valleys," Dr. Ormon said, walking backward to watch the big black birds.

"Host-parasite," Crain said, watching ahead, through the binoculars.

"And what do you think we are?" Dr. Ormon called, gleefully.

Crain didn't answer.

⊸⊙⊷

The zombies at the back of the horde—Crain still preferred *herd*, in the privacy of his head—he'd taken to naming them. The way a primatologist might name chimpanzees from the troop she was observing.

There was Draggy, and Face B. Gone, and Left Arm. Flannel and Blind Eye and Soup.

By the time they got to the horde's victims, there was rarely anything left but the bones with their precious marrow that Dr. Ormon so needed, to prove Crain's second chapter was in need of overhaul, if not reconception altogether.

That night, over a second tibia he'd taken to holding like a champagne flute—Dr. Ormon somehow affected a cigar with his ulnas—Crain posed the question to Dr. Ormon: "If a species, us, back then, adapts itself to persistence hunting—"

"If," Dr. Ormon emphasized.

"If *we* were adapting like that, then why didn't the prey one-up us?"

Silence from the other side of what would have been the campfire, if they allowed themselves fires. If they needed to cook their food.

These were primitive times, though.

In the darkness, Dr. Ormon's eyes sparked. "Gazelles that can sweat through their skin, you mean," he said. "The better to slip our grasp. The better to run for miles."

"The marathon gazelle," Crain added.

"Do we know they didn't?" Dr. Ormon asked, and somehow in the asking, in the tone, Crain sensed that Dr. Ormon was forever objecting not to him, Crain, or to whatever text he was engaging, whatever panel he was attending, but to someone in his life who called him by his first name, whatever that was. It was an unasked-for insight.

"Mr. Crain?" Dr. Ormon prompted.

This was the classroom again.

Crain nodded, caught up. "What if the gazelles of today are, in comparison to the gazelles of six million years ago, marathon gazelles, right?"

"Excellent."

Crain shook his head what he hoped was an imperceptible bit. "Do you think that's the case?" he asked. "Were we that persistent a hunter?"

"It's your thesis, Mr. Crain."

Crain gathered his words—he'd been running through this argument all day, and Dr. Ormon had stepped right into the snare—said, as if reluctantly, as if only just thinking of this, "You forget that our persistence had rewards, I think."

It had a surely-you-jest rhythm to it that Crain liked. It was like speaking Shakespeare off the cuff, by accident. By natural talent.

"Rewards?" Dr. Ormon asked.

"We persistence hunted until that gave us enough protein to—to develop the necessary brain capacity to communicate. And once we started to communicate, tricks of the trade started to get passed down. Thus was born culture. We graduated out of the gazelle race before the gazelles could adapt."

For long, delicious moments, there was silence from the other side of the noncampfire.

Has the student become the master? Crain said to himself.

Does the old silverback reconsider, in the face of youth?

He was so tired of eating stupid marrow.

Just when it seemed Dr. Ormon must have retreated into sleep, or the understandable pretense of it—this was a new world, requiring new and uncomfortable thinking—he chuckled in the darkness, Dr. Ormon.

Crain bored his eyes into him, not having to mask his contempt.

"Is that how man is, in your estimation?" Dr. Ormon asked. "Or, I should say, is that how man has proven himself to be, over his short tenure at the top of this food chain?"

Crain didn't say anything.

Dr. Ormon didn't need him to. "Say you're right, or in the general area of right. Persistence hunting gave us big brains, which gave us language, which gave us culture."

"Chapter six," Crain said. "When I got to it, I mean."

"Yes, yes, as is always the case. But humor me aloud, if you will. Consider this your defense. Our ancient little grandfathers, able to sweat, lungs made for distance, bipedalistic for efficiency, their infants cradled in arms, not having to grasp at hair like common chimpanzees—"

"I never—"

"Of course, of course. But allowing all this. If we were so successful, evolving in leaps and bounds. Tell me then, why are there still gazelles today? Agriculture and the fabled oryx are still thousands of generations away, here. What's to stop us from plundering the most available food source, unto exhaustion?"

Time slowed for Crain.

"You can't, you can't ever completely—"

"Eradicate a species?" Dr. Ormon completed, his tone carrying the obvious objection. "Not that I disagree about us moving on to other food sources eventually. But only when necessary, Mr. Crain. Only when pressed."

"Chapter six," Crain managed.

"Pardon?"

"I would have addressed this in chapter six."

"Good, good. Perhaps tomorrow you can detail how, for me, if you don't mind."

"Sure, sure," Crain said. And: "Should I just keep calling you doctor?"

Another chuckle, as if this question had already been anticipated as well.

"Able," Dr. Ormon said. "After my father."

"Able," Crain repeated. "Crain and Able."

"Close, close," Dr. Ormon said, dismissing this conversation, and then cleared his throat for sleep as was his practice, and, in his mind's eye, Crain could see the two of them from above, their backs to each other, one with his eyes shut contentedly, the other staring out into the night.

Instead of outlining chapter six the next day, Crain kept the binoculars to his face.

If he remembered correctly, 95 crossed another major highway soon.

Would the herd split, wandering down separate ways, or would they mill around indecisively, until some Moses among them made the necessary decision?

It was going to be interesting.

He might write a paper on it, if papers still mattered.

And then they walked up on the most recent group of victims.

They'd been hiding in an RV, it looked like.

It was as good as anywhere, Crain supposed. No hiding place or perfect fortress really worked.

It looked like this group had finally made their big run for it. The RV's front tires were gummed up with zombies. They'd had no choice but to run, really. It was always all that was left, right at the end.

They made it about the usual distance: thirty feet.

They'd been gnawed down to the bone in places, of course.

"If they ever figure out there's marrow in there," Dr. Ormon said, lowering himself to a likely arm, its tendons bare to the sun for the first time.

"They don't have language," Crain said. "It would just be one knowing, not all of them."

"Assuming they speak as you and I do, of course," Dr. Ormon said, wrenching the forearm up.

The harsh creaking sound kickstarted another sound.

In a hiking backpack lying across the center stripe, there was what could only be an infant.

When it cried, it was definitely an infant.

Crain looked to Dr. Ormon, and Dr. Ormon looked ahead of them.

"It's right on the asphalt," Dr. Ormon said, his tone making this an emergency.

"They go by smell," Crain said. "Or sound. Just normal sound, not conductive."

"This is not an argument either of us wants to win," Dr. Ormon said, stepping neatly over to the backpack and leaning forward onto it with both knees.

The crying muffled.

"We're reenactors," he said, while doing it, while killing this baby. "My brother-in-law was a Civil War soldier on weekends. But this, this is so much more important. An ancient script, you could say. One written by the environment, by biology. Inscribed in our very instincts."

Crain watched, and listened, his own plundered tibia held low along his right leg.

Soon enough, the cries ceased.

"You can test your theory about—about methods of child transport—later," Dr. Ormon said, rising up to drive his knees down one last, terrible time. For emphasis, it seemed.

"That was probably Adam," Crain said, looking down at the quiet lump in the backpack.

"If you believe the children's stories," Dr. Ormon said, casting around for his ulna. He claimed their flavor was slightly headier. That it had something to do with the pendulum motion they'd been subjected to, with a lifetime of walking. That that resulted in more nutrients getting trapped in the lower arms.

Crain didn't care.

He was still staring at the raspy blue fabric of the backpack, and then he looked up the road as well.

Left Arm was watching them.

He'd come back. The sound had traveled along the asphalt ribbon of 95 and found him, bringing up the rear of the horde.

It hadn't been scent or pressure waves in the air, anyway; the wind was in Crain's face, was lifting his ragged cape behind him.

So Ormon was right.

Crain looked across to him, one foot planted on a dead wrist, his chicken elbows cocked back, trying to disinter the ulna from its double-helix soul mate of a radius.

"You're right," Crain said across to him.

Dr. Ormon raised his face, waited for the punch line.

"About how they hear," Crain said, pointing with his chin down 95.

Left Arm was still two or three car lengths from Dr. Ormon.

Dr. Ormon flinched back, tangled in the legs of the woman whose marrow he was plundering.

"I got it," Crain said, and stepped forward, past Dr. Ormon, and, when he was close enough, timing it after a clumsy left-arm swipe, he planted the sole of his boot in Left Arm's chest, sent him tumbling, then stepped in neatly to finish it with the tibia as hammer, as axe, as—as tool.

It made his arm feel floppy and chimp-like, as if unaccustomed, as if only using this long bone from sudden, forgettable inspiration.

"Not very persistent after all, are they?" Dr. Ormon said from his corpse.

Crain looked back to Dr. Ormon about this, and then down to Left Arm.

Right beside him was one of thc plundered, the dead, the feasted on. The dead-dead.

Crain lowered himself to this clean corpse, to salvage what he could—pockets first, then the bones, for marrow—and found himself holding Left Arm's left arm. Just to move it away, off.

But then he pulled on it instead.

Because zombies are already decomposing, it came off at the shoulder.

Crain studied it, studied it—*not very persistent, are they?*—and finally nodded to himself, reached through the rancid meat for the bone, liberated it.

The brittle end snapped off under his thumb like a Pez dispenser.

There was still marrow inside.

Crain considered it, considered it *(not very persistent, are they?)*, finally nodded to himself.

"You still into ulnas?" he called across to Dr. Ormon.

"Give them a chance," Dr. Ormon said back, not bothering to turn around.

"Here," Crain said, walking Left Arm's ulna across, careful not to tip the syrupy marrow out. "I broke it already, sorry."

"I really shouldn't," Dr. Ormon said, smiling, taking the ulna between his fingers. "Male or female?" he asked.

He was keeping track. Like it mattered.

"Male," Crain said, loving the truth of it, and watched Dr. Ormon tip the broken end of the bone into his mouth.

Dr. Ormon had already swallowed by the time the taste registered.

He fell to his knees coughing, trying to puke.

Crain pinched his pants up at the thighs to squat down, say it right to Dr. Ormon: "We're not bone suckers, Doctor. We're *persistence* hunters. I think you'll come to agree with me here shortly."

Dr. Ormon tried to respond but could only sputter and gag, swing his arm back and forth for Crain's pants leg.

He was already changing, then.

"This can be chapter six," Crain said. "That sound good to you, sir?"

Dr. Ormon's head bobbed with his regurgitation efforts. With his transformation. With his inevitable acquiescence. Not just to the virus, but to the strength of Crain's argument.

Chapter six, then. It was going to be perfect.

Crain stood, turned to survey his options.

Eighty miles behind him was the campus, with all its vending machines, all its dorm-room toilets to drink from.

All its concrete and asphalt, stretched tight like an eardrum.

The woods, then. Back to the trees.

The soft earth there wouldn't transmit his location to the herd. To any stragglers.

In this particular reenactment, Crain was to be prey, he knew.

Behind him, the all-too-human horde, exhausting the landscape.

This was his thesis in action. His final proof.

He smiled to himself, if smiles still mattered, and was flipping a coin in his head—*trees to the east, or trees to the west?*—when the blue backpack pulled his attention over.

The lump was gently kicking. A small fist, pushing against the fabric. The baby, more resilient than Dr. Ormon had thought. More human.

Crain turned to Dr. Ormon, already trying to figure out how to stand again, into this new world.

Maybe fifteen seconds, then. Ten to be safe.

Crain ran to the backpack, grabbed the infant up.

A girl.

"Oh, *Eve*," he said, and pulled her to his chest, one of her arms more floppy than it should have been, the ribs on that side dangerously concave. But the other lung was working fine. She mewled, was building to a scream.

Crain chose the side of the road where the trees were closest.

Crossing the ditch, the infant held tight in both arms, because he didn't have close to enough body hair for her to clutch on to with her tiny right hand, Crain shook his head to clear the sweat from his eyes.

The gazelles *did* learn to perspire, he said in his head to Dr. Ormon, shuffling into place behind him, and the race, it was on, it had never really ended, not since those first delicate steps, six million years ago.

THIS IS NOT FOR YOU

GEMMA FILES

Three potential sacrifices, just as Phoibe'd predicted, blundering through the woods like buffalo in boots. Mormo broke cover first, naked and barefoot, screaming, with the boys following after, whooping and hollering, straight into the gauntlet, too lust-drunk to see where they were going. Pretty little thing, that Mormo, with a truly enviable lung capacity; the best lure they'd had by far in all the time Gorgo'd been attending these odd little shindigs, and swift enough to keep a good two lengths between her and her closest pursuer as she danced around the tiger-pits. No sooner did this thought register, however, then with a few more steps—plus one wild, deer-like leap—she was gone from sight, entirely: up over the deadfall, rustling the same bushes Gorgo and her girls hid behind, leaving the men in her wake, too shocked not to keep coming.

One took a *thyrsus* to the knee, so sharp Gorgo heard it crack, and pitched headlong, folding up, rolling. More blows caught him from several angles, breaking bones, tearing flesh; he flipped, bellowing, then gave a moaning "whuff!" as Iris came down right on top, astride both hips, club inverted to crack his breastbone and pop at least one lung, squeeze heart against ribcage, bruise liver beyond repair. His skull met a log back-first, brain slammed hard, eyes rolling up; was probably out long before Iris's partners (Scylla, Polyxena) could get on him too, their hands rock-full, looking to make like Cain.

To his left, meanwhile, another lucky winner got Deianira's spear across the top of his ear and recoiled, flinching away only to run straight into Charis's strong grip instead. They were about the same height, but Charis had him from behind, choking him so hard he started to lift off the ground, kicking wildly. He tore at her arm with both hands, drawing blood, 'til she finally threw him down with enough force that Gorgo heard his nose pop, or maybe a cheekbone—then heel-stomped him between the shoulder blades, holding him pinned even as he flailed, trying his level best to swim away. One armpit made a beautiful target for Deianira's next thrust, a goring stab that went in far as she could reach, and the pain made him rear back far enough for Gorgo to slash her scythe across his throat.

The spike of her own kill-pleasure came quickly after that, hot and red and sweet. It was good, but over so soon; just enough to make her want more, something better. *Longer.*

She sat back on her heels, panting, leather tags of her hiking boots cutting into her bare ass as she watched the man's—*boy's*—blood make a flaring collar 'round his slackening, sweat- and dirt-smeared facc. Asking Charis, once she had her breath back: "You see where the last one went?"

Charis shook her head. "Back there, maybe."

On her feet once more, over by the first one, Iris nodded. "Something tripped a pit."

Okay, then. "Praise be," Gorgo said, heaving herself up, unable to quite keep her voice completely irony-free. "Praise be," two new voices chimed in at the same time, from behind her: Aglaia, of course. And Phoibe.

Charis and the others turned, bespattered, grinning—stepped back a bit, all 'round, to display their work to best advantage. Aglaia smiled wide and nodded, proudly, as Gorgo and Phoibe exchanged a small, cool nod of greeting.

"Wonderful," Aglaia pronounced, with the sort of authoritative, maternal warmth that'd've done Mother Theresa herself proud, if she'd worshipped Kali instead of Christ. "*Very* fine. Now... let's go see what She's left us for last, and best."

⊸⊷

The point was to do these things together, not alone. The point was to do them in secret, as much as could be arranged for. The point was to go elsewhere, overnight, and stay as long as it took to get it done. The point was to make it count.

The whole point of a mystery religion, in fact, as Aglaia kept reminding them, was that it was supposed to be—and stay—a *mystery*.

That wasn't her real name, obviously. They'd all taken new ones, first as pseudonyms on the cult's website, then as part of their bonding exercises in "meatspace," as the kids put it; it was to draw a sort of metaphorical line from old to new, a clear path of translation, adaptation. Some of them came from what passed, these days, as "traditional" backgrounds—odd idea, that, all these *mystoi* and Goddess-worshippers apparently long-embedded in between the non-denominationals and the atheists—but for most of them this was just a fantasy, a deep-rooted need, a burgeoning itch they'd never quite known how to scratch before eventually stumbling across the myths, the literature, the site itself, which Phoibe had started, and still maintained. A particular urge which everything around them said was bad, wrong, unnatural, even as that blood-beat voice inside told them it was anything but.

"We shouldn't feel ashamed," Aglaia—an elder stateswoman of some sort of brown persuasion, her graying, loose-curled hair cropped short—had said, during their first real meet-up. "Never. What we do here is older than everything else, all the forces arrayed against us—older than laws, older than rules, older than the inadequate language we use to try and describe it with. It can't be explained. It doesn't have to be justified. And much as we may serve it, may be personally elevated by that service, transfigured even, we are none of us as important as the principle we subsume ourselves to. The tradition survives, always; we may die away—*will* die away—but it survives, always. It doesn't need us. Because even when everything else crumbles, *this* will still endure."

Oh, and Aglaia really did make everything sound so pretty, Gorgo thought, whenever she really started to get her groove on; that was the basic trick, the recruiting pitch, the glue. To frame the reason they were all here as a certain route to spiritual ecstasy, but also make it sound like they were reaching for a goal far more lasting than their own selfish pleasure—something done on this whole sad, stained world's behalf for the unwitting benefit of everyone trapped inside it, exorcising sin while extirpating evil. Like it wasn't any real sort of *crime*, at all.

Aglaia was a true believer, or walked the talk so well as to be nigh-indistinguishable from one; Gorgo simply knew what she liked, and was willing to swallow her share of theosophic psychobabble in order to get a bunch of women with similar interests to not just pitch in at the kill, but clean up after her. Total freaks, in other words, but very useful ones—which was exactly how, in essence, that membership in their little sewing circle continued to hold enough appeal for Gorgo to not just roll her eyes and walk away, even assuming Aglaia and her coterie would let her.

Every meet-up started with a prayer, Aglaia leading, the others reading along off of printout sheets, a different translation every time. This year's went like so—

Preswa, Phersephassa, o Kore Hagne
Wise one, She who stops, She who lives in every harvest
Persipne, Praxidike, o Kore Semele
Wine-maker, Subterranean queen, Most flowery maiden
Persephone, Crown of terror
Beautiful, Fatal, She who consumes
According to Whose will the sacred task is done—
life to produce, and all that lives to kill.

"So what is it you *do*, these days, exactly?" Phoibe asked, under her breath, sidling up at Gorgo's elbow. "Still bending young minds, or did they finally figure out you never actually made it all the way through teacher's college?"

Gorgo shrugged. "Oh, you'd be surprised how little research private schools put in, selecting instructors. We're doing Romantic poets this semester, Keats and all. 'O what can ail thee, knight-at-arms, alone and palely loitering?'"

"You tell them it's a tuberculosis metaphor?"

"On the top layer, sure. Some girls, I push harder; seed an idea here and there, set tests. Try to seek out where their more hidden inclinations might lie."

"I didn't know Aglaia was signing off on any more recruitment drives, especially amongst the underage."

"She's got nothing to do with it, Phoebe."

"Phoibe."

"Whatever."

"Yeah, okay. I mean, what's in a name, right—Susan?"

"Awful mysteries here are ours," Aglaia continued, "so we celebrate them in Your name, which no one may in any way transgress. Happy is she who has seen and believed, both on top of the earth and under it, though she who is uninitiate will never reap a like crop after death, but stay forever buried there in darkness and in gloom."

Think that's my real name you got there, little bitch, just 'cause you hacked it out of my digital footprint? Gorgo projected, while staring Phoibe down, as Phoibe struggled to do the same, and failed. *My original? Think I couldn't change it or anything else about me in a minute, or less, if I wanted to—walk away, disappear off the grid, and not come up for air 'til I stuck my scythe in your tech-savvy spine?*

Think again.

She was a bit of a parody, Phoibe, with her all-black clothes and her hair banded in grown-out dye-jobs like a floppy, cross-cut section of tree—you could practically track her stylistic evolution, or lack thereof, from Manic Panic to Clairol to henna to what Gorgo could only assume was probably her natural shade, a subtle mouse-hide leather tone flecked here and there with the first glints of grey. Deep, slightly keloided dimples bracketing her mouth had once held barbell piercings, just like that scar furling her lip-corner told of a torn-free labrette; she wore a tricked-out pair of granny-glasses with Hipster-thick frames, and tended towards using blush for eyeshadow. But she sure as shit did know how to run a dark-net, so that was something, at least.

Up near Aglaia, everyone was chanting again. Gorgo mouthed the words as Phoibe mouthed them right back at her, a second or two late.

Blood waters it
Blood grows it
Blood alone sees it flower:
Great seed, seed of flesh and bone, Persephone's awful gift
That nurtures and destroys this world one sacrifice at a time
One lover
One child
One king.

Truth was, it *would* be nice to share interests with somebody in private life, Gorgo occasionally caught herself thinking. To be a mentor. She sure wasn't too likely to breed any soft-minded little co-conspirators herself, not at this late date, even setting the problem of stud-stock aside; adoption wasn't really an option either, or fosterage, for similar reasons. Short of walking away from her local maternity ward with a free souvenir, therefore, cherry picking each new class for potentials seemed the next best thing. Hadn't found any thus far, but it was early days still, and she remained hopeful.

Now she set hands on hips and waited, staring down, a whole ten extra years' worth of game-face blankly in place. She had roughly a foot of height on Phoibe, plus a good fifty pounds in heft, not that she expected things would get physical—both of them had a certain investment in returning to work next week, after all, and doing it while looking like nothing worse than the morning after a particularly celebratory girls' night out. But when you'd been looking forward to something all year, sometimes things just happened.

A second later, however, Phoibe shrugged, raising her hands: *no harm, no foul.*

"I'm sure you know what you're doing," she said. "I mean, we're all adults here. What you get up to on your own time's no concern of mine."

"Nope," Gorgo agreed. "So . . . anyone know who the sacrifice's gonna be yet?"

"Whoever gets here first," Phoibe replied. "Same as usual."

"Well, how many candidates in play?"

"Three groups, two to four components each. Maybe four."

"That's short odds."

"Not really; I'd show you the math, but . . . " Here Phoibe trailed off, maybe thinking *I wouldn't want to bore you with it*, or even *you wouldn't understand*, yet smart enough not to voice whichever outright, either way. Continuing, soon enough: "You ever know anybody *not* to show up?"

Now it was Gorgo's turn to shrug. "Not yet," was all she said.

But that, as Aglaia would no doubt say, was where faith came in.

⟜

The place they gathered had been a campground, once upon a time. They arrived singly from every direction, mostly by public transport, then hiked to the meet-point, where Aglaia and her acolytes had already set up most of the necessary infrastructure—dug catch-pits, strung bells, planted weapons (*thyrsi* made on-site, plus whatever else they brought with them), and built the cremation pyre high, for afterwards. People didn't tend to get naked 'til the appointed hour, which suited Gorgo fine, though there were always noticeable exceptions. Right now, for example, she could see tall, lean Charis belly dancing by herself off in the middle distance, pleasantly soft from hormones and with her bush grown full to hide the rest, yet proudly displaying the scars where her implants had gone in every time she back-bent far enough for them to catch the light.

At least one potential "sister" had quit because of Charis, or tried to—made it back almost as far as the north road before Gorgo had caught up with her, dragged her into the bushes and buried her under a deadfall with her flesh flensed sky burial-style, so the animals would come running. It'd been an on-the-fly decision, simple self-preservation instinct twisted into altruism by circumstance, done on behalf of a community Gorgo often questioned whether she needed at all; still wasn't entirely sure Aglaia even knew about it, though she suspected yes, especially since she hadn't found any bones left to crush with a hammer when she'd checked the makeshift grave, last time they met.

In Gorgo's estimation, however, the radfems could say what they wanted, but Charis had always held her end up well enough to merit whatever help Gorgo chose to give her. Once the hunt was on, she was no different than any other gal with an oversized clit—better, considering her sheer stamina, her extra-long reach and strong, militarily-trained grip. When they piled in on the final sacrifice, all together, Gorgo had seen Charis literally work a man's head from his shoulders like some live-action *Mortal Combat* kill, twisting the finger-torn ruin of his throat and neck 'til his vertebrae snapped and spinal cord slithered free.

Sparagmos, Aglaia called it. The Maenad's frenzy, bull sacrifice. A rending apart, followed by *omophagia*, eating the flesh raw. Or, as Gorgo'd always called it, albeit only to herself... fun.

"I know you don't think you're one of us, really," Aglaia told Gorgo, as Gorgo poured herself a bowl of ritual *kykeon*. "But you do keep on coming, don't you? Why do you think that might be?"

"'Cause I like it?"

"You're no great fan of organized religion in general, though, I think; most sociopaths aren't. Yet you must admit it *can* be useful, as a concept, even to those who question it."

Gorgo sighed, steeling herself to stay polite. "Oh, sure," she replied. "Mainly in that it gives us divine permission to go on ahead and do what we were gonna anyways, all wrapped up in a pretty story. Secret knowledge, women's magic, the matriarchy reborn..."

Aglaia shot Gorgo a look, as though unsure if she was being mocked. "So you'll take advantage of the amenities on offer," she said, at last, "but you won't do Her homage."

"If that's the price of staying on the mailing list, sure. Why not?"

"Except that you won't mean it."

At that, Gorgo did have to snort, just a little. "How you ever gonna know *anyone* 'means it,' outside of yourself? Same way I 'know' you do, i.e., not at damn all. Look, lady, I read *The Bacchae*—hell, I've taught it. You really think we can bank on weapons of iron not wounding us when the fit's in full swing, though, no matter how many of those little dried mushrooms you boil the *kykeon* up with? Barley, pennyroyal, psychoactives... it's a nice high, but I don't ever remember getting milk and honey from stones or tearing up trees by their roots while I was on it, let alone wearing snake necklaces, or breastfeeding wolf-cubs."

"Communion wafers aren't made from real man-meat, either. Our feasts are, and *not* metaphorically."

"They weren't, that'd be the deal-breaker right there, for me."

Aglaia chuckled. "I've seen you hunt," she said. "One of our fiercest, when She enters in."

"Hard to stop once I get going, I'll give you that," Gorgo agreed, suddenly tired. "C'mon, though—what I run on's a fetish, not superpowers. I just like to kill people."

"Ah, but you don't just kill *people*, do you, when you have the choice? I'm not talking about self-preservation, or opportunity... I mean pure desire, the perfect victim. The image you touch yourself to."

Gorgo snorted again. Yet the words brought it rising up behind her eyes anyhow, automatic, irrefutable: a man, always, young and juicy for preference. And strong enough to fight hand to hand, take damage from, even—possibly—risk losing to. Not that she ever had.

"... No," she admitted, at last, with reluctance. "You're right. That's never just 'people.'"

"Then you do Her work, and always have. Without even knowing it."

Gorgo shook her head, stubborn. "Dress it up all you want, Aglaia—what I do is what I choose to, that's the whole truth, and nothin' but. 'Cause I *like* it. I don't need any other reason."

"It gets done, however, either way."

Oh yes.

The area of study devoted to those like Gorgo was choked with truisms, creating spaces she'd always found it easy to slip between. Most serial killers, accepted lore went, were white rather than not, middle-class or lower-, organized or dis-... and male, overwhelmingly. Which meant that although there obviously had to be *some* who weren't, by simple process of elimination, nobody really spent a whole lot of time looking for them.

Didn't hurt that women coded societally as victims rather than predators, conferring a weird invisibility on those who didn't worry about becoming somebody else's meal. When men's eyes turned towards Gorgo with ill intent, she met them head-on, smiling. Those unused to the concept turned away; those who didn't had made their bed, and she felt no guilt about laying them down in it.

As it turned out, this attitude formed yet another point of sympathy between Aglaia's lot and herself—since according to the mysteries, sacrifices self-selected through willing, deliberate transgression. They had to *know* there was a taboo in play, even to have some idea of the potential stakes involved, and choose to break said taboo anyways.

Luckily, that was men in a nutshell, or so Gorgo had always observed. Long before the Internet, it had been a truth universally agreed on that whenever somebody started talking about a space being women-only, a segment of the male-identified population would come running with dicks out, ready to mark their territory in the hope no bitch would ever again be dumb enough to believe herself in possession of something *they* couldn't access. It was a winning combination of social mores and genetics, bless their hearts—*just the way we're made, ma'am, now get in the kitchen, etcetera.*

"Everywhere but here," Aglaia claimed, proudly. And so far, her claim had yet to be disproven, there being an undeniable strength in numbers which far outstripped whatever one woman could achieve alone. Everybody wanted community, in their heart of hearts—even those who knew themselves, at base, quite outrageously unsuited to maintain it.

Female serial killers hid behind gender constructs, as a rule. They usually played out the roles people (men) expected them to, then killed inside of that as poisoners, black widows, angels of death . . . caregivers turned toxic. The reason the Maenad myth had been so discounted down the centuries, according to Aglaia, was that the very idea of a woman jumping on somebody and tearing them apart seemed physically impossible. But one had to wonder, like Gorgo remembered doing, even as a child: was there a reason men seemed so wary of "allowing" women to congregate in groups? Could it be they guessed how a pack of women might be indistinguishable from one of lionesses, of hyenas?

Hours passed in chanting, dancing, singing, and the sun dipped low. The *kykeon*, fresh-cooled, got passed around like white lightning; Gorgo drank her next slug in one gulp, watching the newest *mystoi* sip, wince, almost puke. She already felt the drug deep inside her like hooks, opening her wide, letting in the world.

As the dusk began to swim and click around her, she saw Phoibe appear at Aglaia's elbow, night-blooming suddenly, pale out of dark. Watched her murmur in the priestess's ear, then vanish once more, as Aglaia turned to motion Gorgo near.

"Intruders at the perimeter. Mormo has them chasing her already—easy meat, for our best huntress."

Gorgo rose, nodding, to shuck the last of her clothes. She left her footwear on, since running barefoot through the woods was like asking for lockjaw, but Aglaia didn't say anything—possibly since her good right hand Phoibe had apparently decided much the same, albeit sticking with sandals instead of Gorgo's comfortably weighted hiking boots.

Charis handed her one more dose, which lit her up like a punch. Someone she couldn't quite see hugged 'round her from behind, smearing two mud-clay handfuls across both breasts at once, then down over her abs, to cool her thighs' hot vee. Gorgo tossed her hair, and pulled loose; Charis caught her mid-stumble, grinning. "Y'all ready?" she asked.

"Sure am."

"*Thyrsus*, baby girl?"

"Brought my own, thanks." The scythe-handle fit nicely into her palm. "You comin', big sis?"

"Bet your ass," Charis growled, voice dipping lower than she probably wanted it to, not that that mattered: the *ekstasis* was on them both, pumping their blood, stiffening every sinew. Around, Gorgo saw the rest of the pack assembling, all the familiar faces. Iris, Scylla, Polyxena, Deianira...

They took off running, like Artemis Herself led the way.

⊸

And here they were, now. The tiger-pit's displaced covering, lid of the *kiste*, the sacred basket. Gorgo kicked it aside to reveal a third young man—*boy*—staring up, down on one knee and crying with pain, at least one ankle probably shattered from the fall. He was a sweet-looking piece, muscled like a wrestler, hair picked out into a soft natural; his skin gleamed, shade falling somewhere between Deianira's ruddy bronze and Aglaia's warmer, darker hue. Which was a fairly apt comparison, as it turned out—because when he caught sight of Aglaia peering down on him over Gorgo's shoulder his eyes went wide, fixed with shock, and awe, and terrified recognition.

"Mom?" he managed, voice breaking. "*Mom?* What...what're *you* doing...here...?"

Aglaia didn't answer, not immediately. Just drew herself up, turning to stone; crossed her arms and waited, possibly to see what happened next.

"Mom, shit...you have to help me. They're crazy, these women're all—Mom!"

Gorgo back-shifted, waiting as well. Until finally, another voice chimed in: "Well?"

Aglaia, without moving: "'Well' what, Phoibe?"

The woman in question came shoving her way through, pale as a twilit ghost, 'til she stood almost at Aglaia's side—*almost.* But not quite.

"He's penetrated the mysteries, hasn't he?" she declared, nodding downwards, voice pitched to ringing. "Seen things done, heard things said, just like the rest of them. Should the priestess's son go free, and other women's sons pay in his stead? Is this Her will?"

Posturing little hooker, Gorgo thought.

"Didn't hear Aglaia say *what* she wanted done with him, one way or the other, myself," Gorgo pointed out. "And since I'm a hell of a lot more likely to listen to her than to you, on the subject..."

"Ha! The unbeliever speaks." Phoibe threw her arms wide, addressing the whole cult, now flocking in around Gorgo's hunting team. "See how she mocks? Ask yourselves why Aglaia would ever let somebody like this in in the first place, let alone allow her to stay. Then ask yourself if it isn't obvious that the Goddess chose to punish Aglaia for her *hubris*, by sending her first-born to the killing floor! How else could it have happened?"

Defend yourself, idiot, Gorgo tried to project Aglaia's way, watching heads on all sides begin to nod, albeit reluctantly. But Aglaia's eyes stayed on the pit, her whimpering child. She might as well have been a statue.

Murmuring spread in every direction, like a tide.

Time to run, maybe, Gorgo thought, reluctantly, gripping her scythe hard enough to hurt. *Save yourself, before this shit shifts on you; drop out, get gone. This was a bad idea. It's like Missus Gast used to say, my third foster-Mommy—someone like me just needs to stay the hell away from people, I want to keep safe . . .*

(. . . unless I'm killing 'em.)

That was when it happened, sharp as a wound—that same unfurling times ten thousand, the *kykeon*'s blow suddenly felt all over, a general uproar. This lurching, queasy sensation of opening up *so* far it was like her insides were out, skin shifting, one massive neuron blur. Blood broke from her nose, mouth, the corners of her eyes; later, she'd find burst vessels on both eyeballs, a pair of tiny red flowers. For now, however, it was as though *something else* had a hold of her, puppeting her from the gut. Making one hand fly out, scythe's point sticking deep into Phoibe's still-babbling throat, then jerking free again, conjuring a flood. The spurt slapped across Gorgo before hitting Charis, who gasped, and Aglaia, who didn't; a general cry went up, cultists reacting as one. Phoibe fell, flopping, while Gorgo shivered still upright, mouth opening against her will. Words torrented free, garbled, unfamiliar, Greek-accented. Saying—

Fury-source, Wrathful One, All-ruling virgin,
Kore Semele, light-bearer incandescent
Horned Maiden, Earth's vigorous daughter
When Death comes, we go willingly to Your realms
Until again You send us forth, into this world of Form.

She didn't know this prayer, Gorgo realized, unable not to complete what she could only assume was the verse's ancient formula. Not one she'd heard, nor one she'd read. No translation of *The Bacchae* she'd ever taught could have left it behind in her mind's folds, waiting to suggest itself under pressure—no, this was something else. Something Other.

At her boot-tips, Phoibe had almost ceased shuddering. Gorgo found herself pointing at her, mouth stretched Body Snatchers-wide, pronouncing: "How'd it happen? Ask the hacker. The girl with the math. Ask her how she sought him out online, groomed him, brought him and those friends of his here—because she wanted to mount a coup, thought he'd make Aglaia look weak in front of you, that she could turn you against Her chosen. But *nothing happens, ever, except that She allows it.*"

"Praise be," Charis chimed in, wiping Phoibe's blood straight into her mouth; "Praise be," Iris agreed, kicking Phoibe so she flipped, so her last breath went down into the earth itself, Persephone-Perswa's home. To which Aglaia finally nodded, dignified as always, and put her hand on Gorgo's still-shaking shoulder, palm-print burning a hole all the Goddess's presence suddenly drained from once more, leaving her numb and cold, scythe drooping.

"Praise be," Aglaia agreed, approvingly. "I'm so happy for you, Gorgo. It's seldom any of us feels Her grace directly—to have that one be you is a rare honour, and welcome. Especially since I'd've had trouble killing a woman, myself, even one who'd betrayed Her covenant." A lovely smile. "But then, that's what She sent us *you* for."

"The fuck you say," Gorgo replied, all out into a rush, with no time for self-censorship. Her nervous system was still twitching, refusing to obey, or she would've cut Aglaia's throat next—something Aglaia seemed to know, since she glanced at Charis, who gently pried the scythe from Gorgo's limp hand, folding her into an embrace.

"C'mon now, baby girl," Charis said, soothing. "You got nothing to be afraid of. We all want to feel Her hand on our souls the once, like you just did. It's why we're here."

"Not . . . why *I'm* here . . . " Gorgo said, muffled, into Charis's pectoral, her implant-springy breast. But Charis only laughed.

"'Course not," she replied. "We all know *that.* Is now, though—and that's beautiful, don't you see? Hell, it's *divine.*"

"Literally," Aglaia agreed. "Oh, Gorgo! You're a saint to us now, a true Maenad. The very proof of our religion."

And that murmur was back again, eddying right, left, and every which way, whipping the crowd into a frenzy. They seized on Phoibe's body and bore it away, tearing off pieces as it went; probably end up on the pyre with the rest of the meat, fit for the celebratory feast, with the bones all divvied up and buried wherever individual cultists went home to, after.

I'm trapped, Gorgo thought, hanging there in Charis's arms, while Aglaia and the others clapped, cheered, and ululated in approval, each according to their preference. *They've got me now, these freaks, them with their goddamn Goddess. I'm altered, forever changed. Like I don't even know my own self anymore.*

"What about him, down there?" she asked, finally, through trembling lips.

Throughout the preceding action, the still pit-trapped boy—Aglaia's unlucky son—had fallen silent long since, in terms of pleas. Now it was just grunts and cursing, *oh God oh God oh shit, help me please*, with the kid scrabbling at the walls like a crippled badger, trying his level best either to heave himself free or bring the walls' earth in on top of him, so he could suffocate before they pulled him free and ripped him apart. Perhaps having stared enough, however, Aglaia didn't even look, this time. Simply shook her head, curls lifting slightly (softer than his yet similar, Gorgo could now see), and said—

"Phoibe called him, but She made him answer. This is not for him, for any of them, yet still they come: *anathema*, to be dedicated, to be cursed. He chose his own fate."

At that, the scrabbling stopped, as if kicked. Gorgo heard the kid moan out, instinctive, maybe in supplication, maybe in protest: *Mom, oh Mom, Mommy*, no. *Please, God*, please.

True Believers, true belief; not such an arrant hunk of legitimized murder wrapped in bullshit fairytales after all, as it turned out. More's the fucking pity.

No God here, little boy, Gorgo thought, as close to sadly as she was capable of. And closed her eyes.

INTERSTATE LOVE SONG (MURDER BALLAD NO. 8)

CAITLÍN R. KIERNAN

"The way of the transgressor is hard."

—Cormac McCarthy

1.

The Impala's wheels singing on the black hot asphalt sound like frying steaks, USDA choice-cut T-bones, sirloin sizzling against August blacktop in Nevada or Utah or Nebraska, Alabama or Georgia, or where the fuck ever this one day, this one hour, this one motherfucking minute is going down. Here at the end, the end of one of us, months are a crimson thumb smudge across the bathroom mirror in all the interchangeable motel bathrooms that have come and gone and come again. You're smoking and looking for music in the shoebox filled with cassettes, and the clatter of protective plastic shells around spools of magnetically coated tape is like an insect chorus, a cicada symphony. You ask what I want to hear, and I tell you it doesn't matter, please light one of those for me. But you insist, and you keep right on insisting, "What d'you wanna hear?" And I say, well not fucking Nirvana again, and no more Johnny Cash, please, and you toss something from the box out the open passenger window. In the side-view mirror, I see a tiny shrapnel explosion when the cassette hits the road. Cars will come behind us, cars and trucks, and roll over the shards and turn it all to dust. "No more Nirvana," you say, and you laugh your boyish girl's laugh, and Jesus and Joseph and Mother Mary, I'm not going to be able to live in a world without that laugh. Look at me, I say. Open your eyes, please open your eyes and look at me, please. You can't fall asleep on me. Because it won't be falling asleep, will it? It won't be falling asleep at all. We are on beyond the kindness of euphemisms, and maybe we always were. So, don't fall asleep. Don't flutter the eyelashes you've always hated because they're so long and pretty, don't let them dance that Totentanz tarantella we've delighted at so many goddamn times, don't let the sun go down on me. You shove a tape into the deck. You always do that with such force, as if there's a vendetta grudge between you and that machine. You punch it in and twist the volume knob like you mean to yank it off and yeah, that's good, I say. That's golden, Henry Rollins snarling at the sun's one great demon eye. You light a Camel for me and place it between my lips, and the steering wheel feels like a weapon in my hands, and the smoke feels like Heaven in my lungs. Wake up, though. Don't shut your eyes. Remember the day that we, and remember the morning, and remember *that* time in—shit, was it El Paso? Or was it Port Arthur? It doesn't matter, so long as you keep your eyes open and look at me. It's hours until sunrise, and have you not always sworn a blue streak that you would not die in the darkness? That's all we've got here. In for a penny, in for a pound, but blackness, wall to wall, sea to shining sea, that's all we've got in this fluorescent hell, so don't you please fall asleep on me. Hot wind roars in through the Impala's windows, the stink of melting tar, roaring like an invisible mountain lion, and you point west and say take that next exit. We need beer, and we're almost out of cigarettes, and I want a pack of Starburst Fruit Chews, the tropical flavors, so the assholes better have those out here in the world's barren shit-kicker asshole. You'll just like always save all the piña colada ones for me. Then there's a thud from the trunk, and you laugh that laugh of yours all over again, only now with true passion. "And we need a bottle of water," I say. "No good to us and a waste of time and energy, and just a waste all the way round, if she ups and dies of heat stroke back there," and you shrug. Hey, keep your eyes open, love. Please, goddamn it. You can do that for me, I know you can. And I break open one of the ampules of ammonia and cruelly wave it beneath your nostrils so that both eyes pop open wide, opening up cornflower blue, and I think of startled birds bursting from their hiding places in tall grass. Tall grass, there's so much of tall grass here at the end, isn't there? I kiss your forehead, and I can't help thinking I could fry an egg on your skin, fry an egg on blacktop, fry an egg on the hood of the Impala parked in the Dog Day sun outside a convenience store. You ask me to light a candle, your voice gone all jagged and broken apart like a cassette tape dropped on I-10 at 75 mph. I press my fingers and palm to the sloppy red mess of your belly, and I do not dare take my hand away long enough to light a candle, and I'm so sorry, I'm so, so sorry. I cannot even do that much for you. Just please don't close your eyes. Please don't you fall asleep on me.

2.

All these things you said to me, if not on this day, then surely on some other, and if not during this long Delta night, than surely on another. The blonde with one brown eye and one hazel-green eye, she wasn't the first, but you said to me she'll be the most memorable yet. She'll be one we talk about in years to come when all the rest have faded into a blur of delight and casual slaughter. We found her at a truck stop near Shreveport, and she'd been hitching down I-49 towards Baton Rouge and New Orleans. "Sister, where you bound on such a hot, hot, sweltersome night?" you asked. And because she was dressed in red, a Crimson Tide T-shirt and a red Budweiser baseball cap, you said, "Whither so early, Little Red Cap?" And she laughed, and you two shared a joint while I ate a skimpy dinner of Slim Jims, corn chips, and Mountain Dew. Eighteen-wheeled dinosaurs growled in and growled out and purred at the pumps. We laughed over a machine that sold multicolored prophylactics and another that sold tampons. And would she like a ride? Would she? 'Cause we're a sight lot better than you're likely gonna find elsewhere, if you're looking for decent company and conversation, that is, and the weed, there's more where that came from. How old? Eighteen, she said, and you and I both knew she was adding years, but all the better. She tossed her knapsack in the back seat, and the extra pair of shoes she wore around her neck, laces laced together. She smelled of the road, of many summer days without a bath, and the world smelled of dinosaur trucks and diesel and dust and Spanish moss; and I love you so much, you whispered as I climbed behind the wheel. I love you so much I do not have words to say how much

I love you. We set sail southward, washed in the alien chartreuse glow of the Impala's dash, and she and thee talked while I drove, listening. That was enough for me, listening in, eavesdropping while my head filled up with a wakeful, stinging swarm of bees, with wasps and yellow jackets, courtesy those handy shrink-wrapped packets of dextroamphetamine and amphetamine, Black Beauties, and in the glove compartment there's Biphetamine-T and 40mg capsules of methaqualone, because when *we* drove all damn day and all damned night, we came prepared, didn't we, love? She's traveled all the way from Chicago, the red-capped backseat girl, and you and I have never been to Chicago and have no desire to go. She talks about the road as it unrolls beneath us, before me, hauling us towards dawn's early light. She tells you about some old pervert who picked her up outside Texarkana. She fucked him for twenty bucks and the lift to Shreveport. "Could'a done worse," you tell her, and she doesn't disagree. I watch you both in the rearview mirror. I watch you both, in anticipation, and the uppers and the prospect of what will come, the mischief we will do her in the wood, has me more awake than awake, has me ready to cum then and there. "You're twins," she said. It wasn't a question, only a statement of the obvious, as they say. "We're twins," you reply. "But she's my big sister. Born three minutes apart on the anniversary of the murder of Elizabeth Short," and she has no goddamn idea what you're talking about, but, not wanting to appear ignorant, she doesn't let on. When she asks where we're from, "Los Angeles," you lie. You have a generous pocketful of answers at the ready for that oft asked question. "South Norton Avenue, midway between Coliseum Street and West 39th," you say, which has as little meaning to the heterochromatic blonde as does Glasgow smile and Leimert Park. I drive, and you spin our revolving personal mythology. She will be one for the books, you whispered back at the truck stop. Can't you smell it on her? Can't I smell what on her? Can't you smell happenstance and inevitability and fate? Can't you smell victim? You say those things, and always I nod, because, like backseat girl, I don't want to appear ignorant in your view. This one I love, this one I love, eating cartilage, shark-eyes, shark-heart, and black mulberry trees mean I will not survive you, when the truth is I won't survive *without* you. Backseat girl, she talks about how she's gonna find work in New Orleans as a waitress, when you and I know she's cut out for nothing much but stripping and whoring the Quarter, and if this were a hundred years ago she'd be headed for fabled, vanished Storyville. "I had a boyfriend," she says. "I had a boyfriend, but he was in a band, and they all moved off to Seattle, but, dude, I didn't want to fucking *go* to fucking Seattle, you know?" And you say to her how it's like the California Gold Rush or something, all these musician sheep lemming assholes and would-be wannabe musician posers traipsing their way to the fabled Northwest in hopes of riding a wave that's already broken apart and isn't even sea foam anymore. That ship has *sailed,* you say. It's sailed and sunk somewhere in the deep blue Pacific. But that's not gonna stop anyone with stars in their eyes, because the lure of El Dorado is always a bitch, whichever El Dorado is at hand. "Do you miss him?" I ask, and that's the first thing I've said in over half an hour, more than happy just to listen in and count off the reflective mile markers with the help of anger and discord jangling from the tape deck. "Don't know," she says. And she says, "Maybe sometimes. Maybe." The road's a lonely place, you tell her, sounding sympathetic when I know so much better. I know your mind is full to the brim with red, red thoughts, the itch of your straight-razor lusts, the prospect of the coming butchery. Night cruising at 80 mph, we rush past the turnoff for Natchitoches, and there's a sign that says "Lost Bayou," and our passenger asks have *we* ever been to New Orleans. Sure, you lie. Sure. We'll show you 'round. We have friends who live in an old house on Burgundy, and they say the house is haunted by a Civil War ghost, and they'll probably let you crash there until you're on your feet. Sister, you make us sound like goddamn guardian angels, the best break she's ever had. I drive on, and the car reeks of pot and sweat, cigarette smoke and the old beer cans heaped in the back floorboard. "I've always wished I had a twin," she says. "I used to make up stories that I was adopted, and somewhere out there I had a twin brother. One day, I'd pretend, we'd find one another. Be reunited, you know." It's a pretty dream from the head a such a pretty, pretty red-capped girl in the backseat, ferried by you and I in our human masks to hide hungry wolfish faces. *I could turn you inside out,* I think at the girl. And we will. It's been a week since an indulgence, a week of aimless July motoring, letting peckish swell to starvation, taking no other pleasures but junk food and blue-plate specials, you and I fucking and sleeping in one another's arms while the merciless Dixie sun burned 101°F at motel-room rooftops, kerosene air gathered in rooms darkened and barely cooled by drawn curtains and wheezing AC. Strike a match, and the whole place woulda gone up. Cartoons on television, and watching MTV, and old movies in shades of black and white and grey. Burgers wrapped in meat-stained paper and devoured with salty fries. Patience, love, patience, you whispered in those shadows, and so we thrummed along back roads and highways waiting for just the right confection. And. My. Momma. Said. Pick the Very. Best One. And You. Are. It.

3.

Between the tall rustling cornsilk rows, ripening husks, bluebottle drone as the sun slides down from the greasy blue sky to set the horizon all ablaze, and you straddle Thin Man and hold his cheekbones so that he has no choice but to gaze into your face. He can't close his eyes, as he no longer has eyelids, and he screams every time I shake another handful of Red Devil lye across his bare thighs and genitals. Soft flesh is melting like hot wax, here beneath the fading Iowa day. I draw a deep breath, smelling chemical burns, tilled red-brown Bible Belt soil, and corn, and above all else, corn. The corn smells alive in ways I cannot imagine being alive, and when we are done with Thin Man, I think I would like to lie down here, right here, in the dirt between the tall rows, and gaze up at the June night, at the wheeling twin dippers and bear twins and the solitary scorpion and Cassiopeia, what I know of summer stars. "You don't have to do this," the man blubbers, and you tell him no, we don't, but yes, we do. We very much actually do. And he screams, and his scream is the lonesome cry of a small animal dying alone so near to twilight. He could be a rabbit in a fox's jaws, just as easily as a thin man in our company. We found him standing alongside a pickup broken down miles and miles north of Ottumwa, and maybe we ought to have driven him farther than we did, but impatience wins sometimes, and so you made up that story about our Uncle Joe who has a garage just a little ways farther up the road. What did he have to fear from two pale girls in a rust-bucket Impala, and so I drove, and Thin Man—whose name I still unto this hour do not know—talked about how liberals and niggers and bleeding hearts and the EPA are ruining the country. Might he have become suspicious of our lies if you'd not switched out the plates at the state line? Might he have paused in his unelicited screed long enough to think twice and think better? You scoop up fertile soil and dribble it into his open mouth, and he gags and sputters and chokes and wheezes, and still he manages to beg throughout. He's pissed himself and shat himself, so there are also those odors. Not too far away are train tracks, and not too far away there is a once-red barn, listing like a drunkard, and silver grain silos, and a whistle blows, and it blows, calling the swallows home. You sing to Thin Man, *Heed the curves, and watch the tunnels. Never falter, never fail.* Remember that? Don't close your eyes, and do not dare sleep, for this is not that warm night we lay together near Thin Man's shucked corpse and screwed in the eyes of approving Maggot Corn King deities thankful for our oblation. Your lips on my breasts, suckling, your fingers deep inside me, plowing, sewing, and by tomorrow we'll be far away, and this will be a pleasant dream for the scrapbooks of our tattered souls. More lye across Thin Man's crotch, and he bucks beneath you like an unbroken horse or a lover or an epileptic or a man being taken apart, piece by piece, in a cornfield north of Ottumwa. When we were children, we sat in the kudzu and live-oak shade near the tracks, waiting, waiting, placing pennies and nickels on the iron rails. You, spitting on the rails to cool them enough you would not blister your ear when you pressed it to the metal. I hear the train, you announced and smiled. Not much farther now, I hear it coming, and soon the slag ballast will dance and the crossties buck like a man dying in a cornfield. Soon now, the parade of clattering doomsday boxcars, the steel wheels that can sever limbs and flatten coins. Boxcars the color of rust—Southern Serves the South and CSX and a stray Wisconsin Central as good as a bird blown a thousand miles off course by hurricane winds. Black cylindrical tankers filled with corn syrup and crude oil, phenol, chlorine gas, acetone, vinyl chloride, and we spun tales of poisonous, flaming, steaming derailments. Those rattling, one-cent copper-smearing trains, we dreamed they might carry us off in the merciful arms of hobo sojourns to anywhere far, far away from home. *Keep your hand upon the throttle, and your eye upon the rail.* And Thin Man screams, dragging me back to the now of then. You've put dirt in his eyes, and you'd imagine he'd be thankful for that, wouldn't you? Or maybe he was gazing past you towards imaginary pearly gates where delivering angels with flaming swords might sweep down to lay low his tormentors and cast us forever and anon into the lake of fire. More Red Devil and another scream. He's beginning to bore me, you say, but I'm so busy admiring my handiwork I hardly hear you, and I'm also remembering the drive to the cornfield. I'm remembering what Thin Man was saying about fairy child-molesting atheist sodomites in all branches of the federal government and armed forces, and an international ZOG conspiracy of Jews running the USA into the ground, and who the *fuck* starts in about shit like that with total, helpful strangers? Still, you were more than willing to play along and so told him yes, yes, yes, how we were faithful, god-fearing Southern Baptists, and how our daddy was a deacon and our momma a Sunday school teacher. That should'a been laying it on too thick, anyone would've thought, but Thin Man grinned bad teeth and nodded and blew great clouds of menthol smoke out the window like a locomotive chimney. Open your eyes. I'm not gonna tell you again. Here's another rain of lye across tender meat, and here's the corpse we left to rot in a cornfield, and I won't be left alone, do you hear me? Here are cordials to keep you nailed into your skin and to this festering, unsuspecting world. What am I, what am I, what *am* I? he wails, delirious, as long cornstalk shadows crosshatch the field, and in reply do you say, A sinner in the hands of angry gods, and we'd laugh about that one for days. But maybe he did believe you, sister, for he fell to praying, and I half believe he was praying not to Father, Son, and Holy Ghost, but to you and me. You tell him, by your own words, Mister, we see thou art an evil man, and we, too, are surely out and about and up to no good, as you'll have guessed, and we are no better than thee, and so there is balance. I don't know why, but you tack on something about the horned, moon-crowned Popess squatting between Boaz and Jachin on the porch of Solomon. They are pretty words, whether I follow their logic or not. Near, nearer, the train whistle blows again, and in that moment you plunge your knife so deeply into Thin Man's neck that it goes straight through his trachea and spine and out the other side. The cherry fountain splashes you. You give the Bowie a little twist to the left, just for shits and giggles. Appropriately, he lies now still as death. You pull out the knife and kiss the jetting hole you've made, painting sticky your lips and chin. Your throat. You're laughing, and the train shrieks, and now I want to cover my ears, because just every once and a while I do lose my footing on the winding serpent highway, and when I do the fear wraps wet-sheet cold about me. This, here, now, is one of those infrequent, unfortunate episodes. I toss the plastic bottle of lye aside and drag you off Thin Man's still, still corpse. Don't, I say. Don't you dare laugh no more, I don't think it's all that funny, and also don't you dare shut your eyes, and don't you dare go to sleep on me.

Till we reach that blissful shore
Where the angels wait to join us
In that train
Forevermore.

I seize you, love, and you are raving in my embrace: *What the fuck are you doing? Take your goddamn filthy hands off me cunt, gash, bitch, traitor.* But oh, oh, oh I hold on, and I hold on tight for dear forsaken life, 'cause the land's tilting teeter-totter under us as if on the Last Day of All, the day of Kingdom Come, and just don't make me face the righteous fury of the Lion of Judah alone. In the corn, we rolled and wallowed like dust-bathing mares, while you growled, and foam flecked your bloody lips, and you spat and slashed at the gloaming with your dripping blade. A voyeuristic retinue of grasshoppers and field mice, crickets and a lone bullsnake took in our flailing, certainly comedic antics while I held you prisoner in my arms, holding you hostage against my shameful fear and self doubt. Finally, inevitably, your laughter died, and I only held you while you sobbed and Iowa sod turned to streaks of mud upon your mirthless face.

4.

I drive west, then east again, then turn south onto I-55, Missouri, the County of Cape Girardeau. Meandering like the cottonmouth, silt-choked Mississippi, out across fertile floodplain fields all night-blanketed, semisweet darkness to hide river-gifted loam. You're asleep in the backseat, your breath soft as velvet, soft as autumn rain. You never sleep more than an hour at a time, not ever, and so I never wake you. Not ever. Not even when you cry out from the secret nightmare countries behind your eyelids. We are moving along between the monotonous, barbarous topography and the overcast sky, overcast at sunset the sky looked dead, and now, well past midnight, there is still no sign of moon nor stars to guide me, and I have only the road signs and the tattered atlas lying open beside me as I weave and wend through the Indian ghosts of Ozark Bluff Dwellers, stalkers of shambling mastodon and mammoth phantoms along these crude asphalt corridors. I light cigarette after cigarette and wash Black Beauties down with peach Nehi. I do not often know loneliness, but I know it now, and I wish I were with you in your hard, hard dreams. The radio's tuned to a gospel station out of Memphis, but the volume is down low, low, low so you'll not be awakened by the Five Blind Boys of Alabama or the Dixie Hummingbirds. In your sleep, you're are muttering, and I try not to eavesdrop. But voices carry, as they say, and I hear enough to get the gist. You sleep a walking sleep, and in dreams, you've drifted back to Wichita, to that tow-headed boy with fish and starfish, an octopus and sea shells tattooed all up and down his arms, across his broad chest and shoulders. "Because I've never seen the ocean," he said. "But that's where I'm headed now. I'm going all the way to Florida. To Panama City or Pensacola." "We've never seen the sea, either," you tell him. "Can we go with you? We've really nowhere else to go, and you really have no notion how delightful it will be when they take us up and throw us with the lobsters out to sea." The boy laughed. No, not a boy, not in truth, but a young man older than us, a scruffy beard growing unevenly on his suntanned cheeks. "Can we? Can we, please?" Hey, you're the two with the car, not me, he replied, so I suppose you're free to go anywhere you desire. And that is the gods' honest truth of it all, ain't it? We are free to drive anywhere we please, so long as we do not attempt to part this material plane of simply three dimensions. Alone in the night, in the now and not the then, I have to be careful. It would be too easy to slip into my own dreams, amphetamine insomnia helping hands or no, and I have so often imagined our Odyssey ending with the Impala wrapped around a telephone pole or lying wheels-up turtlewise and steaming in a ditch or head-on folded back upon ourselves after making love to an oncoming semi. I shake my head and open my eyes wider. There's a rest stop not too far up ahead, and I tell myself that I'll pull over there. I'll pull over to doze for a while in sodium-arc pools, until the sun rises bright and violent to burn away the clouds, until it's too hot to sleep. The boy's name was Philip—one L. The young man who was no longer a boy and who had been decorated with the cryptic nautical language of an ocean he'd never seen, and, as it came to pass, never would. But you'd keep all his teeth in a Mason jar, just in case we ever got around to the Gulf of Mexico or an Atlantic shoreline. You kept his teeth, promising him a burial in saltwater. Philip told us about visiting a museum at the university in Lawrence, where he saw the petrified skeletons of giant sea monsters that once had swum the vanished inland depths. He was only a child, ten or eleven, but he memorized names that, to my ears, sounded magical, forbidden, perilous Latin incantations to call down fish from the clear blue sky or summon bones burrowing upwards from yellow-gray chalky rocks. You sat with your arms draped shameless about his neck while he recited and elaborated—*Tylosaurus proriger, Dolichorhynchops bonneri, Platecarpus tympaniticus, Elasmosaurus platyurus, Selmasaurus kiernanii,* birds with teeth and giant turtles, flying reptiles and the fangs of ancient sharks undulled by eighty-five million years, give or take. Show off, you said and laughed. That's what you are, a show off. And you said, Why aren't you in college, bright boy? And Philip with one L said his parents couldn't afford tuition, and his grades had not been good enough for a scholarship, and he wasn't gonna join the army, because he had a cousin went off to Desert Storm, right, and did his duty in Iraq, and now he's afraid to leave the house and sick all the time and constantly checks his shoes for scorpions and landmines. The military denies all responsibility. Maybe, said Philip with one L, I can get a job on a fishing boat, or a shrimping boat, and spend all my days on the water and all my nights drinking rum with mermaids. We could almost have fallen in love with him. Almost. You even whispered to me about driving him to Florida that he might lay eyes upon the Gulf of Mexico before he died. But I am a jealous bitch, and I said no, fuck that sentimental horseshit, and he died the next day in a landfill not far from Emporia. I did that one, cut his throat from ear to ear while he was busy screwing you. He looked up at me, his stark blue irises drowning in surprise and confusion, and then he came one last time, coaxed to orgasm, pumping blood from severed carotid and jugular and, too, pumping out an oyster stream of jizz. It seemed all but immaculate, the red and the silver gray, and you rode him even after there was no more of him left to ride but a cooling cadaver. You cried over Philip, and that was the first and only one you ever shed tears for, and Jesus I am sorry but I wanted to slap you. I wanted to do something worse than slap you for your mourning. I wanted to leave a scar. Instead, I gouged out his lifeless eyes with my thumbs and spat in his face. You wiped your nose on your shirt sleeve, pulled up your underwear and jeans, and went back to the car for the needle-nose pair of pliers in the glove compartment. It did not have to be that way, you said, you pouted, and I growled at you to shut up, and whatever it is you're doing in his mouth, hurry because this place gives me the creeps. Those slumping, smoldering hills of refuse, Gehenna for rats and maggots and crows, coyotes, stray dogs and strayer cats. We *could* have taken him to the sea, you said. We *could* have done that much, and then you fell silent, sulking, taciturn, and not ever again waking have you spoken of him. Besides the teeth, you peeled off a patch of skin, big as the palm of your hand and inked with the image of a crab, because we were born in the sign of Cancer. The rest of him we concealed under heaps of garbage. *Here you go, rats, here's something fresh. Here's a banquet, and we shall not even demand tribute in return. We will be benevolent rat gods, will we two, bringing plenty and then taking our leave, and you will spin prophecies of our return. Amen. Amen. Hossannah.* Our work done, I followed you back to the Impala, stepping superstitiously in your footsteps, and that is what I am doing when—now—I snap awake to the dull, gritty noise of the tires bumping off the shoulder and spraying dry showers of breakdown-lane gravel, and me half awake and cursing myself for nodding off; fuck me, fuck me, I'm such an idiot, how I should have stopped way the hell back in Bonne Terre or Fredericktown. I cut the wheel left, and, just like that, all is right again. Doomsday set aside for now. In the backseat, you don't even stir. I turn up the radio for companionship. If I had toothpicks, I might prop open my eyes. My hands are red, love. Oh god, my hands are so red, and we have not ever looked upon the sea.

5.

Boredom, you have said again and again, is the one demon might do you in, and the greatest of all our foes, the *one* demon, Mystery Babylon, the Great Harlot, who at the Valley of Josaphat, on the hill of Megiddo, wraps chains about our porcelain slender necks and drags us down to dust and comeuppance if we dare to turn our backs upon the motherfucker and give it free fucking reign. I might allow how this is the mantra that set us to traveling on the road we are on and has dictated our every action since that departure, your morbid fear of boredom. The consequence of this mantra has almost torn you in half, so that I bend low over my love, only my bare hands to keep your insides from spilling outside. Don't you shut your eyes. You don't get out half that easy. Simple boredom is as good as the flapping wings of butterflies to stir the birth throes of hurricanes. Tiresome recitations of childhood traumas and psychoses be damned. As are we; as are we.

6.

We found her, or she was the one found us, another state, another county, the outskirts of another slumbering city. Another truck-stop diner. Because we were determined to become connoisseurs of everything that is fried and smothered in lumpy brown gravy, and you were sipping a flat Coke dissolute with melting ice. You were talking—I don't know why—about the night back home when the Piggly Wiggly caught fire, so we climbed onto the roof and watched it go up. The air smelled like burning groceries. We contemplated cans of Del Monte string beans and pears and cans of Grapico reaching the boiling point and going off like grenades, and the smoke rose up and blotted out the moon, which that night was full. You're talking about the fire, and suddenly she's there, the coal-haired girl named Haddie in her too-large Lollapalooza T-shirt and black jeans and work boots. Her eyes are chipped jade and honey, that variegated hazel, and she smiles so disarming a smile and asks if, perhaps, we're heading east towards Birmingham, because she's trying to get to Birmingham, but—insert here a woeful tale of her douchebag boyfriend—and now she's stranded high and dry, not enough money for bus fare, and if we're headed that way, could she please, and would we please? You scoot over and pat the turquoise sparkle vinyl upholstery, inviting her to take a Naugahyde seat, said the spider to the fly. "Thank you," she says. "Thank you very much," and she sits and you share your link sausage and waffles with her, because she says she hasn't any money for food, either. We're heading for Atlanta, you tell her, and we'll be going right straight through Birmingham, so sure, no problem, the more the goddamn merrier. We are lifesavers, she says. Never been called that before. You chat her up, sweet as cherry pie with whipped cream squirted from a can, and, me, I stare out the plate-glass partition at the gas pumps and the stark white lighting to hide the place where a Mississippi night should be. "Austin," she says, when you ask from whence she's come. "Austin, Texas," she volunteers. "I was born and raised there." Well, you can hear it, plain as tits on a sow, in her easy, drawling voice. I take in a mouthful of lukewarm Cheerwine, swallow, repeat, and do not let my attention drift from the window and an idling eighteen-wheeler parked out there with its cab all painted up like a Santería altar whore, gaudy and ominous and seductive. Smiling Madonna and cherubic child, merry skeletons dancing joyful round about a sorrowful, solemn Pietà, roses and carnations, crucifixions, half-pagan orichá and weeping bloody Catholic Jesus. Of a sudden, then, I feel a sick coldness spreading deep in my bowels, ice water heavy in my guts, and I want to tell this talkative Lone-Star transient that no, sorry, but you spoke too soon and, sorry, but we *can't* give her a ride, after all, not to Birmingham or anywhere else, that she'll have to bum one from another mark, which won't be hard, because the night is filled with travelers. I want to say just that. But I don't. Instead, I keep my mouth shut tight and watch as a man in dirty orange coveralls climbs into the cab of the truck, him and his goddamn enormous shaggy dog. That dog, it might almost pass for a midget grizzly. In the meanwhile, Ms. Austin is sitting there feeding you choice slivers of her life's story, and you devour it, because I've never yet seen you not hungry for a sobby tale. This one, she's got all the hallmarks of a banquet, doesn't she? Easy pickings, if I only trust experience and ignore this inexplicable wash of instinct. Then you, love, give me a gentle, unseen kick beneath the table, hardly more than an emphatic nudge, your right foot insistently tapping, tap, tap, at my left ankle in a private Morse. I fake an unconcerned smile and turn my face away from the window and that strange truck, though I can still hear its impatient engines. "A painter," says Ms. Austin. "See, I want to be a painter. I've got an aunt in Birmingham, and she knows my mom's a total cunt, and she doesn't mind if I stay with her while I try to get my shit together. It was supposed to be me and him both, but now it's just gonna be me. See, I shut my eyes, and I see murals, and that's what I want to paint one day. *Wallscapes*." And she talks about murals in Mexico City and Belfast and East Berlin. "I need to piss," I say, and you flash me a questioning glance that Ms. Austin does not appear to catch. I slide out of the turquoise booth and walk past other people eating other meals, past shelves grounded with motor oil, candy bars, and pornography. I'm lucky and there's no one else in the restroom, no one to hear me vomit. *What the fuck is this? Hunh? What the fuck is wrong with me now?* When the retching is done, I sit on the dirty tile floor and drown in sweat and listen to my heart throwing a tantrum in my chest. Get up and get back out there. And you, don't you even think of shutting your eyes again. The sun won't rise for another two hours, another two hours at least, and we made a promise one to the other. Or have you forgotten in the gauzy veils of hurt and Santísima Muerte come to whisper in your ear? Always have you said you were hers, a demimondaine to the Bony Lady, *la Huesuda*. So, faithless, I have to suffer your devotions as well? I also shoulder your debt? The restroom stinks of cleaning fluid, shit and urine, my puke, deodorant cakes and antibacterial soap, filth and excessive cleanliness rubbing shoulders. I don't recall getting to my feet. I don't recall a number of things, truth be told, but then we're paying the check, and then we're out in the muggy Lee County night. You tow Ms. Austin behind you. She rides your wake, slipstreaming, and she seems to find every goddamn thing funny. You climb into the backseat with her, and the two of you giggle and titter over private jokes to which I have apparently not been invited. What all did I miss while I was on my knees, praying to my Toilet Gods? I put in a Patsy Cline tape, *punch* it into the deck as you would, and crank it up loud so I don't have to listen to the two of you, not knowing what you (not her, just *you*) have planned, feeling like an outsider in your company, and I cannot ever recall that having happened. Before long, the lights of Tupelo are growing small and dim in the rearview, a diminishing sun as the Impala glides southeast along US 78. My foot feels heavy as a millstone on the gas pedal. So, I have "A Poor Man's Roses" and "Back in Baby's Arms" and "Sweet Dreams" and a fresh pack of Camels and you and Ms. Austin spooning at my back. And still that ice water in my bowels. She's talking about barbeque, and you laugh, and what the fuck is funny about barbeque. "Dreamland," she says, "just like what those UFO nuts call Area 51 in Nevada, where that dead Roswell alien and shit's supposed to be hidden." Me, I smoke and chew on bitter cherry-flavored Tums tablets, grinding calcium carbonate and corn starch and talc between my teeth. "Those like you," says Ms. Austin, "who've lost their way," and I have no goddamn idea what she's going on about. We cross a bridge, and if it's a river below us, I do not see any indication that it's been given a name. But we're entering Itawamba County, says a sign, and that sounds like some mythological world serpent or someplace from a William Faulkner novel. Only about twenty miles now to the state line, and I'm thinking how I desire to be shed of the bitch, how I want her out of the car before Tuscaloosa, wondering how I can signal you without making Ms. Austin Texas Chatterbox suspicious. We pass a dozen exits to lonely country roads where we could take our time, do the job right, and at least I'd have something to show for my sour stomach. I'm thinking about the couple in Arkansas, how we made him watch while we took our own sweet time with her, and you telling him it wasn't so different from skinning catfish, not really. A sharp knife and a pair of pliers, that's all you really need, and he screamed and screamed and screamed. Hell, the pussy bastard sonofabitch screamed more than she did. In the end, I put a bullet in his brain just to shut him the fuck up, please. And we'd taken so long with her, hours and hours, well, there wasn't time remaining to do him justice, anyway. After that we've made a point of avoiding couples. After that, it became a matter of policy. Also, I remember that girl we stuck in the trunk for a hundred miles, and how she was half dead of heat prostration by the time we got around to ring around the rosies, pockets full of posies time. And you sulked for days. Now, here, I watch you in the rearview, and if you notice that I am, you're purposefully ignoring me. I have to take a piss, I say, and she giggles. Fuck you, Catfish. Fuck you, because on this road you're traveling, is there hope for tomorrow? On this Glory Road you're traveling, to that land of perfect peace and endless fucking day, that's my twin sister you've got back there with you, my one and true and perfect love, and this train is bound for Glory, ain't nobody ride it, *Catfish*, but the righteous and the holy, and if this train don't turn around, well, I'm Alabama bound. You and me and she, only, we ain't going that far together. Here's why God and all his angels and the demons down under the sea made detours, *Catfish*. The headlights paint twin high-beam encouragement, luring me on down Appalachian Corridor X, and back there behind me you grumble something about how I'm never gonna find a place to piss here, not unless it's in the bushes. I'm about to cut the wheel again, because there's an unlit side road like the pitchy throat of evening wanting to swallow us whole, and right now, I'm all for that, but . . . Catfish, née Austin Girl, says that's enough, turn right around and get back on the goddamn highway. And whatever I'm supposed to say, however I'm about to tell her to go fuck herself, I don't. She's got a gun, you say. Jesus, Bobbie, she's got a gun, and you laugh a nervous, disbelieving laugh. You laugh a stunned laugh. She's got a goddamn gun. *What the fuck*, I whisper, and again she instructs me to retrace my steps back to 78. Her voice is cold now as the Arctic currents in my belly. I look in the rearview, and I can't *see* a gun. I want to believe this is some goddamn idiot prank you and she have cooked up, pulling the wool for whatever reason known only to thee. What do you want? I ask, and she says we'll get to that, in the sweet by and by, so don't I go fretting my precious little head over what she wants, okay? Sure, sure. And five minutes later we're back on the highway, and you're starting to sound less surprised, surprise turning to fear, because this is not how the game is played. This is *not* the story. We don't have shit, I tell her. We ain't got any money, and we don't have shit, so if you think—and she interrupts, Well, you got this car, don't you? And that's more than me, so how about you just shut up and drive, Little Bird. That's what she calls me, *Little Bird.* So, someone's rewriting the fairy tale all around us; I know that now, and I realize that's the ice in the middle of me. How many warnings did we fail to heed? The Santería semi, that one for sure, as good as any caution sign planted at the side of any path. Once upon a time, pay attention, you and you who have assumed that no one's out there hunting wolves, or that all the lost girls and boys and men and women on the bum are defenseless lambs to the slaughter. Wrong. Wrong. Wrong, and it's too late now. But I push those thoughts down, and I try to focus on nothing but your face in the mirror, even though the sight of you scares the hell out of me. It's been a long time since I've seen you like that, and I thought I never would again. You want the car? I ask Catfish. Is that it? Because if you want the car, fuck it, it's yours. Just let me pull the fuck over, and I'll hand you the goddamn keys. But no, she says. No, I think you should keep right on driving for a while. As for pulling over, I'll say when. I'll say when, on that you can be sure.

7.

Maybe, you say, it wouldn't be such a bad idea to go home now, and I nod, and I wipe the blood off your lips, the strawberry life leaking from you freely as ropy cheesecloth, muslin ectoplasm from the mouth, ears, nostrils of a 1912 spiritualist. I wipe it away, but I hold it, too, clasping it against the loss of you. So long as I can catch all the rain in my cupped hands, neither of us shall drown. You just watch me, okay? Keep your eyes on my eyes, and I'll pull you through. It looks a lot worse than it is, I lie. I know it hurts, but you'll be fine. All the blood makes it look terrible, I know, but you'll be fine. Don't you close your goddamn eyes. Oh, sister, don't you die. Don't speak. I cannot stand the rheumy sound of the blood in your throat, so please do not speak. But you say, *You can hear the bells, Bobbie, can't you? Fuck, but they are so red, and they are so loud, how could you not? Take me and cut me out in little stars...*

8.

So fast, my love, so swift and sure thy hands, and when Catfish leaned forward to press the muzzle of her 9mm to my head and tell me to shut up and drive, you drew your vorpel steel, and the razor folded open like a silver flower and snicker-snacked across coal-haired Haddie's throat. She opened up as if she'd come with a zipper. Later, we opened her wide and sunk her body in a marshy maze of swamp and creek beds and snapping-turtle weeds. Scum-green water, and her guts pulled out and replaced with stones. You wanted to know were there alligators this far north, handy-dandy helpful gator pals to make nothing more of her than alligator shit, and me, I said, hey this is goddamn Mississippi, there could be crocodiles and pythons for all I know. Afterwards, we bathed in the muddy slough, because cutting a bitch's throat is dirty goddamn business, and then we fucked in the high grass, then had to pluck off leeches from our legs and arms and that one ambitious pioneer clinging fiercely to your left nipple. *What about the car? The car's a bloody goddamn mess?* And yeah, I agreed, what about the car? We took what we needed from the Impala, loaded our scavenged belongings into a couple of backpacks, knapsacks, a pillowcase, and then we shifted the car into neutral and pushed it into those nameless waters at the end of a nameless dirt road, and we hiked back to 78. You did so love that car, our sixteenth birthday present, but it is what it is and can't be helped, and no way we could have washed away the indelible stain left behind by treacherous Catfish's undoing. That was the first and only time we ever killed in self defense, and it made you so angry, because her death, you said, spoiled the purity of the game. What have we got, Bobbie, except *that* purity? And now it's tainted, sullied by one silly little thief—or what the hell ever she might have been. We have us, I reply. We will always have us, so stop your worrying. My words were, at best, cold comfort, I could tell, and that hurt more than just a little bit, but I kept it to myself, the pain, the hollow in the pit of my soul that had not been there only the half second before you started in on purity and being soiled by the thwarted shenanigans of Catfish. Are you alright? you asked me, as we marched up the off-ramp. I smiled and shook my head. Really, I'm thinking, let's not have that shoe's on the other foot thing ever again, love. Let's see if we can be more careful about who we let in the car that we no longer have. There was a moon three nights past full, like a judgmental god's eye to watch us on our way. We didn't hitch. We just fucking walked until dawn, and then stole a new car from a driveway outside of Tremont. You pulled the tag and stuck on our old Nebraska plates, amongst that which we'd salvaged from the blooded Impala. The new ride, a swank fucking brand-new '96 Saturn the color of Granny Smith apples, it had all-electric windows, but a CD player when all we had was our box of tapes, so fuck that; we'd have to rely on the radio. We hooked onto WVUA 90.7 FM outta Tuscaloosa, and the DJ played Soundgarden and Beck and lulled us forward on the two-lane black-racer asphalt rails of that river, traveling dawnwise back to the earliest beginnings of the world, you said, watching the morning mist burning away, and you said, *When vegetation rioted on the earth, and the big trees were kings.* Read that somewhere? Yeah, you said, and shortly thereafter we took Exit 14, stopping just south of Hamilton, Alabama, because there was a Huddle House, and by then we were both starving all over again. There was also a Texaco station, and good thing, too, as the Saturn was sitting on empty, running on fumes. So, in the cramped white-tile fluorescent-drenched restroom, we washed off the swamp water we'd employed to wash away the dead girl's blood. I used wads of paper towels to clean your face as best I could, after the way the raw-boned waitress with her calla-lily tattoo stared at you. I thought there for a moment maybe it was gonna be her turn to pay the ferryman, but you let it slide. There's another woman's scabs crusted in your hair, stubborn clots, and the powdery soap from the powdery soap dispenser on the wall above the sink isn't helping all that much. I need a drink, you say. I need a drink like you would not believe. Yeah, fine, I replied, remembering the half-full, half-empty bottle of Jack in the pillowcase, so just let me get this spot here at your hairline. You go back to talking about the *river,* as if I understand—often I never truly understood you, and for that did I love thee even more. The road which is the river, the river which is the road, mortality, infinity, the grinding maw of history; *An empty stream, a great goddamn silence, an impenetrable forever forest. That's what I'm saying,* you said. *In my eyes, in disposed, in disgrace.* And I said it's gonna be a scorcher today, and at least the Saturn has AC, not like the late beloved lamented Impala, and you spit out what the fuck ever. I fill the tank, and I mention how it's a shame Ms. Austin Catfish didn't have a few dollars on her. We're damn near busted flat.

Yeah, well, we'll fix that soon, you say. We'll fix that soon enough, my sweet. You're sitting on the hood, examining the gun she'd have used to lay us low. Make sure the safety is on, I say. And what I think in the split second before the pistol shot is *Please be careful with that thing, the shit our luck's been,* but I didn't say it *aloud.* An unspoken thought, then bang. No. Then BANG. You look nothing in blue blazes but surprised. You turn your face towards me, and the 9mm slips from your fingers and clatters to the oil- and anti-freeze-soaked tarmac. I see the black girl behind the register looking our way, and Jesus motherfucking-fucking-fuck-fuck-fucking-motherfucker-oh fuck me this *cannot* be goddamn happening, no way can *this* be happening, not after everything we've done and been through and how there's so much left to do and how I love you so. Suddenly, the air is nothing if not gasoline and sunlight. I can hardly clear my head, and I'm waiting for certain spontaneous combustion and the grand *whump* when the tanks blow, and they'll see the mushroom cloud for miles and miles around. My head fills with fire that isn't even there, but, still, flashblind, I somehow wrestle you into the backseat. Your eyes are muddy with shock, muddy with perfect incredulity. I press your left hand against the wet hole in that soft spot below your sternum, and you gasp in pain and squeeze my wrist so hard it hurts. *No, okay, you gotta let go now, I gotta get us the fuck outta here before the cops show up. Let go, but keep pressure on it, right? But we have to get out of here now.* Because, I do not add, that gunshot was louder than thunder, that gunshot cleaved the morning apart like the wrath of Gog and Magog striding free across the Armageddon land, Ezekiel 38:2, or wild archangel voices and the trumpet of Thessalonians 4:16. There's a scattered handful of seconds, and then I'm back on the highway again, not thinking, just driving south and east. I try not to hear your moans, 'cause how's that gonna help either of us, but I do catch the words when you whisper, *Are you alright, Bobbie? You flew away like a little bird,* and isn't that what Catfish called me? *So how about you just shut up and drive, Little Bird.* And in my head I do see a looped serpent made of fire devouring its own tail, and I know we cheated fate only for a few hours, only to meet up with it again a little farther down the road. I just drive. I don't even think to switch on the AC or roll down the window or even notice how the car's becoming as good as a kiln on four wheels. I just fucking *drive.* And, like agate beads strung along a rosary, I recite the prayer given me at the End of Days, the end of one of us: Don't you fucking shut your eyes. Please, don't you shut your eyes, because you do not want to go there, and I do not want to be alone forever and forever without the half of me that's you. In my hands, the steering wheel is busy swallowing its own tail, devouring round and round, and we, you and I, are only passengers.

THE CULVERT

DALE BAILEY

My brother never had a grave. No funeral service. Not even a real obituary. Just a handful of articles I scissored from the front page of the city's newspaper when I was thirteen years old. I have them still. I can fan them out like a hand of poker, yellow as old ivory, fragile as pressed flowers: Local boy goes missing, Still no sign of missing child. Parents cleared in missing child case.

Soon after the authorities gave up on finding Danny, we moved to a town three hundred miles away. My father retired from a lucrative profession to take a job at a fencing company, wrestling coils of wire. I spent my adolescence there, friendless as a leper. So I learned the shape of loss, its scope and its dimensions.

Danny was exactly two minutes and thirty-two seconds older than I was. Even our mother could not tell us apart.

Grizzled men that smelled of cologne and cigarettes interviewed me in the days after Danny disappeared. Over ice cream. In the park. They seemed impossibly old to me, though I suppose they couldn't have been much older than I am now. As the years slip by, old age perpetually recedes before you. In our hearts we never change.

Sometimes I dream of the tunnels.

We lay each alike in our twin beds, watching the closet door, ajar like a fissure into the night, our hands crossed atop our chests like dead men, and drew in the same breath and blew it out into the blackness in accidental harmony and whispered to one another almost below the threshold of sound. Sometimes now I wonder if we really spoke at all, if we didn't have access to one another's thoughts themselves, if we didn't share the same geographies of boyish desire.

I've drifted from job to job all my life. I suppose it was inevitable that I'd drift back to the city sooner or later. But this barren apartment over an empty storefront doesn't feel like home.

Did you see your brother get into a stranger's car? they would ask. Did he have an accident? What happened, Douglas? How was it that I could not recall?

That was the worst thing of all, losing my best friend and my brother in a single blow.

I used to ride my bike to Deet's Grocery, on the corner of Main and Hickory, to exchange a handful of grubby coins for a hoard of green-apple Jolly Ranchers or Double-Bubble bubble gum, with the riddle inside the wrapper—but it wasn't the same without Danny. After that I'd hike up to the highway and stare at the cars zipping by, aching to be somewhere, anywhere, else.

We'd stolen flashlights from our father's toolbox. They felt heavy and reassuring in our hands.

Everything is dead here.

I remember the day we discovered the culvert. Icy rain needled our slickers. Mountains shouldered up around the highway, dun-hued mud squelched underfoot, dank trees turned their leaves to clouds the color of soured milk. Yellow headlights smeared the mist, the blur of cars rocketing past. The culvert beckoned like a dark eye, cloacal and alluring.

When we were seven years old, we stood naked in front of our bedroom mirror and gazed at the mystery of ourselves, twins twinned. I occasionally find myself before one of those three-paneled department-store mirrors and stare at myself replicated to infinity, wondering which, if any of them, is me.

We fascinated our classmates. Sometimes they ran cool fingers across our face.

Inside the culvert, a flood gushed around our feet, sweeping before it a wrack of clotted leaves and sticks. At the near end, rain hammered the culvert's concrete apron; at the far, an ashen circle of light disclosed an arm of deeply forested mountain. As our eyes adjusted to the silky darkness in between, a rift of more tenebrous gloom summoned itself into being: a cleft just wide enough to slide through sidewise. We felt its clammy breath upon our face. The dark seemed suddenly ominous and strange.

I haven't thought of them in years, those bikes. After Danny disappeared, his leaned untouched on its kickstand in the garage for months. Then we moved, and I never saw it again.

I remember the sky, a soulless arc bleached the color of bone by the heat.

In the glare of the flashlights, the culvert unveiled itself: moss grown and functional, without beauty. Half an inch of coffee-black water stood in its leaf-choked channel, emitting a rich, peaty stench. Shadows fled before us like flights of bats. Traffic thundered overhead. The dread of underground places, the burden of the planet bearing down upon us.

That was the summer of our thirteenth birthday.

The cleft was choking, claustrophobic. Four or five feet of sliding sideways, sucking in your belly, your head wrenched to one side. It narrowed until we thought we could neither pass nor return. Panicked, we strained forward. Abruptly, the walls fell back. Darkness cradled and embraced us.

My parents fell silent in the months after Danny disappeared. I think his loss broke something inside them. They had a way of looking past me, like they were looking for the part of me that wasn't there.

The sweep of our flashlight beams revealed a perfectly arched atrium a dozen feet in circumference. A dry, level floor. Twin archways that opened into intersecting corridors. We shone our flashlight into each of them. Black and unrelenting, they gave nothing to the light.

I've been divorced three times.

I remember my father's work-thickened knuckles, nicked and scarred with the dozens of tiny wounds inflicted by coils of wire.

We chose the left-hand way.

The tunnel spiraled deep into the earth. Cold pimpled our skin and frosted our breath. The air smelled of stone and time. Our sneakers scuffed the floor, unleashing choruses of whispers. The gravity of the tunnels drew us inexorably downward. The enchantment of the secret and the subterranean.

Deet's Grocery is gone. There is little commerce here anymore, just blocks of abandoned storefronts, windows soaped over, sun-faded For Lease signs taped up outside. Traffic swishes by in the mountains above the valley. Few cars renounce the highway to descend into these empty streets. I will leave this city soon. There is nothing for me here.

Still the passage spiraled down, deeper, deeper, until at last, impossibly, it deposited us through the neighboring tunnel into the arched atrium where we had begun.

We celebrated our thirteenth birthday at a restaurant that catered to children. I can't remember how many of our schoolmates attended, but I still recall the red bunting our parents draped around the room where dinner was to be served. A clown ushered us screaming into a towering maze of plastic ducts where we chased one another breathless. Afterward, our father distributed tokens for skee-ball and video games. We measured our winnings in tongues of extruded tickets, and traded them for plastic trinkets at a counter manned by bored teenagers. We ate two slices of pizza at dinner and shared a single chocolate-glazed cake with thirteen candles. We blew them out together, as though we had not lived twenty-six full years between us.

We chose the right-hand path. It spiraled ever upward. Surely it must soon pass beyond the asphalt surface of the highway into the daylit world beyond. Yet it did not. It spilled us into the atrium instead. This time we emerged from the left-hand tunnel. We turned back to follow it a hundred yards or so, and found that it descended as far as we could see.

Like all children, we had our secret lives. We orbited a star of our own, as isolate and self-sufficient. Secrets were our watchword, lies our sigil of conspiracy.

We rarely spoke of the tunnels. But at night in our dark bedroom, with the closet door ajar like a portal into a labyrinth, we shared the same uneasy dreams.

The tunnels were utterly silent.

At the party, my mother knelt to hug me. Tears glinted in her eyes. When she drew me close to whisper in my ear, her voice broke. It's so hard to see you grow up, Danny, she said. Her embrace was suffocating.

Time did not pass there. No matter how long we spent exploring the maze of corridors, when we emerged once again from that fissure in the concrete, the world was unchanged. The sun shot its rays at the same angle into the culvert's mouth. Stepping out into the air, we saw the same clouds hanging unmoved in the same blue and depthless sky.

We used to test our mother. I'm Danny, I would say, and Danny would respond, No, I'm Danny, you're Doug, and you're Danny and I'm Doug, and so on, until finally we could not be certain even ourselves which of us was who.

One morning we squeezed through the cleft to discover an even dozen archways radiating from the atrium. By then we'd procured supplies for exploring the corridors: sweatshirts against the cold, knapsacks to carry spare batteries, a snack, a thermos of our mother's tea. And though we'd grown confident that all paths circled back to the atrium by some mechanism we could not understand, we did not that day care to venture the dark.

After that, we used red spray paint to blaze the walls with arrows, like Hansel and Gretel scattering breadcrumbs to mark their way.

I parked in the gravel turnout where Danny and I had once stashed our bikes and climbed toward the highway. I heard it before I saw it: the rumble of behemoth trucks downshifting on the long grade out of the mountains, the tire-hiss of cars darting among them, nimble as pilot fish. I scrambled up the final slope, digging for purchase, and stood at the guardrail, watching the traffic slip eternally past.

Our mother insisted that we dress identically. Even afterward, she shopped in duplicates.

We were too old for that kind of party.

I had trouble finding the culvert. I had to work my way through dense brush before I stumbled upon the drainage ditch that paralleled the highway. I walked alongside it for fifteen minutes, studying the embankment. Even then I almost missed it. A thicket of weeds and junk trees had sprung up in the stony breakwater below its concrete apron, obscuring the culvert's black and abiding eye.

The last time we pushed through the crevice, there was but a single archway in the atrium. The tunnel beyond was broader than any we'd yet taken. As we walked it broadened still, so that we could no longer touch the walls with our outstretched hands. After a long time, it steered us into an immense square. An elaborate fountain—angels with trumpets, long dry—stood in the center, Italianate buildings and arcades to either side. Winding streets branched off here and there, lined with vacant shops. If there was a ceiling, our flashlight beams could not reach it.

That was the day after our thirteenth birthday.

We crossed the square and took a narrow street. At each intersection we marked our way. Meandering alleys delivered us into lavish piazzas, endless colonnades, stately domes and galleries: the city of our dreams.

I stood at the mouth of the culvert, knuckles nicked and scarred from the climb. Ducking my head, I stepped inside. Nothing had changed. The same half-inch of stagnant water, the ruin of rotting leaves.

Danny! I called. Danny! The culvert shouted back at me in diminishing echo, until it no longer sounded like a name at all.

We walked the cobbled streets and after a time they became the same streets, crowded and narrow, with the same turnings of the way and the same buildings leaning over them and the same fathomless sky between. Time and again we found ourselves in the same square with the same ornate fountain at the center. No matter how many forking paths we took away from that place, they always led us back.

When I took my first college girlfriend home to meet my parents, she studied the photos of my brother and me that my mother had propped in their dozens around the house. I didn't know you had a brother, she said. I didn't know you were a twin. We broke up six months later.

How long we wandered that labyrinthine city, I cannot say. We ate the last of our snacks on a balcony overlooking that central plaza, we drank the last of our tea. Exhaustion took us. We slept curled together in the anteroom of an opulent palace, and woke unrested, to terror and despair.

I remember a time my father took my mother in his arms. I want to know what happened to him, she wept.

I must have slipped ahead of Danny—a few steps, half a dozen yards or so, no more, that is all I can know or surmise. But when I turned to find him, a maze of branching streets intersected where before there had been but a single way. My brother was gone. The red arrows had evaporated. Jackdaws had eaten our crumbs.

I have studied the blueprints for the city's drainage system. The highway sweeps out of the mountains far above. There are no tunnels there.

They are there. They are.

No photos of me without Danny adorn my parents' house.

How long I sought my brother among those shifting streets, I do not know. I called for him until I grew hoarse. But the city's acoustics betrayed me:

my voice boomed back at me down empty avenues and across abandoned courtyards. His name sounded like any other name.

Sometimes I think of all the things Danny never got to do.

She was a pretty girl, lithe and blond. I can't remember her name.

The way narrowed, the city fell behind me. I descended a cramped defile, the arched ceiling close above me. It wound finally back to the atrium. Twin tunnels converged there. The fissure cleaved the stone on the other side. Danny! I called. Danny! The corridors threw my voice back at me, the name indistinct; it could have been any name. It could have been mine.

Perhaps he was waiting for me on the other side, I recall thinking as I squeezed through the crevice, but he was not there. When I turned to look behind me, the fissure was gone.

Three times I walked the culvert end to end. Two dozen times I have walked it since. The walls are smooth and uninterrupted. If there is a crevice in its concrete length, I cannot find or see it.

I will never leave this city.

I wish I'd never had a brother. Sometimes I think I never did.

Two of us went in. Only one of us came out. And dear God, I don't know if it was me.

PAST RENO

BRIAN EVENSON

I.

Bernt began to suspect the trip would turn strange when, on the outskirts of Reno, he entered a convenience store that had one of its six aisles completely dedicated to jerky. At the top were smoked meat products he recognized, name brands he'd seen commercials for. In the middle was stuff that seemed local, with single-color printing, but still vacuum packed and carefully labeled. Along the bottom row, though, were chunks of dried and smoked meat in dirty plastic bags, held shut with twist ties, no labels on them at all. He wasn't even certain what kind of meat they contained. He prodded one of the bags with the toe of his sneaker and then stared at it for a while. When he realized that the clerk was staring at him, he shook his head and went out.

I should have known then, he thought hours later. At that point he should have turned around and driven the half-mile back into Reno and gone no further. But, he told himself, it was just one convenience store. And it wasn't, he tried to convince himself, really even that strange. It just meant people in Reno liked jerky. So, instead, he shook his head and kept driving.

It was the first time he'd left California in a decade. His father had died and he'd been informed of it too late to attend the funeral, but he was driving to Utah anyway, planning to be there for the settling of the estate, whatever was left of it. He was on his own. His girlfriend had intended to come along and then, at the last moment, had come down sick. What it was neither of them were quite sure, but she couldn't stand without getting dizzy. To get to the bathroom to vomit she had to crawl. The illness had lasted three or four hours and then, just as suddenly as it had come, it was gone. But she had refused to get in the car after that. What if it came back? If it had been bad while she was motionless, she reasoned, how much worse could it be if she was driving? He had to admit she had a point.

"Do you even need to be there?" she had asked him. "Won't they send you your share wherever you are?"

Technically, yes, that was true, but he didn't trust his extended family. If he didn't go, they'd find a way to keep him from what he deserved.

She shook her head tiredly. "And what exactly do you deserve?" she asked. Which was, he had to admit, a good question. "And didn't your father tell you never to come back?"

He nodded. His father had. "But he doesn't have any say," he said. "He's dead now."

But in any case she had not come with him. And maybe, he thought now as he drove, his girlfriend's illness—miles before Reno—was the first indication the trip would turn strange. But how could he have known? And now, well past Reno, already having gone so far, how could he bring himself to turn around?

⟜

Back at the beginning, just past Reno, he drove, watching Highway 80 flirt with the Truckee River, draw close to it and then pull away again. Then he hit the scattering of houses called Fernley and the river vanished too. For miles there was almost nothing there, just a ranch or two and bare dry ground. He watched a sagging barbed-wire fence skitter along the roadside, then, when that was gone, counted time by watching the metal markers that popped up every tenth of a mile. After a while those disappeared, too, leaving only the faded green mile markers, numbers etched in white on them. He watched them come, his mind drifting in between them, and watched them go.

He thought of his father as he had been when he was young, a man who wouldn't leave the house without ironing a crease in his jeans. His boots he made certain were brought to a high polish before he left, even if he was just going to the back acres, even if he knew they'd be dirty or dusty the moment he stepped off the porch. That was how he was. Bernt hated it. Hated him.

He remembered his father lashing a pig's hind legs together and running the rope over the pulley wheel screwed under the hayloft floor and winding the rope onto the handcrank. His father had made him take the crank and said, "You pull the bastard up and hold it and don't pay no mind to how it struggles. I'll get the throat slit and then that'll be the worst of it done. Your job's nothing. You just keep hold to it until the fucker bleeds out." Bernt had just nodded. His father said pull and he had started cranking. There went the pig up, squealing and spinning and flailing. His father stood there beside it, motionless, knife out with his thumb just edged over the guard and touching the side of the blade, just waiting. And then, with one quick flick of his arm, he opened its throat from ear to ear. The pig still struggled, the blood gouting from the wound and thickening the dust. Bernt couldn't understand how his father didn't get blood on his boots or his pants, but he just didn't.

It was always that way, every time he killed something. Never a drop of blood on him. Uncanny almost, it seemed to Bernt, and he had spent more than one sleepless night as a teenager wondering how that could be, why blood would shy from his father. The only possibilities he could come up with seemed so outlandish that he preferred to believe it was just luck.

That was the kind of man his father had been. Now, dead, what was he?

⟜

He shuddered. He watched the mile markers again—or tried to, but they simply weren't there any more. For a moment he thought he might have left the highway somehow, by accident. But no, he couldn't see how he could have, and whatever road he was on had every appearance of a highway. Then he flicked past a sheared off metal stub on the roadside and wondered if that wasn't what had once been a marker, if someone had been systematically cutting them down. Bored kids, probably, with nothing to do.

He gauged the sun in the sky. It seemed just as high as it had been an hour before, not yet starting its descent. He checked the gas gauge: between half and a quarter tank. He kept driving, wondering if he had enough gas to get to the next station. Sure he did. How far could it possibly be?

He opened the glovebox to take out the map and have a look, but the map wasn't there. Maybe he had had it out and it had slipped under the seat, but if it had it was deep enough under that he couldn't find it, at least not while driving. No, he told himself, there would be a gas station soon. There had to be. He couldn't be that far off of Elko. It was less than three hundred miles from Reno to Elko and he'd filled up in Reno. And Winnemucca was somewhere in between the two. Had he passed that already without realizing it?

He had enough gas, he knew he had enough. He shouldn't let his mind play tricks on him.

His father had told him that if he was going to leave he should never come back.

Fine, Bernt had said. *Wasn't planning to come back anyway.*

And then he had left.

Or wait, not that exactly. It had been so many years ago now that it was casicr to think that that was how it had ended, but it hadn't been quite so simple. He hadn't said, *Fine*. He hadn't said, *Wasn't planning to come back anyway.* What he had said, "Why the hell would I want to come back?"

His father had smiled. "Thought you'd never ask," he said. "Come along," he said, and made for the door, waving to Bernt to follow him.

Perhaps an hour later—maybe more, maybe less, it was hard for him to judge time driving alone—he called his girlfriend to tell her that she had been right, that he shouldn't have come after all. He was hoping that maybe she would talk him into turning around, inheritance be damned.

But she didn't answer. Or no, not that exactly: the call didn't go through. It seemed like it was going through—he dialed the number, he heard it ring a few times and then the call disconnected. His phone had no reception.

Well, what's strange about that? a part of him wondered. He was out in the middle of nowhere: of course service was bound to be bad. He'd have to wait until he was near a town and then he'd try her again.

All that sounded right, rational, correct. And yet another part of him couldn't help but worry that something was wrong.

⟜

The radio, too, faded in and out, the same station one moment seeming quite strong and the next little more than static, and then quite strong again. *Not strange*, a part of him again insisted. Must be the mountains, he told himself, the signal bouncing around in them. He told himself this even though it seemed to happen just as regularly when he was in open country as when he was skirting a mountain or when one had just hove into view.

There were moments, too, when there was nothing but static. When he turned the knob slowly but found nothing. When he could press the search button and his tuner would go through the whole band from beginning to end without finding anything to settle on, and would start over again, and then again, and again, and again. It might go on for five minutes or even ten, and then suddenly it would stop on a frequency which, to him, still seemed to be nothing but static, but it stayed there. After a while he became convinced that there must be something beneath the static, a strange whispering, that surely would slowly resolve itself into voices. Though it never did, only stayed static.

⟜

He checked his gas gauge. It read between a quarter and a half a tank. Hadn't it read that before? He tapped on it with his finger, softly at first and then harder and harder, but the reading didn't change.

When he came to Winnemucca, he would stop for gas, just in case the gauge was broken. He probably didn't need gas to make it to Elko, but he would stop anyway. He tapped the gauge again. Had he already passed Winnemucca? He felt like he should have, but surely he would have noticed?

⟜

He watched his father check the crease of his trouser leg. He watched him stop on the porch and raise first one boot and then the other to the rail, quickly buffing them with the yellow-orange cloth draped there, and then he stepped off and went down the path leading out to the road.

Bernt followed.

"This here is all mine," his father was saying, gesturing around him. "This, all of this, belongs to me."

But of course Bernt knew this. His father had been saying things like this ever since Bernt was a child. It was not news to him. When his father turned to see how Bernt was taking it and saw his son's face, his lips curled into a sneer.

"What in hell do you know about it?" he asked Bernt.

"What?" asked Bernt, surprised. "I know you own the land. I already knew that."

"Land," said his father, and spat. "Shit, that's the least of it," he said. "I own anything that comes here, plant or animal or man, including you. If you leave, it's because I let you. And if I let you, you sure as shit ain't coming back unless I say."

Almost before Bernt knew it, his father's hand flashed out and took his wrist in a tight, crushing grip. Bernt tried to pull away but his father was all sinew. He nodded once, his mouth a straight inexpressive line, and then he cut off the path, toward the storm cellar, dragging Bernt along with him.

⊸

No, he should have reached a town by now. Something was wrong. The sun was still high. It shouldn't still have been high. It didn't make sense. The gas gauge was either broken or for some reason he wasn't running out of gas. He tried again to call his girlfriend and this time, even though his phone didn't have any bars, the call went through. He heard it ring twice and then she picked up and she said *Hello*, her voice oddly low and almost unrecognizable—probably because she was sick, he told himself later. He said, "Darling, it's me," and then the call disconnected. He couldn't get it to reconnect when he called again.

⊸

His father took Bernt across the yard, pulling hard enough on his arm that it was difficult for Bernt to keep his balance. Once he stumbled and nearly fell and his father just kept pulling him forward and he had to struggle to stay upright. He got the impression from his father that it didn't matter to him if Bernt stayed upright or not.

They went past the barn and around to the back of it, to where the storm cellar was, a single wooden door set flat into the ground and kept closed with a padlock. Bernt had always known it was there, but he had never been inside. His father let go of his arm and thrust a key out at him. "Go on," he said to Bernt. "Go and look."

II.

Just when he started to panic, he came to a town. He didn't catch the town's name: perhaps the sign for it had been vandalized, like the mile markers. He came over a rise and around a bend and suddenly saw the exit sign and the scattering of buildings below, windows shimmering in the sun. He had to brake and slide over a lane quickly, and even then he hit the rattle strip and came just shy of striking the warning cones before the concrete divider. But then he was on the ramp and going down, under the bridge and into town.

He drove in to the first gas station he saw. He stopped at the pumps and turned off the car and clambered out, only then realizing that the shop was abandoned and empty, the pumps covered with grime, the rubber hoses old and cracked. He got back into the car and turned it on again, then drove through the streets of the town looking for another station. But there didn't seem to be one.

⊸○⊷

What had he seen in the storm cellar? He still wasn't quite sure. He unlocked it and went down, his father standing with his arms crossed up top. It smelled of dust inside, and of something else—something that made him taste metal in his mouth when he breathed the air. It made his throat hurt.

He went down the rickety wooden steps until he came to a packed earth floor. There was just enough room to stand upright. Even with the door open, it took a while for his eyes to adjust, and once they had adjusted, he didn't see much. The floor was stained in places, darker in some places than others—unless that was some natural property of the earth itself. He didn't think it was. There was, in the back, deeper in the hole, a series of racks and there was something hanging on them. He hesitated and from up above heard his father say, "Go on," his voice cold and hard. He groped his way forward, but because of the way his own body blocked the light it wasn't until he was a foot or two away that he realized that what he was seeing were strips of drying meat. Hundreds of them, sliced thin and sometimes twisted up on themselves, and with nothing really to tell him what sort of animal they had come from. Though it was a large animal, he was sure of that.

His mouth grew dry and he found himself staring, his eyes flicking from one strip to the next and back again. He almost called out to his father to ask him where the dried meat had come from, but something stopped him. In his head, he imagined his father answering the question by simply reaching down and swinging the door shut and leaving him in darkness. The feeling was so palpable that for a moment he wondered if he wasn't in darkness after all, if he wasn't simply imagining what he thought he was seeing.

He forced himself to turn around very slowly, as if nothing was wrong, and climb up the stairs. His father watched him come, but made no move to reach out and help him as he scrambled out of the shelter.

"You seen it?" asked his father.

He hesitated a moment, wondering what exactly his father had meant for him to see—whether it was the strips of meat or perhaps something else, something behind the racks, even deeper in. But almost immediately decided that it was safer to simply agree.

"I saw it," he said.

His father nodded. "Good," he said. "Then you understand why you have to stay."

Bernt made a non-committal gesture that his father took as a yes. His father clapped him on the shoulder and then began walking.

Why his father felt he understood, what his father thought he'd seen, what he'd thought the storm cellar had done to him, Bernt couldn't exactly say. Indeed, he would never be sure, and ultimately felt it might be better not to know. He went after his father back to the house and retreated to his room. From there, it was a simple matter to wait until dark and then pack a few things, climb out the window, and leave for good. He had never been back.

⟜

After a while he gave up looking: the gas gauge read between a quarter and a half full still; probably he had enough to make it into Elko.

He parked in front of a diner on Main Street and went in. It was crowded inside, all tables full. He sat at the counter. Even then, it took a while for the waitress to get around to him. When she finally did, he asked her about a gas station, felt it was par for the trip when she told him there wasn't one.

Used to be one, she said, *but gas here cost too much. Nobody used it, not with Elko nearby.* No, the nearest one was up the road at Elko.

"How far away is that?" he asked.

The question seemed to puzzle her somehow. "Not far," she said.

He asked what she suggested and she recommended the soup of the day, which he ordered without thinking to ask what it was exactly. When it came it was surprisingly good, a rich, orange broth scented with saffron and with strings of meat spread all through it. Pork, probably. It made his mouth water to eat it. It seemed a sign to him that his trip was finally becoming less strange, or at least strange in a way that was good rather than bad. When he finished he used the edge of his thumb to scour the sides of the bowl clean.

He sat there, far from eager to get back on the road. The waitress brought him a cup of coffee with cream at the end without his asking for it, and before he could tell her he didn't drink coffee she was gone again, off to another customer. He let it sit there for a while and then, for lack of anything better to do, took a sip. It was rich and mellow, different from coffee as he remembered it, and before he knew it he had finished the whole cup.

It's okay, he told himself, and found he more or less believed it. *The strange part of the trip is over. Everything will be all right from here on out.*

⟜

He had written twice to his father from California. The first time was maybe a year after he'd arrived. He'd wanted for his father to know that he was all right, that he'd landed on his feet. He'd also wanted to gloat a little. Perhaps, too, he had still been curious. *What exactly was it that you thought showing me the storm cellar would do? What was it in there that you thought would keep me?*

For a month, maybe two, he had waited for a reply. But his father had never answered the letter. The only way he knew for certain his father had received it was because when his father died his aunt had written to let him know, saying that they'd finally gotten his address off a letter he'd written his father.

The second letter, years later, had been more measured, calmer. It was, as much as he could bring it to be, an attempt at reconciliation. It had come back to him unopened, *Return to Sender* written across it in his father's careful block writing.

⟜

Everything will be all right, he was still telling himself when he got up from the stool and made his way to the bathroom. He peed and flushed, then stretched. While he was washing his hands, he noticed the mirror.

Or *mirrors*, rather. There were two of them, one suspended over the other, a larger one with a small one screwed in over it so that the larger one looked almost like a frame around it.

He looked at himself in it, his haggard face, but his eyes kept slipping to where one mirror ended and the other began. Was it meant to be that way? Some sort of design scheme? Was the center of the larger mirror cracked or foxed and the small mirror had been hung to cover that? Was there some kind of hole that the second mirror was hiding?

He reached out and grabbed the edges of the top mirror. It was affixed in each of its four corners by a screw that went through the corner of the mirror and then through a thin block of wood and then through the mirror behind it. He could just get the tips of his finger in the space left between the mirrors. He tugged, but it was bolted firmly in place.

When he let go, the tips of his fingers were black with dust. He washed his hands again, more slowly this time. His face, when he looked up this time, looked just as haggard. He turned off the taps, dried his hands, and left the bathroom.

⟜

A moment later he was back in. He had the penlight on his keychain out and was shining it at the gap between the top mirror and the bottom one. He pressed his eye close, but no matter where he looked, no matter where he shone the light, the mirror behind it looked whole and complete.

III.

At first, he lied to his girlfriend, claiming he had gone to Utah and to his father's ranch for the reading of the will, but had received nothing. But then, when the box came, he finally came clean. It was an old box, starting to collapse, and smelled dank. It was very heavy. The words "Bernt's Pittance" were written on the side of it in his father's careful hand.

He left the box sitting on the table for a day and a half. The evening of the second day, they were both sitting in bed, both reading, when she asked him when he was going to open it. He had put the book down on his chest and had begun to talk. She had let him, had interrupted only once, and when he was done she had curled up beside him one hand touching his shoulder softly, and said nothing. That had surprised him—he thought she might be angry that he had lied to her. But if she was angry, she kept it to herself.

Of course, he told her, *nothing was really going on, it was just my imagination. It was just an ordinary trip. I was just noticing the things that under normal circumstances I wouldn't notice.* But as he told the story, moved bit by bit across the landscape between Reno and the small town whose name he had never quite figured out, it was all he could do not to panic again. He didn't believe it was a normal trip. He believed it was anything but. And he believed that, somehow, his father was to blame.

The hardest part was explaining why seeing that, seeing the one mirror placed atop the other mirror, had been the thing that had turned him around and made him drive back to Reno, made him stop and rent a hotel room and drink himself nearly blind until he ran out of liquor and sobered up enough to realize enough time had elapsed to give his girlfriend the impression that he had gone to Utah. There hadn't, he had to admit, been anything really wrong with the mirrors—but that, somehow, had been *exactly* what was wrong with them.

That had been the one time she had interrupted him. "Was it like what you saw in the storm cellar?" she asked.

But what had he seen in the storm cellar? He still didn't know, and never would. Was that like the mirrors? No, that had been a hole in the ground containing curing strips of dried meat. How could twinned mirrors be like a hole in the ground and strips of meat? No, the only thing they had in common was that he felt like he couldn't quite understand what either one was telling him. That he felt he was missing something.

He left the café, climbed into the car and drove. His intention at first, despite the way he was feeling, was to keep driving, to continue on to Utah, to see the trip through. But as he took a left out of the parking lot and headed down Main Street, he felt like he was being stretched between the mirror and wherever he was going now. That a part of him was caught in the mirror and the link between that and the rest of him was growing thinner and thinner.

⤙⊙⤚

And so instead of getting back on the highway, he circled back to the café. He took the tire iron out of the kit nestled beside the spare tire and walked into the café and straight into the bathroom. He gave the top mirror a few careful taps with the tire iron and broke out each of the four corners, and then lifted it down and set it flat on the floor. The mirror beneath was complete and whole. This mirror he simply broke to bits, just to make sure there wasn't something behind it. There wasn't. Only blank wall. So he broke the first mirror as well. And then he left just as quickly as he had come, the waitress staring at him open mouthed and the burly cook hustling out of the building and after him, cursing, just as he turned the key to his car and drove away.

Even then, he might have kept going, might have kept on to Utah, he told his girlfriend. But the trip—all of it, not just that last moment of finding himself doing something he'd never thought he'd do—seemed to him a warning. It was a mistake, he felt, to go on. So, he turned around.

And indeed, almost before he knew it, he was back in Reno, the car all but out of gas. He found a gas station, then found a hotel and settled down for a few drunken days to wait. Both because he was ashamed that he hadn't gone all the way to Utah and because, to be frank, now that he was back in a place that seemed fully real to him, he was afraid to get in the car again.

⤙⊙⤚

But then at last, head aching from a hangover, he had climbed into the car and drove. A moment later he had crossed over the state line. He wound up into the mountains, went past Truckee, skirting Donner Lake, through Emigrant Gap and then slowly down out of the mountains and into more and more populated areas, ever closer and closer to home. By the time he had pulled into their driveway, it almost seemed like he had made too much of it, that he just wanted an excuse not to go to Utah after all.

The more he talked, the more he tried both to explain to his girlfriend how he felt and to dismiss it, to relegate it to the past, the more another part of him felt the event gather and harden in his mind, like a bolus or a tumor, both part of him and separate from him at once. He did not know if speaking made it better or made it worse.

⤚o⤙

When he was done, he lay there silent. His girlfriend was beside him, and soon her breathing had changed, and he could tell she was asleep. He was, more or less, alone.

There was the box still to deal with, he knew. He knew, too, that he would not open it. He did not want whatever was inside it. In his head he planned how to get rid of it. Just throwing it away did not seem like enough.

Careful not to wake her, he got up. He slipped into his jeans and found his car keys. He put on his socks and a shirt, and at the door he slipped on his shoes.

No, he needed to get it as far from him as he could. He would take it back to Utah, back to where it came from.

⤚o⤙

Or maybe not, he thought a few hours later, well into the drive and recognizing nothing as familiar, completely unsure where he was. Maybe not as far as Utah, but certainly somewhere past Reno. That would have to be far enough.

THE COAT OFF HIS BACK

KERIS MCDONALD

"Hello, Geoff," said Dr. Archwin, and he watched the skin around her eyes wrinkle into lines of sympathy. "How are you?"

"I'm fine." Geoff Leighton had to say that. It was the correct social formula. He noted that she was still waiting with that warm concerned look, so after an awkward beat he added, "Thank you for asking, Joyce."

"Well, it's good to see you back."

"There's been a rush job on, has there?" That was a little in-joke, and he saw her relax a touch. Working here, deadlines were not something to worry about. Funding and manpower, yes—but not time. They were standing in the main materials conservation lab of the York Castle Museum and were surrounded by labelled boxes, all filled with artefacts and items of antique clothing scheduled for immediate inspection and possible remedial action. Behind this room was a humidity-controlled storage facility which Dr. Archwin tended to refer to as The Backlog; it was full, always—so much so that parts of the collection had to be kept in warehouses out on the Clifton Moor industrial estate. And down the corridor from where they stood now was the public area where the actual displays began; glass cases full of gowns and breeches and shoes, masks and purses, combs and jewellery and hats—all dimly spot-lit in rooms sealed away from the natural light that would rot fabric and fade colour. The items that the Great Unwashed got to see counted for a tiny percentage of those within the museum collection.

"We've actually had a new donation in," Dr Archwin said. "It's over by your desk. I thought you'd find it interesting."

"What about that WRAF uniform I was working on?" Leighton asked as he followed her across the room. He could see that the white expanse of his desk had been cleared and it made him feel faintly anxious, as if his services had been dispensed with.

"I had Louise finish it off for you. Nice fresh start."

Leighton blinked. *It's not like I've been ill. It was compassionate leave, that's all.* "Thank you," he said again, without conviction. Then; "Is this the bequest?"

"This" was a chest about a metre long. One glance told him that it was a mass-produced object of little value to a museum: early Victorian, brass corners, with cheap leather cladding over the panels that was now torn and curling up. And he thought he could detect a musty smell.

Dr. Archwin looked pleased. "It came out of a sealed attic in Heworth, when the owners had the roof re-tiled. They didn't even *know* they had an attic until then, apparently. But it's the contents we're interested in, not the box."

"I'm glad to hear that."

"Probably eighteenth century, most of them. Someone was a collector."

"*Probably?*" It wasn't like Dr. Archwin to be vague on dating. If she'd accepted the bequest for the collection, it was because it was of historical value. As Textiles Curator, she was forever fending off worthless old clothes that the public tried to donate, telling them regretfully that their gifts were "not within the scope of our collections policy."

"You'll see. Not exactly fashion pieces."

Leighton was intrigued, despite himself. He put his case carefully on the desk, and leaned with palms flat down either side.

"You'll find the accessioning information all up on file. The items are in surprisingly good condition," Dr. Archwin added cheerfully, "despite the old-lady-smell."

He thought of the hospice room with its pastel colours; his mother's hands, grey already, peeking over the edge of the duvet like trapdoor spiders waiting to pounce. And the smell of age, and disinfectant, and adult nappies.

"Oh—" said Dr. Archwin. "I'm so sorry, Geoff! That was..."

"That's okay." His voice was calm and emotionless. He was pleased with himself for that.

"I'm an idiot."

"Honestly, it's not a problem. We were never close. And she went peacefully in the end."

"If you need anything . . . " Dr. Archwin was older than him, but like most English people of her class had no idea how to deal with bereavement. She put her hand awkwardly on the back of his and gave it a squeeze. It was the first time in eight years they'd ever touched.

He snatched that hand away as if her nervous warmth burnt him. Offence flared in her eyes.

"I'm sorry," he stuttered, half-aware that he was cradling his hand to his chest protectively. "I . . . I just don't like being touched suddenly."

"Of course." She was, he saw, as flushed and dismayed as he was, but for her the clash was tainted with guilt and now the admixture was curdling to pity. "Geoff, whatever you . . . Just take the time you need. And let us know if there's anything we can do . . . "

"Thanks."

"I lost my own father, to cancer. I know how hard it is."

This was excruciating. Couldn't she just leave him alone? He shook his head, forcing a smile. "Like I said, we weren't close."

Dr. Archwin's eyebrows rose slightly. She probably wasn't even aware of her expression of disapproval. "She was your mother," she said gently.

Just go away. "I'm fine. I'll get to work."

"Okay."

"Okay."

"Keep me up to date with the new acquisition," she said as she walked off.

⤙⊙⤚

Leighton slipped on clean cotton gloves after opening the chest. That was one of the things he really liked about this job: the need for care and cleanliness. In this lab, dirt was the enemy. A rust-stain, a grease-spot, the subtle acid etch of a fingerprint—any contamination could cause inexorable damage to delicate historical fabrics. Dirt abrades. It attracts moisture, and provides a base for fungus to grow on. Silk and cotton threads do not last forever, but neither does bone nor iron. Everything in nature decays. Everything is transmuted, molecule by molecule, in the slow-burning alchemical crucible of time.

The chest opened easily, releasing a wave of the musty scent he'd already noticed.

Not an old-lady-smell, he said to himself sourly. *More like... Something agricultural. Earthy.* That wasn't a good sign; he braced himself for maggot-frass and mould.

But the layer revealed in the open box wasn't dirty sheepskin or anything similar. It was a dark blue brocade, hand-embroidered with symbols of some sort. And on top was a small piece of paper upon which was written, in elegant Victorian copperplate:

From the house of Dr. Marmaduke Palmes,
surgeon of the City of York
I will have none of it
Lev 13:52

Leighton took careful photos before touching anything. He opened the accessions file on his computer and added the page for conservation notes, prepped a new box and layers of acid-free tissue paper, and only then gently drew the garment out for inspection.

It was a robe with an open front: made from thin woollen cloth with an irregular weft that argued it had been hand-loomed. The base weave was rather fine. He was almost sure that it was a traditional Bedouin *bisht*—he'd have to look that up on their photographic database—but it had been customised with what looked like Hebrew letters on top, executed in much coarser style and thread by someone, he suspected, unused to wielding a needle. The garment was noticeably heavy, and when he laid it out for inspection Leighton realised that small lumpy objects of some kind had been sewn into the broad lower hem.

What they were would have to await further inspection.

In the meantime, what he needed to do was appraise the piece and remove surface dust. Using a small hand-held vacuum-cleaner with fine muslin stretched across the nozzle to catch loose objects such as beads, he hoovered the garment inside and out. Not much dirt came off, and there was little discolouration about the neckline where one might expect it. He suspected the robe was not often worn. He laid it within its new box and padded it with scrunched-up acid-free tissue to round out the arms and skirt; the ideal was to have no folds and no creases left in during storage.

Beneath the robe was a large square silk cloth that had started out black, he suspected, but was faded now to a mottled purple, the colour of old bruises. It was stitched with a red wool circle, more quasi-Hebrew letters, and some symbols that he tentatively identified as a chalice, a knife, a heart, and an eye from which lines of light or possibly flame were streaming.

He took pictures and measurements of everything.

Beneath the altar-cloth, if that was what it was, was a pair of beaded man's slippers—definitely eighteenth century in style—a skullcap embroidered with more amateurish Hebrew, a shallow silver-edged bowl of yellow ivory, a dagger without a sheath, a plain wooden stick as long as Leighton's forearm with a leather grip at one end, and a lead cross scratched with sigils that he didn't recognise at all.

His area of conservation expertise was clothing, so he boxed up the hard artefacts and set them aside for Louise. Ritual kit for a magician, was his disdainfully amused surmise. He looked through the accession numbers on file, but only the date, donor, and the barest of descriptions had been logged so far. Perhaps Dr. Archwin found it faintly risible too, or wanted to avoid sensationalist statements. In every century magic lingered on as a kind of minority interest, sometimes vigorously condemned by the establishment and sometimes treated as a peculiar hobby for the not-quite-respectable. The eighteenth century was, after all, the era of the Hellfire Club. And the materials here—an imported Oriental robe, silk and ivory and gilding—suggested a well-to-do amateur. Perhaps even the Dr. Palmes fingered by the Victorian collector.

Leighton was a conservator, not a curator. Only the structural integrity of the items mattered to him, not their purpose or history. Dr. Archwin had been right about the state of preservation: aside from some fading, which was to be expected from natural dyes, the fabric looked to be in good condition. He taped a clean layer of acid-free paper over his desktop before starting on the final garment. Cleanliness was king in this place.

The very bottom layer of the chest's contents proved to be the source of the smell. It was a riding coat, and as soon as he unfolded it upon his desk Leighton made an educated guess at the first decades of the 1700s, just from the style of the cut—those deep cuffs, that collarless neck, the ranks of buttonholes, the broad skirts. He was, however, a little nonplussed by the material. He'd expect to see a gentleman's coat made up in good cloth, not large patchwork pieces of leather.

Too thin to be a cavalry coat, he thought: *that's not armour.* Perhaps it was intended to afford some protection from rainfall or wind, but it had no lining or padding of any kind, nor any sign that any such had once been attached.

It didn't seem to fit with the rest of the box's contents at all. Instead of the near-fetishistic ornamentation of the ritual clothes, this was unadorned. It smelled strongly, but then a lot of leather did. Leighton wrinkled his nose. He was doubly glad for his gloves by now. Not just because they protected the coat from him, but because they kept his hands from unwanted contact with *it*.

He wasn't fond of leather, as a material. Too damp and it got clammy and unpleasantly soft; too dry and it went grotesquely crispy; exposure to the sulphur dioxide of gas-lighting could disintegrate it to powder. Leighton never wore leather gloves in his private life, and his winter coat was a heavy tweed.

But he was almost pleased to spot a faint white bloom on the beige panels of the coat-skirts. Fungal infestation would account for the musty smell, and that he could deal with. He got to work cleaning with dilute acetone on a cotton bud, rolling the wet head over an unobtrusive patch below a fold. The leather had a rich sheen once the matt layer of mould was removed.

That'll do nicely, he thought.

It was only when he happened to slip a hand into the square coat pocket that he found a second, smaller piece of paper. Unfolding it revealed another handwritten message:

John Palmer: his Innocent Coat

An innocent coat? Leighton wondered. *What's that then?* Then he noticed the coincidence in names, Palmes and Palmer, and wondered if he'd misread one or the other. A re-check did not clear up the question. The two notes did not look to be in the same hand, and neither thin, browning script was entirely clear. It was possible that they were meant to be the same name, but perhaps not.

"It's one thirty. Don't forget to have lunch," said Louise, passing behind him. Leighton glanced up, noticing for the first time the faint gnawing in his guts. It was so easy to forget to eat, he'd found over the last week. So easy to just get lost among his own thoughts. In that hospice room, time had seemed irrelevant. The murmur of distant voices, the faint rise and fall of the coverlet, the regular hiss of the plug-in air-freshener—those things were constant, all day and night.

He'd thought she'd never die.

It's not good for you, though. Going without food. He knew he'd lost weight, because he'd had to shave again for the first time this morning and he'd noticed the hollows of his own cheeks. And baggy, tired eyes, too.

He went out for a sandwich, walking past Clifford's Tower into the centre of town and casting a glance over the first yellow daffodil heads that were starting to dot the steep banks of the motte. Another spring on its way, he told himself. The daffodil display was always a pleasure.

When he returned twenty minutes later, he received an unpleasant shock. For just a moment, as he walked into the bright colourless space of the lab, he thought that someone was sitting at his desk, shoulders hunched and head down. Then he realised that it was the tan leather coat. It was supposed to be lying out on his work-desk, but someone had hung it over the back of his chair. Its broad skirts trailed on the linoleum.

Alarm washed through his veins. Fragile clothing could be damaged by hanging. Besides which, he'd left the coat spread out flat and no one should have altered that.

"Louise!" he snapped. "Did you move this?"

"Move what?" she asked, not looking up. She was bent over her own desk, painstakingly stitching a disintegrating Edwardian wedding dress to a net backing that would keep its shape.

"This coat!" Leighton couldn't help but find her irritating to look at. Why was it that she insisted on wearing a T-shirt to work instead of a proper long-sleeved blouse? Did she really have to have so much flesh on display? Her upper arms were plump and shapeless, and the sight of her flabby mole-speckled skin was not enticing.

"Nope," she said, through a mouthful of pins. "Not me."

"Well, did anyone else come in here?"

"Uh-uh."

Leighton narrowed his eyes. Interfering with a colleague's ongoing work was very bad form—and Louise was only a junior conservator. Clearly, allowing her to tackle that WRAF uniform last week had given her ideas above her station. He should really complain to Dr. Archwin.

But he wasn't the sort of man who kicked up a fuss. He didn't like to complain.

Bottling up his irritation, he lifted the nasty antique coat very carefully from the padded back of the swivel-chair, laid it back on the worktop, vacuumed out the inside once again to remove foreign lint, and then got on with cleaning off the mouldy patches.

⊸

By the time five o'clock rolled around, the musty fungus smell had almost cleared under the sharp tang of the acetone and Leighton was pleased with his progress. He laid the coat out in a new box, to be finished off in the morning. Then he joined his colleagues for the farewell presentation to Yvonne from Accounts, who was going off on maternity leave—a bit of a pity he hadn't missed that while away himself, he couldn't help thinking, but there was no helping it—and slipped out forty minutes later, while most people were still chatting, to catch his bus home.

The rush-hour traffic was as bad as ever. Perhaps he should walk home now that the nights were getting lighter, he pondered; it could hardly take longer to cross the city on foot than to creep by bus round the outside of the medieval walls and then out along Bootham and Burton Stone Lane. The Council should do *something* about the traffic, for goodness sake. And why were the lights so slow to change each time?

As he descended from the bus he heard someone call out behind him.

"Scuse me, mate, is this your—?"

The door wheezed shut. Leighton turned and looked up to see a man half-standing from the seat that must have been just behind his own, holding up a beige mac. They stared at each other through the window as the bus lurched away from the kerb. Leighton shook his head and lifted a hand to mime *Thanks, no, that's not mine.*

It was good to know that some people were still polite, he told himself as he walked home.

His house was a tiny end-terrace, two-up and two-down. The front room was full of the boxes he'd brought back from the hospice. Leighton looked at them coldly, and went through to the kitchen to make his tea, which consisted of a chicken fillet, peas from the freezer, and boiled potatoes. While he was paring the potatoes the peeler caught the tip of his left index finger and took a sliver of skin clean off. Leighton cursed and plunged the wound into cold water, watching the blood furl out like a tiny swatch of silk. He wadded a tea-towel around his fist and left it to staunch itself as he wandered back into the living room.

The silly accident had put him in a dark mood. The cardboard boxes full of junk—old-woman clothes, old-woman ornaments, yellowed paperbacks that no charity shop would want—seemed to stare at him in baleful reproach. He could imagine that his mother's smell still clung to them, that it was seeping into his home even now.

He remembered the day she'd turned up on his doorstep, asking to be let in, begging for the chance to talk. How he'd slammed the door in her face. The sense of relief then, as if he'd finally done something positive.

He remembered much further back; the way she used to gather him into her lap as a child when he was angry, when he was making too much noise, whenever they had a falling-out. Sometimes for no reason at all. The heaviness of her arm around his shoulders. The warm soft press of her palm against his face. The way she rested her cheek against the top of his head.

Rage burned in his guts—good, clean rage like the day he'd slammed the door—and he began to carry the boxes out the front, to the grey wheelie bin in the tiny front yard. There were too many to fit so he shook the contents out into the bin instead: underwear and cardigans and toiletries and shoes and photograph albums and over-the-counter medicines and all the tatty crap of a tatty crap life. He pressed it down and leaned in, creating layer after compacted layer of detritus. He was sweating by the time he smashed the last cardboard box flat with his tea-towelled fist and forced the bin lid down on top of it.

I will have none of it, he said to himself, triumphantly quoting the note in Dr. Palmes's box.

The phrase had a rather satisfying ring to it. His finger stung, but he didn't care. He looked around as he turned back toward his front door, defying any of his neighbours to be watching, but nothing stirred in the dusk-stained street except for a half-glimpsed gingery flick of a cat disappearing over a wall.

Leighton took his dinner to his computer desk that night. Cradling his hurt fist in his lap and clicking to Google, he typed in *Marmaduke Palmes*

York awkwardly with one finger of the other hand, his fork dancing over the keys.

It was an easy search; everything was on the first page. 'Palmes' turned out to be a very old Yorkshire name indeed, brought over from Normandy in William the Conqueror's retinue. The family had lived for centuries in Naburn Hall, just outside York. And a Marmaduke Palmes of the eighteenth century—Leighton rather doubted there could be many men with a name like that—showed up in the first volume of John Burke's 1834 tome, *A Genealogical and Heraldic History of the Commoners of Great Britain and Ireland enjoying territorial possessions or high official rank, but uninvested with heritable honours*—which was probably a thrilling best-seller in its day—wherein he and several siblings living in Naburn were listed tersely as having "died unmarried."

A gentleman surgeon of the city, confirmed bachelor, indulging in a little magical tinkering on the side. That didn't seem implausible.

Chewing a mouthful of chicken, Leighton reflected that historical research was ridiculously easy nowadays. He would have looked up the Biblical allusion, assuming that *Lev* stood for *Leviticus*, but he couldn't recall the relevant chapter and verse numbers.

⟜

That night Leighton slept badly. His cut finger had stopped bleeding, but it throbbed hotly with just enough insistence to keep him in the shallower waters of sleep. Which meant that he dreamed all night; exhausting, dreary dreams that made no sense and gave no satisfaction. The only one that he could really remember when he woke the next morning wasn't even a whole dream, just a scene. Two men were meeting in the dark corner of a pub. One of them was youngish and broad-set and looked like he really needed a shave and a bath. Under the stubble and the dirt his face was heavily pockmarked. The other was older, with smooth cheeks and grey hair and the air of someone who wanted to be elsewhere. This second man placed upon the wooden table a buff-coloured bundle, but kept his hands pressed down upon it.

"Is that it?" asked the first.

"Indeed it is," the old one told him.

"And will it do the trick?"

"I swear it will. You shall go blameless, though your sins be scarlet. Neither will any harm come to your life."

"You swear all this on my mother's name?"

The older man pursed his lips. "She would turn in her grave if she knew you had come to this."

With a grunt, the younger man reached inside his coat and pulled out a small leather pouch. "I think you would have occasioned her the greater shame, Uncle," he muttered, passing it over.

The recipient weighed the purse in his hand, but negligently as if the whole thing was too distasteful to care about, then pushed the folded bundle across the table top. "Be sure to wear it against your own skin," he answered. "Do not take it off."

"I am surprised that you do not wear one yourself," said the swarthy man.

"They are not so easily come by. Besides, there is a price to pay. There is always a price for such things, beyond the trouble that you have already put me to."

That was all the dream. It left a sour taste in Leighton's mouth and an itch in his brain, so that he couldn't help thinking about it as he showered in the morning. But that was all of it he could recall.

No, there was one other dream, he realized—though it hadn't seemed to be connected to the first. It had kept looping 'round, like a clip from the worst home video in the world. He'd dreamed over and over that he got up out of his bed and went to the top of the stairs, waiting for someone who was ascending from below. Moonlight lay on the half-landing, and he'd stood and watched that square of carpet with a feeling of great discomfort, knowing that at any moment someone was going to climb into view. And then, yes—there they were; lying flat on the stairs and crawling up, hand over hand over hand.

He never saw their face. The dream looped back and started again before that became clear. He wasn't even sure there was a face to see.

That recollection made him feel clammy despite the cascade of hot water.

When Leighton got to work, the Innocent Coat was missing.

⊸

At first he couldn't think where he'd left the coat. Its storage box lay open, ready to receive the padded garment, but the box contained only a few flat sheets of tissue paper. Had he replaced it in the surgeon's chest the night before—and if so, why?

Then he brought back to mind the events of the day, and he knew he'd definitely not shoved the garment away. He'd put it in its box there, just so. He knew he had. Someone else must have removed it.

Leighton ground his teeth and started a methodical search—not because he thought the coat would turn up in the wrong place, but because he had to be able to say, "Yes, I checked there." He found the Oriental robe and the altar cloth in their proper boxes, labelled up correctly. He found the magician's implements boxed on Louise's *pending* shelf where he'd left it; she looked up at him curiously as he glared at the contents, but went back to her wedding beads.

"You okay?"

"Fine." Beneath a flesh-coloured plaster, the cut on his finger burned.

He checked back in the bequest trunk. The slippers were still in there, along with the two pieces of paper and the hat. All was as it should be, except for the Innocent Coat. There wasn't even the lingering aroma of the old leather.

Slowly, Leighton sat down at his desk. For a moment he covered his face with his hands, but that unthinking action made him shudder and he sat up straighter. His stomach cramped, and he recalled dimly that he'd eaten no breakfast.

He had to tell Dr. Archwin. He didn't want to—she would be furious, quite rightly, and the thought of incurring her blame made him feel physically sick. But he had to. Once formally accessioned, an object belonged to the museum in perpetuity, like it or not. They had no legal right to sell it, to throw it out or to give it away, even if it was deemed a waste of space and resources. It could not just *disappear.*

He had to flag up the loss.

Could someone have stolen it, he wondered? Louise was the only one with obvious access, but he had no reason whatsoever to suspect her. Or anyone else for that matter, he had to admit. By historical costume standards it had been a noisome, unattractive object. He'd disliked it, he had to admit, from the moment he'd lifted it out and laid it like a corpse upon his desk.

Did it have some hidden value he knew nothing about?

He logged onto the Web and did a search for *Innocent Coat.*

Nothing. He forced a deep breath, though his chest felt constricted.

"Louise... Do you know what an Innocent Coat is?"

She stood upright, stretching her back. "What context?"

"Seventeen-hundreds."

She scrunched her face up in a doubtful grimace and started to shake her head.

Reluctantly, he added, "Possibly something to do with ritual magic or folklore."

"Oh—you've got something magicky, have you?" She brightened. "Let's have a look."

Well, that was the problem, wasn't it? He didn't have the coat to show her. He bent into the chest to retrieve the smaller slip of paper, simply to save face.

"If it is occultish, you probably want to e-mail the witchcraft museum at Boscastle," Louise said as she ambled over. "I can't remember the guy's name, but it'll be on file. He helped us out with that dead cat in the farmhouse wall at Pocklington, remember?"

The mummified cat had made the local papers, he recalled. He watched Louise take the piece of paper, and wished her fingers weren't so disgustingly plump.

She blinked, and then her eyebrows rose. "Dunno about the coat, but I know a John Palmer."

It was Leighton's turn to be surprised.

"Seventeen-thirties, say? That's Dick Turpin."

"I'm *sorry*?"

"The highwayman?"

"Yes—I know who Turpin is." Actually, Leighton's associations with that name were a lot of vague "stand and deliver" jokes. And hadn't there been some rubbishy TV series back in the seventies, all cheap sets and bad romance?

"Well, he fled to York when he was wanted for double murder in Essex. Lived in the East Riding for over a year under a false name—John Palmer—then got himself hanged on the Knavesmire for horse-stealing. And he's buried about two hundred yards that-a-way." She pointed toward the inner ring-road and looked pleased with herself. "I did a module on Turpin for my degree."

Leighton just frowned.

"Oh come on, Geoff—you must have seen his condemned cell in the museum?"

"Uh, yes. I suppose." The Castle Museum sprawled across several buildings including the old city prison, but he hadn't walked around it in years.

"The bloke was a total thug really; nothing like the legend. No Black Bess, no overnight ride from London, no chivalry. House-breaking and torture and sheep-rustling, more like. But he's a big name." Her eyes widened. "If we've turned up his coat that's *fantastic* publicity."

"We haven't got his coat," Leighton said grimly. "We might have had it yesterday. But it's gone missing."

"Oh . . . arse," said Louise. Then; "You need to tell Joyce."

⤙

The confrontation with Dr. Archwin was horrible. Leighton could feel his shirt clinging to him in sweaty patches by the time he walked away, and the first thing he did was go to the gents and dry-heave into the sink.

It wasn't what she'd said. It was the way she'd looked at him.

The same way his mother had looked at him when she was angry, all those years ago. That cold disappointment that presaged colder punishment.

Leighton caught a glimpse of himself in the bathroom mirror as he splashed cold water across his face. His skin was pasty-white. He thought of his mother's grey face against the hospice pillows, and the tears crusting in the corners of her eyes.

You were always a horrible boy, but we've got to forgive and forget after all these years, she'd whispered. *Come here, Geoffrey. Give me a kiss.*

He remembered the papery feeling of her cheek against his fingers. Her skin already drying out to fine leather.

He washed his hands again, scrubbing with soap.

When he went back to the lab Louise looked up from her copy of the *Museums Journal.* "You all right?"

He nodded, though the movement brought back his nausea. "She says she's treating it as an internal matter at the moment. We have to double-check this whole place."

Dr. Archwin had said—*Are you absolutely sure you never took it out of the lab, Geoff? At any point?* And she'd looked at him with narrowed eyes nested in lines of doubt. He could feel his throat closing up, just at the memory.

Louise gave him a cautious smile that looked sympathetic but meant nothing.

So they searched the lab for a misplaced coat, in every drawer and corner and box, all in vain. Then they went back to their respective desks. Leighton supposed he was meant to carry on working on the contents of the Palmes box, and he managed that for a time. But the coat was preying on his mind. He made a phone-call to an answer-machine in Boscastle, and in a fit of frustration went back online.

It was all there: the history of Dick Turpin. The trial proceedings had been taken down at the time and published in pamphlet form, along with a contemporary account of his final days and death on the gallows. To Leighton's mind *The Trial of the Notorious Highwayman, Richard Turpin, at York Assizes, on the 22nd Day of March, 1739* was full of peculiarities. Turpin had taken the name Palmer when he fled north because he claimed it was his mother's maiden name. He'd lived in the manner of a gentleman, yet without visible income, for a year and more, and somehow that didn't rouse suspicion until he lost his temper one day, shot his landlord's cockerel in the street and then threatened to shoot the man who protested. At that point he could have walked away scot-free, yet he refused to be bound over to keep the peace. Only when in York prison did his true notorious identity come out by sheer fluke—someone recognised his handwriting—and even then he failed to make any serious attempt at defending himself. He didn't even take the opportunity to call on witnesses, which the judge himself found bizarre:

Prisoner: Several Persons who came to see me, assured me, that I should be removed to Essex, *for which reason I thought it needless to prepare Witnesses for my Defence.*

Court: Whoever told you so were highly to blame; and as our Country have found you guilty of a Crime worthy of Death, it is my Office to pronounce Sentence against you.

It was, Leighton thought, as if Turpin assumed he could get away with anything. As if he were immune to condemnation—to the point of recklessness—until it all went terribly wrong.

Even when he ascended the scaffold, Turpin had seemed to be possessed by what was described as an "amazing Assurance" and "undaunted Courage" that the situation hardly merited. He bantered insouciantly for half an hour with the hangman—*Half an hour?* Leighton thought. *What were they all waiting for?*—and only went to his fate when he jumped off under his own volition to die "in about five Minutes."

How long would *about five minutes* feel to a man strangling on a short noose? Leighton thought sickly. He felt worse when his eye fell on the name *Palmes*.

A few days after death, Turpin's body had been robbed out of its grave. Not an uncommon occurrence in those days when bodies for medical dissection were hard to come by; the city mob soon tracked it to the house of a local surgeon, Dr. Marmaduke Palmes, where the corpse was discovered in a garden shed and carried back "almost naked, being only laid on a Board, cover'd with some Straw" and buried again, this time in slaked lime.

Despite the near-riot provoked by his theft, Dr. Palmes seemed to have got away with his misdemeanour. Reading all this, Leighton felt clammy, as if something damp were pressed up against him.

He tried to bury the thought, but another search turned up a quote from a report in *The Gentleman's Magazine* of June 1737 that made things worse. In it a reward of £200 was offered for the discovery of Richard Turpin, murderer-at-large, who was described as "broad about the Shoulders," and "very much mark'd with the Small Pox." The coincidence with his dream made Leighton's throat feel as if his ribcage was heaving to draw in air.

"You all right?" Louise asked. "You look awful."

"Just a touch of asthma," he whispered.

"Go home if you're feeling sick. We weren't expecting you back this week anyway."

He went home early, as suggested, walking instead of taking the bus. But he made a detour first of all, to the tiny graveyard of St. George, to see Turpin's plot. The stone was large and clearly marked:

John Palmer otherwise
RICHARD TURPIN
The notorious highwayman and horse stealer

Why had Palmes stolen the body? For illicit anatomical study, as everyone assumed? Or did family loyalty extend even to illegitimate and disgraced relatives? Why had Turpin been sent back for reburial naked, when it was recorded that he had specifically sent for a coat for his hanging?

The thin grass and grey stones offered no answers and the blustery spring wind seemed to cut right through his clothes to claw at his skin. Leighton couldn't bear to stand there long, so he headed back across the city. His route took him up High Petergate, and as he passed the small shops and pubs of that medieval street, the sign of the *Three-Legged Mare* caught his eye. The "horse" in question was the tripod shape of the Tyburn-style gallows that had stood on the Knavesmire, and the painted sign depicted the crowd staring at the condemned men about to be hanged.

Pulling his coat tighter about him, Leighton passed under the thick walls of Bootham Bar and waited at the road crossing with the other pedestrians. Fatigue made him close his eyes momentarily.

"Why did you not wear it always, as I instructed you!" a man's voice hissed behind him. "See what a pass it has brought you to!"

"Stop your mouth, Uncle." The second man's voice was a good deal rougher, almost a bark. "The thing gave me evil dreams and I wanted respite. My head was a-pounding with their damnable voices. You never warned me of that!"

Leighton froze, shoulders hunched.

"I told you there would be a price, did I not? But you assured me you were man enough to pay it without fear. Now it all comes crashing down upon your head, braggart. You have no coat to keep off the winds of ill-fortune, only a hempen scarf that is prepared for you in the morning. Tell me where you have left it."

Leighton cracked an eye open cautiously, but the traffic surged on before him and the voices went on behind.

"Why should I tell you?"

"Do you think that I made the thing, only to leave it hanging behind a door for any villain to pick up?"

"Any villain, Uncle? Do not concern yourself: I know where it is."

"Then tell me! It will do you no good now."

"Ah, that is where we disagree. Did you not tell me that the coat will save me from condemnation?"

"It is too late for that!"

"Is it? I think the Innocent Coat will save my neck, even at the last drop. They have told me so."

"Who has?"

"The ones who come and lie beside me at night, and whisper into my dreams. They promise me freedom. They tell me they need a strong fellow like me to wear the coat and walk them abroad. They tell me to trust them."

"Richard—*tell me where the coat is*."

"I have sent for it. You might see it on the morrow, if you care to watch."

A foul smell of badly-tanned leather rolled over Leighton and he couldn't help it: he jerked around to face the men who had been conversing behind him, and nearly stepped backwards into the road in doing so.

There was no one there, of course. Only a young mother with a pushchair, looking at him gyrating on the pavement as if he were some kind of nutcase.

It's stress, he thought, with a sickly apologetic smile. *I should never have gone back to work this week.*

⤚

When he opened his front door, his first thought was that there was a body lying on the stairs just inside; stretched out flat, one arm crooked above its shoulders as if it had fallen face down while descending.

Then he realised it was worse than a body. It was the Innocent Coat.

In a moment he was inside, slamming the door and switching on the light. He didn't want the world to see that Dr. Archwin had been right after all—that he had taken the coat home yesterday, just as she'd suspected. Well, he must have. Who could argue? He must have taken it home *without realising it*—because there it was. He had *stolen* it.

What was he supposed to do now?

What was wrong with him?

The unfairness of the situation made his heart hammer and his eyes blur over. He couldn't possibly take it back now that he'd declared it missing—"Here we are, sorry about that, it turns out I'd gone off with it after all, no hard feelings, eh?" Could he smuggle it back into the lab and hide it in some dark forsaken corner where it could be found later?

That was hardly better. She'd still know he was to blame.

Wheezing a little, Leighton bent over the treads to pluck up the fallen coat. For a moment his tear-blurred eyes made the leather seem to quiver. Then it was in his hands, heavier than he remembered and a little clammy. The smell was faint but distinctive, and turned his stomach.

He carried the vile garment at arm's length, to keep it away from his body. Averting his twisted-up face, he stalked through into the living room, wondering how he was going to get rid of it—because he surely didn't want it in the house.

I will have none of it. The phrase sparked in his memory. Three strides took him to the desk where his laptop waited. *Leviticus 13:52*—he could remember the verse numbers now, since a second glance earlier today. Laying the coat across the top of his seat, he typed in the reference and picked an online version of the King James Bible.

The words were stark:

> *He shall therefore burn that garment, whether warp or woof, in woollen or in linen or any thing of skin wherein the plague is, for it is a fretting leprosy; it shall be burnt in the fire.*

A bitter laugh tore itself from Leighton's throat, leaving the flesh raw. Even the Web concurred with his desire to get rid of the thing! Burning it sounded like a great idea. Quickly he bundled the coat into a wodge that he stuffed into the open grate of his fireplace. He would need matches from the kitchen and logs from the lean-to out the back. He would burn the horrible object to ash, and Dr. Archwin would never know of his guilt.

He was out of the room for perhaps three minutes. When he got back, the Innocent Coat was no longer there. Faint ash-marks on the hearth suggested that it had been dragged out onto the rug.

Leighton stood in the centre of the room and turned slowly on his heel, mouth agape. Where could it have gone? Had he suffered another blackout and stashed it somewhere? The shadows behind the furniture looked full of uncertainty, as if things were moving within them, and the hair crept on the back of his neck. He could not thrust away the uncanny mental image of the coat sliding flat behind the big bookcase, or creeping under the old-fashioned sofa. He found he didn't want to kneel down and check beneath. In fact he didn't want to breathe out, in case the sound masked the furtive approach of soft leather from behind or above.

A fretting leprosy, he thought.

When his cell phone rang he nearly jumped out of his skin. He did go as far as dropping all the logs on the carpet. "What?" he demanded as he retreated towards the kitchen where the light was so much better. "What is it?"

It was the man from the witchcraft museum, returning his call and wondering what he wanted to know about Innocent Coats.

"What are they?" Leighton asked, slamming the kitchen door and backing up towards the sink. "What do they do?"

"Um . . . they're like . . . have you heard of the Hand of Glory?"

Leighton scrunched up his eyes, trying to think straight. "That's some sort of candle made out of hand, or something?"

"It was a candle of human fat gripped in the severed hand of an executed criminal. A form of thieves' magic. It was supposed, when lit, to make the inhabitants of the house unable to wake or move, so that housebreakers could carry out their raid without raising an alarm. Well, an Innocent Coat was a similar idea—but rarer, and more potent. Anyone who wore one was supposedly immune to suspicion or the attention of the law. He could literally get away with murder, and no one would blame him."

Leighton tried to swallow. "What would it look like?"

"I've never seen one. If they ever did exist, I don't think there are any left—certainly not in museums, though maybe in a private collection somewhere. But I assume it would look like a leather coat. It had to be made from the skins of hanged men, you see. And they had to be murderers."

John Palmer: his Innocent Coat.

Leighton ended the call without another word. Then he simply stood, and stared at the kitchen door. The clock ticked. Behind him, the light faded out of the afternoon.

That coat was out there, somewhere in the house. On top of a wardrobe, perhaps, or behind a chest of drawers, or under the bed. Somewhere, waiting. He knew that now. It had waited decades in that sealed attic, and now it could afford to be patient, he supposed. It would wait for him to fall asleep, or to shrug the whole affair off and convince himself that nothing had really happened. Then it would make its move.

He wondered briefly what it would look like. Would it slide, like a snake? No . . . he rather thought it would crawl arm over arm, like in his dream; that thin cold leather malignantly inexorable.

He could escape now, out the back. Escape to . . . he could not think where. But he suspected it would just keep following. It wanted him. When he was off-guard, then it would appear. Its soft sleeves would brush over him, groping for his face . . . just like his mother used to. She'd gather him into her lap when he was small, and press her hand over his mouth and under his nose, cutting off all air. He'd squirm and struggle as his lungs started to ache, but she was so much stronger than him, then. Fear would become panic, discomfort would become agony. He'd even try to bite, but it never worked. Darkness would flood in around the corners of his vision as consciousness faded, and his stillborn shrieks were muffled in her implacable palm.

That memory was enough to send sweat running down his back and thighs.

It was years before he was big enough to resist her choking embrace. Years before he stood up to her. Even now, the recollection of her face in the hospice bed made him shake. Her gummy saliva had smeared the flat of his palm as she'd tried in vain to fight him off, spasming weakly. Her eyes had opened wide and bloodshot and she'd pissed herself under the duvet.

His regret that day was that he hadn't had the foresight to bring gloves. The texture of her skin had very nearly been enough to make the task impossible. Skin against skin—just unbearable. And it had taken *so long*.

Why had she taken so long to die?

The Innocent Coat would be the same, he knew. That thin leather would feel like his mother's crêpey hide as it piled onto his face and throat. As it slithered its sleeves over his arms, and spread its skirts over his legs, and clung to him like a second skin.

He couldn't stand that: the feeling of skin against skin. The soft and intimate smothering. The *touch*. That thought was simply . . . unbearable.

So he would not bear it.

Shaking, Leighton took the potato peeler out of the kitchen drawer, and began the long hard task of stripping himself of the terrible stuff.

the worms crawl in

LAIRD BARRON

The worms crawl out. The worms play Pinochle on your snout.

We chanted that at mock funerals when I was a kid. Shoot your sister playing cowboys and Indians and she fell dead, that's your dirge. The playground bully challenges you to a duel after class, that's the ditty your friends hummed as the hour of doom approached.

Hadn't heard the worm song since I was twelve, but it's coming back into style, thanks to my wrath. I've been done a great wrong, you see. Done a great injustice by a man named Monroe. However, I've come to think of him as Fortunato. It makes me smile to do so.

He "tricks" me into going on the hiking trip. I've always had a hate-hate relationship with the great outdoors. Bad enough I'm stuck working nine to five in the weather; camping is a deal breaker. My feelings don't matter. He's as slick as a magician or a shrink: talks about one thing, shows you one thing, but there's always something up his sleeve. He knows his con, short or long. Can't dazzle 'em with brilliance, baffle 'em with bullshit, is his motto. Much as the hand is quicker than the eye, Monroe's bullshit usually defies my perception of it until after the fact when it's time to cry.

Phase one of the scam, he invites Ferris and me over to the house for a barbeque. Optimistically, I assume that's merely a cover to regale us with his latest sexual exploits, and yep, Monroe does chortle over a couple of girlfriends he has squirming on the hook, each completely ignorant of the other. But it turns out that this gloating is actually a pretext to maneuver me into a conversation about Moosehead Park and its fabulous game trails.

So, Elmer, you hunt, right? You lived in the woods when you were a kid. The only way he could know that, since I've never mentioned it, is from Ferris. And of course, I correct him. My dad had been the big white hunter in the family; the rest of us were simply dragged along for the ride. Nonetheless, Monroe believes in education via osmosis. It isn't hunting that intrigues him. He is far too much of a wilting flower to lay hands on a rifle, much less put a bullet into the brainpan of some hapless animal. He needs street cred, as it were, wants to butch up his resume with the ladies, and a brief foray into the swamps of south central Alaska is just the ticket. First rule of disappearing into the wilderness is, always bring a buddy.

We chew some ribs, toss back a few brews, and thus plied with meat and drink I agree to tag along this very next Saturday for an overnight campout. It has to be me. Not a chance any of his colleagues will blow a perfectly good weekend with the shifty motherfucker. Plenty of them will gather for a free feed and trade shop gossip, but that is the extent of it. Dude probably thinks he's really clever, manipulating his lummox of a pal, albeit pal might be too strong a word.

Joke's on him. I'm not as dim as I pretend. The trip is exactly what I want. It's my big chance to settle the score.

Ferris doesn't say anything. She *looks* plenty worried. I pretend not to notice. Can't have her suspecting that I suspect she suspects I *know* there is something going on between her and Monroe. In that unguarded moment, her expression says she thinks her boyfriend is out of his gourd, putting himself at the mercy of a paranoid husband who can load a six-hundred-pound engine block barehanded. Alas, Monroe's downfall is his unremitting narcissism. He doesn't want to get away with snaking my wife, he wants to rub my nose in it.

If Ferris were to get a whiff of my true mood she'd forbid Monroe's excursion under no uncertain terms and spoil everything. Although, even in her most febrile visions, it's doubtful she could imagine I plan to off him in some devious manner and drop the body into a deep, dark pit. One of my flaws is jealousy. Not the biggest of them, either, not that she has the first inkling.

We've been together since our late twenties. Going on fifteen years, and parts of me remain Terra Incognita to my lovely wife.

See, there are some things you should know about me, things I should get out in the open. I won't, though. Not until later.

⊸⊙⊷

Ferris worked as an administrative assistant at the high school where Monroe taught English. Fancied himself a poet, did our man Monroe. A skinny, weepy fella who preened as if his scraggly beard made him kin to Redford's liver-eating-Johnson and that his sonnets were worthy of Neruda.

Yeah, sonnets.

Ferris started bringing the shit home in a special folder, wanted my "professional" opinion. I'm no expert, I drill wells for a living. But yeah, I published a few pieces in lit journals over the years, had one chapbook about blood and vengeance picked up by Pudding House when I was younger and angrier. I read Monroe's poems, told her what I thought of them, which wasn't much. Classic poseur artiste. The kind of asshole who upon learning he can't strum a guitar to any effect minors in poetry or fiction to impress the doe-eyed girls who hang around coffee houses and the bored ones at faculty parties. One of those, *I'm writing a book*, shitheads who isn't really doing any such thing.

Yeah, everybody hates those guys.

Guys who kiss married women on the mouth aren't too popular either. Even though I was likely the last to know, I'd finally gotten wise at Monroe's Fourth of July house party. A fateful glimpse of him and Ferris in a window reflection was a splash of cold water for sure. Shielded by an open refrigerator door, both of them leaning in for a beer, and by god, Monroe laid it on her. The door swung closed and they acted casual. Cheeks a bit rosier, laughter a notch too sharp, and that was all. I played the oblivious fool. Wasn't tough; waves of numbness filled me, that big old local anesthetic of the gods. It was as if the enemy had dropped depth charges. Those bombs sink real deep before detonating. First time I'd ever thought of Ferris as an enemy.

I didn't fly into a rage or fall into despair. Nah, my reaction was to get chummy with Monroe. I fucked my wife more often and a lot more vigorously than was my habit. Also, I took some dough from a rainy day account and paid a private eye to tail those lovebirds for two weeks. The results were inconclusive. No motel rendezvous, no illicit humping in their cars, but they did frequently meet for drinks at the tavern on 89 when she told me she was shopping for office supplies or groceries. Practically mugging each other in the photos. The detective offered me a cut-rate package to tap their phones and intercept email communications. I declined, paid him, and sent him on his way. He'd shown me enough. My imagination would do the rest.

Then I took that thumb drive of photos and locked myself in a room and brooded. As my dad would've said, I went into the garden and ate worms.

Moose have learned to steer wide of Moosehead Park. Hunters and redneck locals blast the poor critters the second one pokes its muzzle out of the woodwork. The park isn't all that park-like; really just an expanse of marsh and spruce copses in the shadow of the Chugach Mountains that got designated public use. Basically, the feds looked around for the armpit of the great outdoors and said, Fine, peasants. Enjoy! Thanks a lot, Jimmy Carter.

The government hacked a path through it, east to west. Take a step left or right and you're ass deep in devil's club or bog water. You would not believe the mosquitoes that rise in black and humming clouds. Spray on the chemicals, layer your clothes, throw netting over that and spray it too for good measure, and you're still fucked. Those tiny stabbing bastards will find a way to your tender flesh.

I stop by Monroe's house at dawn, load him and his gear, and then drive us to the trailhead. My truck is the only vehicle in the lot. Camping season is kaput and man-eating bug season has begun. This is early fall before the first hard freeze or fresh termination dust on the mountains. Any second now for one or both, however.

Monroe is a willowy fellow of Irish descent, so he slathers his pale skin with sunblock, then slips on a fancy vest he probably snagged off the rack the night before, and squeezes himself into a high-tech pack with a slick neon yellow shell and enough elastic webbing to truss a moose, if we see one. It looks heavy and probably is since he's stuffed all of the camping gear in there. I carry my meager supplies, including a sixer of suds, in a rucksack. In my left hand I heft a fishing rod. Trout run in the streams yonder and I've a mind to hook a couple for dinner if the opportunity arises.

Ominous clouds sludge in from the east as we begin our trek. The plan is to hike a few hours, pitch the tent, and maybe recon the surrounding area. In the morning we'll head home. Nothing fancy, nor prolonged or grueling.

We rest periodically. I slug water from my dented canteen and lover boy pops the top on a wine cooler. The trail winds through barren hills and stands of black spruce. Gloom spreads its wings over the land. The air tastes damp, and yes, sir, the mosquitoes and the gnats taste us.

No point in making this an epic: At last we reach a patch of dry ground on a hill and set camp. Tent, fire pit, the works. Monroe asks about bears, and he asks about them a lot. I'm not too worried as they tend to be fat and complacent this close to winter. Spring, when the beasts emerge lean and starved, is the dangerous time.

Nonetheless, I tell Monroe that dearie-me, we'd best be on guard against those man-eaters. I instruct him to keep trash and scraps in a sealed container to minimize ursine temptation, which is a sound idea, but fun to watch him perform as he casts worried glances into the underbrush. I scan the horizon and judge that indeed a storm is approaching, although the weather forecast has made no such mention.

I grab my fishing rod and tell him to fall in.

"Fishing? In this weather?" He cups his hand to catch the first raindrops.

"Morning is better. But it's okay. A little rain won't keep them from biting."

His expression is glum as he zips his fancy yellow pastel slicker that matches the glaring yellow backpack shell. The idea of hooking a fish doubtless hurts his tender feelings. I try not to sneer while thinking that Ferris had certainly gone the whole nine yards to find my opposite.

The map indicates a creek within a mile or so and I wade into the bushes, hapless Monroe on my heel. The possibility of a fresh trout fillet appeals. Moreover, it amuses me to let branches whip back at his face and hear his muffled exclamations. I chuckle and think of the skinning knife strapped to my hip. It's the journey, not the destination, right?

I almost trip headlong into the hole. Monroe saves me. He snatches my belt as I teeter on the crumbling brink, and yanks me back. Faster reflexes than I'd have guessed. He has to use his entire bodyweight, and thus counterbalanced, we fall awkwardly among the alder and devil's club.

"What the hell is that?" he says.

"A hole in the ground," I say. Thorns in my shin, rain trickling down my neck, mosquitoes drilling every available surface, all conspire to provoke my ire. Not just a hole. Not a sinkhole, or an animal burrow, or anything of nature. Upturned clay rings the pit. Water seeps gray and orange from its rude walls.

"You know, it looks like a grave." He gains his feet and peers into the hole. "Holy shit. Somebody dug this thing not too long ago."

"It's not a grave. The shape is fubar."

"Yeah? That a rule? Gotta be six by six on the nose? Maybe they were in a hurry. Digging around big rocks. I'm telling you."

"Maybe a retarded hillbilly dug it."

Sarcastic as I might be, he has it right. This is a grave, albeit an oblong, off-kilter grave, six or seven feet deep and freshly dug. It doesn't matter that the shape is wrong; the hole radiates unmistakable purpose. I don't see a shovel or tracks. The latter bothers me. Should be tracks in the wet dirt. Should be more dirt. Should be broken branches. Anything. I'm not a tracker. Still the consistency of the clay, the wisps of steam, convince me that the mysterious digger did the deed and left within the past hour or two.

"Man, what do you think?" Monroe says with less worry and more eagerness than I like.

"I think we should mind our own business and get back to camp. Call it a day."

"Hold on." He swats away a cloud of mosquitoes. "I'm curious. Aren't you?"

"No, Monroe, not really. Either it's a grave, or it's not. If not, then who gives a shit? If it is, then presumably someone will be along presently to dump a corpse. I'd prefer to be elsewhere." I don't wait around to hold a debate. Hell with fishing. Nightfall looms and I want to put distance between us and that site. The need to get away is overpowering.

We make it back to base without incident. I feel Monroe's sulky gaze the whole way. I consider pulling stakes. The idea of folding the tent is unappetizing and impractical. Blundering through the forest in darkness is how tinhorns and Cheechakos wind up with busted legs or lost for a week. No thanks. I light a fire and boil water for the MREs I brought. Keep my trusty .9mm pistol handy, too. Rain starts pissing down for real. We huddle under a makeshift canopy of spruce boughs and a tarp. Blind and deaf, and choking on campfire smoke.

Isn't until after supper and a third brew that I realize I've forgotten about my half-assed plan to kill my little buddy.

⟜⊙⟝

Late that night I wake to the drum of rain on the tent fabric. Pitch black.

"Elmer," Monroe says. He sounds tense.

"Yeah?"

"Why'd you bring me here?"

"I didn't. You wanted to."

"Uh-uh. *You* wanted this."

"Monroe, shut the fuck up and let me sleep."

"Something occurred to me when I saw that grave. You made it. You made it and then brought me to it."

I lie very still. I smell the fear on his breath.

"Elmer?"

"Yeah?"

"Great minds think alike. This is for Ferris."

He breathes heavily next to me in the dark before smashing the rock down on my head.

⟜⊙⟝

You are stripped utterly naked when confronted by your own mortality. You are stripped utterly naked when you are dropped to the bottom of a hole and buried in the mud, handful by handful, and left to rot. The worms crawl in.

⟜⊙⟝

Two items from the grim days of my youth.

Dad and his brothers were into cockfighting. Many a blue-collar paycheck was won and lost on his prize Lubaang and Asil warrior birds. My people spent generations in El Paso and they'd picked up the sport from the Mexicans. Gorgeous destroyers, our fighting roosters. These weren't simple chickens like you see on a farm. A damn sight bigger and meaner than their domestic kin. Orange and black and sheened emerald, tall as a man's knee, and eager for violence. One glimpse and you could see the devil in them, you could trace the line of descent back to dinosaur raptors.

Dad taped razorblades and jags of glass to their spurs and turned them loose in a killing pit. Hell of a lot of blood and feathers, afterward. I liked the blood and the smell of the blood. The black feathers were my favorite. I gathered a bunch and made a war bonnet. A boy at school offended me and I pursued him in my war bonnet of orange and black feathers and threw him down and rubbed his face in the playground dirt.

In retrospect, Mom and little sister flying the coop, so to speak, when I was four, the cockfighting, boozy gambling, and a procession of whores that followed my dad around might've had an effect on me. Also, we relocated from Texas to Alaska. The main difference between the two states is the distinct lack of an electric chair in the Land of the Midnight Sun.

The other thing is, I could do a weird trick with my mind. Got hooked on the idea of telekinesis after reading an old science fiction novel called *The Power* about some dude with superhuman abilities. God alone can say how many hours I spent squinting in concentration. And it worked, sometimes. I tipped water glasses and caused electronic devices to go haywire without touching them. I could stop a clock by beaming death-thoughts at it. Once I concentrated hard enough to levitate a cinderblock about six inches above the garage floor. Dad stumbled upon me; I was out cold, bleeding from my nose and ears. A three-day coma followed; doctors diagnosed it as epilepsy. Dear lord, the apocalyptic nightmares I suffered: Oceans of blood, rivers of maggots, the damned leading the damned across plains of fire and ash. The damned pointing their crisped, skeletal fingers at me and wailing in unison.

Shot a silver streak through my hair. At least the girls thought it cute. I was too scared to screw around with ESP and telekinesis after that. Set it aside with other childish things.

⊸

There's nothing dramatic about the transmogrification of lowly Elmer D. from dead meat into a walking and talking abomination unleashed upon the hapless people of the Earth. It occurs between one drip of rain from a spruce bough and the next. An owl glides in and snatches a squirrel. A cloud smokes across the face of the moon. The night takes a long breath, and then I am among all that is.

I have no memory of clawing up out of the muck, although it would be keen if my cadaverous hand had thrust free of the soil like in all those hoary old movies. One moment I lie interred in smothering blackness, the next I find myself striding through a twilight forest where mist hangs from evergreen branches. Gray upon gray. In this instant, I question nothing, I ponder nothing. My only goal is to plow forward into the infinite grayness.

A strange sensation to be plugged into every birdcall, every snapped twig, every stir of grass in the breeze, the scents of dead leaves, loam, and moose droppings; yet disconnected, numb. My body is a lead float, adrift. It oscillates between here and there, fat and thin. Hideously immense, yet helium light. I lurch, dragging my left foot. My power is enormous. I brush tree trunks and they crackle and uproot and crash.

Flames leap from a pile of logs. This clues me in to the fact it isn't sunset or dawn, but rather the dark of night. My sight penetrates spectrums beyond the human norm. Constellations flare, white against gray. I *hear* the stars as a celestial chorus, molten atoms colliding and chiming.

Three hunters squat around the fire as men have done since saber tooth tigers prowled the land. A motor home is parked nearby. Electric light streams from the windows. I've crossed many miles in a blink to arrive in the parking lot. Sweat, beer, gun oil, I smell it all. Seven hundred yards to my left, an owl regurgitates the pellet of the squirrel it gobbled for dinner. I smell that too.

None of the hunters notice my apparition at edge of the cheery circle of their fire. Unlike me, they can't see in the dark. Soap bubbles form above the head of the nearest man. The bubble shimmers and expands. It contains images of a blue-collar truck commercial: happy children, barking dogs, muddy Fords, him sighting down on a bighorn ram and blasting it off a ledge. Him plowing his stolid wife, blowing out the candles on a cake. That sort of deal. Once glance tells me the life story of Hunter Numero Uno.

A phantom approximation of his face swells the bubble. It whispers to me in the language of electron particles, "Master!"

I nearly swoon in an ecstasy of desire and my tongue lolls to my grimy navel. I am starved.

One by one, I seize them and crack their skulls and scoop out the brain matter and gulp it whole. Sparks sizzle and drip down my chin, light me up from the inside. For a few moments, before the incredible rush fades, I, as Whitman said, contain multitudes.

⊸o⊷

This transformation started long before the inciting incident in the hole. Maybe it had been occurring my entire life. Ten bucks says Dad's sperm was already mutating when it plowed into Mom's egg. He'd gotten spritzed with Agent Orange during his tour in Vietnam and suffered all kinds of health problems afterward. He drank, and so did Mom. There was also a sense of cursedness haunting the family line. Dad went in a wreck. Dad's cousin was an ace Alaskan bush pilot who death spiraled his Cessna into Lake Illiamna. An uncle was eaten up by cancer despite living a clean, Presbyterian life, no smokes, no booze. An aunt did ten years in the pen and got hit by a motorcyclist three days after her parole. Somebody else got shanked in a brawl at the Gold Digger, back when it *really* was a saloon with sawdust and a mechanical bull and full of motorcycle club thugs and crankheads looking to stab you in the kidney. My sister, she joined the FBI. Her name was Jeanie and last I saw her she was eighteen months and counting. Rumor is she went down in a corruption sting and sliced her wrists.

Dumb luck I didn't pop out of the womb with two heads.

I like the idea that death is a transitory state; my passage from pupa to final instar. I'm a whole new insect. While the notion I've become posthuman sends my nerves a twanging, I'm not exactly afraid, or even concerned. Oh, a tiny fragment of the old me mewls and screeches in its cage, but to no greater effect than the whine of a fly under glass.

The Usurper deigns to answer my imprecations at one point.

We are the next big thing. This whisper issues from inside me; it oozes forth. The whisper is blood welling from a puncture. Sexless, dispassionate. *We are Omega, we are Kingdom Come. We have always been, we will always be.* I receive a picture, muddy and flickering, of warm seas and green light, of trilobites and worms and moss. Dinosaurs have not been invented, but the devil is everywhere.

We are the apparatus. We are the apex. We are first.

I cannot reply. I'm trying to decide if apex means precisely what it intimates and if it's something I want to be (*of course you do, you ninny!*). Again, images coalesce from the ether, like bursts of speech through shortwave static. The future unravels in an arc of projectile vomit from the jaws of Saturn: an approaching tsunami of blood and peeled flesh and more blood. A thousand feet tall, rolling at a thousand miles per hour. The first of many such waves.

Wave after wave of carnage, and me in gigantic repose atop a heap of bones. My friends and foes, beneath me at last!

Ferris is fucking Monroe. We don't have to take that kind of bullshit. We should fix their wagons. We are the apparatus. We are the way.

That sounds reasonable. A man should attend his priorities. Family comes first.

⟜

I loved monster movies as a kid. Don't all boys love monster movies?

Dawn of the Dead. Evil Dead. Reanimator. From Beyond. The Fly. The Thing. Right on. I dug it, especially zombie flicks. The shambling undead did it for me.

Had my first hot-and-heavy teen make-out session with Julie Vellum during a screening of *Night of the Living Dead* at her dad's split-level Girdwood house. I'd seen the movie plenty of times, but this was super-fucking-hot cheerleader Julie Vellum, shag rugs, a leather couch, and her pop's brand-new sixty-inch television we were talking about. That's why Mr. V tolerated me sniffing around his princess that lost summer of my junior year in high school—like me, he was a devout fan of classic fright features. Val Lewton and George Romero were unto gods in Mr. V's estimation. Death gods, I thought, but kept such smart-ass observations to myself by concentrating upon the sky-high hemline of his daughter's skirt.

The three of us camped on that giant couch. Me on one end, Julie on the other, her dad, larger than life, occupying the middle. We kids sipped bottles of Coke while Mr. V blasted his way through a fifth of Maker's Mark and talked over all the good parts. Soon, he slurred and blessedly lengthy gaps interrupted his monologue. He rose and staggered toward the kitchen in quest of more booze. There followed a series of thuds and then a crash that shook the living room.

"Holy shit!" I said.

"Oh, don't worry. That's just him passing out. He does it all the time." Julie gave me a cat-eyed look. Two seconds later we met in the middle. She kissed me as my hands went roaming places they had no business, and then she jacked me off like she'd done it before.

I made it with Julie a half dozen times before school started again. Once the frost set in, she dropped me like a bad habit. Despite my momentary anguish, it was for the best. White trash, both of us. However, she had a little money, and that made all the difference. She also carried a torch for the quarterback on our football team. Beating his ass wouldn't have been a problem; I was really good at inflicting pain by then. Size and meanness were on my side, although I made certain to keep the latter under wraps. My gambit was to smile and keep my mouth shut whenever possible. Didn't matter. Most everyone was piss-scared of me for reasons they couldn't express. The assholes voted me most likely to wind up in prison or in an early grave.

This was why I suppressed my rage, and why I let JV saunter into the sunset with her trophy jock. The things I envisioned doing in the name of love would've landed me in Goose Bay Penitentiary or a nuthouse. Instead, I went into the garden and ate worms and went quietly mad exactly as the moldy poets from pen-and-quill days had done.

Nightmares afflicted me with a vengeance I hadn't experienced since adolescence. Who knows what precipitated them. Stress? Hormones? Whatever the case, these were the stuff of legends. Imagine being trapped inside a waxworks dedicated to atrocities, and all the doors sealed. Horrors from pre-adolescence reinvented themselves into subtler, more sophisticated iterations freighted with guilt and shame. My nightmares had *matured* and they took a cat o' nine tails to my psyche. I was visited every night for several months.

The phenomenon leaked into waking life. I became gaunt, pallid, and terser than ever. I forced myself to wear a shit-eating grin while secretly worrying that I'd gone around the bend. I began to hallucinate. At school I caught glimpses of my classmates and teachers wearing death masks. Some were pale and serene, others contorted and agonized, and still others dripping blood, or caved in, or sheared away entirely to expose the cavern of the mind.

The unexpected result of this being that I got better with my own mask, more scrupulous about tightening the bolts. Even so, it's a miracle I kept a straight face while gazing at exposed brains or punctured eyeballs. I got good at nodding and smiling.

Nonetheless, a particular incident almost undid me. One morning during passing period Julie's locker door was open and for some reason, don't know what the hell I was thinking, I eased on over to chat her up. Second week of school, me being lonely and horny, not in my right mind, which covers any teenage boy, but me moreso. The door swung shut and there she stood, enfolded in the jock's arms, playing tonsil hockey. The bell broke up their tryst and they sauntered away, not acknowledging my presence as I stared after them.

I didn't feel anything, the exact same way I didn't feel anything the time Dad got drunk and slugged me in the jaw and laid me on my ass. The same lights flickered in the dark regions of my mind, the same roar of distant wind rose in my ears. The locker and a section of the concrete floor dissolved as if by acid. A hole bored into the earth and I had an erection that nearly split my pants. No nose bleed this time around. I was afraid, though. Terrified enough that I got away and got drunk on Dad's stock of Old Crow, damn the consequences were he to discover the theft, and I made myself forget. But the nightmares. Jesus. Jesus.

Dogged, simple-minded stubbornness got me through the autumn more or less intact, and largely unscarred.

What *scarred* me was getting ejected face-first through the windshield of Dad's 1982 Chevy that winter. He hit a patch of ice and left the road doing around sixty-five and smacked a berm of snow packed tight as concrete by the state road graders. Never a compulsive buckler of seatbelts, I flew over the berm and burrowed into the virgin snow beyond. Dad burned up with the Chevy. Odd, how of all the folks that were rendered a horror show in my visions, I hadn't ever seen his death mask until I glimpsed him through the flames and melting glass.

No more nightmares for a long, long time after that incident. No dreams of any kind. Sleep became a chrysalis.

⤙◦⤚

Apparently, a side effect of apex prowess is peckishness. The Glenn Highway spreads before me, a glistening buffet table strung with cozy sodium lights for mood.

Whatever manipulates me is not traveling of its own volition so much as being pulled as a steel filing by the mother of all magnets. The delays and digressions are but zigzag deviations of a neutron star as it's dragged into a black hole.

In any event, I zig through a rest stop near Eagle River and am compelled to annihilate the dozen or so inhabitants. Well, I *say* compelled—it's not as if I require much arm-twisting.

I wrench doors from semi-trucks, and peel the roofs off compact cars. I am a beast cracking oyster shells. My need is overwhelming, my appetite is profound. I lick eyes from sockets, then the brains, the guts, the cracked-from-the-bone marrow, and even swallow a few bones whole. I expand and contract, I divide and reform. I squirm and slash. I am a pit that is everywhere. Light bends around me, or it is consumed.

A handful of survivors flee into the dour Plexiglas-and-cement octagon with a stylized eagle blazoned on the sloped roof. My reflection warps against the glass, or perhaps warps the glass itself. A cockscomb of jagged flint erupts from the sundered dome of my cranium. Spurs of razor-tipped basalt extrude from my wrists, elbows, and knees. Even as I take it in its ghastly splendor, my physiognomy alters and is transfigured into something far worse, something that overwhelms my capacity to articulate its awfulness.

I am resplendently dire. I am a figure of awe. I am a horror.

They barricade the entrance with soda machines and that delays me for a few seconds once I finish outside. I find them cowering and gibbering prayers under Formica tables and in bathroom stalls. Somebody stabs me with a hunting knife, somebody else plugs me with a small-caliber handgun. Six or seven teeny popgun flashes in the dark among the roaring and screaming. It hardly matters.

Toward the end, I flop, maw agape, on the concrete floor at the end of the demolished gallery and let that sweet hot stream of blood and viscera roll down my gullet. Overhead, the lights flicker crazily and shadows rip themselves apart.

When it's finished, I shamble forth from the despoiled building. Pasted in gore and excrement, crowned by a garland of intestines, I strike a Jesus Christ pose in the center of the highway.

Traffic routes around me, makes me consider the legend of the stampeding buffalo herd breaking around a man if he remains motionless and tall in his boots. The sun arcs across the sky four times, and so swiftly it sheds tracers of flame. A green-gold ball of bubbling gas, a bacterium in division. The amoeba sun segments in rhythm with my own squamous brain cells. The sun strobes and vanishes. The sliver of moon swings down and sinks into my breast, cold as a fang of ice. That which nests within my DNA blooms and reticulates as it rewrites parameters of operation.

The city awaits.

I project myself forward along a corridor of alternating light and darkness, contract through a crimson doorway, and into a dance hall. My need to gorge is satiated and replaced by an urge I don't recognize. A wormhole opens behind my left eye. The void shivers and yearns; it lusts for sensation.

Music dies as the DJ apprehends me with his bemused gaze. Then the dancing. All heads turn toward my dreadful countenance.

What happens at the Gold Digger Saloon. I cannot speak of it. The ecstasy is the sun going nova in my brain. Nova, then collapsing inward, a snow crystal flaking, disintegrating, and then nothing left except a point of darkness, the wormy head of a black strand that bores its way to the core of everything.

⟜

We aren't rich. The pool house is our compromise—as long as Ferris didn't push for a mother-in-law cottage, I'd see she had herself a full-length heated pool to do laps. Ferris was on the swim team in high school and college and she's tried valiantly to maintain her form. The YMCA is a no go. Too many sluggish old people in the lane, too many screaming kids, too many creepy dudes in the bleachers. Thus, the pool house. A gesture of defiance in the face of brutal Alaska winters.

I enter through the skylight. A long-dead star field turns and burns over my shoulder. The coals that were stars sigh.

Ferris lies naked and icy pale against the dappled green water. Her eyes are closed. Occasionally her arms and legs scissor languidly. Beneath her, is her seal shadow and the white tile that slopes away into haziness. Vapors shift across her body and carry its scent to me, sharp and clean amid the faint tang of chlorine. She daydreams on the cusp of sleep and I taste the procession of phantoms that illuminate her inner landscape. Mine is not among them.

I descend as if a great spider on its wire, then stop and hang in place. This thing that has hijacked and reconstituted my body, reduced my consciousness and placed it in a bell jar, is drawn to her. More specifically, that which I have become is drawn to something *within* her. I don't comprehend the intricacies. I can only bear mute witness to the spectacle as it unfolds.

A black spot stains at the bottom of the pool. The spot spreads across the white bed, a ring of darkness widening as pieces of tile crumble into the depths. It is a pit, slackening directly below my lovely, frigid wife. My betrayer wife, my arm extending, my claw, hollow as a siphon, its shadow upon her betrayer's face, and the abyssal trench an iris beneath. Wife, come along to Kingdom Come, come to the underworld.

Her eyes snap open.

"I didn't fuck him," she says. "I fantasized about it, plenty."

Monroe is absent from the scene, and that's a shame. Every pore in me longs to drink his blood, to liquefy him, fry him, to have his heart in my fist. To ram his heart down her throat.

"I didn't fuck him. Elmer, I didn't. I should've."

Her blood. His blood. Their atoms.

I open my mouth (maw) to accuse, to excoriate, and the dead song of the dead stars worms out. But she doesn't blink, she repeats that she hasn't fucked him, hasn't fucked him. She projects her innocence in an electromagnetic cone meant to kill. She is entirely too composed, this fragile sack of skin and water.

She says, "Are you here to hurt me, Elmer?" Her smile is pitiless, it cuts. "The time you came home drunk and forced me? There's a word for you, hon. Don't you remember what you've done?"

I don't remember. I seethe.

Difficult to concentrate through the interference of her thoughts that explain via pointillism how Monroe opportunistically slaughtered me and then so much like the narrator of the "Tell-Tale Heart" had succumbed to guilt and paranoia and eventually fled the country. The FBI hunts him in connection with my disappearance. He could be anywhere. She suspects Mexico. Monroe always had a romanticized notion about Mexico and what he could do there, a super gringo lover man.

The little shit swallowed her teary stories of my cruelty and violence. He'd done me in as an act of vengeance. An act that only earned Ferris's contempt. She is utterly my creature and let no man cast asunder what all the powers above and below had seen fit to forge.

I convulse with a complicated longing and snatch for her. She's too quick. She rolls, sleek and white, and flashes downward amid a cloud of bubbles into the pit. Fool that I am, I follow.

⤙⤚

We meet in darkness, each illuminated by a weak spotlight that dims and brightens with our breathing. I sense immense coldness and space pressing against the bubble where we reside. I am whole. My cloven skull and rotting flesh are restored. My mind is papered over with gold star stickers and crepe.

She points an automatic pistol at me. I understand that it's a present from her would-be lover. The barrel aligns with my eye. I have traveled through the barrel and been deposited in this limbo.

"I warned him. Told him he'd never succeed. If I couldn't kill you, then there was no hope for him." She laughs and shakes the wet hair from her eyes. "Arsenic in your coffee every day for three months. Nothing. For God's sake, I frosted your birthday cake with rat poison."

Now that she mentions it, now that her thoughts bleed into mine, I recall the bitter coffee, the odd aftertaste of the icing on my last cake. A skull and crossbones has hung over our marriage for years. Yet, I remain. What does it mean?

"I hurt you, but I couldn't kill you. Monroe couldn't. Nobody can. You died in childhood. Maybe you were never born. Maybe the parasite that fruits your corpse is the only true part of you that existed."

Am I merely a figment? If so, I am the most rapacious, carnivorous, and vengeful figment she will have the misfortune to encounter. I strike aside the gun and reach for her. A black halo of light manifests around Ferris. Her arms spread wide and she becomes the very figure of a dread and terrible insect queen. The enormity of her eclipses my own.

She clutches me and the sting slides in. "It was always here, love. In all of us, always."

It's apparent that I've miscalculated again.

⊸

Reality has bent and bent. I look past the nimbus of black flame into her cold eyes. Reality just goes right ahead and comes apart.

Darkness rolls back to daylight. It's spring and balmy. The breeze is redolent with sweet green sap and the bloom of roses. Guests and children of the guests clutter a lawn that's too bright and too green to be real. "Death to Everyone" by good old Will Oldham crackles over the speakers. I'm stuffed into a poorly fitted tux. At my side, Ferris shines as radiantly white as the Queen of Winter.

I have seen this, relived this, in a thousand-thousand nightmares.

My hand overlaps hers as we saw the blade into that multi-tiered cake. She opens her mouth and bites through the icing, the bunting, and my brittle soul. I shudder and kiss her. It feels no different than kissing ice bobbed up from the bottom of an arctic lake. She inhales my heat and my vitality before I can inhale hers. She's always been stronger, in the only way that counts. She always will be stronger.

Oldham's voice fades and the guests stare at us in hushed expectation.

Nearby, a little girl in a black funeral dress begins to sing the "Hearse Song" to the boy she's tormenting with malice or affection, take your pick:

"They put you in a big black box
And cover you up with dirt and rocks.
All goes well for about a week,
Then your coffin begins to leak.
The worms crawl in, the worms crawl out,
The worms play pinochle in your snout,
They eat your eyes, they eat your nose,
They eat the jelly between your toes."

This time around, I do what I should've in the first place all those lost years ago. Instead of cutting a piece for the first guest in line, I grip the knife and slice my throat. Blood fans the cake and Ferris's white dress. She throws back her head and laughs. I sink to my knees in the thirsty grass. The sun pales and contracts to a black-limned ring. Red shadows pour through the trees, drench the lawn, and reduce the paralyzed spectators to negatives. I try to speak. Worms crawl out.

⟜

Ferris's parents loved me. I first met them during Thanksgiving when she and I stayed over at the family casa—Ferris slept in her old room with the Justin Timberlake poster and a mountain of heart-shaped pillows and teddy bears while I bunked in the basement on a leather sofa between her old man's pool table and a gun safe.

There was a tense moment when she removed her shades and revealed the Lichtenburg flower of a purple knot under her eye. Ferris was so very smooth. She spun a story about getting kicked in the face during swim practice, and her family bought it. She wasn't speaking to *me* except as required, probably hadn't even decided whether to stay with me or toss her engagement ring into the trash.

Hell of it was, at that early stage in our romance I didn't care much either way.

Turkey, gravy, pumpkin pie, and afterward, a quart of Jim Beam passed around a circle of a half dozen of Ferris's menfolk. Salt of the earth bumpkins who raised coon dogs and revved the engines on four-wheelers at the gravel pit and picked through piles at the dump for fun.

You like John Wayne? one truck-driving uncle wanted to know. Shore as hail, I love the Duke! And with that, I was in like Flynn. My lumberjack beard, plaid coat, and knowledge of professional football didn't go amiss, either.

Her dad welcomed me to the family with teary eyes and a bear hug. I wasn't "nothin' like them pussies she usually brings home from college." How right my future in-law hillbillies were! Not three days before that Clampett-style feast I'd beaten a UAA fraternity brother within an inch of his life for giving me the stink eye as I staggered home from the Gold Digger Saloon. I made the letter-sweater-wearing jock try to eat a parking meter. The whole time Ferris's family exchanged jocular crudities at the supper table, my hand was in my pocket, caressing thc frat boy's braces, with a few teeth still stuck in them, like a God-fearing Catholic fondling his rosary. It was the only thing that kept me from stabbing one of those bozos with a steak knife.

I gave the lot of those silly, inbred bastards my best aw-shucks grin, and daydreamed about how lovely and charred their slack-jawed skulls would shine from the cinders of a three a.m. house fire.

Aided by booze and a vivid imagination, I survived dinner and into the following day. Driving home, the stars were blacked. Snow fell like a sonofabitch. Every now and again the tires slipped against ice and the truck shook. Dad's ghost muttered in my ear. My heart knocked and I forgot to blink for at least forty miles. The high-beams carved a tunnel into the blizzard. Patsy Cline came on the radio out of Anchorage. Patsy sang "Crazy" and that was our song, all right.

Ferris reached across the gulf from the passenger side and held my hand. Her fingers clamped cold and tight over mine. In the rearview there was nothing but darkness, snowflakes endlessly collapsing in our wake, and a black slick of road painted red in the taillight's glow.

THE DOG'S HOME

ALISON LITTLEWOOD

Sometimes, the cruellest thing a creature can give you is love. I get up and Sandy the retriever is there. He comes running when I go downstairs and tries to lick my face. I feel sad, or irritated, depending on my mood, and then I go out and the last thing I see is his head tilted to one side, surprised to see me leaving him all over again. I get back and he's there, tail wagging—I can hear it, beating the radiator by the door—and it begins again. There's no end to his love. It's capacious; it's infinite. It was the first thing I was told about him, and it was true, and every day I'm surprised to see that it's true. You'd think both of us would have got used to it by now, but we haven't. I suppose, in that, I'm more like him than I realise.

"You wouldn't stand a chance if it wasn't for the dog," my mother had said when she raised the question of visiting Aunt Rose. At first I didn't know what she meant, though I remembered my aunt from when I was small; she'd come on a duty visit. I was about five years old. She'd loomed over me in the hall and dropped her bag next to her feet, which were clad in brown brogues that I could see my snotty little nose in. She'd leaned down, her scrawny hands reaching for me, and she'd touched both my cheeks. Her hands were cold, I remember that too, and then she leaned in closer, pursing her lips. I'd waited for the touch of her tight mouth on my cheek, but it never came. Instead she'd whispered, her voice dry and fierce but her breath surprisingly warm against my skin, "Wash your face before you greet your elders and betters."

I'm not sure my mum even heard; certainly, I never saw her react. And that was how I remembered Aunt Rose, crone-like, tall, thin, claws for hands and a death rattle voice. I filed her away in a mental box with *Do not open* on the lid, and left her there. Or so I thought.

"It'll go to the dogs' home," my mother said.

She had no love of my aunt. She had no love for my dad, either. He'd left the two of us a long time ago and I thought we'd managed all right, got along without too many problems; until she'd said that about the dogs' home.

Aunt Rose had "married rich," Mum always said, and she always had a note of resentment in her voice when she said it. Better still, judging from her tone: Rose had "married dead," the guy popping it soon after, leaving her loaded. A big inheritance with nowhere to go. No wonder Mum had pound signs in her eyes.

That was when she'd said, "Course, Andrew, you wouldn't stand a chance if it wasn't for the dog." She looked at my blank expression and snapped, "Rose doesn't like people. But that dog—that dog likes people. So Rose tolerates them. She'll visit folk just because the dog likes to see them. She'll stop and chat to people on their walks, because her dog likes *their* dog. If it wasn't for that animal—" She clicked her tongue in disapproval. "And now," she added with a note of triumph, "the dog's home all alone, isn't he? The neighbour's feeding him and that's about it. So she needs someone to go and stay. She needs *you* to go and stay."

I opened my mouth to protest. I saw the look on my mother's face and closed it again.

"Make sure that dog loves you," she said. "Make him love you and *she'll* decide she loves you too."

⟜

Sandy wasn't at all the kind of dog I'd expected. I'd thought Aunt Rose would have some sniffy little thing, a chihuahua or a peke, but when I collected her key from the neighbour and let myself in, there he was: a flurry of tail, big paws and weight behind them, all joy and enthusiasm. There was a volley of barks but not a second's hesitation before he was all over me, licking, covering my sweater in hair and drool. I couldn't reconcile the idea of Aunt Rose and this living, breathing, messy creature; it didn't seem they occupied the same universe, let alone the same house. But occupy it Sandy did. I could smell him there, a cooped-up smell that was unmistakably dog, and I sighed and set down my bag at my feet. It looked like I wouldn't just be staying in her house; I'd be cleaning it too. But first, it was time to visit Aunt Rose.

⟜

The hospital's antiseptic smell, barely masking what lay beneath, was a sharp contrast to the shut-in, musty house. Rose was in a room of her own and I was thankful for that. I'd never been around illness, not really. I didn't look at the wards to either side as I went towards number seven and I found it a small, narrow box, a metal bed clearly visible through a large window. In the bed was the collection of bones and skin that Aunt Rose had become. Looking at her there, I had no idea how I could ever have thought of her as tall. She seemed barely larger than a doll, and when she let her head fall to the side, looking at me from hollowed sockets, she seemed to move like one too.

"Hello, Aunt Rose," I said, and she rolled her head back again with a little grunt. I'd intended to play it carefully, but found myself blurting, "I came to look after Sandy. Mum said you might need some help."

Some help. I knew, looking at her, how inadequate those words were. She needed more than help, would soon pass beyond the kind of help that anyone could give. But she didn't appear to think about what I said. She made a brief gesture and I recoiled from it, then realised she had indicated the plastic chair next to her bed. I slid into it. The legs scraped against the tiles and her lip twitched.

Aunt Rose stared at the ceiling. I didn't know if she was waiting for me to speak, but I tried. I told her that Mum was fine. I said she'd have come herself, but she couldn't get away from work—I almost found myself saying that Mum couldn't afford to have her wages docked, but I wasn't sure how that might sound. I thought of the slight body in the bed in front of me, hidden under a single sagging sheet, and all the money it possessed. It seemed terribly unlikely.

"Sandy's fine," I said. "He was happy to see—"

The breath was shocked out of me when she grasped my hand. I looked down. Her fingers, narrow and putty-coloured, held mine, which had turned white under their pressure. I tried to pull away but she held on, moving with me, and I had a sudden image of it being like that forever, her cadaverous hand closed on mine.

"Bring him to me," she said.

"What?"

Pardon, is what I expected her to say—the remnant of some childhood memory, perhaps—but she did not. "They won't let him in," she said, "and they won't let me out. I want to see my dog." Her eyes met mine. "It's *all* I want. You understand?"

Her eyes were pale blue and weak-looking, but a cold strength shone through them. It didn't appear natural. I looked away.

"I want to see my dog." She sank back against the pillows. Her face was blank, as if the life had already gone out of it—*already*, that was what I thought—and then a nurse came in talking about changing the sheets, smiling at me a little too brightly, in a way that told me it was time for me to go.

⊸

Sandy greeted me when I got back to the house. It was as if he hadn't seen me in years. I was surprised by his love. It was capacious; it was infinite. I imagined the look on Aunt Rose's face if she could see it being bestowed upon me.

⊸

"He'll understand," she said, the next time I went to see her. I tried to tell myself I didn't know what she meant, but I did.

"They'll think he'd jump all over me," she said, "but he won't. He'll know. He'll take one look at me and he'll know." Her head lolled, her gaze moving towards—but not quite meeting—my own.

"He's a smart dog. He always knew me and I knew him. He just needs to see me, so he knows—he knows I haven't—"

Abandoned him, I thought. In my pockets, my hands curled into fists. I'd spent the morning cleaning out her fridge. The smell had been indescribable. Then I'd started on the cupboards, but not before I'd walked the dog; *her* dog.

He was too joyful a creature to be her dog.

I told myself that Sandy wouldn't give two shits if he thought she had abandoned him, not now, but how could I know that was true? A dog is not a person.

A dog is not a person. I curled my fists tighter when I remembered what I'd found in the cupboard in the lounge. I scowled, just as I might have when I was five years old, but she didn't notice.

"I thought I'd have to make an awful choice for him one day," she said. Her throat was working, as if she was holding back tears. "That's the only thing that makes it bearable now. Going first, I mean. I know I won't have to do that. I'll never have to look at him while he goes to sleep. And he'll forget, won't he? After he's seen me. He can move on."

You're damned right he can, I thought. That morning I'd taken him to the park. He'd gone scurrying after all the sticks I threw.

She grasped my hand again. This time her grip was weak. "Please," she said. "If you do anything for me. Do this."

That night Sandy curled up on the floor and stared up at one of the chairs. No one was sitting in the chair. I scowled at him. I went and sat in the chair. After a while, he came and sat at my side and rested his head on my knee. I whispered to him while his eyes closed and he slept like that, the breath catching noisily in his throat.

How easy it is for a dog to love you. How hard it is, for a person. Sometimes people don't even love their own family. It just isn't in them. It wasn't in Rose's small, wasted body; it never had been. I knew that from the letters I found. Not hers, of course; I never saw whatever answers Rose had sent, but I know we never received anything more than words.

I always thought we'd got along all right, me and Mum. But I was a child, and children don't always know. They aren't like dogs. They can't take one look and understand. I wasn't even sure I understood after I'd read the letters I found stashed out of sight in Rose's cupboard.

He grows so fast, Mum had written. *He already needs new shoes. The trousers I got him last month are too short already. He looks a bit like Dad, have I mentioned that? You'd love him if you saw him now. I don't suppose you might be able to . . .*

But she never had, had she? Aunt Rose hadn't helped us. She never helped her own sister. She'd read these letters and she didn't love me. She'd seen me when I was five and she didn't love me then and here I was taking care of her house and her dog and visiting her in hospital because that was what family did, and she hadn't even noticed. Mum had been right, but she had been wrong too. The dog may have got me in, but I never had stood a chance, not really. There was only one way Aunt Rose was ever going to notice me; one way I might be able to persuade her to help.

⊸

Aunt Rose was right. She'd never actually said it, but it's true. A dog can break your heart.

⊸

"Five minutes," I said. "Five minutes, or maybe not even that if anyone finds out." The papers shook in my hand. My fingers had dug into them, claw-like, gripping too tightly. "But you have to sign first. And it has to be witnessed. We'll find a couple of nurses to do it." She stared at me. Mostly she stared at the ceiling, but this time she never took her eyes from mine. Hers were small, the pupils constricted, the pale blue almost blending with the greyish whites of her eyes. It was horrible to see, but I didn't look away. She was family, after all.

If there's any way you could help—he has to start school next week. He needs a uniform. I've been offered more hours but it means I can't be with him. I'll have to leave him with a neighbour, and he screams the place down when I'm not there…

I shook the thought away and forced myself to focus on the will. "Are you going to sign it?"

"But—"

"You don't need to worry about Sandy." I thought about how he'd been that morning, watching me leave, his head poking through a gap in the curtains, his tongue lolling in a wide doggy smile. I forced myself to stroke her hand. We both looked down at our fingers. "I'll make sure he's okay." I thought about telling her about his love, how he had enough for everyone; about how he'd be comforted. I stopped myself just in time.

"Will you sign?" I repeated.

Her head rolled away, but I could still make it out when she nodded.

⊸

Back at the house, I read the letters once more. It wasn't so much the words that got to me, but their frequency. My mother had written to her sister once a week. Her hope—no, her faith—had never wavered. Family; she had believed in family, in their love.

Sandy rested his chin on my knee while I went through the letters, and occasionally I paused long enough to stroke his head. His fur there was a little shorter but softer than on his back. Long whiskers jutted from the side of his head, besides the ones that grew around his nose; others formed extra-long eyelashes. I listened to him breathing, the little catch where the air was constricted in his throat. His posture must have been uncomfortable, but he still didn't move.

Sandy was a big dog. He wasn't the kind that could be smuggled inside a handbag or under a coat. He was big and full of life and anyway, he loved me now.

But a promise is a promise.

⊸

The last time I visited Aunt Rose was the first time I'd seen her smile. I got there a little late, because by then the nurse at the door tended to be occupied with other visitors. I waited until she turned her back before I slipped down the corridor and into Aunt Rose's room. It was easier than I'd thought, though my heartbeat felt as if it would trigger alarms. I listened to the steady *beep—beep—beep* of my aunt's monitors, and calmed myself. Her rhythms sounded strong and steady, as they had for the last couple of days; as they had since I made my promise. *A turn for the better*, the nurses had said. *Who knows...?*

I pictured it, Aunt Rose back in her house, in her favourite chair, the dog gazing up at her, adoration in his eyes. It wouldn't happen. It *couldn't.*

I shook my head. A promise is a promise, especially to family. Because promises to family are mainly unspoken, aren't they? The ones about love, especially. The ones about help.

I smiled when I turned to face my aunt. She was sitting up in bed, looking brighter than she had in days. Her eyes were shining; there was joy in them. She knew I'd keep my promise—that was what families did—and now I was here.

"Where is he?" she asked.

My smile became a little wider. It took her a moment longer to see the expression in my eyes.

⊸

I get up and Sandy is there. I live in Aunt Rose's house now, though it isn't her house any longer. It's mine. He comes running when I go downstairs and tries to lick my face. I feel sad, or irritated, depending on my mood, and then I go out and the last thing I see is his head tilted to one side, surprised to see me leaving him all over again. I get back and he's there, tail wagging—I can hear it, beating the radiator by the door—and it begins again.

The thing I see, though, when I look at him, is Aunt Rose. Aunt Rose, little bigger than a doll, her limbs desiccated, covered by a single sagging sheet. Her eyes lolling back in their hollowed sockets, the emptiness in them. The *nothing* in them. It was the only thing left that she had really wanted, and once I gave it to her—once I opened the bag and leaned towards her and let her look inside—I guess she'd done.

It had been hard to cut. He wouldn't hold still, for one thing, and I couldn't see what I was doing because the fur on his neck was longer than that on his head. It was still golden, though, and it spilled over my fingers. He licked me when I got hold of his collar. He tried to jump up at me, excited, not understanding.

It wasn't easy to cut; I think I said that, but it really wasn't.

I thought I'd have to make an awful choice for him one day, she'd said. And I remembered the relief on her face when she'd said it. I understood it. I took one look, and I understood.

I couldn't see for crying.

Make him love you, Mum had said, and I had. The awful thing was, I loved him too. I took a knife to his neck and I pushed it in. The noise he made was terrible. Pain, yes. But mostly, it was the sound of betrayal.

It didn't kill him, not at first. He bucked in my hands, and the knife slipped out. It took me a while to gather myself. He struggled. It was a while before I could do it again.

When Aunt Rose looked inside the bag, at first, she didn't do anything. She just froze, me trying to hold it steady so that she could see his eyes, not the bloody part, the matted fur, just those adoring eyes—and her own eyes swivelled and she looked at me. She looked at me for a horrified second before she opened her mouth—to form words or take a breath, I wasn't sure which—and then she started to claw at her chest.

Aunt Rose didn't get better. She didn't come home. She did get to see her dog, though, or what remained of him, before she died. I didn't want to do it, but he was a big dog. He wasn't a dog that would fit under a coat or in a bag. Not all of him, anyway.

Sandy comes to greet me whenever I get home. He wraps himself around my legs, and on some level, I can feel his touch, though the house never smells of dog any more. It doesn't smell of him because he isn't really there. I remind myself of that whenever I look into his eyes and see the adoration written in them. Sometimes the cruellest thing a creature can give you is love. I'd rather see *her*. Aunt Rose, the last look she ever gave me, her face twisted in pain and her eyes—the coldness in them. The hatred. It's what I deserve, but I tell myself; it's what she deserved too.

The dog was only caught between us.

There's no end to his love. It's capacious; it's infinite. It was the first thing I was told about him, and it was true, and every day I'm surprised to see that it's true. You'd think both of us would have got used to it by now, but we haven't. I don't think I ever will, and that's a pity, because I have the feeling we're going to be living together for a long, long time.

TREAD UPON THE BRITTLE SHELL

RHOADS BRAZOS

The vehicle pressed through a cloud that thickened into terracotta, and for a moment the desert track disappeared. In the passenger's seat, Charlie squeezed her knees with both hands, but Yileen didn't seem too concerned. He turned his dark, weathered face to her, grinned, and refocused on the track with a languidness that jabbed at her gut.

"Have you ever—" Charlie stole a glance at the speedometer. "Gotten stranded out here?"

Yileen snorted. "Many times. Once a month?"

The Australian outback wasn't as flat as the Nullarbor—as if anything could be—but seemed somehow even less forgiving. Charlie picked up her canteen and felt its weight.

Yileen laughed, ending with a dry cough. "Don't be concerned. I drive this road so many times. See—boulder coming up on the right."

There it was, melting out of the veil.

"Patch of corkwood over the ridge."

A twisted grove rose up on both sides. In the haze, the stunted trees looked like black bolts of lightning, arcing up out of the ground.

"We'll make a meal of their seeds—pray that help arrives."

This time she caught Yileen's jest. That faint curl to his lip sealed it—wry Aboriginal humor. The truck dipped into a sandy trough, spun its tires a bit on the rise and was once again on flat ground. Grit hissed against her window. Pebbles and light debris pecked at the glass.

"Being true, I wouldn't normally suffer this," Yileen said, motioning to the road. "But he's dead set on having you back."

It made Charlie smile inside. *Yes, Mum. He's a doctor.*

Charlie had discovered the cave—per Dr. Fosberg's cryptic directions—but she doubted many would have recognized it. It was less than obvious. Curiously so.

"Sounds like they're really stuck," she said.

"Been for a while. You're gonna crawl in those tunnels some more?"

"It's what I do best."

"But you are a very tiny girl."

Though that was a glancing insult, she'd let it slide—Yileen meant well. "When caving, you'd be surprised how many blokes wish they were too."

Yileen chuckled. "Right! I wouldn't do so well down there." He patted his stomach and then squinted down the track. "Told ya we were close. We live another day."

The camp was ahead—a half-dozen large tents, khaki canvas splotched calico with the desert. Their sides whipped and cracked with the gusts. The helicopter that had served as transport for her previous trips was tarped down behind them—a small fleet of trucks too. That angular structure at the site must be the winch for the lift. Good, they'd listened.

"Tent on the end is yours," Yileen said, coasting slower.

"Good, but can you let me off at the drop?"

Yileen grunted and down-shifted. After another minute, he eased the vehicle to a stop alongside the pit. He put his hand on her shoulder. It surprised Charlie; Yileen had always kept his distance.

"Be very careful." His wide features were turned down, his brow sagging.

"I always am," Charlie said. She pulled her goggles in place before stepping into the desert's fury.

From within the cage, Charlie watched the pit's receding mouth, her way lit by yellow bulbs graced with rusty halos of silt. Thick cables hung alongside her, trailing down into the earth. The air took on a chalky coolness that put her at ease.

It must have been a half-kilometer ride, or close to it, when the cage finally clanked onto a platform at the upper end of a well-lit cavern. A chapel-sized channel dipped away to a yawning cathedral with boulders for pews. Cabling twisted away to junction boxes powering floodlights and computer equipment stacked on folding tables.

"Miss Wenham?" A reedy voice.

Charlie hadn't seen him sitting there, a narrow man with the stature of a bent stick of cane. He rustled up from a paper-littered table and offered a handshake.

"I'm Dr. Fosberg."

"Oh, of course. It's nice to finally meet you."

Was it? Somehow she'd pictured somebody a little more imposing—a little more Nordic. He had the blond hair and the fair skin, but it didn't look like his pillaging went beyond the cappuccino bar.

"Likewise," he said. "Thank you so much for coming. May I call you Charlotte?"

"Charlie, please." She looked about, letting her interest in the environment mask her disappointment. Indulging in flights of fancy—always a mistake. "The drop was astounding, but—too bad. You'd have the Mecca of base jumping if it were wider. Where are your helpers?"

Fosberg slumped back into his chair. "Exploring. Mapping. For what that's worth. I'm not expecting anyone for another . . ." he checked his watch, "six hours, or thereabouts. And the following team won't arrive until late tomorrow."

"How many?"

"Twenty-five." Fosberg patted her wrist. "Twenty-six."

Charlie smiled weakly and somehow avoided wrenching her hand away. As Fosberg spread out a rolled map, she silently scolded herself. He was just trying to be welcoming. His attention was more on his equipment than her. She knew the difference. How many times during Cocklebiddy tours had she been sized-up by guys with a schoolgirl fetish? Their eager agitation was palpable. With the way she was judging Fosberg . . . maybe they had been right; she *did* have something in common with them.

"I'm glad to be back," she said.

"Excellent."

"Show me what you've found."

He motioned to the map. It was a detailed outline of the caves. The system reached downward in one massive limb that zigzagged and narrowed, before fracturing into long, twisting fingers.

Charlie scrutinized the layout while Fosberg pointed to key features and traced out the paths of his expedition teams. The two of them chatted a long while, the discussion varying from fully explored sections to treacherous spots that may have more to offer.

"So, are you ready to look around?" Fosberg asked. "Satisfied with payment?"

"Yes—yes, it's good, and appreciated, but I'm curious."

"Yes?"

"What are you really looking for?"

Fosberg rolled up the map and tucked it away. "What do you think?"

Charlie flipped through a stack of sketches. Each was a gridded outline of a cavern—numbered, indexed, and clipped with color photos. She studied them closely.

"Well," she said, "you're a geophysicist."

"Partly. My focus is seismology, geomorphology, in addition to historical studies."

"Strata. Something to do with tectonics. The island's position and all that."

"Eh." Fosberg brushed the question away.

"Come on now. I'm for the game of it all, but how'd you know there was a cave here?"

"Research."

"I've found a few before this one, down south," Charlie said. "Just new entrances to established systems. Nothing earth-shattering. Nothing like this."

"Personal pride. Commendable."

"I suppose. This is definitely a new find, but, Dr. Fosberg—"

"Call me Kristof, please."

"Kristof—this system was hidden. Not undiscovered, lying away from eyes. It was buried. Someone had sealed it."

After two days of searching the desert, she'd found the entrance more or less where Fosberg claimed it to be—an equal distance north of *Uluru* and *Kata Tjuta*. Yileen had traveled out with her in the 'copter, made sure she set foot on the coordinates, and not on any mulgas or adders. While Yileen yabbered on about how this wasn't really a desert, and with the two monuments just peeking over the horizon, she'd found it.

"The capstone, you mean?" Fosberg asked. "It didn't surprise me."

"Well, I've never seen such a thing."

"You were very bold to dig under it. I appreciate your daring, your insight. The data you sent allowing—" Fosberg motioned at the equipment around him. "This. That's why I've asked you back. I need someone with bold ideas." He leaned over the table. "This cave goes down *deep*, like nothing you've ever seen."

"Sounds like Jules Verne."

Fosberg grinned wide. "A bit, perhaps."

"If I find it, you'll put my name on the final drop?"

"As I said, yes."

"And you get?"

"Recognition, much like yourself, but of a different sort. I'm proving a theory. Let's be a team of two. I can explain on the way down."

Charlie appraised him carefully. So, he wanted to get his hands dirty? That was to be respected. And he was eager to explore. She could relate to that. "You know the ropes? I don't dawdle."

"I've had training. I'm not a speleologist, but I can follow your lead."

"You're absolutely sure there's another drop?"

"My research guarantees it. I know you weren't convinced before, about the location, but... here we are. It was waiting for us."

"And what do your studies say about the depth?"

Fosberg stared at empty space. "A tremendous distance."

"Fine. Let me gear up and I'll take you to it."

⊸⊙⊸

Once they were both properly outfitted, progress was quick. The forward cavers had left ample lines. Charlie was a bit chagrined to see every pitch bolted where trad gear could easily have been placed, but it did keep matters simple.

The two of them made short work of the boulder field, descended through several shallow drops, and crossed a sluggish river via an overhead traverse.

Fosberg was capable—a bit hesitant—but he knew the basics.

"This is the epicenter of my studies," Fosberg said, somewhat winded. "Though that isn't the proper term for it."

Charlie set a spring-loaded cam in place of a bolt she wasn't willing to trust. Fosberg must have hired amateurs, maybe some club. Somebody rube enough to drill next to a severe horizontal fault. "Earthquakes?" she asked.

"Yes. They center here, but they don't originate here. It's very strange. They start along the coasts, north and south, and then converge. Two subtle waves of such precision."

Charlie made a quick abseil down and Fosberg followed. She took a second to survey the newest cavern. A domed ceiling sloped down to a cataract running through the far wall.

"There's a spike," Fosberg continued, "clearly noticeable as the waves overlap, right here. It's plain on the seismometer. The north wave continues along with the south, and each ends where the other began. The whole continent ripples."

"Never heard of that. Here, hold this." She tossed him a line.

"The newer instruments show it discretely. But, if you examine the old data—" Fosberg scratched at his chin. "Even with less stations, poorer resolution—it's there too."

Charlie backed down a long, steep grade. Fosberg met her at the bottom.

"Nine-year intervals," he said. "At first I thought it was some sort of global rhythm. Perhaps the sub-plates oscillated in hierarchical tessellations. But at that speed? Ridiculous, I know. It was just a theory."

The conversation faded as they worked down a dry streambed, retracing team five's route. Fosberg grumbled about that fact but kept following.

"Could it be tidal?" Charlie asked.

"What?"

It had been an hour since the last conversation.

"The waves," Charlie said. "They start at the coasts."

"No, no. I don't see how."

Charlie sat on a loose boulder and Fosberg joined her. His breath rasped. He might have studied the equipment and technique, but he'd skimped on the cardio. She offered him her canteen, which he eagerly took.

"You didn't tell the others about the... what did you call it, the capstone?"

Fosberg wiped at his mouth. "This is a dead end. I told you. Team five turned around here."

"Yes, but you didn't tell them."

"The capstone? No. I saw no reason to."

Charlie loosened her pack and let it slip to the floor. Fosberg gave a questioning glance.

"You know what I think?" Charlie asked. "I think you're not being entirely honest, with them or me."

"That's a bit rude of you."

"Maybe. It's just an honest observation. What does a cave have to do with earthquakes? Not much, I say. And measuring away from *Uluru* and *Kata Tjuta*? You can't get any more Aboriginal and off-limits."

Fosberg squinted down hard.

"And who would have sealed this place if not the Aborigines?" Charlie said.

"The Pitjantjatjara tribe?"

"Or their cousins."

"I'm quite free to operate without a permit. This location is outside of the park."

"Only because nobody knows about it. Anymore."

"So you don't wish to help?"

"I brought you here, didn't I?" Charlie said. "Behind you."

Fosberg turned.

"Those photos were a great idea," Charlie said. "If you would have informed your teams, they would have seen it."

Fosberg pressed his hands against the wall. "I don't—"

"Look at the wall's structure—just like the capstone. See how the leftward surface ripples? But it doesn't touch this section. Unusually smooth. Well, except for the chiseling."

Fosberg's hands trembled on the stone.

"Here!" He fell to his knees and rubbed at the wall. "A crack running, turning..." He traced his fingers up and around.

Charlie folded her arms and watched him work. It wasn't easy; she wanted to tear at that wall alongside him.

"This is it! Help me."

"I want the *whole* story."

"I've told you."

"How did you know this was here?"

Fosberg pounded on the wall. He tried to force his fingers in the crack. He spun back to Charlie and glared.

"All right. It's going to seem... you're not going to believe me."

"Try me."

"The Earth is hollow."

Charlie pressed her lips tight.

"Not the way its proponents believe. They truly are insane. Portals at the north and south poles? Ha! Besides, I looked. There's nothing there. But—"

Fosberg took a step closer to Charlie. She didn't budge.

"There is too much evidence," he said. "Too many legends of the Underworld across too many cultures. The Mayans call it *Xibalba*. The Buddhists call it *Agharti*. The old Hebrew, *Sheol*. *Hel*, in the Anglo-Saxon."

"Hell?" Charlie laughed nervously. This guy's theories weren't as funny as they should be when you were alone with him.

"I think the Christian interpretation is... a bit extreme. In the Old Norse, it was *Hellir*. Something concealed, like a cave."

"How'd you select this spot?"

"I crossed Aboriginal myths with Norse myths. The *Nyaviah Vahs*, the *Place of Exile*, was renamed the *Never-Never*. Boyd used the term in 1882, but didn't originate it. It's the typical Aussie grab and slang. No offense."

Charlie shrugged.

Fosberg continued, his words flowing quicker and quicker. "It corresponds to the Icelandic *Nifl*, or what my ancestors called *Niflheim*. I found multiple references of two stones separated by a dozen seven-fold thousand cubits. There was a point, northward equally far from both. It formed a triangle—the *Apex of Providence*. They—" He stopped abruptly and sighed. "You don't believe me."

"Doesn't sound much like seismology."

"I became interested in the subject when my colleagues found the Beijing Anomaly. It dampens tremors, you see. A sea the size of the Arctic Ocean, but underground. That area is open. Hollow. And there's another one here. Our presence proves it."

"Back to that."

"I'm going to go see it. I want, *need*, you to go with me. I need your expertise."

Charlie pressed her palm to the false wall. Flakes slipped away that had been loosened by other hands. Hands that had struggled to blend this stone into its surroundings. Hands that wanted to keep her out. There was something special here. A hidden place.

She opened her pack and removed her equipment.

⊸⊷

They whittled away at the stone's mortar. From all sides, they chipped and scraped until they found the widest gap.

Charlie worked at a deep gouge in the mortar with her knife. She blew away loose silt. "Kristof, I'm through."

Fosberg dropped his tools and huddled close, his cheek against hers. "Do you see anything?"

"No, but feel."

He wiggled the blade about and pulled it back free. "Ten centimeters?"

"Just a shell compared to the capstone."

"We need a new approach."

"Go back to camp?" Charlie asked. "We can bring in tools and some more hands."

"That would take hours. I'm betting we can get it loose. Can you set an anchor in the ceiling?"

She eyed the distance. "Boost me up."

After some delicate balancing, she wedged in two tricams, locked a carabiner on each, and, following Fosberg's instructions, looped a line through. Together, they rolled a hundred-kilo stone before the wall, tied the line in place, and hoisted the stone off the ground.

"A pendulum," Fosberg said. "You see?"

The two of them pushed the stone high and released it. It arced downward and pounded into the seal's base.

Fosberg examined the point of impact. "A few more times."

Ten minutes later, her arms were numb. Fosberg couldn't have been doing any better, but he was too excited to stop. The stone slammed home again. The top of the seal buckled outward as the bottom shoved in.

"Yes!" Fosberg leapt about.

Weariness was forgotten. Another dozen drops and the seal pivoted top to bottom and crashed to the floor. Fosberg grabbed his camera and began snapping photos.

Charlie rubbed her forearms and inhaled the passage's draft, moist and fetid. The flash from Fosberg's camera strobed away. It slowed. It stopped. He let the camera rest against his chest.

The passage sloped away into darkness. Charlie moved closer and the light from her headlamp joined Fosberg's own. "Well?" she asked. "Are you set to—"

She'd had unnerving encounters before, but always when alone, far forward of any group. Once, in post-war *Abkhazia*, she'd been lowering herself down a chokingly tight chimney, deep in the back of the *Krubera* system. She was days away from the cave entrance. Nobody else had been that way; she just knew it. She was just gathering herself to wedge down lower, when something from below tugged at her leg.

Her normal response was to back out and call it a day. Act casual and blame overexertion for her loose imaginings. It wasn't worth mulling over.

Until this moment. Now every dubious encounter was racing back.

It sat a short jog ahead, a figure at the edge of the light, slumped forward in the center of the passage, its face turned toward them.

"Hello?" Fosberg actually talked to it.

Charlie grabbed Fosberg's elbow. He was trembling. He called out again. "Hello?"

The worst part was knowing that he saw it too. How was she supposed to justify this?

Fosberg slipped into the passage. Though he was a physical disappointment and a mediocre caver, he did have determination.

Charlie held herself tight and followed. Her footsteps were hollow, like the earth. *So absurd.* She clenched her teeth.

The man sat cross-legged. Time had reduced his body to little more than stiff leather with a shock of white hair. His only clothing was a twisted cord, bound about his waist. He clutched a long spear.

A flash. Fosberg's camera again.

"Look at that boomerang," he said. "Blue with white stars. He's a patriot." He chuckled and flashed away from other angles.

"Don't touch him," Charlie said.

"Oh, I won't. I—" Fosberg stared down the passage.

Charlie followed his gaze.

There was nothing there.

"I never doubted," Fosberg whispered. He grabbed Charlie's hand. "Ready?"

She squeezed back, not even considering avoiding his touch. Seeing the emptiness looming before her, there was nothing she wanted more than to know she wasn't alone. They walked to the edge together.

⊸

The radio crackled. "Anything?"

Charlie set her feet comfortably against the rock face and leaned back on the line. She grasped the radio about her neck. "No. I'm about to take another reading."

"Affirma—" Fosberg cut out. His voice whistled and snapped through the static. "—holding up?"

"I'm fine. Drop another line."

The radio was quiet. She tried again before switching channels.

"Dennis?" she called.

After a brief pause the radio answered, "Yeah, Buttercup?"

"Tell the doctor I'm out of line."

"Your wish is my command."

Team four had joined them in the two days since they'd found the pit. *The* pit. Nothing else even compared to this. Years ago, she'd visited the *Cave of Swallows*. It had been imposing, the jungle suddenly falling away into a shaft so deep and wide that it could be stuffed with ocean liners. Or *Son Doong*, wide enough to hold its own jungles. But they were just grot-holes compared to this. Empty a thimble of water into the ocean.

The ceiling sloped toward the far side, supposedly. The instruments lost track of it. Fosberg had Yileen bringing in a new shipment of surveying equipment. Some sort of military scopes used for locking howitzers on Chechens, Fosberg had joked. Twenty-kilometer range. Charlie didn't really consider that surveying.

She tied the line down, pulled her own rangefinder from her pack, and scanned the far wall. Nothing, of course. She did a slow arc to the right and back to the left. It had a 2000-meter distance, but she might as well have been scanning the moon. A quick check upward read a little over 1800 meters.

She did a brisk bit of math. "Dennis, let Kristof know I'm at 2525."

The radio clicked twice and answered. "Like the song?"

"What are you talking about?"

"Nothing. He wants you back up. They'll have the lift set up by the time—" Silence. "—sometime tomorrow?"

"I'm not setting records in an elevator."

The radio faded out and back in. "—see the bottom?"

"Give me a second."

She tucked the radio away and pulled loose a flare. Fosberg should have supplied magnesium, something that burned in water—but, too late now. She pulled the cap and struck the tip on the wall. Sparks hissed forth, rapidly building to a jet of red in a haze of pink-lit smoke, making the forward wall look like a slab of meat. The stench of sulfur covered the ever-increasing swampiness from below.

Charlie wiped the sweat from her face.

"I see you," Dennis said over the radio. "—a speck."

She held the flare straight to the side and released. It tumbled downward and bounced off the wall, spotlighting the surface in a ball of light. As the wall receded, the flare tumbled through empty space. It faded to a spark. It was gone.

"Seven-second drop," Charlie called.

"Seven?" Dennis said. "Uh... hold on." After an interminable wait. "That jibes. Doc says—" The radio faded. "Two hundred—"

One more time. She couldn't turn back now.

"Send another bundle. I really need it."

The supply line next to her rustled upward.

The radio chirped and Dennis came through again. "In motion."

⟜

Charlie fastened multiple anchors at strategic points. Two for her own line and another two for the supply. She ran doubled webbing between each with a twist and clip. Standard technique. If one anchor failed, her line would still be secured by the second.

After a half-hour wait, the supply line returned, two massive coils of rope knotted at its end. Her hands shook as she made the attachments and lowered the ropes down. She stilled herself and breathed slowly. Mustn't lose focus now.

Once she was latched into position, she tried Fosberg again.

"I'm going now." She waited for the response. There was none. She might as well tell him while he couldn't argue. "The surface concaves. It's a free pitch from here on. It'll take a long while to climb back, so... be patient."

She checked her harness and the descender one last time. There was a rattle from the radio. She turned it off and kicked away from the surface.

Absolute nothing.

To all sides a blackness pressed in with a physicality. She couldn't even tell if her headlamp was on. There was nothing to illuminate.

Trying to lower steadily wasn't easy. With the air so humid and slick, the rope wanted to slip. She leaned back and increased the angle to compensate for the lack of friction. The halfway point of the line drifted past.

She could hear it now. With each measured descent, it drew closer. Lapping. There was a soft rhythm to it, like waves along the beach. She'd get a little closer and touch it. She'd dip her toes into the River Lethe and forget life's problems.

Suspended in a cloud, floating down like a lost angel, her headlamp traced out a glowing cone. She tried another reading, but it was difficult to get a bead on the ceiling. The rangefinder was nearing its maximum and the mist scattered the beam. She'd just have to mark the end of the rope and calculate it later.

She tried to pace her descent, but the rope slipped. Liquid wrung over her gloves and down her arm. She was sliding faster and faster, her pulse accelerating with her speed. Did she stop-knot the end? She couldn't have forgotten such a thing.

God! To fall off—to spill into the earth.

The air thickened. Charlie kicked her leg out and around, looping the lower line against herself, and leaned back hard.

She slammed to a stop and warmth flowed up and over her.

She lay very still, gasping in shock as much as in confusion. Her hands stung. The whole world tilted so that it felt as if she were standing, and then lying, and then tipping with her toes in the air. Somehow, she managed to prop herself up on her elbows. A viscous liquid ran down her face.

Take slow breaths.

She brushed her cheek and studied her fingers. It wasn't blood. Thank you.

She was in a pool, a handwidth deep and crystal clear. Her impact hadn't even raised any sediment. The waters were tepid and feather-light. She turned her head left and right. There was no end. A glassy sea extended in all directions. Her stomach lurched.

There was no floor below the waters, just a blackness that went on without end.

Charlie flipped to her hands and knees and stared downward. Water dripped from her soaked clothes. Of course there was a bottom, but it was as black as onyx. The abyss at the bottom of the world. She pressed downward and it yielded like wet clay. When she pulled her hands back, her prints stayed, but only for a moment. They smoothed to a perfect flatness.

She stood, untangled the line from her leg, and pulled it loose from her harness.

"Hello, Dennis?" she called out over the radio. "I'm—"

Here, victorious, afraid?

Something wasn't right. She turned to a different channel. That familiar crackle of activity was gone. Shorted out by the waters, no doubt. Just great.

Her lips were salty.

"The Sea of Charlotte." She smiled. This could never be taken away.

After drying her camera lens, she took a few pictures. She tried to take a step but her feet wouldn't move. They were ankle deep in the clay.

The muck sucked noisily at her shoes. With a cry, she wrenched one foot free, and then the other. Her footprints shrank and flattened even as she began to sink again.

Enough of this. They must be going crazy up there. She needed to get out of the mist and try a flare—hopefully they were still good. Dennis would pick that up and relay her state back to Fosberg and the others. It would be a tedious climb with the line so slippery, but she could do it. She turned to the rope.

It was gone.

She spun left and right.

She hadn't moved from where she'd landed. The rope had been right at her feet. There had been at least ten meters of slack. The supply line had been here too, just off to the side. She shuffled about, aiming her light in all directions.

Finally, she saw it, overhead. On her toes, she could just touch it with fingertips, but knifed into the seafloor from the effort. She reset her stance. Now the line was out of reach.

"Are you joking?" She stretched higher, but without luck. "What are you doing!"

She yanked her feet free again and tore her pack from her back. After dropping it into the waters, she stepped on it, trying not to think how she was going to do this without equipment. She leapt up and seized the line with both hands.

It might as well have been soaked in oil. It had been directly in the waters; its every fiber dripped with the stuff. She slipped back to the bottom, only that final knot giving her purchase. Now she was even higher above the waters. They were still pulling the rope from above, but she couldn't hold on—not like this.

"Stop!" she screamed up into the mists, the darkness. "I can't—"

She tumbled back into the sea.

⊸

It had been hours. Charlie turned off her lamp to conserve battery. Her supplies were gone, buried in the clay. Though she made nervous attempts to dig down, she couldn't find the point from where she'd jumped. Who knew how far her equipment had sunk by this time?

She sat in the waters with her legs stretched flat before her to slow the sinking. Every ten minutes she moved.

Shift to another spot. Listen to the waves slosh. Wait.

She tilted her head back and stared into emptiness.

⊸

She awoke with a start. Dozing should have been impossible, but with the exhaustion of the climb and the stress, she'd done it. She tried to sit up, but couldn't budge. Curiosity turned to horror. She'd sunk down to her waist.

Echoless screams. She clawed at the surface, raking away clay in handfuls. She was just starting to make real progress when a touch brushed her face.

The tension at her brow told her that her eyes were wide open, but in this void that meant nothing.

Again, a slow motion, tracing down to her lips.

She reached up to her headlamp. As she debated whether she really wanted to see what lived down here, it touched her neck. She lashed out with both hands and wrung it tight. Her body seized, like she'd caught herself from falling. She flicked on her lamp.

It was the rope, hanging down from the mists. She pulled hard, kicking against the bottom until she had tugged herself free. Her body shook. The end of the rope was at the sea's surface. What kind of game were they playing?

She fed the line back through her harness and tied it off. The last fifty meters had been slick, but—she gave a test pull—she could do it. A little less than two hundred meters straight up. She'd climb as high as she could and then wrap the line around herself to rest. Once she—

The seabed shook. Charlie looked down. The place where she'd freed herself wasn't sealing; it was a twisting gouge in the clay's surface. From its deepest edge, an iridescent film bubbled up and over the waters.

She threw herself at the line and yanked herself upward.

The sea rippled in long waves and the mist thinned. Charlie clawed higher. It wasn't easy; she had to clench tight. She wound the line around her leg to increase the friction. Her forearms ached, but she didn't falter. One hand above the other, pull, wrap the leg, and reverse the hands.

As the line swayed, she saw the waves, much taller than before, spaced farther apart. She kept her ascent steady and quick. The line was drier now and she was able to pull hard, yet the sea's surface wasn't that far below her feet. The crests of the waves surged to the height of houses before crashing back over each other in a roar of spray, each pass taller than the last.

Her foot was briefly submerged. She redoubled her efforts.

She raced upward at a reckless speed, but it didn't seem to matter. Each following wave caught her higher. Now it passed by at her knees. She was slipping.

The next wave submerged her. She spit and choked as it receded. Quickly wrapping the line about her wrists, she tried to climb again. It was no good. Another wave hit her.

"Got you! Up, up!"

It was a blur of motion. Hands pulled at her and she was lying on cold metal. A clank and shift, and she was rising above the waves. She coughed and sputtered. Fosberg knelt beside her.

"I'm so sorry," he said.

"No, I—" Charlie wheezed and forced herself to her knees. "I almost didn't make it."

"You didn't."

A deep reverberation swelled from below. It wasn't the tides; it was something much bigger.

"What are you—"

"Nobody's walking away from this," Fosberg said. "The others ran off, as if that would help. But I couldn't leave you."

"They . . . ran? What—"

"I evacuated the climb. We were going to get you with the lift, see? But when they saw. When I realized—"

Fosberg sobbed and shook his head.

"Kristof, I don't understand."

"Look."

They were almost high enough to lose sight of the waves. The crests of each just caught the little light that reached so far.

A deep rumble wrapped about them, its intensity swelling. Charlie pressed her hands over her ears. Fosberg fell to the platform and pulled at her arm. She could just make out his words.

"Hold on!"

It swept across the sea from the north. A glittering surface that sliced the waves into nothing. Charlie gripped the grated floor as the lift careened back and forth, tipping ominously. From the south, an identical surface approached.

"No." She clutched tight and wept.

They connected with a crack like thunder. Charlie could feel the impact within her, shaking her bones. She had never felt so small.

A blink. The lids receded from a sea of tears.

Kristof spoke softly at her ear. "The Eye of Providence."

⊸

The quakes were everywhere now. No one knew how many people had been lost along the world's coasts. Hundred of millions was the estimate—such optimism. The entire Ring of Fire had erupted. Pacifica was only a memory.

"I don't trust this architecture," Fosberg said. "Loose building codes."

Many of the older structures in the city had already collapsed.

"The radio says the Yellowstone Caldera erupted," Fosberg continued. "It was much bigger than they thought." He leaned back in his chair and looked out from the balcony at the jagged peaks of the Andes. "So much for those fellows. Sad, I would love to study the data. Another?"

"Sure," Charlie said.

They had stocked up on food and alcohol after arriving in *La Rinconada*, right before things really started to get bad. At five kilometers above sea level, the view would be great. There wasn't much to do now other than sit back and enjoy the altitude—while there was one.

Fosberg choked on a stale cigar. He stubbed it out. "Didn't miss much with that habit."

"You're celebrating," Charlie said.

"I am not. I just wanted... to know." Fosberg gasped and scratched furiously with his pencil at a pad of paper. "*Níðhöggr* chewing at the roots of *Yggdrasill*, coiled about the *Tree of Knowledge*. Thus ends Eden. *Ragnarök*. Of course!"

"I guess." She thought she might understand his point, but didn't feel like saying it.

The ground shook again.

Charlie had thought about warning her family, getting them out too, but Fosberg made a good argument against it. They were better where they were. It would end quicker, less drawn out. By coming here, the two of them were volunteering for much worse, but they were too curious not to.

"Maybe we deserve it," Charlie said.

"Perhaps." Fosberg took a slow swallow from his beer. "I wish I would have learned to dance."

"I can show you some steps, if we have time."

"Thank you. I'd like that."

"Wish I could have gotten Yileen to come with us."

When they finally reached the surface, Yileen had been sitting cross-legged at the edge of the pit. Charlie gave him the boomerang. She didn't know why she had picked it up, but she was glad she did. Yileen studied it in his lap, but didn't say anything.

"I don't think he wanted to go," Fosberg said. He turned quickly and dashed back into the hotel room.

Charlie popped the cap from her own beer and held the bottle against her forehead.

Southeastern Algeria had been shaken into gravel. Fosberg claimed that was the tail end of it.

Jörmungandr was known by many other names: *Uroboros*, *Borlung*, *Yurlunggur*. A serpent of immense size from the Old Norse, the Aboriginal, the Hindu, the Egyptian, and so many other cultures.

The Rainbow Serpent. Once, long ago, everyone had known it was there, though they now told themselves it was only a story. But every tale, no matter how fantastic, holds a little truth.

"Snakes don't have eyelids."

"Snakes?" Fosberg sat down again beside her. "More of a legless lizard, I'd say. And here she is!"

It was a moonrise, rising up past scores of horizons, half a world away. A single eye with a shimmering rainbow body trailing behind. Oceans and fire flowed in its wake, into the upper atmosphere, and so much farther. The shattered remains of a continent showered ever upward.

"We'll heal. Give it ten thousand millennia or so. Life will try again."

Charlie drank deeply. Maybe she should go chisel a warning on a cave wall.

PERSISTENCE OF VISION

ORRIN GREY

I want you to act like this is all a movie. That'll make it easier.

If it was a movie, it would open with darkness. No credits, no titles, just a black screen that you stare into waiting for something to appear, waiting for the darkness to resolve into a picture. Instead, there's a voice reciting familiar words: "911, what is your emergency?"

Then another voice; a woman, crying, terrified: "There's a man in my house. He's in my bedroom."

"Are you in a safe place?"

"Now he's in the living room. He's in whatever room I go into. He's standing in the corner, pointing at me. He's talking, but I can't hear what he's saying."

At this point, you'd get the titles.

⤙o⤚

It wasn't the first 911 call. No one knows what the first one was. There's no way to separate it out from the others, even if anyone had wanted to. There's no way to draw the line and say, "This is the first real one. All the ones before this were just hoaxes, crazy people, misunderstandings." And then there's the question, of course, about how many of the ones before *were* crazy people, hoaxes? How long had it been going on, before we even knew?

And once it started, it took everyone so long to figure it out, because how do you figure something like that out? What do you do with that call, the one that played there in the dark, when the police and the EMTs arrive and find the woman crammed under her couch somehow, huddled up there like a frightened cat, dead from shock, the phone still gripped to her ear, the house otherwise deserted? What do you do with the call from a college kid who says that his fiancée went into the closet and never came out? When you look in the closet and find that it's maybe two feet square, just enough room for some clothes and the vacuum cleaner and no place for a person to go? You dismiss them at first, of course. You take the kid into custody, notify the woman's next of kin. But after a while, there are too many. After a while, people are no longer calling 911. After a while, the phones don't work anymore, and when you pick them up all you hear is voices, hundreds of them piled atop one another, all whispering your name.

⟜

If this was a movie, we'd have to have some kind of song playing over the opening credits, right? Something at once unexpected and appropriate. Not Johnny Cash, because Zach Snyder's *Dawn of the Dead* remake beat us to that punch, and besides, "The Man Comes Around" isn't quite right. So let's go just one step to the side, and get Nick Cave and company singing Dylan's "Death Is Not the End."

And while the music plays, there'd be snippets of footage in the background. Stuff from security cameras, blurry cell phone videos, clips of news shows. You'd see hands coming out of a shadow where a light was just shining, showing an empty corner. You'd see a window filling with bloody handprints. You'd see a girl, being pulled into what looks like a solid wall, sliding up it, into the ceiling. Someone is running, holding the camera. The door is just a few feet away, and they look behind themselves, turning the camera with their gaze, and there's nothing behind them to be afraid of, but as they turn back the door is gone, bricked up in those few half-seconds, and then you hear a scream, and the camera goes to static.

Yeah, that's the opening credits.

⟜

The trick, when you're trying to compress any story into a couple of hours, is how to handle the exposition so it's not so clumsy. We'd want to avoid a text crawl or an opening narrator, because those are old-fashioned; reserved, nowadays, for more epic films, or things that purport to be "based on a true story." And while we want verisimilitude here, we also want to distance you from what's happening. That's kind of the point. Hence the song, right?

If this was an indie film, or something from overseas, we'd probably not give you any exposition at all right away. You'd just get dropped into the middle of the action, and you wouldn't have any idea what was going on. Just like in real life. Nobody knew what was happening. Most people died without ever knowing, they explained it whatever way they had to, or no way at all. There were street-corner preachers and politicians alike saying that it was God's judgment, there were cults that sprang up in the last days. There were people who were trying to give it some kind of scientific explanation—hallucinogens and black holes—even as the walls were bleeding and doorknobs were disappearing under the sweaty grasps of desperate hands. Outside my window, someone had spray-painted across the side of an office building, "Now 'tis the very witching hour of night, when churchyards yawn and hell itself breathes out contagion." It seemed as good an explanation as any, at the time.

The studios wouldn't stand for that, though, so your protagonist would be someone who worked at the facility. Or maybe someone who was married to someone who worked at the facility. Someone like me.

(I'm lying to myself, of course. If Hollywood had the purse strings, we wouldn't be married, we'd be dating. And fifteen years younger. And our genders would be flipped, so that I was the one working at the facility and she was the one at home, tapping out movie reviews on her laptop in the kitchen window. We probably also wouldn't be in Montreal, but hey, maybe. They're filming more and more movies in Toronto these days, or they were, back when they were still filming movies.)

Maybe she'd tell me about the project in the evenings, over plates of spaghetti, like she really did. Or maybe she'd keep it all secret from me, but I'd read some notes or something, after the whole thing started. One way or the other, I'd discover how they found the machine in a bricked-up basement underneath an abandoned insane asylum. (The studios would love that!) They thought it was some kind of computer, maybe one of the first computers ever built. Not really a computer at all as we know them today, but something more like a difference engine, like the ones Turing worked on. All brass and levers and numbered keys, like a cross between some kind of ancient cash register and a pipe organ. All the project was ever supposed to do was to see what this thing did, what it was. This was going to be a big break in the history of computing, but, instead, it was the end of the history of anything.

They knew that something was wrong the minute they started the machine. There wasn't some slow build-up, it all happened at once. When they turned it on, there was a wave of poltergeist activity that swept out from the machine throughout the entire lab, across the river, and through all of Montreal. Every table and chair in the lab was shoved against the wall farthest from the machine. In the lunchroom a few floors up, chairs and tables overturned, plates slid off shelves to smash on the floor. Silverware magnetized. Every electronic device in the building shut down, and the entire city suffered a massive power failure.

In our apartment, all the doors slammed shut simultaneously, and the handful of VHS tapes that I still had in a box under the entertainment centre all melted.

Things went to shit from there.

Following on the heels of the poltergeist activity, so close behind it that no one in the lab had even reacted, the ectoplasm began to materialize out of the valves of the machine, flowing down the sides, forming a sort of barrier around it, something that shimmered and moved almost like water. Nobody in the lab had any idea what it was then, of course, but the first one who touched it died instantly. His hair turned white, he fell to the floor choking and slapping at his chest. By the time anyone else got to him, he'd ossified, and there were hundreds of spiders crawling out of his mouth and nose.

⊸⊙⊷

In the movie version, the machine would have been the heart of everything. Its destruction would have been the end of the film, the salvation of mankind. That makes for a better ending, sends the folks in Peoria home happy. In real life, though, the machine was just the key that turned the lock. Once the door was open, there was no closing it.

They did manage to destroy the machine, eventually, and when they did, they found a corpse in the middle of it. The mummified body, hooked to thousands of copper wires, of a woman named Katrina Something, the rest of the name illegible, a powerful physical medium, born 1899, died 1916. We only know any of that because there was a plaque on the inside of her abstract coffin that told us.

By then, the handful of people who were left from the facility had figured out sort of what the machine did. Or, at least, what it *had* done. By then, almost everyone had kind of figured it out. Everyone knew, at least, what was happening, even if a lot of them didn't give it a name. Some did, though. The Internet, when it still worked, came to our rescue, prepared to turn anything, even the end of the world, into a kind of meme. They called it the Ghost Apocalypse.

It's funny, in a way, because we had all been culturally preparing for the dead to come kill us for years by then. We just expected it to be their bodies, not their restless spirits. We had zombie apocalypse survival guides, and over on the US side of things the CDC supposedly had a disaster plan for a zombie outbreak. Nobody had a plan for ghosts, and they proved a lot harder to deal with than zombies because, frankly, nobody knew how they worked. You couldn't lay them to rest or settle their unfinished business, destroy the fetters that bound them to this mortal plane. They were pouring through now, this was their world. And you certainly couldn't just shoot them in the head. Sometimes they already didn't have a head. Sometimes they were just a voice, or a shape, or a cold draft, or the elevator door suddenly closing on you no matter what you did, and then the rest of the elevator dropping twenty-seven stories to the underground parking garage, killing everyone on board.

We only had one movie that predicted this. Well, two if you count the remake. It was *Kairo* in Japan in 2001, *Pulse* in the US in 2006, during the height of the J-horror boom, starring that girl from *Veronica Mars* and that guy from *Lost*. Well-known prognosticators of the end of the world.

(Did *Ghostbusters* and *Ghostbusters 2* predict a kind of ghost apocalypse, albeit one staved off, twice-over, by a more Hollywood-friendly happy ending? Maybe a little bit.)

It was from *Pulse* that we got the idea that saved those few of us who got saved long enough to see what a world was like populated mainly by the dead. Some kid figured it out, disseminated it on Reddit and everywhere else. After most of the power went down, people started spreading the news with hand-lettered flyers written on red paper.

It wasn't just red tape, like in the movie, though that was a great touch, guys. It was red *anything*. Something about the colour red kept them out. Some people speculated it was a spectrum thing, that ghosts were some kind of light or energy themselves, and that the red spectrum disrupted them somehow. Others thought that red was the colour of life, of blood and the heart and human passion. That maybe it reminded ghosts of mortality, or that it protected those who still pulsed with living blood and heat. People brave enough to do research in the big, abandoned, spooky libraries full of books that floated off the shelves or opened themselves up to thematically relevant passages turned up records of Victorian-era "ghost traps" that were just red-painted rooms, or even containers with red interiors, designed to cage spooks.

Whatever the proof of it, it seemed to work, and so those of us who survived did so by painting the insides of everything red. Red walls, red floors, red ceilings. Painting over windows. When paint wasn't at hand, we used red paper, red markers, even red ballpoint pens, though those didn't work so well, it turned out.

From inside our red rooms we sent out parties dressed in red clothes to try to bring back food, fresh water, more paint. Most of them didn't return.

That's not a very good Hollywood ending, is it? All of us sitting in our red rooms, waiting to get picked off one by one and join the ranks of our oppressors? What they don't tell you about surviving the apocalypse is that it's really not worth it. Everyone you care about is probably dead, there's nothing fun left to do, and not a whole lot to live for. With the zombie apocalypse or whatever, at least you'd have some hope, however naïve. You could imagine a cure being found, or the zombies eventually all just rotting, if only you could outlast them. What are you supposed to do when the dead really do come back, though, and not just their carcasses? What's the endgame on *that*? They're not going to rot, get bored, go away. They're not going to sleep, or die again. There's nothing left to do, except delay the point at which they get you, a line of hopeless desperation that stretches out forever into the horizon, like a hallway in a Kubrick film.

⊸

I'm not going to tell you how Georgiana died. That was her name, though everyone just called her Georgie, me included. If this was a movie, you'd see it. If this was a movie, and I was the protagonist, *I* would have seen it. It would have been dramatic, would have happened at some climactic moment. I would have been there, inches away from saving her, clutching at her hand as her fingers were pulled from mine, one by one. But this isn't a movie, and that's not how it happened.

I'm not going to tell you how she died, because I don't know. I wasn't there. Am I even sure that she's dead? Well, I'm pretty sure. One of her co-workers told me she was gone. Those were his words, "Georgie's gone," just before he himself was gone, pulled around a corner and just *gone*, the hallway empty for a hundred feet in both directions.

I didn't give up on her, even then. I went out looking, after the first of the red rooms got put up. In my red clothes, red hood pulled up, I went searching like I was on my way to Grandmother's house. And maybe I finally found her, or she found me. I don't really know, not for sure, not anymore.

I won't tell you how she died, but I will tell you this. One last bit, and maybe it'll make for a better ending. I still go outside to smoke. How crazy is that, right? But I don't see any reason to quit anymore, and sometimes it's worth maybe being dragged down into a storm drain, or disappearing into the street, or just suddenly turning white and weeping blood. Sometimes I just want to be outside again, and there's no death horrible enough to make staying in that goddamned closed-up red room worth it for even one more minute.

On nights like that, I go out behind the building where we've been staying—it used to be a hospital, we painted up an entire wing—and I smoke a cigarette while I look out over the river. And lately, every time, I see Georgie there, standing on the edge of the water. I know that it's her, even though I can't really see her face. I'd know her in a crowd, by now, from the way she stands, the way her hair falls. I've seen her against the back of my eyelids every day since she was gone, and I'd know her backward, blindfolded. I know that it's her, and I know what she wants. Not to drag me away, not like the others, not yet. Give her time, maybe. For now, though, she just wants me to follow her. To go willingly into that good night. To grind out my cigarette and walk down into the freezing water of the St. Lawrence. And I know, as surely as I know any of this, that one night soon, I will.

Roll credits.

IT FLOWS FROM THE MOUTH

ROBERT SHEARMAN

I'd been flattered when asked to be the godfather of little Ian Wheeler, of course, but I'd had certain misgivings. When I'd met up with Max in the pub, something we'd liked to do regularly back then, I'd tried to explain at least part of the problem. "Oh, don't worry about the whole spiritual adviser nonsense," said Max. "Lisa's no more religious than I am, this is just to keep her parents happy." So I caved in, and went along to the christening, and watched Ian get dipped into a font, and afterwards posed for photographs in which I must admit I passed myself off quite successfully as someone just as proud and doting as the actual father and mother.

But my real concern had nothing to do with any religious aspect, and more with the discomfort of shackling myself for life to a person I had no reason to believe I would ever necessarily like. I'd had enough problems when Max started dating Lisa—Max and I had been inseparable since school, and now suddenly I was supposed to welcome Lisa into the gang, and want to spend time with her, and chat to her, and buy lager and lime for her—and it wasn't that I *disliked* Lisa, not as such, though she was a bit dull and she wore too much perfume and I had nothing to talk to her about and she had a face as dozy as a stupefied cow. It was more that she had barged her way into a special friendship, with full expectation that I'd not only tolerate the intrusion but welcome it. She never asked if I minded. She never apologised.

And so it was with little Ian. I'm not saying he was a bad child. It was simply that he was a child at all. I'd never been wild about children, not even when I had been one, and I had always been under the impression that Max had felt the same, and I'd felt rather surprised that he wanted one. Surprised and, yes, disappointed. But then, Max had done lots of things that had surprised me since he'd met Lisa. And my worst fears came to be realised. On the few occasions I went to visit, I would be presented before Ian, as if he were a prince, and every little new thing about him was pointed out to me as if I should be entranced—that he had teeth, or that he could walk, that he'd grown an inch taller—sometimes I was under the impression I was supposed to give the kid a round of applause, as if these weren't all things that I myself had mastered with greater skill years ago! I just couldn't warm to my godson. It seemed to me that he was constantly demanding attention, and I could put up with that if it was only his mother he was bothering, but all too often he'd pull the same stunts on Max. Still, I tried to be dutiful, and at Christmas and on birthdays I would send Ian a present. But is it any wonder he made me uncomfortable?—this infant who had crept into my life, though his birth was none of my doing, though his existence wasn't my fault. With his strangely fat face and his cheeks always puffed out as if he were getting ready to cry. I played godfather the best I could, but I felt a fraud.

When Ian was killed at the age of three, knocked down by a car (and safely within the speed limit, so the driver could hardly be blamed), I was, of course, horrified. The death of a child is a terrible thing, and I'm not a monster. But if a child was going to have to die, then I'm glad it was Ian.

Max and I had always been rather unlikely friends, or so I was told: at school he was more popular than I was, more sporty, more outgoing. I suspect people thought he was good for me, that's what my mother said, and I resented that—I'd point out that, in spite of appearances, he was the one who had sought me out, who wanted to sit next to me in class, who waited to walk home with me. I'd been there for him when he failed his French O-levels, when he got dumped by the cricket first XI, when he first smoked, drank, snogged. I'd been best man at his wedding to Lisa, and I'd arranged a very nice stag night in a Greek restaurant, and given at the reception a speech that made everybody laugh. And I tried to be there for Max when Ian died. We'd meet up at the pub, at first it was just like the good old days! And I'd get in a round. How was he feeling? "Not so good, matey," he'd say, and stare into the bottom of his pint. "Not so good."

We drifted apart. And I'm sorry. I would have been a good friend if he had wanted me to be. But he didn't want me to be.

Max and Lisa sold their house and moved up north. We exchanged Christmas cards for a couple of years. In the last one, Max told me they were moving again, this time overseas. He promised he would write to me with his new address. He didn't.

One evening I was at home reading in my study when there was a phone call. "Hello? Is that you, John?" The number was withheld, and so I'm afraid I gave a rather stiff affirmation. "It's Max. You remember, your old friend Max? Don't you recognise me?"

And I did recognise him then, of course; and he sounded like the old Max, the one who'd call me every evening and ask for help with his homework, the one who always had a trace of laughter in his voice.

He told me he was down in the city for a "work thing," and the firm had given him a hotel for the night. "Would you like to meet up on Thursday?" he said. "We could go to the pub. No problem if it's too short notice. But we could go to the pub."

It was rather short notice, to be fair, but I didn't want to let Max down.

The pub was heaving with businessmen, it was just after the banks had shut, and the pub Max had chosen was right in the financial district. And I felt a sudden stab of discomfort—what if I couldn't remember what Max looked like? What if I couldn't tell him apart from all these other smart suits? (What if he couldn't remember me?) But he'd arrived first, and he was guarding a small table in the corner, and I knew him at once, he really hadn't changed a bit. He was standing up, and laughing, and gesticulating wildly to catch my attention. No, I was wrong—he *had* changed, a bit, just a bit, actually—as I got closer I could see he'd put on some weight, and his hair was grey. But I'm sure just the same could be said of me, I'm sure that's true, I'm not as young as I was, though I try to keep myself trim, you know? I stuck out my hand for him to shake, and he laughed at that, he was laughing at everything. And he pulled me into a hug, and that was nice.

"What are you drinking?" was the first thing he said. "My round, I'll get the drinks."

We stayed rather late that night, and we had a lot of beer, and I suppose we got quite drunk. But that was all right. For a while we had to shout over the crowd to make ourselves heard, and that was a bit awkward, but pretty soon all the bankers began to go home to their wives and left us in peace. He asked me what I was up to these days, and I explained it the best I could, and my answers seemed to delight him and he laughed even more. I asked him how long he would be in England.

"Oh, we've moved back now," he said. "Mum's dying, I wanted to be close. Well, not too close. But the same country is good. Back over last year, sorry, should have been in touch."

I told him that it didn't matter, he was home now, he'd found me now—and I expressed some sympathy for his mother, I remember quite liking her, when I went to Max's house she'd give me biscuits.

"We've got this lovely house in the countryside," Max said. "A mansion, really. Almost a mansion. And the garden's fantastic. Lisa has been designing that, but of course, no surprises there!" I wondered why it was no surprise, I wondered whether Lisa was famous for designing gardens, I supposed she might have been. It was the first time he'd mentioned Lisa, and I said I was glad they were still married.

We shared anecdotes about our schooldays, some of the ones Max told me I had no memory of whatsoever, so they were quite fresh and exciting. I asked him how Lisa was, and he said she was well. I didn't bring up Ian at all, and I felt a bit bad about that—but then, Max didn't bring up Ian either, the evening was mercifully free of dead children.

I said I'd walk him back to his hotel.

"You should come and stay," he said to me as we walked the streets. He hung on to my arm. It was raining, and Max didn't seem to notice, and I didn't care. "Come and stay this weekend. It'd be lovely to see you properly. And I know Lisa would just love to have you." Before I knew it he was all over me with practical details—the best train I could catch, that they'd pick me up from the station. I said I wasn't available the next weekend, I was too busy—I wasn't as it happens, but I still didn't want him to think he could just swan his way back into my life and be instantly forgiven. I promised to come up the weekend after.

Now, I am aware that I don't come out of the following story too well. I can't pretend I understand more than a fraction of what happened when I visited Max, so I'll just tell it the best I can, warts and all. And I think you'll accept that the circumstances were very strange, and perhaps, to an extent, extenuating.

⊸o⊷

Max met me at the station in his car. I asked if it were a new car, and he smiled, and said it was. Then we drove to his house through the rolling countryside, and he talked about his new car all the way. He'd said that he lived somewhere conveniently situated for occasional commutes into London, but I'm glad I hadn't got a taxi, the drive was half an hour at least.

Lisa was standing in the driveway to welcome us. I wondered how long she had been standing there. I had been concerned she might remember that I had often shown her a very slight resentment, but she gave no indication of it. She smiled widely enough when I got out of the car, she opened her arms a little in what might have been the beginnings of a hug. I didn't risk it, I offered her my hand. She accepted the hand, laid hers in mine like it was a delicacy, gave a little curtsey, tittered. I still didn't like her very much.

I had to admit, she looked better than I'd expected. Some women grow into their faces, do you know what I mean? They just age well, their eyes take on a certain wisdom, maybe, they just look a bit more dignified. (Whereas I have never known that to be true of men—we just get older: flabbier or bonier, it's never better.) I had always likened Lisa to a cow, and it wasn't as if she had totally thrown that bovine quality off, but the fleshier parts of her face that I had once dismissed as pure farmyard now had a certain lustre. She was beautiful. There was a beauty to her. That's what it was, and I was surprised to see it.

At first I couldn't see why Max had referred to his house as a mansion. It wasn't especially grand at all—bigger than my house in the city, of course, but you'd expect that in the styx. They showed me their kitchen, and the stone aga that took up a whole half of the space. They showed me the lounge, the too-big dining table, the too-big fireplace. I made the right sort of approving noises, and Max beamed with pride as if I were his favourite schoolmaster giving him a good report card.

"Let me show John the garden!" said Lisa. "Quickly, before the light fades!" And she was excited, impatient.

And now I understood the use of that word "mansion"—because though the house was unremarkable, the gardens at the back were huge. "It's just shy of two acres," boasted Max, and I could well believe it, it seemed to stretch off into the distance, I couldn't see an end to it. But it wasn't merely the size that was impressive—on its own, the size was an anomaly, a vast tract of land that had no business attaching itself to a house so small, like tiny Britain owning the whole of India. What struck me was the design of the thing, that it was truly *designed*, there was honest-to-God method in the placing of all those shrubs and hedges, the garden was laid out before us like a fully composed work of art. Even in the winter, the flowers not yet in bloom and the grass looking somewhat sorry for itself, the sight still took my breath away.

"I did all the landscaping myself," said Lisa. "It was a hobby." We walked on pebbled paths underneath archways of green fern. One day the paths would lead to big beds of flowers—"I've planted three thousand bulbs of grape hyacinth," Lisa told me, "and, behind that, three thousand of species tulip—so, in the spring, there'll be this sea of blue crashing on to a shore of yellows, and reds, and greens! You'll have to come back in the spring." And every archway opened out to another little garden, different flowers seeded, but placed in ever-winding patterns; there was a topiary, there was even a faux maze: the design was intricate enough, I could see, but the hedges were still four feet tall, only a little child could have got lost in there.

And then, through another archway, and Lisa and Max led me to a pond. There was no water in the pond yet, this was still a work in progress. And, standing in the middle of the pond, raised high on a plinth, a statue of an angel—grey, stone, a fountain spout sticking out of its open mouth.

The wings were furled, somewhat apologetically even, as if the angel wasn't sure how to use them. Its face was of a young cherub, and I stared at it, trying to identify it—it seemed familiar, and I wondered what painting I'd seen that had inspired it, was it Raphael, maybe, or Michelangelo?

"It's Ian," said Max helpfully. And I had a bit of a shock at that. But now I could see it, of course—the infant hands, body, feet; the strangely fat face; those puffed-out cheeks he had always had, now puffed out in anticipation he'd be gushing forth a jet of water.

"We gave a photograph of him to a sculptor," said Lisa. "Local man. Charming man. Excellent craftsman. Can you see the detail in that?"

"This way," said Max, "it's like Ian is always here, watching over us."

I said I could see the effect they were aiming for. And I couldn't help it, I actually laughed, just for a moment—I remembered that nasty, sulky godson of mine, and thought how unlikely an angel he would have made. If there's an afterlife, and I have no reason to believe in one, God wouldn't have made Ian Wheeler an angel, he wouldn't have wasted the feathers on him. And I thought too of how, had he lived, he'd be a teenager, or nearly a teenager?—if he were still about by now he'd be even nastier and sulkier. Instead here he was, preserved as a three-year-old, forever in stone, with wings sprouting from under his armpits.

I apologised for laughing. "No, no," said Lisa. "The fountain of remembrance is supposed to make you happy."

We went back to the house. Lisa had prepared us a stew. "Only peasant stock, I'm afraid!" she said. The meat was excellent, and I complimented her on it. She told me it was venison. We opened the bottle of wine I had brought, and disposed of it quickly; then Max got up and fetched another bottle that was, I have to admit, rather better.

After we had eaten we settled ourselves comfortably in the lounge. Max took the armchair, which left me and Lisa rubbing arms together on the sofa. Max smiled, stretched lazily. "I like being the lord of the manor!" he said.

"It suits you very well!" said Lisa, and I agreed.

They placed another log on the fire, and we felt safely protected from the winter outside. But I thought there was still not much warmth to the room. It felt impersonal somehow, as if it were the waiting room for an expensive doctor, or the lobby of a hotel. It was neat and ordered, but there were no nick-nacks to suggest anyone actually lived there. No photographs on the mantelpiece.

There were more anecdotes of our childhood, and Lisa listened politely, and sometimes even managed to insinuate herself into them as if she had been part of our story all along. The wine was making me drowsy, so I didn't mind too much.

I said how happy I was they were back in England.

"Oh, so are we!" said Max, quite fervently. "Australia was all well and good, you know, but it's not like home. You can only run away from your past for so long." It was the only time Max had ever suggested he had run away at all, and Lisa frowned at him; he noticed, and winked, quite benignly, and the subject was changed.

"It's a lovely community," said Lisa. "There are village shops only ten minutes' walk from here, they have everything you really need. The church is just over the hill. And the local people are so kind, and so very like-minded."

At length Max did his lord of the manor stretch again, and smiled, and said that he had to go to bed soon. "Church tomorrow," he said, "got to be up nice and early."

"Max does the readings," said Lisa. "He's very good. He has such a lovely reading voice. What is it tomorrow, darling?"

"Ephesians."

"I like the way you do Ephesians."

I expressed some surprise that Max had found religion.

"Oh, all things lead to God," said Max. "It was hard, but I found my way back to His care."

"Maybe you could come with us in the morning, John?" said Lisa. "You don't have to believe or anything, but it's a nice service, and the church is fourteenth century."

"And my Ephesians is second to none," added Max, and laughed.

I said that would be very nice, I was sure.

"I'll show you upstairs," said Max. "Darling, can you tidy up down here? I'll show John to bed."

"Of course," said Lisa.

I thanked Lisa once again for a lovely meal, and she nodded. "A proper peasant breakfast in the morning, too!" she promised. "You wait!"

"We've put you in Ian's room," said Max. "I hope you enjoy it."

I must admit, the sound of that sobered me up a little bit. And as Max led me up the stairs, I wondered what Ian's room could be—would it still have his toys in, teddy bears and games and little soldiers? Would it still have that sort of manic wallpaper always inflicted upon infants? And then I remembered that Ian had never lived in this house at all, he'd died years ago—so was this something kept in memorial of him? And I had a sudden dread as we stood outside the door, as Max was turning the handle and smiling and laughing and ushering me in, I didn't want to go in there, I wanted nothing more to do with his dead son.

But I did go in, of course. And it was a perfectly ordinary room—there was nothing of Ian in there at all as far as I could see. Empty cupboards, an empty wardrobe, a little washbasin in the corner. Large bay windows opened out on to the garden, and there was an appealing double bed. My suitcase was already lying upon it, it had been opened for me in preparation, and I couldn't remember when Lisa or Max had left me alone long enough to take it upstairs.

"It makes us happy to have you here," said Max. "I can't begin to tell you." His eyes watered with the sentiment of it all, and he opened his arms for another hug, and I gave him one. "Sleep well," he said. "And enjoy yourself." And he was gone.

I went to draw the curtains, and I saw, perhaps, why this was Ian's room. I looked out directly upon the garden. And from the angle the room offered I could see that all the random charm of it was not so random at all—that all the winding paths, the flowerbeds, the arches, all of them pointed towards a centrepiece, and that centrepiece was the pond, and in the centre of that, the fountain. Ian stared out in the cold, naked with only bare feathers to protect him, his mouth fixed open in that silly round "o."

I pulled the curtains on him, got into my pyjamas, brushed my teeth, got into bed. I read for a little while, and then I turned off the light.

I felt very warm and comfortable beneath the sheets. My thoughts began to drift. The distant sound of running water was pleasantly soporific.

I vaguely wondered whether it were raining, but the water was too regular for that. And then I remembered the fountain in the garden, and that reassured me. I listened to it for a while, I felt that it was singing me to sleep.

I opened my eyes only when I remembered that the pond was dry, that the fountain wasn't on.

Even now I don't want to give the impression that I was alarmed. It wasn't alarm. I didn't feel threatened by the sound of the water, anything but that. But it was a puzzle, and my brain doggedly tried to solve it, and its vain attempts to make sense of what it could hear but what it knew couldn't be there started to wake me up. I don't like to sleep at night without all things put into regular order, I like to start each day as a blank new slate with nothing unresolved from the day before. And I recommend that to you all, as the best way to keep your mind healthy and your purpose resolute.

Had Max or Lisa left a bath running? Could that be it?

I turned on my bedside lamp, huffed, got out of bed. I stood in the middle of the room, stock still, as if this would make it easier to identify where the sound was coming from. It was outside the house. Definitely outside.

I pulled open the curtains, looked back on to the garden.

And, of course, all was as it should have been. There were a few flakes of snow falling, but nothing that could account for that sound of flowing water. And poor dead Ian still stood steadfast in the pond, cold I'm sure, but dry as a bone.

I was fully prepared to give up on the mystery altogether. It didn't matter. It wouldn't keep me awake—far from it, now that I focused on it, the sound seemed even more relaxing. And I turned around to pull closed the curtain, and go back to bed.

If I had turned the other way, I know I would have missed it.

The window was made up of eight square panes of glass. I had been looking at the garden, naturally enough, through one of the central panes. But as I turned, I glanced outside through another pane, the pane at the far bottom left, and something caught my eye.

There was a certain brightness coming from it, that was all. A trick of the light. But it seemed as if the moon was reflecting off the pebbles on the path—but not the whole path, it was illuminating the most direct way from the house to the memorial pond. The pebbles winked and glowed like a cat's eyes caught in the headlamps of a motor vehicle.

And there, at the end of that trail of light, at the very centre of the garden, there was the fountain. And now the fountain was on. Water was gushing out of Ian's stone mouth, thick and steady; I could see now how his posture had been so designed, with his little hands bunched up, and pressed tight against his chest, to suggest that he was *forcing* out the water, as if his insides were a water balloon and he was trying to squeeze out every single last drop.

There was nothing even now so very untoward about that. If the fountain was on, so it was on. But I changed the direction of my gaze, I looked out at the garden through the central pane again—and there the fountain was dry once more, the garden still, the pathways impossible to discern in the dark.

I'm afraid I must have stayed there for a few minutes, moving my head back and forth, looking through one pane and then through another. Trying to work out what the trick was. How one piece of the window could show one view, the other, something else. I'm afraid I must have looked rather like an idiot.

And I tried to open the window. I wanted to see the garden without the prism of the glass to distract me, I wanted to know what was real and what was not. The catch wouldn't give. It seemed to freeze beneath my fingers.

Then there was a knock at my door.

It brought me back to myself, rather; it wasn't until then that I realised it, that I was on the verge of hysteria, or panic at the very least. I don't know whether I had cried out. I thought I had been silent all this while, but perhaps I had cried out. I had woken the house. I was ashamed. I forced myself to turn from the window, and as I did so, with it at my back, I felt like myself again. I smoothed down my pyjamas. I went to open the door. I prepared to apologise.

Lisa was outside in a white night dress. She came in without my inviting her to do so, smiled, sat upon my bed.

"Hello, John," she whispered.

I said hello back at her.

"Did you never want children of your own? I'm curious."

She began unbuttoning her night dress then. I decided I really shouldn't look at what she was doing, but I didn't want to look through the window again either, so I settled on a compromise, I stared at a wholly inoffensive wardrobe door. I said something about not really liking children, and that the opportunity to discover otherwise was never much likely to present itself. I was aware, too, that something was very odd about her arrival and the ensuing conversation, but you must understand, it still seemed like a welcome respite from the absurdities I had glimpsed through my bedroom window.

She seemed to accept my answer, and then said, "Would you help me, please?" Her head disappeared into the neck of the night dress, its now loose arms were flailing. I gave it a tug and pulled the dress off over her head. "Thank you," she said. She smiled, turned, pointed these two bare breasts straight at me.

"What do you think?" she asked. "Are they better than you were expecting?" I endeavoured to explain that I had had no expectations of her breasts at all. She tittered at that, just as she had when she'd curtseyed to me in the driveway, it was a silly sound. "They're new," she said, and I supposed that made sense, they seemed too mirror perfect to be real, they seemed *sculpted*. And they didn't yet match the colour of her chest, they were white and pristine.

I wanted to ask her about the view through the window, but it seemed suddenly rather impolite to change the subject. What I did ask, though, was whether she was quite sure she had the right bedroom? Didn't she want the one with her husband in it? And at this her face fell.

"Max hasn't told you, has he?"

I said that he hadn't, no.

"Oh God," she said. "Bloody Max. This is what we... This is why. God. He's supposed to tell. Why else do you think he brought you here?"

I said that we were old friends, and at that she screwed up her face in contempt, and it made her rather ugly. I suggested that maybe he wanted to show me the house and the garden.

"Max hates the fucking house and garden," said Lisa. "He'd leave it all tomorrow if he could." She grabbed at her night dress, struggled with it. "Bloody Max. I'm very sorry. We have an agreement. I don't know what he's playing at. This is the way *I* cope." She couldn't get her arms in the right holes, she began to cry.

I said I was sorry. I asked her whether she could hear running water anywhere, was it just me?

"I've always liked you, John," she said. "Can't you like me just a little bit?"

I said I did like her, a little bit. More than, even.

"Can't you like me for one night?"

I tried asking her about Max, but she just shook her head, and now she was smiling through the tears. "This is the way we cope. Can't you help me out?" I said, yes. I said I could help her out. I said I was puzzled by the fountain outside, but by this stage the night dress was back over her head again, maybe she couldn't hear.

She said, "Now, don't you worry. I'm not going to do anything you won't like." Then she climbed on top of me and gripped me hard between her thighs. She let her long hair fall across my face, then she whispered in my ear. I expected her to say something romantic. She said, "I won't get pregnant, I've been thoroughly sterilised."

I hadn't touched a woman in years. Not since I was at school, not since Max had discovered girls, and had started touching them, and I had touched them too so he wouldn't leave me out.

But even accepting my unfamiliarity with the whole enterprise, I don't think I did an especially good job. To be honest, I let Lisa do all of the work, the most I contributed was a couple of hands on her back so that she wouldn't fall off and sprain herself. And I listened to the sound of the fountain outside; sometimes the mechanical grunts of Lisa would drown it out, and I'd think maybe it was over, but then she'd have to pause for breath, or she'd be gnawing at my neck with her lips, or she'd be sitting tall and gritting her teeth hard and screwing her eyes tight and being ever so quiet, and I could hear the fountain just as before.

At length she rolled off, and thanked me, and kissed me on the mouth. The kiss was nice. I grant you that, the kiss was nice. She curled up beside me and went to sleep. Then she turned away from me altogether and I was alone, so alone.

The curtains were still open, but there was no light spilling into the room, it was just black and bleak out there. And from my position I couldn't crane my head to see whether there was any light coming through the pane on the bottom left.

I didn't want to wake Lisa. I got out of bed very gently. It was cold. My pyjama trousers had got lost somewhere. I'd have had to have turned on the bedside lamp to find them. I wasn't going to turn on the bedside lamp.

I went straight to the pane, I looked out.

As before, the pathway to the centre was lit by sparkling pebbles. But this time the snow was falling in droves, big clumps of it, and every flake seemed to catch the moon, and each one of them was like a little lamp lighting up the whole garden. The flowers were in bloom. It was ridiculous, but the flowers were in bloom—the blanket of red and white roses was thick and warm, and the snow fell upon it, and the roses didn't care, the roses knew they could melt that snow, they had nothing to fear from it. I looked out at where Lisa had planted the hyacinths and the tulips—it was, as she'd said, like a wave of blue breaking upon a brightly coloured shore.

And at the fountain itself. Ian was throwing up all the water he had inside him, and he had so *much* water, he was never going to run out, was he? But I would have thought his face would have been distressed—it was not distressed. The worst you could say about the expression he wore was that it was resigned. Ian Wheeler had a job to do, and he was going to do it. It wasn't a pleasant job, but he wasn't one to complain, he'd just do the very best he could. And the flowers were growing around him too, and vines were twisting up his body and tightening around his neck.

Over the sound of the fountain I heard another noise now. Less regular. The sound of something dragging over loose stone. Something heavy, but determined—it seemed that every lurch across the stone was done with great weariness, but it wasn't going to stop, it might be *slow*, but it wasn't going to stop. And I can't tell you why, but I suddenly felt a cold terror icing down my body, so cold that it froze my body still and I could do nothing but watch.

And into view at last shuffled Max. He was naked. And the snow was falling all around him, and I could see that it was falling fast and drenching him when it melted against his skin, but he didn't notice, he was like the roses, he didn't care, he didn't stop. Forcing himself forward, but calmly, so deliberately, each step an effort but an effort he was equal to. Farther up the path, following the trail of sparkling pebbles to the fountain. Following the yellow brick road.

I tried looking through the other panes. Nothing but darkness, and the snow falling so much more gently. I only wanted to look at that garden, at that reality. But I could hear the sound from the other garden so much more clearly, I couldn't *not* hear it, the agonised heave of Max's body up the path. The flow of running water, the way it gushed and spilled, all that noise, all of it, it was pulling him along. I had to look. I did.

Once in a while the bends of the path would turn Max around so that he was facing me. And I could see that dead face—no, not dead, not vacant even, it was filled with purpose, but it wasn't a purpose I understood and it had nothing to do with the Max I had loved for so many years. I could see his skin turning blue with the cold. I could see his penis had shrunk away almost to nothing.

And now, too soon—he had reached the statue of his dead son. At last he stopped, as if to contemplate it. As if to study the workmanship!—his head tilted to one side. And maybe his son contemplated him in return, but if he did, he still never stopped spewing forth all that water, all the water there was in the world. Then—Max was moving again, he was using his last reserves of energy, he was stepping into the freezing pond, he was wading over to the stone angel, raising an arm, then both arms, he was reaching out to it. And I thought I could hear him howling. He was, he was howling.

I battered at the window. I tried again to open it. The catch wouldn't lift, the catch was so cold it hurt.

But Max had his son in his arms now, wrapping his arms about him tightly, he was hugging him for dear life, and he was crying out—he was screaming with such love and such despair. And then, then, he fell silent, and that was more terrible still—and he put his mouth to his son's, he opened his mouth wide and pressed it against those stone lips, and the water splashed against his face and against his chest, and yet he kissed his son closer, he plugged the flow of water, he took it all inside and swallowed it down.

The window gave. The rush of cold air winded me. I called out. "Max!" I shouted. "Max!" But there was nothing to be seen now the window was open, nothing but dead space, dead air, blackness.

"Darling," said Lisa.

I turned around. She was awake.

"Darling," she said. "Darling, close the window. Come back to bed." She patted the mattress beside her in a manner I assumed was enticing.

I closed the window. I looked through the pane once more, I looked through every pane, and there was nothing to make out, the moon was behind the clouds, the darkness was full and unyielding. I went back to bed. I did as I was told.

⊸

I had fully intended to go to church the next morning. I had made a promise, and I keep my promises. But when I woke up the house was empty. Max and Lisa had gone without me. I made myself a cup of tea, and waited for them to come back. Eventually, of course, they did. All smiles, both looking so smart, Max in particular was very handsome in his suit. "Sorry, matey," said Max. "I popped my head around your door, but you looked like you needed the extra sleep! Hope you don't mind!" And Lisa just smiled.

Neither of them said a word about the adventures of the night before, and neither treated me any differently. Lisa had told me she'd cook a big peasant's breakfast, and she was as good as her word—bacon, eggs, and sausages she said were from pigs freshly slaughtered by a farmer friend she'd made. Then we settled down in the lounge, and shared the Sunday newspaper, each reading different sections then swapping when we were done. It was nice.

Some time early afternoon, though, Max looked at the clock, and said, "Best you get back home, John! I've things that need doing!" And I hugged Lisa goodbye, and Max drove me to the railway station, and we hugged too, and I thanked him for the weekend.

We drifted apart. I don't know who drifted from whom, I doubt it was anything as deliberate as that. No, wait, I sent them a Christmas card, and they didn't respond. So they're the ones who drifted. They drifted, and I stayed where I was, exactly the same.

⤚⊙⤙

That would be the end of the story. I had heard from an old school friend that a couple of years later Max and Lisa had separated. It was just gossip, and I don't know whether it was true or not, and I felt sorry for them just the same.

That was maybe six months ago. Recently I received a letter.

Dear John,

You may have heard that Max and I have gone our different ways! It was quite sad at the time, but it was very amicable, and I'm sure one day we will be good friends.

But sometimes when something has died, you just have to accept it, and move on.

I still have the house. Max was very generous, to be fair. All he wanted was half of the money, and the fountain from the garden. We had to dig it up, and I'm afraid it has made the garden a bit of an eyesore! I tried to tell Max it won't work, it was specially designed to fit with all our underground piping, but as you know, there's no talking to Max!

I'm going to rethink the garden. I'm sure I can make it even better.

All the locals have been very nice, and they're attentive as ever in their own way. But I don't know. I think perhaps they liked Max more than they ever liked me.

If you would like to stay again, that would make me very happy.

Maybe I shouldn't say this. But that night we spent together was very special. It was a special night. And I think of you often. Sometimes I think you're the one who could save me. Sometimes I think you could give me meaning.

But regardless. Thank you for always being such a good friend to me and Max, and for being best man at the wedding, and any other duties you took on.

Best regards,

Lisa Howell (once Wheeler)

I haven't written back yet. I might.

WINGLESS BEASTS

LUCY TAYLOR

The first thing I tell people headed out here is just this: Go someplace else. I mean, Death Valley got that name for a reason, right? And the Mojave, of which Death Valley's a part, is especially dangerous in ways most people don't even suspect. I know, because I've seen the results of somebody's wrong turn or ill-considered adventure. And even though I live out here and own Joe's Towing Service—which comes in handy at times—I don't patrol the off-road areas on a regular basis, just when I'm edgy or restless or when I've got reason to believe someone may be in need of assistance.

Then I lock up my double wide and head out to the back country, checking salt pans and arroyos and lake beds where those afflicted with hubris or just old-fashioned stupidity are most apt to meet with disaster.

Tragic deaths and mysterious disappearances don't deter people, though. They keep turning up, charging off into blast furnace heat, not taking along enough food or water or gas, and sometimes, inevitably, a few meet with misfortune.

Case in point: the gimp with the cane at the Bun Boy Diner this morning. Only a little after six a.m and I'm just pulling into Baker, California, a pit stop for tourists traveling on I-15 between Barstow and Vegas. The town's claim to fame is having the world's biggest thermometer (like you need that to tell you it's hotter than the devil's butthole here), which rises 134 feet over a main drag lined with two-star motels, gas stations, and shuttered convenience stores. I park my truck and amble into the Bun Boy for my usual breakfast of egg, hash browns, and grits before I head out to Barstow to visit my girl.

Right off the bat, though, the creep at the counter gets under my skin.

Soon as I see him, a squat, toadish little man, with a shiny bald dome looks like it's been polished with Pledge and hear him yakking to Margo the waitress about his plans to go off-roading in the Mojave, I peg him for the kind of know-it-all who'll be in deep shit by sundown.

I know his type: the obnoxious braying voice of a small man trying to sound imposing, the sardonic roll of his dishwater eyes when Margo suggests that the desert is best left to the young and the able-bodied, the puffed-up way he tries to pretend the cane's not really necessary, that he only carries it "in case I encounter a rattlesnake."

"Well, no rattlers in here," I tell him and ask which of the vehicles out in the lot belongs to him.

I figure him for the owner of the Subaru Outback or the Ram1500 or even the goofy-looking Baja Beetle I saw coming in, but he slurps his coffee and says, "Mine's the red Camry. Oh, I know, go ahead and laugh, but it's got me where I need to go plenty of times."

Which amuses me, because the kind of serious off-roading he's talking about demands a lot of a vehicle—at minimum, you need a flexible suspension, high clearance, and big tires with deep open treads.

"That's the wrong ride for your purposes," I say, taking a stool next to him. "You want a vacation, forget the Mojave. Just stay on 15 north. Three hours from now you can be laying bets at a crap table in the Bellagio or getting a lap dance at Spearmint Rhino Cabaret."

He grunts, but whether it's in response to my unsought advice or to some other pain in his pancake-flat ass, I can't tell. He upends the sugar bowl into his coffee and says with disdain, "Vegas is where Satan vacations when he gets bored with hell. Myself, I prefer the purity of the desert."

Now that takes me aback, because he sure doesn't seem like a man who'd know much about purity or aspire to it or respect it, for that matter. But then, I suppose, neither do I, yet it was the austerity of the desert, the vast silence and uncompromising indifference to all human fears that lured me out here almost ten years ago, and I've never been tempted to go back to my old bad-ass life on the streets of L.A., not once.

"Joe Fitch," I say, extending a hand, which he shakes with a prissy distaste suggesting he thinks I may have recently used it for wiping my ass. I shrug off the attitude and go on. "If you're hellbent on going out there by yourself, at least know what you're getting into. You break down, you get stuck, or your GPS lies to you—and let me tell you, a GPS will lie like a ten-dollar whore—any of that happens and, in this heat, you are goddamn dead."

Maybe still worrying about our handshake, he taps a squirt of hand sanitizer from a tube on the counter into his palm, which is thick and red as a slab of raw liver. "Otis Hanks. And, no offense, but I'd prefer you not curse."

"I won't," I tell him, "except to say if you go off half-cocked in the desert without the right experience and equipment, then you are well-fucked and royally so."

Hanks scowls and I figure I'm about to get chastised for the cussing, but what he says is, "Your name's familiar. Do we know each other?"

I assure him we don't. I wonder if we might've done time together, but I'm not about to bring up the nickel I did in Lompoc for a bar fight that ended up with a manslaughter charge or the lesser run-ins I've had with the law on various occasions. My past is what I moved to the Mojave to forget.

His comment about my name rankles, but still, in the interest of fairness, I try to put some fear into Hanks, pointing out that the sun's barely up and the giant thermometer already reads over a hundred degrees, and if he has any sense at all, he'll rethink his plan for an off-road adventure in the middle of goddamn July.

But I doubt that he will, because guys like him never listen. They're like my old man, railing about sin and salvation from the pulpit of the Wrath of God Methodist Church back in California; they already got all the answers. To hear folks like that tell it, God Himself comes to them for advice.

So I tell Hanks about just a couple of the tragedies that have taken place here over the past few years; about the skeleton that was found in a desert wash by a group of kids looking for arrowheads, just west of Newberry Springs along Interstate 40 and how it turned out to be the remains of a tourist from Munich, who must've thought the Mojave was some kind of Disney World, but without the A/C, and then proceeded to stroll off into the fiery furnace with just a half gallon of water, wearing thong sandals, a tee shirt, and shorts. When they found him, his mouth and nostrils and every other orifice was stoppered with sand and the vultures had pillaged his insides like conventioneers at the Golden Nugget's buffet.

And I tell him about the woman from Huntsville, Alabama, who got the terrific idea to take her eight-year-old son camping in the Mojave a couple of summers back and how, when the road ran out and her GPS cheerfully instructed her to turn right and continue another eighteen miles into a waterless hellhole, she followed directions. A ranger found the car and the kid dead nearby a few days later. The mother's body wasn't found for months, not much more than a pile of bones, hair, and vulture scat, or so I heard.

Margo swings by with the coffeepot then and refills my mug, saying, "You setting him straight, Reverend Joe?"

This makes Hanks's squinty eyes in their nests of wrinkly, sun-cured skin flicker with curiosity. "Don't tell me you're a man of the cloth, Mr. Fitch?"

Margo grins as she pours a steaming black stream. "Old Joe here's a reverend like I'm a pole dancer, but folks here gave him that name 'cause he lives out in the nowhere by hisself like one of them—monasticians?"

"Monastics," I say, "and I'm far from that. But my father was a minister with an interest in such things. I grew up listening to him preach about the religious tradition of men who turned their backs on civilization and went out into the deserts of Egypt and the Sinai. Men like Abba Macarius and Anthony the Great who were looking to deepen their spiritual life through isolation and physical hardship. Guess I got inspired by that." I shrug. "In hindsight, it seems naive to me now, but finding God was my aim when I moved out here years back and I guess what started out as a bit of a joke at my expense . . ."

". . . is still a joke," chuckles Margo, "but we like you now. You're one of us."

Hanks raises a brow so pale that it's almost translucent. "And did you? Find God?"

The question pokes me like a sharp stick as I fork up my eggs. "Of course not. There was nothing to find."

We sit in silence then, shoveling food into our pieholes, but I keep dwelling on his comment about my name. After a while, I get up and amble out to my truck, noting with some amusement that the Camry belonging to this guy who only requires his cane for warding off rattlesnakes is parked in a handicapped spot. I get a map from the glove compartment and come back inside.

Hanks's mouth twists in annoyance when I unfold the map, like he's worried I'm going to dip the northeast corner of Nevada into his biscuits and gravy, but I take out a pen and draw him a route through the back country to a remote, beautiful area I call the Cauldron. "It's a straight shot from the paved road. No need to even get out of your car. Other side of the salt pan, there's a Joshua tree forest and beyond that, a dune field that'll make you think you're on Mars." I pause before adding, "Probably best not to try climbing them, though."

Hanks studies the map the way a prude eyes pornography, with distaste and a thinly veiled craving, then folds it up.

"I appreciate your concern, Mr. Fitch, but as I was explaining to our waitress here while you were outside, I'm a bit of an amateur eremologist—" he sees of my puzzled expression, "—one who studies the deserts. Since my retirement, I've visited quite a few, the Gobi, the Sahara, the Atacama. I've hiked some of the world's most desolate regions and come back none the worse for it." He glances down at his right boot, which is built up higher than the left one, and yanks up a pant leg, offering a glimpse of an off-white prosthesis. "Well, except for the incident with the leg, but that was due to a sin of lust, not a hiking mishap."

Right about then Margo notices some people across the room need more water and goes hurrying over with a pitcher while I try to dispel some unpleasant images about what kind of kinky sexual shenanigans—an amputee fetish perhaps?—might result in the loss of a limb.

Hanks notes our reactions and has the grace to redden a bit. After some awkward silence, he allows as how, since he has what he calls "a flexible itinerary," he just may hang onto the map anyway. "Wouldn't mind seeing that Joshua tree forest," he says, and there's a wistful note in his voice that I haven't detected before, as though he's longing—maybe not so much to see Joshua trees—but to be somewhere, anywhere else, besides here.

When Hanks dons his safari hat and gets up to pay his tab, I throw down some bills and walk with him outside. Even with the cane, which is a striking piece of handiwork—mahogany with an intricately carved ivory handle—he creaks laboriously along, huffing like one burdened by more than just a physical disability.

My tow truck, parked a few spaces down from his Camry, catches his eye. "Joe's Towing Service. Now I recall how I know you."

I look at him quizzically.

"Two nice people I met on a trip recently said you towed their car when it stalled in the desert. Maisie and Claude from Modesto. Said if I saw you to send their regards."

I turn away and gaze up at the eyesore thermometer, which now measures a hundred and four, as ice crystals clink in my chest. "Names don't ring a bell."

Hanks sighs, as though my failure to remember the couple confirms for him some basic belief about human nature. We shake hands again and I watch him drive off, then hightail it back into the Bun Boy and make it to the can just in time to puke up a thick slop of greasy coffee, potatoes, and eggs.

What Hanks said isn't possible. No fucking way.

The last time I saw dear ol' Maisie and Claude, they were stone fucking dead and I was towing their Mazda 280z with their bodies in the back seat.

⊸⊷

Part of me, the impulsive, hot-headed ruffian whose misdeeds inspired some of my old man's more graphic sermons wants to go after Hanks right then and there, but I choke down the urge. That was the old me. Now I know how to hang back and be patient, bide my time. That's a skill the desert has taught me.

So I climb into my truck and roar out toward Barstow, knowing I'll catch up with Hanks in due time. Right now, I need to spend time with my girl.

Opal isn't her real name, of course. I call her that, because her blue-gray eyes remind me of opals, flecked with tiny motes of cobalt and daffodil gold. She was found by a sheepherder, wandering up near Red Mountain, half naked and near death with deep, infected gashes on her shoulders and neck, like at some point she'd collapsed, and the vultures had done a little taste testing before she fought them off and got moving again. Far as anyone knows, she hasn't spoken to anyone since. The heat and the trauma of her ordeal, including whatever led to her being in that situation in the first place, has parboiled her brain. Now she occupies a room at the Rohr Convalescent Center in Barstow, a Jane Doe waiting for somebody to come forward and give her a name.

Today when I slip into her room, she's propped up in bed, a little fuller in the face than the last time I saw her, but still stiff as a scarecrow, with that tiny mummified smile on her lips that never twitches or flags, that seems to hint at a cache of secrets she's hoarding. The only part of her that moves are her half-closed, feral eyes, which scan back and forth, tock-tick-tock, as though she's mesmerizing herself by following the path of an interior metronome.

After chitchatting with one of the nurses, who stops in to say hi, I take a comb and brush from the night stand by the bed and set about braiding her hair, which has gone white over the months that I've known her. To pass the time, I talk to her like I always do, just random stuff that she's heard before, about how it was when I first moved to the desert, how that ocean of emptiness both fascinated and horrified me. Something about that burnt, hostile terrain, so purged of anything conducive to sustaining life, gave me a strange kind of solace born of pain and familiarity. I realized that my addled, punitive parents had given me something valuable after all—the ability to survive in a place so barren that few people even come here and those that do, generally don't stay very long.

And although I didn't find God in the way most people know Him, I found deities of my own understanding—hundreds of them, winged carrion-eaters reigning over a savage landscape. I recognized them from my father's sermons, these vulture-gods, and I named them after the archangels: Moloch and Charon, Metatron and Uriel and Gabriel. I recognized them at once for what they were, creatures old as the rocks and the salt pans, ancient as the bones of the finned creatures that once lived here sixty-five million years ago when the Mojave was a vast, inland sea.

I knew they must see us as we really are—wingless beasts lumbering across a destroyed landscape, while they soar on the updrafts, patient and cunning, knowing that we're here for only an eyeblink in their eternity.

The great birds appalled me at first—with their plucked, scarlet heads and seething black eyes—and their habits struck me as ghastly. After startling one outside my trailer one day, I watched it take clumsy running hops, flapping furiously to get airborne, then regurgitate a gut full of stinking carrion all over the hood of my truck in an effort to lighten the load. That one, the Leaver of Offerings, was the first, and soon others came. They'd soar on the thermals for hours within sight of my home, silent and watchful, until I'd come outside and let them lead me to whatever they'd found that was dying or injured: a burrowing owl, a tortoise, a chuckwalla . . . a vagabond from Munich or a mother desperate to find help for her boy.

Opal shivers then and exhales a sound, not much more than a thin hiccough of dread. I wonder if she's been hearing me. Doesn't much matter, she knows who I am.

Her hair looks good when I finish it, the long braids sliding over her shoulders in smooth, ghostly ropes that stand out against her dark, ruddy skin. But when I hold the mirror up so she can admire herself, her eyes ignite like a cornered bobcat's and a snarl corkscrews between her bared teeth.

I lean close, stroke a wisp of hair back off her face and whisper the same thing I always do, "Next time I come here, I'm going to kill you."

⊸

Now it's Hanks's turn.

On the way back toward Baker, I take a seldom-used exit and follow an unmarked dirt road until I come to the edge of the Cauldron. Here the remnant of road peters out at the edge of a cracked lake bed and I blaze across it, raising a roostertail of white sand sparkling with tiny grains of feldspar and quartz. For miles around, there's no pavement, no signs, and no help if you need it. No indication that Hanks has passed this way, either, so I head south, where the desert floor splits into a snake's nest of arroyos and the earth is so dry that sections lurch up, overlapping each other like a shelf of ceramic tiles. When my tires crunch over the baked clay, the noise is an escalation of tiny explosions and the air turns the color of cinders and chalk.

I'm following the approximate route that I mapped out for Hanks, but when I see the outline of Joshua trees in the distance, a sudden sense of unease washes over me. I've always found the trees spooky—the way the branches claw and arch in grotesque, twisted shapes, like the broken limbs of men who've been crucified. But now, when I get out of my truck to survey the terrain through binoculars, I spot the outline of a vulture amid the tree's deformed limbs. At the sight of me, the bird hisses softly. Its neck swivels around and a beak so red it might have been dipped in a wound lifts into the yellow-white glare.

It takes off, flying out toward a formation of orange sandstone that juts to the east. I follow its flight through the binoculars and zoom in on a dust-caked red fender—Hanks's Camry, left at the base of the rocks in a puddle of dwindling shade.

Towing a car so you don't damage the transmission requires care and the right implements, but not ruining Hanks's ride isn't high on my list of concerns. I hook it up to the back of my truck, tow it a half mile away and offload it behind a low rise bristling with pinon and creosote. On the passenger seat I find a modest supply of water and energy bars; a key is hidden under the floor mat. I stuff my backpack with bottles of water and granola bars, lock up the car, and pitch the key into the scrub.

What I've found is that people whose vehicles disappear in the middle of nowhere generally do one of three things: they assume they've screwed up and returned to the wrong place and commence a futile and increasingly frantic search. Or they stay calm, keep their wits about them, and try to hike out. Either dehydration and heat stroke fell them or I do the job with the crowbar I keep in my truck next to the phony maps, but either way, the birds feed. A third, smaller group, those with a naive belief in the goodness of humanity, huddle in whatever shade they can find, presumably praying for help to come, and thank God when they see me approaching—at least until they realize I'm not there on a mission of mercy.

The Modesto couple Hanks mentioned fell into that last category.

Hanks, though, does none of these things. When I hike back to the sandstone formation, there's nothing to indicate he's returned to the place where his car ought to be, no helterskelter footprints of the kind a panicked person generally leaves, no indication he's attempted to follow my tire tracks. I clamber onto the highest ridge of sandstone and do a sweep with the binoculars. I don't see him at first—his khaki clothing and tan safari hat blend in with the dun-colored sand—but the lazy swoops of vultures mark his place on the desert floor like a giant red X. He's about a mile away, heading toward the dune field, puttering along like a geezer perusing his garden. Everything catches his fancy: a thorny cactus pad, a stretch of orange dogweed, the green, tapering shafts of a cluster of desert candles.

As I watch, he looks up abruptly. Although I know at this distance, he can't possibly see me, our eyes seem to lock, and his flaccid lips smack with what an over-imaginative mind might interpret as relish. Real or not, the gaze is unsettling and I turn away. A few seconds later, when I focus the binoculars again, he's no longer there. All I see are the bristly contours of a cluster of teddy bear cholla and the slow rotation of obsidian wings against a searing hot sky.

Has he stumbled into an arroyo or collapsed in the meager shade of some creosote bushes? I press on, expecting to catch up to him quickly, but the desert seems to have licked up his life like spilled water. It's not until mid-afternoon that I spot him again, when the temperature in this part of the Cauldron must be approaching a hundred and twenty and the heat waves the vultures are riding look like curtains of shimmering gauze.

To my astonishment, the distance between us hasn't narrowed at all. If anything, Hanks has pulled farther away.

The heat's pummeling him, though, exposing his decrepitude. His head's bowed, shoulders sagging, and the hand clutching the cane by turns stiffens and then undergoes bouts of violent trembling. He no longer stops to investigate this flower or that sparkly mineral. Nor does he seem to notice the grim entourage that spirals above him like smoke rings expelled from the simmering earth. A check of my compass tells me what I already suspect, that his meandering course has begun to veer north. The straight line he undoubtedly thinks he's walking has begun to curve drastically, taking him not to the place where he left his car, but toward the Joshua tree forest.

For the next hour, I'm able to keep him in view, expecting him to drop any minute, but he soldiers on and the distance between us barely shrinks. Finally, frustrated, I break into a furious run and briefly enjoy the satisfaction all killers must feel when closing in on their prey. Yet just when I'm almost upon him, something shifts as though a key's clicked in a door of the universe, and his outline flickers and fades. What just moments ago seemed so obviously flesh and bone blurs away into shadows and sand. The vultures disperse, and a deathly stillness ensues. Suddenly I'm the only thing left alive on the earth and the single sound is the rasp of my breathing.

I check the number of full water bottles left in my pack, am shocked to discover there's only one left and that it's less than half full. I've been drinking water throughout the day, but my throat feels like I've gargled with sawdust and brine, and my lungs burn like I've inhaled the desert. Still, I'm not ready to turn back, a determination that's strengthened when I find a bright gob of blood on the rubbery pad of a prickly pear cactus. From the looks of Hanks's tracks, it appears he's faltering badly, leaning so heavily on the cane that it punches into the sand an inch or two deep.

Even as Hanks fades, so does the day. The shadows elongate and the sun blowtorches the horizon with bands of vermillion and deep mustard blue.

And the wind picks up, scouring my exposed skin and hurling huge, tangled masses of tumbleweed around like bizarre beach balls. Its bluster plays tricks with my hearing. A woman's voice—plaintive and whimpering—plays counterpoint to its keening. A second voice joins in and initiates a fevered duo—my father raging about the temptations of demons and the abyss of the damned where fallen angels feed on their prey. It's a rant as lunatic and mindless as the woman's, but more disturbing for notes of threat and contempt underlying it.

The sky suddenly looks too big to be real, a painted backdrop meant to deceive me. The gritty wind, full of sadistic trickery, is bent on erasing Hanks's tracks.

To the west, a cloud of bats rises up from a nest of creosote bushes and takes to the sky like a flurry of semaphores from the pen of a demented scribe. Instinctively I duck down and cover my head as their dark mass swarms by. The rush of their passing distracts me; the warring voices subside. My head clears, and in the distance, I see the stark outlines of the Joshua trees.

In the fading daylight, the grotesque trees appear eerie and blighted. Black, oval blooms freight their branches, giving some trees the appearance that they are ready to uproot from the earth under the weight of the vultures that roost in them. The stench of carrion wafts toward me, and a low murmur makes the hair stiffen on the back of my neck. It's the voice of a woman begging for help. Pleading for water.

Then it changes, and Hanks cries for water.

The sound, unmistakably real this time, echoes from far back in the trees. I catch a glimpse of Hanks's khaki hat as it flies off his head, of a body tumbling and falling, hitting the ground amid puffs of sand and a cascade of stones. For a second, the wind and Hanks mourn in unison. Then silence.

I run toward him, but the sunset fires scalding light into my eyes, and my strides are unsteady and blundering. A shadow coiled beneath one drooping, heavy-laden tree brings to mind a fetally curved body. I grab for it and recoil as one hand disappears into flesh so decomposed that it slides off the bone in clumps of powdery fur, while the other grasps a jawbone missing most of its teeth—the scraggly remains of a coyote or fox. Other, larger bones, flecked with threadbare scraps of cloth, suggest deaths older and feedings more savage.

"Mr. Fitch?" The words, coming from behind me, aren't so much spoken as spat, and I whirl around, arms raised but not fast enough, too late and too slow to block the knob of the cane before it staves in the flesh between my brows.

⊸o⊷

"Well, finally. There you are."

I don't know how much time has passed, ten seconds or a day, but Hanks's gravelly voice is edged with impatience and thwarted intent. The cane he brandishes is slick with blood and a caterpillar-like tuft of something I recognize to be one of my eyebrows adheres to a carved notch in the ivory.

I want to seize him by his wattled neck and wring the life from him, but when he squats down and turns his vexed gaze on me, I can taste his loathing and feel the spikes imbedded in his every word, and I shut my eyes.

"You didn't hear what I was saying, did you? You were . . . elsewhere. No matter. I was speaking of the deserts of Norway and New England and Brazil. Can't tell you their names, because they don't exist yet. But they will. You'll see. Oh, just give it time."

I try to swallow, find my throat clogged. "I want . . . water."

He sneers. "Oh, don't we all!"

In the bruise-colored dusk, he hobbles back and forth, hunched and scowling like a traveler on a subway platform awaiting a long-delayed train he knows in his heart never will come.

Suddenly he spins around and wags the cane a few inches away from my face; the sudden, violent motion in front of my eyes off-kilters a slice of my brain, blurs my vision, and stymies my tongue. When I try to speak again, my parched throat produces only a feeble croak that elicits a look of disgust.

"You think you're so unique, don't you?"

He rolls up the right pant leg, reaches down and pops off the prosthesis, revealing a chewed stump of something oozing and raw, like what you'd see in some third-world butcher shop. The charnel house smell of that suppurating stump makes me gag, but what's worse is that Hanks doesn't seem unduly discomforted. Like he's been existing this way for a very long time.

He lays a paternal hand on my shoulder. "We're not so different, you and me. That woman you named Opal, the one you found near Stovepipe and chose to keep for yourself, I understand how that happened. No place lonelier than the desert, and a man has needs that a lap dance in a gentlemens' club won't satisfy. I took a woman once too for my personal use—she was a Berber girl from the Tenere whose family threw her out for being unchaste. Unlike you, though, I kept her tightly bound, so she couldn't escape into the desert where some sheepherder could find her." He exhales a snort. "A sheepherder, for God's sake! Like such occupations even exist in this day and age!"

He hops backward, stork-like on the one leg, teeters a bit, then reattaches the prosthesis. "Didn't surprise me I had to forfeit a limb. I took what didn't belong to me after all. Bitch of it was, the leg was still attached when the birds ate it."

The tears spurting through my lashes shame and shock me. They're also precious drops of moisture that I try to capture on my tongue, a futile effort that makes Hanks's eyes crinkle with contempt.

But the tears produce more tears and, after that, words that are old and dreadfully familiar. "I'm sorry, so sorry. I won't do it again. I promise I'll stop. I won't kill anyone else!"

Hanks cocks his head, perplexed and peeved-looking. Then he stands up, his creased face sad, avuncular, and kicks me in the head.

When my vision clears, Hanks is bent over me, studying my face while a black ant the size of a paperclip navigates the ruts in his forehead.

"You misunderstood me," he says, as though there's been only a slight, inconsequential interruption in our conversation. "My purpose isn't to stop you from killing. It's what you do, and you're good at it. Gifted even." He gestures toward the trees with his cane and the vultures roosting there stir, hissing softly, their naked necks stretching and curving into question marks. "Not here, though. Not anymore. From now on, yours are the deserts of the interior lands, the hellscapes of your creation. Deserts so vast you can wander for eons before finding someone to kill. Or to fuck. But don't worry. You won't be alone. After you left her this morning, someone helped Opal take a sheet into the bathroom and showed her how to hang herself from the shower curtain. She could be free now, but she'd rather be angry. She wants revenge for what you did to her. And she's still so very thirsty."

He gazes around at the skeletal trees with their dark, restless fruit and lifts up the cane. At once the vultures' hissing grows louder, unnatural, imperative.

Some of them take to the air, swooping so low that I can feel the foul breeze from their passing rustle my hair. I know there is very little time.

"The people you met in the desert," I blurt out, "Maisie and Claude, did they . . . ?"

"Talk about you? Of course they did. But don't worry about your mama and daddy too much. They were headed to their own desert anyway. You just sent them there sooner."

Hanks's grin is inhumanly wide. His mouth creaks open like a rusty-hinged crypt and belches forth a bevy of soft, struggling things, tarry and mewling, that flee into the darkening sky and are plucked from the air by the vultures. They are the souls of the lost and the damned and I know one of them is my own.

"Safe journeys," he says, before his face is obscured beneath a barrage of obsidian wings and stabbing beaks.

⤙○⤚

When my screaming stops and I risk opening my eyes, the sun is still setting and constellations unknown to mortal astronomers swarm in the dome of a blazing red sky. I'm alone in a Joshua tree forest and, a few yards away, an assembly of vultures is squabbling over the remains of my foot.

Hanks is gone, but his cane lies within reach.

The birds bolt down their feast and take to the air, one by one, as a woman's voice, familiar and piteous, cries out for water. She sounds as near as my heartbeat and as far away as the other side of the moon.

After a while, I pick up the cane and start hobbling along, knowing I have all eternity to find her.

DEPARTURES

CAROLE JOHNSTONE

I saw his feet first. Not before I saw any other part of him; I *only* saw his feet. I forgot it later, and only remembered at the end—that in the beginning it was his feet that terrified me. More specifically, it was his shoes.

I was tired, mooching around the shop, restocking and tidying in a lull between flights. Picking all the crap up off the floor, returning unwanted books, magazines, drinks, you name it, to their rightful places. You'd be amazed (or maybe you wouldn't; depends on where you work, I suppose) at how messy, how disrespectful, how fucking rude people are outside their own homes. They leave everything at their arse because it's someone else's job to tidy it up for them. They don't need to see you do it, just knowing that you will seems to be enough, and it can't be blamed on laziness or lack of time when the shop in question is less than thirty feet by ten.

After I'd filled a bin bag with empty coffee cups, cans, wrappers, and receipts, rescued a rolled-up copy of *Heat* and the latest James Patterson from a half-price smoothie bucket, and a suspiciously limp and squashy Cornish pasty from the souvenir aisle where it had been wedged between boxes of tablet and tartan dishcloths, I made myself a second permitted coffee of the day and went back behind the till to have both it and a sneaky Mars bar.

It was very quiet. I liked working the domestic gates, partly because foreigners had an even greater capacity for rudeness, but mainly because the hours were better (there were no flights after ten p.m.) and the quiet lulls were longer. I could hear the annoying calliope jingles of all the puggies down towards gates six through two, hysterically shrieking and jostling for attention that was very rarely won. They weren't the benign penny slots of town centre amusement arcades, these were airport slot machines: hardcore behemoths with embedded bill acceptors and terrible odds, whose profits relied solely upon delays and stopovers and the fidgety boredom of the trapped. The occasional PA announcement was far poorer competition; the way in which airports strove to make the trivial deafening and the important incomprehensible never failed to cheer me up. Behind me, I could hear the squawk of easyJet walkie talkies as they got ready to leave Gate 1A, and I looked across at the slow-turning orange-and-white jet, its engines low whining and lethargic.

I stood, drinking my horrible coffee, eating my stolen Mars bar, and watching the turning wings of the plane until it disappeared from sight. The sky was pinkening up, low red at its edges, orange behind high thin clouds. A nice evening. No turbulence for the EJC432Y bound for Stansted. When it reappeared on the runway: a dark shadow delineated by its small lit windows, its engines kicking up a gear, I followed the line of its departure automatically, pulling my gaze along the wide bank of windows. The easyJet staff broke into both my reverie and view, nodding at me without really looking as they went past, heading for the distant departure lounge, lanyards whipping left and right, walkies still squawking. And that was why I saw him, I think. That moment of broken concentration, a tired awakening that was aware but not quite aware, like the weird borderland between dozing and sleep.

But that first time, of course, it was just his feet. Just his *shoes*. They were black and scuffed old leather. I was seeing them from behind, and the heels were worn down at the sides as if he favoured his instep. They were planted straight and close enough to touch but not quite. They were very still. Very, very still.

I couldn't see anything else of him at all. I understood that this was because he was bent over in his seat, too low for me to see him over its back, but it was disconcerting all the same. He was sitting in the middle of a long central bank of plastic seats running parallel to the shop but facing the windows. The easyJet plane took off with a tremulous shriek, and I flinched, spilling still-hot coffee.

"Shit!" The sound of my voice echoed a little too loud, and I glanced back over at those shoes fast. Neither they nor their owner had moved. I found myself looking instead at the darkening reflections inside the long stretch of glass, searching for his and hoping I wouldn't find it. I didn't. There was a strange smell in the air, a little like plastic long ago burned. It wasn't strong enough to water my eyes, but it was close. I was suddenly very aware of how alone we were—a ridiculous concern, considering the hundreds milling around in the departure lounge alone, but there it was all the same. He and I, for the moment—in that weird borderland lull—were completely alone.

There were many, many reasons why he was there. Perhaps he'd wandered into the wrong place, and was now stupefied with choice and indecision. Perhaps he'd missed his flight. Perhaps he'd fallen asleep in his chair and *then* missed his flight because no one had thought to wake him up; it was every man and woman for themselves in departures. Perhaps he'd come through to the gates before being prompted to do so. People did the strangest of things in airports. The screens, the announcements, the barriers, the queues, the crowds; the check-in, bag-drop, security, shop, eat, drink, and wait of it never failed to engender the very worst in them. Airports made people anxious, nervous, angry, and above all stupid. Perfectly sane folk would find themselves carried off flights kicking and swearing; others would be prepared to argue the toss over rules that had never been set in anything less than stone since time immemorial, surprised and dismayed again and again by their inability to emerge victorious from battle.

I looked over at those shoes again. Still no movement. If he had any hand luggage, I couldn't see it. Of course, it might have been sitting on a seat next to him, but people travelled with cases big enough to accommodate the kitchen sink these days. And I *knew* that he didn't have anything with him. I felt it with all the certainty of a dream.

"Boo!"

"Holy Jesus Fuck!" This time the coffee cup fell right out of my hands, ricocheting off the side of the till and splattering brown all over the tiles and my own shoes.

"Nice to see you too." Nicky cocked her head to one side, a long feathery earring following the line of her cheekbone. "Long day?"

"Sorry. Shit." The coffee was already seeping through my tights to touch my skin. "What are you doing here?"

Her head stayed cocked, her frown blowing at those feathers and making me want to slap them away from her face. I realised that my hands were shaking. They were hot and they were clammy, and they were shaking. I also realised that Nicky was talking, and all I'd heard was a nasty rush deep inside my ears. "What?"

"I said I'm covering the last three hours of your shift, remember? You asked me last week—are you alright, sweets?"

"Yeah. I'm fine. Sorry." I tried on a smile, and it seemed to convince because her frown became a conspiratorial grin and those horrible feathers disappeared back behind her hair.

"Dicky taking you out, is he?" Nicky came around the counter, and when I didn't answer, she kicked her hip against mine, showing her teeth. "Or maybe a dirty weekend away, is that it? Diggler taking you to paradise in a Travelodge?"

Nicky and *Dicky* got on—that had always been fairly inevitable. Sometimes I'd wished that they got on a little better than that, but Nicky had been dating a very married consultant software developer for more than five years, and she was a girl who made it her business to know which side her bread was buttered on. Rich was a hospital porter—an extremely temperamental hospital porter.

"Christ, where the hell's *he* going? Hang on." She disappeared around the corner and I almost shouted out to stop her, convinced at once that the *he* was the man with the shoes, and that she shouldn't be going anywhere near him. It wasn't him—but it took me two long blinks and a queer shift of focus to realise it. I almost lost those shoes again in a third blink; looking at them was like staring into one of those Magic Eye pictures. When Nicky walked into my line of vision again, I *did* lose them, but I wasn't sorry to.

She had an arm around the shoulders of a very decrepit old fossil, who was dragging a carpet bag behind him that looked about as old—and as big—as he was.

"I think you've come through too soon."

The fossil cocked a white-furred ear in her direction. "What, Jeanie?"

"I said, I think you've come through too soon, sweets. Have you got your boarding pass?"

This was greeted with an earnestly blank expression. The carpet bag drew to an exhausted halt.

"Where are you travelling to?"

"What, Jeanie?"

Nicky bent low and gave him her best nightclub voice. "Where Are You Going?"

"Belfast." Said in a faintly belligerent tone, as if Nicky should have been well aware of where he was bloody going. As he and his carpet bag resumed their dogged shuffle, Nicky's arm still clamped around his shoulders, his gaze suddenly found mine in a dazzlingly sweet and toothless grin. "My Jeanie's a good girl."

If it was a question, I didn't answer it. I'd spent most of the encounter still trying to slide my gaze beyond it, as if seeing those shoes had become a compulsion. Or maybe it was no more than the need to know that a huge spider hadn't moved away from its home on the skirting board.

Nicky gave me a cheerful wink. "Yeah, I'm a regular saint."

Once they had disappeared in the direction of the departure lounge, I tried not to look in the direction of those shoes again. I went about mopping up the spilled coffee with great diligence, wiping down the till, the counter, the tiles, myself, and all the while I pretended that I wasn't looking, that I couldn't smell that rank residual stink of burnt plastic, that I wasn't afraid of a bloody pair of shoes.

"Well?"

I almost banged my head on the counter's underside and took a few seconds to breathe before standing up. "Well what?"

"You, Dicky, and the heady delights of an all-you-can-eat Premier Breakfast?" The cocked head and frown were back.

"No, Christ." I only resisted the *as if* because I wanted to get away quickly. Away from the cocked head and the frown (both of which had been making far too many appearances lately), away from the breathy slide of those horrible feathers—most of all, away from those black scuffed leather shoes. I grabbed my bag and my coat. "I've got to go."

"All right, I can take a hint. Hey, wait—babes, wait!"

I had the shakes again. I wanted fresh air. I wanted to be standing in the No. 35 bus shelter, looking up at the red-and-white winking sky, breathing in cold, dark air. I'd already made it around the counter and halfway to the waiting area before I stopped. "What?"

"Till key."

"Right, sorry." I walked back fast, unhooking it from my belt as I went.

"You sure you're all right?"

"Yeah." I tossed the key and it skittered across the counter, its spiral chain bouncing. I turned back around before she could say anything else, and only stopped when the soles of my feet hit the softer carpet of the waiting area. I looked across at the bank of seats. The shoes were still there, and though I probably should have gone over to speak to their owner—if only for curiosity's sake (or more probably for opening the wardrobe door and letting the light in's sake) rather than solicitude—I didn't. What I did concede to was going back into the shop.

"Look, there's a guy over there. He's been there a while, hasn't moved." When Nicky only blinked at me, I felt compelled to keep going, God knew why. It seemed a mean trick at best: to pass on my own fears to the relief, but I did it anyway. My nan (not averse to passing on the odd horror story herself) had always set much store by fear. It was *a damn sight better to be afraid than a-dead*, and you can't argue with logic any more than senile repetition.

"Look, see over there, in the overflow seats next to 1A?"

She leaned over the counter, looked. If she saw him—if she saw his shoes anyway—she didn't react in the way I'd expected. Which is to say, she didn't react in the same way that I had done. Instead she shrugged, nodded, frowned again.

"He kind of gives me the heebie jeebies, that's all."

"A freak and unique in an airport, Christ, what next: a perv teaching Sunday school?" She grinned when I didn't. "I'll get Jimbo to check him out next time he waddles over to these parts. Go."

When I only stood there, looking at her and the black hint of feathers inside her hair, she gave me that half-frown, half-grin again. "Go, woman!"

I did. Feeling a little like I was leaving her to her doom aboard a sinking ship, I tossed a high-pitched "Nice earrings!" over my shoulder. This made me feel a little worse. The cheerful shouted "Thanks, sweets!" that chased my spongy retreat across the length of the waiting area made me feel a *lot* worse. Night had finally taken hold, and as I resolutely marched towards the brighter lights of the corridor leading back to the departure lounge, refusing to look at any reflections in the dark glass alongside as I did, I belatedly realised that—just like Nicky—none of the easyJet staff, with their swinging lanyards and squawking walkies, had really *seen* those shoes either.

⊸⊙⊷

Monday was a spectacularly bad shift. Part of that was the staggering rudeness of early-week suits seeking retribution after hours of impotent queuing and probing and waiting. Two Christmases before, Nicky had hung a giant multicoloured piñata above the counter, and either the suits didn't see it or didn't get it, or didn't care either way. But most of it was Rich. Most of it was almost always Rich.

Late afternoon, I watched a passenger, head down and doggedly sprinting towards Gate 1B, past all the other passengers sitting and waiting to board the same flight (which wasn't due to board for another twenty-five minutes), waving his boarding card and passport above his head as if he feared being left behind on a planet doomed to imminent destruction. Sipping another horrible coffee (this a forbidden third of the day), I watched as the easyJet staff tried to convince him not to sprint through the gate but to sit the hell down, and I watched as panic whispered through the sitting ranks; as they got up in ever-increasing increments to join a queue that would stand and jostle and crane around itself in self-inflicted fury for the next twenty-five minutes.

A little old lady dumped what looked like a dozen boxes of Edinburgh Rock onto the counter, balancing the latest Catherine Cookson on top where it wobbled precariously. She thrust her boarding pass at me.

"It's okay, I don't need that."

She blinked suspiciously at me.

"It's only for international duty free."

She poked it into the underside of my wrist as I started scanning the boxes. When I still didn't take it, she started poking it hard enough to hurt. I stopped, snatched the bloody thing out of her hand, and smiled while pretending to actually do something with it.

A suit with a very unhealthy roadmap of veins across the bridge of his nose and cheeks shoved through to the front of the queue, stopping just shy of elbowing the little old lady out of the way as well.

"My flight's boarding."

"It's not boarding until 17:00."

"They're fucking queuing, love!"

"That might well be," I handed the boarding pass back to the little old lady, who stashed it between the pages of her passport with comical, head-swivelling furtiveness, "but the flight's not boarding until 17:00."

He held up a bottle of water and two packs of chewing gum, smacked them furiously together. "One-sixty and fifty-five fucking pence times two." He tossed three pound coins onto the counter, one of which rolled instantly off, probably never to be seen again. He glared at me. "Fucking daylight robbery."

The little old lady watched him storm off in the direction of Gate 1B. Behind her, the queue was growing ever more rebellious. "Do I get the book for free, dear? Look at all the rock I'm buying." She leaned closer, her gaze myopically earnest. "In duty free, you get money off for buying in bulk."

There was another of those blessed lulls in the aftermath of the 17:15 to Gatwick and the 17:35 to Manchester. I sat on the stool behind the counter, half of my mind on stealing something from the chocolate display, the other half on Rich. Bad weekends were nothing spectacularly new, but it seemed to me that the bad were most definitely outnumbering the good these days. And how much weight did three years really carry when measured against months of repetitive and jealous vitriol, and nights spent lying back to back, drunk and angry and upset? And afraid. There was that now too. I wasn't stupid. I was angry and upset—and afraid—but I wasn't stupid. I just didn't know yet whether that made any difference.

I slid off the stool, ostensibly to stretch my legs and pilfer another Mars bar, but I found myself walking out into the waiting area instead. It was quiet again; all quiet on the western front, as Nicky was fond of saying, even though the domestic gates were in fact east-facing, out towards the darkening estuary.

I looked at the vast windows, started walking in their direction—for diversion and little else—and then I saw him. I saw him, and promptly remembered that I'd forgotten ever seeing him in the first place. My low heels drew to a stop together, the carpet giving way beneath them. This time I was far enough forward that I could see what I couldn't from inside the shop. He was still in the same seat—it suddenly seemed incomprehensible to me that I hadn't noticed him at all during the previous four hours, though I hadn't—and he was still in the same position. I'd been right in thinking that he'd been hunched over: he sat facing those dark windows, a black donkey jacket obscuring his arms where they hung low over his knees, his head bowed beneath a flat cap, the jacket's collar sitting high against his neck and face.

I felt the stillness again. I felt the silence again. That acrid smell returned to burn behind my eyes and throat. In that weird, alien *nothing*, I felt the rush of everything. I could hear the desperately shrieking octaves of the puggies, the garbled messages of the loudspeakers; I could see the distant lights of the gate corridors and their yellow-lit signs, the slow-blinking alarms of the mobile stairways and baggage trucks out on the tarmac. But all of it was very far away—the almost muted sound of a TV, the sodium glow of streetlights through bedroom curtains when sleep has almost stolen them away. I looked back across at that donkey jacket and flat cap, at the long, low reach of those arms. It felt like I was treading water; as if time was running too slowly to accommodate me, or I'd rushed on too far ahead of its reach.

My hands were shaking again, their palms sweaty cold. Still standing just shy of the end of that bank of plastic seats, I stood and looked and shuffled and sweated. It suddenly occurred to me that he might be dead. That he had been dead all this time. A new low, even for an airport, I was telling myself even though I knew it wasn't true. And then that flat-capped head started rising up from the shadowed valley of his shoulders.

I couldn't move—that much was obvious from my immediate attempts to do just that—but what I could do was turn my gaze from that bank of seats to the reflection of them in the dark window opposite. I saw myself first: a hunched and flinching silhouette in pencil skirt and flouncy blouse. And then I saw him: a profile of head and shoulders. And then eyes. I could have sworn that I saw his eyes.

I glanced left again, in the hopes of seeing Jimbo or even an eastern European with a domestic trolley (to glance right was only to see the deserted Gates 1A and 1B—and of course, that donkey jacket, scuffed leather shoes, flat cap, maybe even *eyes*), but there was no one. Nothing. An *absence* of nothing.

I pretended to myself that it was only my job and a fear of losing it that made me walk towards the window, that made me wheel right at that bank of seats, that made me walk along its length until I was standing in front of that hunched donkey jacket and flat cap.

I cleared my throat, but the voice that came out of it was still horribly high-pitched and unrecognisable as my own. "Can I help you?"

His head had blessedly dropped back down between his shoulders so that all I could see was the dusty top of his flat cap and the matted suggestion of hair beneath. His chuckle rumbled the carpet under my feet like a taxiing jet. A nasty buzzing started up inside my ears and my legs felt suddenly weak. The stink of burnt plastic mingled with something else—something warm and metallic. I didn't know what it was, but I knew what *kind* of smell it was:

the kind that came from inside. I glanced again towards gates six through two and the corridors beyond. Nothing. No one.

"Are you my daughter?"

"What?"

A hand snatched out towards my legs and then thought better of it, drawing into a long-nailed, grimy fist. I flinched backwards anyway—fast enough to trip on my heels. That flat, inflectionless question came again. It sounded somewhere high above my head, as if it had come from a hidden speaker. "Are you my daughter?"

The stink of burnt plastic—maybe rubber—roared suddenly louder, clawing and choking at my throat. I staggered backwards again, taking the hand that I'd unconsciously reached out towards him with me.

He stood up slowly, head still nodding low onto his chest, but it seemed to me that he became suddenly *huge*: his arms spreading too wide a span inside that nasty donkey jacket, his legs trunk-like and juddering as they came towards me. I backed up again and again, only stopping when the cool damp of the window met my shoulder blades.

"I'm waiting for my daughter."

That made better sense, I tried to tell myself—as I pretended not to look, as I pretended not to smell, as I pretended not to hear the horrible buzzing inside my ears and the flat malign voice above and behind and everywhere else around me. Maybe he was a mad old dad come to intercept his mortified daughter, and maybe he'd missed her. God knew, the domestic gates were demented cattle markets at the best of times: arrivals forced into battling their way past the crowds who would leave on the same plane minutes later. Maybe he'd been one of those arrivals. Maybe he'd bought a ticket only as a means to reach the gates. Maybe she hated him; maybe she was afraid of him. Maybe she'd thought that this time she'd managed to escape. Maybe, maybe, maybe.

I made myself push away from the window and move towards him—and I made myself ignore the puckering crawl of my skin as I did it. Those long donkey jacket arms widened, lengthened, but still stopped short of touching. I watched the flat cap come up and *out*, like a tortoise head from its shell, and when I thought about screaming, I was only surprised that I didn't.

"Are you my daughter?"

I saw his eyes. In the instant I realised that the buzzing wasn't inside my ears after all, but orbiting close around his head in frenzied black relays, I saw his eyes and those eyes saw *me*: a hunched and flinching silhouette in pencil skirt and flouncy blouse caught inside slit pupils that blinked once, twice, before hiding that me behind translucent third eyelids. The eyelids of a shark.

I backed away again, too slow, too late. Where his left cheek and lips should have been there was only a gaping hole, beneath that the yellow shine of bone, and beneath *that* the ugly pulse of black tumour. All of a sudden, I could smell it too—over the stink of burning something, and the stink of blood, waste, exudate, fuck knew what else (I knew what else, but wasn't about to add *that* to the list)—the nauseating stink of his rotting face.

"You're not my daughter." I got a flash of long teeth embedded inside yellow jawbone as he tried to grin. "But you'd do."

I ran. My neck cricked, shudders running the full length of me and back again, and I staggered away, muttering, sobbing, screaming—again, God knew which, but I was doing at least one of those things if not all three. It was only when the going got harder instead of easier that I came back to myself a little and realised that I was caught inside an urgent wave of bodies. The sounds of the airport rushed at me as if I'd just broken through the surface of a lake. I flailed, screamed, terrified of going back under. The buzzing, the smells, the sense that I was somewhere else entirely—that weird borderland between what was real and what should never be—slowly receded as I pushed my way up through a stampeding crowd that was at best annoyed, at worst indifferent. Over my head, a more familiar disembodied voice:

"The 18:15 to Cardiff is now boarding through Gate 2. Please have your ID and boarding passes ready for inspection."

"Hey." A heavy hand on my shoulder that wrung another of those alien screams from me. "Hey! You're disturbing the natives."

Jimbo pulled me out of the stampede for the Cardiff flight, earning himself a few of those annoyed or frighteningly indifferent stares as he did it. His florid face was half concerned and half mortified. He let go of me just as soon as he could.

"What the hell's up with you, Lorna?"

"Look, for Christ's sake, there—over there! In the overflow seats for 1A and B—there!"

Jimbo looked. As the Cardiff flight thinned, disappearing down the funnel of Gate 2, he went on looking, screwing up his eyes like Mr. Fucking Magoo, his mouth half open and exposing black-filled incisors.

"Do you see him?" When Jimbo didn't answer, but instead went on peering, mouth still hanging open in that moronic underbite, I grabbed hold of his upper arm. *This* he reacted to, shaking me loose like I'd tried to hit him. "Do you fucking *see* him, Jimbo?"

He turned to look at me, and just about managed to disguise a shoulder shrug. Just about. "Yeah, I see 'im."

I tried another tack, now juggling a whole plethora of things that I wasn't going to think about—the latest being that Jimbo couldn't see *him* either. Not properly. Not as he really was. "Please, Jimbo, he's a nut job and he's been there for days—will you just get fucking rid of him?"

"Alright, I'll get rid of 'im." Jimbo moved off too quickly, and in the wrong direction. I was too late in grabbing for him again, and his relief was obvious as he picked up speed.

"Jimbo!"

"I'll be back in five," he muttered over his shoulder, waddling fast towards the departure lounge corridor, keys jangling at his waist. "Got a call for check-in."

I stood, just shy of Gate 2, legs still shaking, hands still shaking, bad-smelling sweat sliding down my back in cold, fat rivulets that soaked into the waistband of my skirt. A particularly excitable puggy sped through a gamut of high-pitched notes and then back again, making my shoulders hunch. Slowly—slower than I wanted to, but my body was doing its own thing again—I turned around.

I squinted, blinked, felt that nauseating slide in perspective again. And there he was. The black sheen of his eyes found me (*full nictitating membranes*, some madly sane voice inside me said), and then he pulled his flat cap off in a flurry of scattered flies and bowed low, exposing a skull as yellow as his jawbone or teeth. There was an eye sitting inside the crown of that skull—I saw it before darker spots danced a reel across my vision and my body turned itself fast back around. A small, grey, blinking oval eye.

I left. Before the easyJet staff and their squawking walkies had a chance to vacate the now empty Gate 2, before I managed to forget what I'd seen, before I allowed myself to be trapped in the borderland with *him* again, I left. I wasn't treading water anymore—I was drifting, flailing, tethered to nothing but black empty space.

⤚o⤙

That night, I got horribly drunk. I shouldn't have done—it was possibly the very worst thing that I could have done—and I paid for it in more than just nightmares. Rich saw to that.

I didn't go back to work for almost a week. Nicky phoned often, and I only talked to her because the alternative was seeing her. Lying is always a lot easier when the person who's being lied to can't see your face. Can't see the lie.

I only went back because staying at home became the uglier prospect. It's amazing what the human brain can convince itself of; all those subconscious and even conscious prompts filtering what it wants to believe from what it doesn't. A disregard for logic so blatant that it seems hardly credible. I went back. This time I still remembered. I remembered those eyes (those *full nictitating membranes*); I remembered the smells, the flies, the rotting tumour sitting inside yellow gleaming bone. I remembered the "you'd do," and I remembered that third fucking eye, and still I went back. And as I walked down the long, rain-framed corridor from the departure lounge to the domestic gates, all I was thinking of was Rich and something I'd read somewhere once. *She was to be had for the taking.* Even then, with that sentence drifting unimpeded—*unfiltered*—through my brain, I was still only thinking of Rich.

The shoes weren't there. *He* wasn't there. Not hugely surprising since the overflow seats were packed, impatiently awaiting the boarding of two rush-hour flights, but it was a fact all the same. Nicky was waiting for me, hopping foot to foot, looking down at her mobile and up at the digital clock on the wall. When she saw me, she came around the counter fast, dropping her phone onto it before throwing herself against and then around me, digging her nails into my back. She was wearing feathery earrings again—this time red—they tickled my cheek, but I forced myself not to flinch.

Words came out of her in a breathy rush. "Oh thank God you came thank God you're alright I said to Ian I said to him if she doesn't come tonight I'm going 'round to find out what's wrong are you alright you *are* alright sweets?"

"I'm alright." Through a mouthful of hair and red feathers.

She drew back, took her nails away and moved her hands to my shoulders. Her smile stopped before it started, leaving an ugly, lipless grimace in its stead.

"Jesus Christ, what did he do to you?"

I touched my cheekbone, appalled first that I'd done it, and then latterly that make-up and time hadn't been enough to erase the lie.

Nicky's grimace became deliberate. "Fucking Dicky—fucking, shitting, *fucking* Dicky."

I didn't say anything. Now the hands at my shoulders started digging their nails in too. The red feathers bounced in and out of her hair.

"You've fucking left him." I didn't know if it was a question or a statement, but when I didn't respond to that either, Nicky's eyes grew wide. There was some measure of contempt in them; I don't know if she knew it was there, but it was. "*Have* you fucking left him?"

"We've got a flat together, Nicky. We've got... stuff together."

"Stuff?" She let go of me, and even though her embrace had hurt, I felt the absence of it acutely.

"I will. I am."

Her eyes narrowed. "Good. Ian and I'll come 'round tomor—"

"It's okay, Nicky. I can take care of it myself."

Those still faintly contemptuous eyes believed otherwise, but her grimace had gone. "You're sure?"

"I've got to get used to doing things on my own."

She liked this answer. Her eyes softened and her hands reached for mine. "Okay, sweets." Those eyes hardened again. "He's a bastard." I wondered how much of that fury was for herself and for what she might once have thought of him. Dicky. Diggler. "He's a fucking bastard."

⊸⊷

In the end, she stayed an hour over the end of her shift, helping me do not very much at all. She didn't hold my hands again, but I caught her looking at me far too many times while pretending that I hadn't, and she pretended to believe everything I'd said while she very obviously didn't.

Before she left, she kissed my made-up cheek. "Take care of you, sweets."

This time I knew it was a question, and so I hugged her close, closing my eyes against those red feathers. "I know you will."

She left, but she didn't want to. *I* didn't want her to. Very suddenly—like the terrible snap of a rope tethered to the safety of home—I didn't want her to go anywhere at all. Instead, I smiled, waved her off, and turned my attention to the nearest scowling customer.

⟜

I felt the lull come before it arrived. While the 20:45 to Belfast still boarded to the accompaniment of the usual feverish racket, I could feel that silence—that nothing—like the creep of a ghost not yet dead. I tidied and I restocked and I served dwindling groups of customers until I heard the tremulous shriek of the departing Belfast jet, and then the dwindling squawks of easyJet walkies.

I didn't venture out of the shop. Didn't even look towards the windows across from its entrance. I drank two coffees, ate two Mars bars, flipped blindly through a magazine, all the time pretending that I wasn't there yet. Wasn't inside the lull—that empty, soundless borderland.

Grimy, long-nailed fingers pushed a three-pack of souvenir tea towels across the counter towards me. I didn't look up, not when the puggies' cries diminished into distant echo to be replaced by the angry buzz of flies, not when I tasted all those rank smells up close again. Not when I saw the long streaks of blood on the cheap weaves of cloth.

My hands shook as I searched for and then scanned the barcode; my voice shook harder when I asked for five pounds fifty. I didn't hold out my hand. And I still didn't look up.

A breath, then the audible and hideous swallow of muscles too atrophied or rotten to realise their function. That inexhaustible buzzing. The sickly sweet stink of dead or putrefying flesh.

"Are you my daughter?"

I let go of the tea towels, retreated until my back met the cigarette shelves in a hard smack, and then I finally looked up.

In the better light of the shop, his eyes were black shining marbles; I could see my head and shoulders inside both. What skin he had left was peeling away from the bone beneath like well-cooked chicken. The stink of him was incredible; my stomach squeezed and squeezed inside an invisible fist, and only terror and a reflexive clench of my diaphragm stymied its convulsions. Worst of all was that tumour—that cancerous, pulsing mass of black. Sitting inside the yellow gleam of his jawbone like chewing tobacco. He suddenly grinned—I saw his naked jaw fight hard to do it—and a piece of that rank necrotic tissue fell foul of his teeth, spilling black goop over what was left of his chin before disappearing into the high collar of his donkey jacket.

I swallowed bile and saliva, my own jaw clicking loudly in that terrible nothing. His grin persisted. "You're not my daughter." Those three-lidded eyes found the bruise along my cheekbone. "Not yet."

I ran. I banged through the counter's side hatch, and I ran. He followed me. I could hear the wheeze of his breath, and I could smell the rank stench of his exertions as I sprinted past Gate 2 and the shuttered Costa Coffee alongside it. The carpet became deeper between Gates 3 and 4; by the empty Gate 5, it had become a sticky tar that sucked at the soles and heels of my shoes. I was sobbing, crying, slapping at the slow buzzing air around me as if that might be enough. After Gate 6, I became stuck. The more I struggled to move, the more entrenched I became, as if I'd wandered blindly into quicksand.

He put his hands on me. Their heat crawled through my blouse to my skin. They turned me around, and the quicksand parted in accommodation. I didn't look at him. Instead, I stared down the dark throat of Gate 6—a throat that led into another empty nothing, until the next hungry orange-white roar became its temporary belly.

"Leave me alone." I whispered it.

Those nails let me go. Out of the unwilling corner of my eye, I saw the arms of his donkey jacket reach out and then up. I saw his flat cap hit the carpet, chased by a black cloud of flies before the quicksand swallowed both. I heard the creak of his bones as he bent low and the wet blink of that third-eye. And God help me, I looked. I looked. At the patchy gleam of skull through matted islands of hair. At that grey, pupilless eye sitting inside his crown. It narrowed, it puckered—and in another wet sigh, it blinked.

The flanking walls started to sprint towards each other in a breathless rush. I screamed, hunching down, hands outstretched as if I meant to stop them. They shuddered to a halt less than ten feet apart. Above me, the ceiling dropped and curved. I could still see the departure lounge corridor up ahead, but I had to squint too hard to do it; it was dwindling into distance like a landmark long passed. I glanced right, towards the wide bank of terminal windows, but now they had become deep-set plastic ovals, the night beyond them absolutely dark.

The floor that suddenly gave way beneath me—pushing my pulsing belly up into my thundering chest—was still carpet, but only just. An alarm screamed in my ear as I ricocheted off what seconds before had been Gate 6's admittance desk. I smelled burning something—its stink choked my throat. There was a man next to me. He grabbed for my hand and then let it go when yellow masks fell out of that low curved ceiling above our heads. I stood, lurched, screamed some more (though I now had better competition), and then the lights went out.

I staggered through dwindling space, grabbing for headrests and bodies. Lines of white pulsed along the floor like a frantic motorway diversion, and when the way became a sudden and steep incline, I gritted my teeth and kept on going, as if salvation might be waiting for me at the summit.

And I followed those white lights. On my hands and knees, suffering the assault of too-large suitcases, and the stampede and shove of screaming bodies both behind and ahead, my belly dropping and rising, dropping and rising, I followed those little white lights. There were barely authoritative shouts somewhere behind them, and frightened milling bodies that had no clue what to do at their finish, but the only thing able to stop my dogged crawl was a tight-fisted punch that scraped nails along my cheek in its wake.

Still crawling, still pummelled by screams and bodies and falling suitcases, still choked by that suffocating alien smell, still fighting against that ever-heightening incline, I reached shaking fingers to my face and then looked down at my bloody hands. Hands that had never been mine.

And then in the dark. In the suddenly breathless and silent plummet of dark, a voice that was not my own either: "Daddy?"

When I came back, I was standing again, propped up against the sweet rotting stink of his donkey jacket. I shoved him from me with a guttural scream. The teeth inside his jawbone gleamed; his flies buzzed around my head before returning to their home.

"I am not your fucking daughter." My voice was hoarse, almost a whisper.

That laboured grin flashed bone and black wet tumour again. "Not yet."

I backed away. While the carpet under my feet remained carpet and not sucking quicksand, I kept on doing it, hardly caring how far I might be from the departure lounge corridor—only caring that I was getting farther away from the grinning spectre of *him*. I looked across at my hunched reflection inside the dark bank of glass, and wondered whether it was still me. Still *all* me.

My right shoulder suddenly hit something blessedly solid, and I turned around, clinging to the corridor's beginning with a sob. I looked up along the length of that wide walkway with its yellow-lit Keep Rights and go heres, go theres dwindling into endless repetition and shadow. And then I looked back. The hairs on my neck and scalp still standing to attention in stiff bunches, I turned around and I looked back. He was a black juddering shadow inside buzzing fog. Trying to see him from a distance was like trying to see a 3D image inside a 2D picture again. But I could do that now. Whether I wanted to or not, I could do it now without even trying.

He wasn't going to leave me alone. I'd *seen* him. He wasn't ever going to leave me alone. I remembered those scuffed black shoes, close enough to touch but not quite. And I saw too that one day he would get his wish. The "you'd do" that even in my initial terror I'd recognised as impotent threat was impotent no longer. Neither was the "not yet." I was already closer to both—almost within their reach. One day I really would be his daughter, in the same way that the demented *pick me! pick me! pick me!* of the puggies was always certain to get the better of someone eventually.

And so I gave him the finger. I gave him the finger, and I turned around, and I ran. I ran faster than I'd ever done before. And I never once looked back at what I was leaving behind.

⊸

The *stuff* I'd told Nicky about didn't amount to very much at all. I packed and boxed it while Rich was suffering through a double shift at the hospital, and all of it fitted easily into a hired 4x4 in one trip.

My new bedsit was small and cold and damp. I watched endless reruns of *CSI* while eating steaming chips out of paper from the takeaway downstairs. When the equally endless *pick me's!* of my mobile became too much to bear, I dropped it into a skip more than a hundred yards from the flat, and never thought of it again.

Only at night—in that breathless borderland between dozing and dreaming—did I let myself remember anything at all. And even then, only fleetingly. My liberation was two-fold; I had much to both protect and hide from. But I'd come to recognise something else too. *His* daughter's escape had been far better than mine. From a father who would stalk her into the burning hell of her death; who would wait for her, rotting and grinning inside it. That was the kind of love worthy of a better escape. There was cold comfort in that at least. He might still be waiting for her, but even with that rank third-eye he'd never find her. Not her. Always the last thing that I heard before sleep carried me into the breathless and silent plummet of dark was his whispered, creaking grin. "But you'd do."

The final voicemail message that I'd listened to before ditching the phone had come from Jimbo. Nicky hadn't turned up to any of her shifts either; *what the bloody fuck was wrong with either of us*? I remembered the old fossil and his carpet bag, headed for Belfast. I remembered that dazzlingly sweet and toothless grin too. "My Jeanie's a good girl." Nicky's cheerful wink over the white fluff of his head. "Yeah, I'm a regular saint." And last—always last—I remembered those black scuffed leather shoes, close enough to touch but not quite. And that gleeful, hopeful, hungry question. "Are you my daughter?"

Regret is a surprisingly easy bedfellow. Even guilt can be borne if it must be. *Better to be afraid than a-dead*. And after all, it's every man—and woman—for themselves in departures.

YMIR

JOHN LANGAN

"I saw how the night came, Came striding like
the color of the heavy hemlocks."

—Wallace Stevens

I

There was a child standing in the road.

Even as Marissa was jerking her foot from the gas, feathering the brake so as not to throw the Hummer into a skid, she was registering the child's threadbare clothes—rags, really—its bare arms and legs, its uncovered head, all impossible here, a hundred some miles south of the Arctic circle. The Hummer shimmied on the ice. From its back seat, Barret—Barry, he insisted she call him—said, "What is it?"

The child's hair was thick, black, long enough for a girl but not too long for a boy. Its wide eyes were brown; its exposed skin was an olive that had been sun-darkened. Although the Hummer was slowing, it was not doing so quickly enough to prevent it running over the child, the child who could not be here, in the middle of a road across a wide, frozen lake in northwestern Canada, twenty miles from the nearest human settlement.

"Marissa?" Barry said.

What else could it be but a hallucination, a manifestation of the PTSD she prided herself on managing so well since her return from the sand, from Iraq? "It's nothing," she said; though she did not return her foot to the gas, yet. "I thought I saw something in the road."

"Up here?" Barry said. "Not likely. At least, I don't think it is. Do they have caribou in these parts?"

"I don't know."

The child was ten yards in front of her. History prepared for its first, tragic repetition.

"It wasn't a polar bear?" Barry's voice betrayed his eagerness that it was.

"It wasn't."

She lost sight of the child beneath the hood. There was no thud of metal striking flesh, no barely perceptible tremor in the steering wheel. When she checked the rearview mirror, no small form lay crumpled and bloody on the ice. Her vision wobbled as her heart surged with relief. She let the Hummer coast until her pulse did not feel as if it were going to burst her throat, then put her foot back on the gas.

II

"You saw some crazy shit over there," Delaney said. They were on the beach, sitting on the lounge chairs the resort stationed there, passing a bottle of Kahlua back and forth. Delaney had wrinkled his nose at the sight of the liquor, said he preferred his alcohol to taste like alcohol, not candy, but Marissa said it was what she had at hand, and if he didn't like it, he didn't have to drink it. After a night of screwing in her air-conditioned hotel room, they had ventured into the steaming air to watch the sun rise over the Gulf. A pleasant lassitude, yield of the last week's drunk and the last three nights' furious sex with Delaney, suffused her.

His words, however, curdled her satisfaction. She said, "Says who?"

"Says you." He drank from the Kahlua, grimaced. "Jesus." He held the bottle out to her. "You talk in your sleep."

Marissa took the liquor. Across the Gulf, the line of the horizon was becoming more distinct, the sky fading from navy blue to pearl. "What did I say?"

Delaney shrugged. "Nothing too specific. You sounded pretty upset."

The drink was suddenly too sweet. She swallowed hard and returned the bottle to Delaney.

"I'm guessing you were Army," he said once it was clear she wasn't speaking. "I know women aren't supposed to be in combat roles; I also know things don't always work out that way. What was that girl's name? Jessica something."

"Lynch—Jessica Lynch."

"Right."

In the thickets to either side of the beach, songbirds were anticipating the dawn, their whistles long and liquid. She said, "I wasn't in the Army. I was a driver—private contractor for a group called Stillwater."

"Weren't they—"

"They did a lot of security work around Baghdad. But they had their fingers stuck in all flavors of pie. I was in West Virginia, Charleston, driving tankers full of you-don't-want-to-know-what from one coal plant to another. The money wasn't nearly as good as you would have expected. Stillwater put out the word they were looking to hire drivers to transport supplies from Baghdad to points all over. Starting pay was three times what I was making stateside, with gold-plated benefits, as well. It was no secret the situation over there wasn't nearly as rosy as the President and his cronies were claiming, but the Stillwater rep assured me we'd be using only secure roads. I knew it was a risk, but I figured I'd do it for a year, two at the outside—long enough to accumulate a nice little nest egg for myself. I thought I might be able to parley this position with Stillwater into a better one, maybe driving a limo for some corporate bigwig. I had my livery license; just wasn't anyone interested in hiring me to use it in Charleston.

"Anyway, Iraq was a fucking disaster. Since the roads we were driving were supposed to be safe, they were lightly guarded, if at all. How long do you suppose it took the insurgents to figure that out? The second day I was in Baghdad, the guy who was in charge of my convoy, a big Texan named Shea, took me aside and handed me a duffle bag. Inside it was an AK-47, with half a dozen magazines. 'This'll come out of your first paycheck,' he told me. Called it a mandatory expense. He offered to show me how to use it, but I said I was fine. My daddy'd taught me how to rifle-hunt; I guessed I could work out this thing if I had to. Shea had no trouble with that. He insisted, on penalty of automatic dismissal, that I have the AK on the seat beside me for the duration of any and all runs I made as part of his team. If we stopped at any location that was not secure, which was every place between Baghdad and our destination, I was not to leave my cab without that weapon. Doing so was a fire-able offense.

"Intense, right? Most of the guys I drove with were like that. The Army said they'd do what they could for us, but they'd invaded with too few troops in the first place, far from enough to occupy the country, and with the insurgents popping up all over the place, there generally weren't enough of them available to accompany us. Once in a while, we'd luck into a couple of Humvees with .50 cals. They didn't do much to reassure me, themselves, but I assumed if we came under fire, we had a better chance of getting rescued with them than we did without them."

Above, clouds caught the light of the imminent sun and kindled white and gold. Below, the ocean went from slate to deep blue. Marissa held out her hand, and Delaney pressed the bottle into it. She raised it to inspect its contents, said, "When I started drinking alcohol, this was my drink of choice, this and Bailey's. This was in high school, senior year. Girly drinks, the guys called them, but what the fuck did they know. Girly," she pfffed her disdain. "They'd stand around someone's car or pickup, drinking their cheap, crappy beer, showing off their varsity jackets like a bunch of goddamn peacocks flaunting their tails. One kick, and the biggest of them would've been down with a broken leg, a set of busted ribs."

"Tae kwon do?" Delaney said.

"Tang soo do," Marissa said. "Third-degree black belt. *Sam Dan.*"

"Huh. You keep up with it?"

"Not formally. I train on my own, for what it's worth. What about you?"

"A little of this, a little of that. I'm more a learn-as-you-go kind of guy."

"Is that so?"

"It is."

The Kahlua was still too sweet, but drinking it no longer made her feel as if she was going to vomit.

"I'm wondering," Delaney said, "if you'd be interested in a job."

III

The Eckhard Diamond Mine was a collection of Quonset huts set back from the rim of a titanic hole in the endless white. Barry leaned forward for a better view of it, whistling appreciatively. "Isn't that something? How far across would you say that is?"

"A quarter-mile," Marissa said.

"I expect you're right."

She stopped the Hummer at the front door of the metal shed closest to the pit. The light green paint that had coated the structure was visible only in scattered flakes and scabs. She left the motor running: the digital thermometer on the dash measured the outside temperature at forty below, and she didn't want to risk the engine not starting. For the same reason, she was carrying the heavily oiled .38 revolver in a shoulder holster under her coat. She zipped and buttoned the coat, pulled on the ski-mask and shooting mittens lying on the passenger's seat, and tugged her hood up. She half-turned to the back seat. "You ready, Barry?"

He had encased his bulk in a coat made of a glossy black material that made her think of seal skin. The gloves on his large hands were of the same substance. He drew a ski-mask in the gray and electric green of the Seattle Seahawks down over his broad, bland face. "Ready," he said. "Let's go look at my new investment."

Marissa had expected their arrival to draw some kind of reception from whoever was inside the hut. The moment she stepped outside, however, into cold that shocked the air from her lungs, that she felt crystallizing the surfaces of her eyes, she understood why those inside and warm might prefer to reserve their greetings for her and Barry joining them. The cold seemed to take her out of herself; it was all she could do to keep track of Barry as he lumbered the fifteen feet to the hut's entrance. Without bothering to knock, he wrenched the door open and squeezed through the frame. Marissa followed, giving the area surrounding this end of the building a quick once-over. She wasn't expecting to see anything besides the Hummer with its schoolbus yellow paint, a steady cloud of exhaust tumbling from its tailpipe, the great hole in the earth in the background. Nor did she.

IV

"His name is Barret Langan," Delaney said. "He was friends with a guy I used to work for."

"Why don't you take the job, then?"

"I'm happy where I am."

"What makes you think I'm not?"

"Maybe you are." Delaney accepted the bottle from her. The rising sun had ignited the sea to platinum brilliance.

She said, "What's the job?"

"He's looking for a driver, mainly. But it wouldn't hurt if you knew how to take care of yourself, which it sounds like you do."

"Why? What is this guy, some kind of gangster?"

"He's a man with a lot of money," Delaney said, "a little of which he inherited, more of which he married into, and most of which he made by taking the money that had come his way and investing it."

"So he needs, like, executive protection?"

"Not exactly. From what I understand, the guy spends maybe fifteen minutes a day working—talking to his investment manager, that kind of stuff. The rest of the day, he... wanders around."

"What do you mean?"

"I mean he wanders around. He's in Olympia, right? In Washington. Say he watches something on TV about a donut shop in Portland: he goes to Portland."

"In Oregon?"

"Yeah."

"Is that far?"

"For a fucking donut, it is."

"Is he married?"

"Macy, yeah."

"And she's okay with him taking off for Boise?"

"She's got her own things going, charities, mostly. She's out of the house as much as he is."

"Is this her idea? Get him a babysitter?"

"Don't know. From things I overheard him saying to Wallace—my old boss—he's walked into some pretty dodgy places. Bars so far off the beaten track, they aren't even a rumor. Ghost towns that were never on the map to begin with. Old industrial sites. I gather he's run into some less-than-wholesome characters. Could be he's just being prudent. Funny thing is, the guy's enormous, six-eight, three-twenty, easy. Hands like canned hams.

You'd think the sight of him would be enough to steer most trouble in the other direction."

"Size isn't everything."

"That's not what you said last night."

"Really?"

"Anyway," Delaney said, "the job's there if you want to look into it."

The sun had lifted over the horizon, lighting the landscape to gold-tinted colors. Marissa said, "If I were interested in this position, how much are we talking? Fifty? Sixty? I heard some of the guys who ferried around the Stillwater execs drew down as much as eighty."

"You'd have to do your own negotiating," Delaney said, "but I can guarantee you'd be making three times that, at least."

"Jesus," Marissa said. "Are you serious?"

He nodded. "Understand, you'd have to be available twenty-four/seven."

"For that kind of money, I'll sleep at the foot of his fucking bed."

"You want me to put you in touch with him?"

"Might as well. What's the worst that could happen?"

"Don't say that," Delaney said.

V

Inside, the Quonset hut was a poured concrete floor and metal ribs arching overhead. It had to be warmer than outside, but not by enough to matter. By what light the cloudy windows admitted, Marissa saw that, with the exception of a large, metal cage at its center, the structure was empty. Without hesitation, Barry strode to the cage, which appeared to contain another cage—an elevator, Marissa realized, it was an elevator. Barry swung open the cage door, and stepped into the car, which creaked with his bulk. A black box with a row of rectangular switches had been mounted to his right; he snapped all up at once. Within the elevator, a pair of halogen lights hung in opposite corners flared to life, while the air filled with the nasal hum of electricity. After making certain the door to the place was shut, Marissa crossed to the elevator. It shifted slightly with her weight. A narrow black box with two buttons set one below the other attached to the wire to her left. Barry nodded his ski-masked head at it. "If you would…"

She stabbed the lower button with a mittened finger. The car clattered, shook, and commenced a shuddering descent. Although her face was covered, she supposed her skepticism was evident. She said, "I was under the impression this place was more of a going concern. How long has it been since it was active?"

"As a diamond mine, thirty years, give or take. From the start, it was never as productive as its backers predicted. What diamonds were here were dug out almost immediately. The operation chugged on for a few more years, after which, it was leased to a pair of scientists."

"Scientists?"

"I met one of them; though I didn't know it at the time. At one of Manny and Liz Steiner's parties, a Dr. Ryoko. He and his colleague used the lower reaches of the mine for some type of subatomic research. Had to do with exploiting the layers of rock to slow down the speed of some exotic particles enough for them to be measured. After they left, the mine lay dormant for a decade and a half, until a man named Tyler Choate paid a ridiculous sum of money to have the use of the location for three months."

The elevator lowered past an unlit tunnel. Marissa said, "What for?"

"That is a very interesting question. No one I talked to—and I spoke with a number of people—could answer it. I had to turn to a woman who's good with computers to find out exactly how much his rental cost Mr. Choate. I'm used to large amounts of money. This was enough to impress me.

"To make matters more perplexing," Barry said, "Tyler Choate undertook this course of action while an inmate at a maximum-security prison, where he was serving twenty-years-to-life for some especially nasty sex-crimes. Where, as far as I've been able to ascertain, he continues to pay his debt to society."

Marissa was about to ask him if he was sure, stopped herself. Of course he was. When Barry became interested in something—truly interested—he researched the subject as thoroughly as any scholar. Instead, she said, "I'm guessing that Tyler Choate led you to this place, and not the other way around."

"That's right," Barry said. "You're wondering why."

"Yeah."

"When Delaney informed you I was looking to hire someone, he told you that he knew me through his employer, Wallace Smith. Did he tell you what happened to Wally?"

Another dark tunnel rose in front of the elevator door. "Just that he was dead. And," she added, "that he had nothing to do with it. To be honest, he seemed kind of spooked by the whole thing."

"As well he should have been. No one has been able to say with any certainty what became of the man—of him and Helen, his wife. She had suffered a grievous injury and was being cared for at their house. One morning, she, Wally, and her nurse disappeared. Most of them did, anyway. There were . . . pieces of them left behind. Strictly speaking, there's no definite proof that Wally is dead—that any of them is. But it doesn't look good. The police were treating it as a probable multiple homicide."

"So Tyler Choate's some kind of crime boss, and your friend crossed him."

"That sounds as if it should be what occurred," Barry said. "I'm pretty sure it's the theory the cops are working from. From a distance—from what I've told you—it's the reasonable explanation. Wally's wife was injured in a barn that was connected to the Choates. This set him off in search of information about them. He hired a private detective, a man named Lance Pride; he was the one who located Tyler Choate."

"Wait," Marissa said, "the guy's wife was hurt in a barn? What happened?"

Barry considered the latest tunnel that had opened before them. "A horse kicked her in the head. Split her skull open. A freak accident, but it left her with massive brain damage."

"Ouch. I guess that explains why he was so keen to get hold of whoever owned the barn."

"The horse kicked Wally, too—ruined his hip, left him unable to walk without a cane. That didn't matter as much as the wound to Helen, though."

"What became of the horse?"

"Delaney shot it."

"Oh."

"Anyway—what I started to say was, when I began to poke around into Wally and Helen's disappearance, into the weeks leading up to it, what appeared to be the reasonable explanation fell apart right away. For one thing, the Choates weren't your typical crime family. Almost the opposite, in fact. Pig farmers and super-scientists. I know, it sounds bizarre, but several of the men in the family had careers of some note. In physics, mostly. They also raised pigs on their property, to no great profit, from what I could determine. Members of the family came and went from view. Sometimes this was because they were visiting universities, research labs, think tanks, consulting on theoretical problems and their practical applications. I'll be honest: I couldn't tell you what the hell they were studying, and I flatter myself I'm intelligent. Some of the projects had to do with fairly exotic subatomic particles, which may explain Tyler's interest in this mine."

"You said he was in prison," Marissa said, "Tyler."

The air had warmed sufficiently for them to remove their ski-masks, which Barry did, leaving tufts of his fine hair half-raised. "He is. I gather he was as gifted as the rest of the family, but chose a career in law enforcement, instead. Presumably, to allow him a safe vantage point from which to pursue his less-wholesome activities."

"He was the bad apple," Marissa said. "The rest of the family was okay—weird, but okay—and he was into bad shit. Your friend messed with him, and Tyler had him taken care of. If he's important enough, then him being in prison doesn't matter. He wants to reach out and touch someone, he can do it."

"All very rational," Barry said, "except, there's no evidence linking him to any larger criminal network, not even in rumor. He appears to be a model inmate; at least, his warden thinks so."

Marissa pulled off her ski-mask, stuffed it in her coat pocket. "Okay," she said. "I want to say maybe the Choates are a dead-end, but we're here, so I assume they're not."

They passed the entrance to a larger tunnel. "He called me," Barry said. "Tyler Choate. Last week. I've spent a lot of time and treasure on this matter. I've investigated the Choates as extensively as did Wally. Hell, I succeeded in laying hands on the transcript of a cassette tape Lance Pride sent to Wally about a supposed visit he paid to Tyler Choate in his prison cell. It's nonsense, but I read it half a dozen times. I've had Wally and Helen's histories put under the microscope, too. I've stood in the room where the pieces of them were found. It's been scrubbed clean, of course, but I swear, there is a feel to that space... It's as if, when you notice the walls and ceiling out of the corners of your eyes, they aren't meeting the way they should. But what other effect would you expect the site of such violence to have?

"The problem is, none of what I've found fits together. Despite my best efforts, I've been unable to arrange the information I've gathered into a coherent whole that will explain my friend's fate. From what I understand, the police have encountered the same difficulty. I've kept on searching—it was what led me here, to Eckhard. I did my homework; I knew that the mine was tapped out decades ago. I suspect the consortium who've purchased it intend to set it up as some type of tax dodge. I don't judge them; I've done the same thing, myself. What caused me to reach out to them was the fact that Tyler Choate had made use of the mine. In turn, this drew his attention to me."

"What did he say?"

"He asked me if I was a student of mythology."

The entrance to the next tunnel was smaller. "Mythology?"

"I said I'd read Bullfinch when I was younger, Edith Hamilton. Good, he said, I was familiar with the story of Ymir."

"Ymir."

"It's part of the Norse creation myth. Ymir is a giant, inconceivably huge. The god, Odin, together with his brothers, Vili and Vé, kills Ymir, then uses the pieces of his corpse to build the world. His skull becomes the sky, his blood the sea—you get the idea."

"Lovely."

"These are the Vikings we're talking about. They weren't famed for their refined sensibilities."

"Okay—what does this have to do with anything?"

"Picture, Choate said, a being that size, vast enough that the inside of its skull could form the entire sky. How long did I suppose it would take for a creature that enormous to die? Eons as we measure time, even as our gods do. All the time Odin and his kin were carving up Ymir, tossing his brains up into the air to make the clouds, they were surrounded by his dying thoughts. When Ragnarok—their apocalypse—came, and everything went down in fire and ruin, it was only the last of those thoughts, coming to its end."

"That's pretty trippy," Marissa said, "but I don't—"

"Suppose," Barry went on, "you could drill into that giant skull, through to whatever remained of its brain. A sublime trepanation, he called it. Wouldn't you need a plane for that, I said, if we were inside the giant's head? That was taking the myth too literally, Choate said. What it described was the fall of a being—the catastrophic fall, the Big Bang as the original murder—in whose remains all of us were resident. We—everything was living inside this dying titan. Our solar system was a bacterium subsisting on its cooling flesh. Quite a hopeless situation, he said, no less for him and his family. The Choates had scaled the evolutionary ladder, climbed so high above their fellow apes they could no longer see them below, but for all that, they were little better than tapeworms gorging themselves in the loops of the giant's rotting intestines."

How many tunnels had they passed? All full of darkness that had a curiously flat quality, as if it had been painted on the rock face. Barry said, "There are points, however, where the tractability of the quantum foam might permit you to pierce the giant's forehead, to expose the surface of that great brain. You might stand at one end of an unbelievably long tunnel and watch thoughts light Ymir's cerebrum like chains of bursting suns. If you could decode those lights, who could say what you might learn?"

"All right," Marissa said, with sufficient force to interrupt Barry's reverie. "We've moved from trippy to batshit insane."

"I know, I know." Barry shook his head. "The man's voice... it was as refined, as precise, as an Oxford don's. It seemed to surround me. I wanted to ask him about Wally, say, How are you connected to my friend's death? But as long as he was speaking, I couldn't force the words out. They were trapped by Choate's voice. I had the sense that he knew exactly what my question was, but he never answered it. Instead, he invited me to meet him here, today. I agreed. I knew he was still in prison—and I double-checked, after the call ended—but I also knew I would keep our appointment. And," Barry opened his hands to take in the elevator, the surrounding rock, "here we are."

Half a dozen comments competed for Marissa to voice them, ranging from piteous ("Oh, Barry.") to scornful ("Seriously? This is why we drove to the ass-end of nowhere?"). All were choked off when movement to her left drew her eyes to that corner of the elevator, where she saw the same child who had stood in front of her on the ice road. Its eyes were wide, its mouth open.

VI

After her breathing had returned to normal, Marissa rose from the bed, pulled off the baseball cap and sunglasses Delaney had asked her to wear, and tugged on a t-shirt. Rather than returning to the king-sized bed, she settled in one of the chairs beside the small table that served as her personal bar. Most of the bottles ranged on it were down to a film tinting their glass bottoms, but the Baileys sloshed when she hefted it by the neck, and that was fine. She wasn't certain Delaney was awake; she didn't bother checking before she started to speak.

"On the beach," she said, "earlier, I never finished what I was saying to you."

He mumbled what could have been, "Doesn't matter," his words already half a snore.

She swallowed a mouthful of Baileys. It had been a week since she had not been drunk. Each day's biggest challenge lay in consuming enough alcohol to maintain the pleasant version of the state, without tipping over into anger and self-pity. She said, "This one day, my convoy was caught in an ambush. Textbook example of how to spring one. There were eight of us, traveling west to one of the bases, there. I was third in line. The country was flat, which somehow registered in how big the sky felt. We stuck to the middle of the road, which ran through neighborhoods of squat, sand-colored houses, past palm trees and these big bushes whose name I couldn't remember. The ground was dry; the rigs pulled up rooster-tails of dust as they went. There wasn't any speed limit—well, none that we kept to. In front of some of the houses, groups of men in white robes and red headscarves watched us pass. A few of them threw rocks; although it was more the kids, teenagers and younger, who did that. They had a pretty good aim, too. I'd adjusted to the crack of a rock striking the windshield, the bang when it struck the door. We hadn't been driving that long when the guys ahead of me slowed, fast. Over the radio, I heard Grant, in the lead truck, say, '—in front of me,' and then the IED detonated.

"I saw the explosion, the jet of smoke; I heard the boom, like one of those big fireworks they set off toward the end of Fourth of July displays, the kind of sound you feel deep in your chest. It blew out Grant's windows, shredded his tires, tore the shit out of his engine. Probably concussed Grant, too; although, the insurgents shot him, so who knows? Everything came to a halt. I knew we'd been hit, and when the shooting started, I knew it wasn't over. After the bomb, the gun sounded almost tiny, like strings of firecrackers. I wasn't sure, but I thought we were being targeted from the windows of a couple of houses on either side of the street. Crossfire, right? Most of the fire concentrated on the first truck, but I heard McVey, who was in the second truck, screaming that his windshield was full of holes, and he was pretty sure they'd hit his engine, too, because it was dead.

"Everyone was on the radio at the same time. Shea, the head driver, who was fifth in line, kept trying to raise Grant. 'Grant,' he said, 'move ahead.' Finally, McVey told him Grant was dead, and things weren't looking too good for him, either. 'All right,' Shea said, 'you're going to have to pull around him.' 'No can do,' McVey said, his rig was not moving. Shea couldn't—this was the guy who'd come off as such a badass the first time I met him. Now that the shit was burying the fan, he couldn't process what was happening. He must've told McVey to drive around Grant half a dozen times. McVey said he would love to, but his truck wouldn't move.

"The whole time, the insurgents kept firing, pop pop pop. A bullet punched through the top of my windshield. My AK was on the passenger's seat; I was waiting for Shea to tell us we were going to have to leave our trucks and take the fight to our attackers. At the very least, I was expecting him to direct us to rescue McVey. Because it would have to be us. Someone had radioed the Army for assistance—it must have been Shea—and the woman on the other end told him to wait for an answer that still hadn't come. My heart had shrunk somewhere deep down in my gut. Thc basc of my throat hurt. I was wearing the flak jacket and helmet the company had issued us, but I didn't rate its chances of stopping a bullet from an AK too high. Any minute, I expected the insurgents to leave their windows, or start targeting the rest of us. But all they did was empty magazine after magazine into Grant and McVey's rigs. McVey had gone from demanding help to repeating this kind of prayer, 'Jesus, Jesus Christ, oh Jesus, save me, Jesus Christ.' There was room to the right of his truck, maybe enough for me to squeeze through. I thought I might be able to roll up beside him, use my truck as a shield to let him escape from his and climb in beside me. I could picture myself doing this, but I couldn't do anything to make it happen. My left hand was on the wheel, my right was on the gearshift; my left foot had the clutch pressed in, my right was over the gas—and I sat where I was. Shea was speaking to me, had caught up with the situation and was saying I had to pull around McVey and lead the group out of there. I didn't."

Her throat was dry. She took a generous pull on the bottle. "They had started kidnapping contractors, the insurgents. They were posting videos to YouTube of these guys sitting cross-legged on the floor, their hands tied behind their backs, surrounded by men in black ski-masks. All of them denounced the occupation, a few made requests for ransoms. One guy was murdered, there, on camera, his throat slashed and his head cut off while he was dying. Afterward, the murdering fuck who'd done it held up the poor guy's head like it was some kind of trophy. There was this expression on the dead man's face . . . I don't know how to describe it. He looked sick, as if he'd been choking on his own death. I want to say that this was what was keeping me from moving. Maybe it was. Shea was telling me to put the truck in gear and step on the gas. McVey was crying, 'Jesus,' over and over again. My nostrils were full of the burnt stink of gunpowder. The insurgents' guns rattled on, blowing out another of McVey's tires. 'Move,' Shea was saying. I couldn't believe how level his voice was. 'You have to move.'

"Then I was. I can't say what happened. One moment, I was paralyzed; the next, I had the truck in first and was spinning the wheel to the right. It was a tight fit between McVey's truck and a couple of those heavy bushes, but I cleared it. Bullets smacked the passenger door. One punched through and drilled the seat beside me. I didn't slow beside McVey's cab. I didn't look over at it, or at Grant's rig, still burning. I focused on the road before me, and that allowed me to see the child standing in the middle of it in plenty of time. I couldn't say if it was a boy or a girl. It was young—six, seven—dressed in rags. Barefoot. I thought about Grant's sudden stop. There had been reports of insurgents putting children in the way of approaching convoys and, when the trucks slowed, hitting them. I hadn't believed the stories—hadn't wanted to—but it appeared that was precisely what had occurred, here.

"Passing Grant's truck, I steered left, in an effort to avoid the remains of the IED scattered across the road. This set me straight toward the child. I wanted to turn right, but I had to wait for the truck's back wheels to clear the bomb wreckage, and by the time they did, I was already too close. I pulled the wheel around, anyway, shouting at the kid to get out of the way, but even if it had heard me over the roar of the engine and the popping of the guns, I doubt it understood English. It stood there, its eyes wide, its mouth open, its arms hanging at its sides. I could have stomped the brake and done what I could to miss the child, but I didn't. It was like, now that I had put myself in motion, I wasn't about to stop.

"There should have been no way for me to feel the truck striking something that small. Yet I'm positive a slight tremor ran through the steering wheel as I sped past the place where the child was standing. I didn't check my mirrors for anything lying in the road.

"Later, after we'd pulled into our destination and were sitting around the mess hall, I asked Shea if he'd noticed a child's body a little way past Grant's truck. Yeah, he said, he'd seen a body there that must have been a kid's. Motherfuckers must have stationed it there to stop Grant, then, when they set off the IED, it was killed in the blast. 'Savages,' he said. 'Motherfucking savages.' I said nothing to contradict his version of events."

The bottle of Baileys was empty. Marissa turned it in her hands. She thought Delaney was asleep, but she wasn't certain. She sat where she was, and did not say anything else.

VII

With a shuddering clash, the elevator came to a halt.

"End of the line," Barry said, and slid back the door.

The child was still in the car, its expression of horror unchanged.

Barry stepped out into darkness. For a moment, Marissa was alone in the car with the child. *Not real*, she thought. *It's not real. There is nothing standing there.* Then the tunnel at whose end they had arrived filled with pale, flickering light as Barry flipped the switch that turned on the fluorescent lights set in its ceiling. "It's this way," he said and, without waiting for her, set off.

Pulse thudding, she fled the elevator, rushing ahead of Barry. She swallowed, said, "You should let me go first."

He grunted.

To give her hands something to do, she unsnapped the row of buttons fastening her jacket over the top of its zipper, pinched the zipper's tongue, and eased it down far enough to allow her access to her pistol in its shoulder holster. She considered tugging off her mittens, but decided that the air, while warmer than it was at the surface, was not that warm. Although she could sense the child at her back, she did not turn her head. Instead, she said, "This Wallace—you guys must have been pretty close."

"Oh?" Barry said. "What makes you say that?"

The tunnel was surprisingly finished, its floor and rounded walls concrete. The lights buzzed. "Well," she said, "I mean, here we are, right? I'd have to check the odometer for the exact mileage, but we've come pretty far. Not to mention, all the other stuff you've been up to. You don't do that for just anyone."

"I suppose not," Barry said, though the tone of his voice was threaded with doubt. "Wally was a friend, of course. We certainly drank enough of one another's Scotch. There wasn't a function amongst our set that the two of us didn't attend, and exchange a few words at. He'd traveled quite a bit, and if we were stuck for conversation, we would compare notes on Finland, or Egypt, or Mongolia. We were forever going to do something together, plan a return trip to one of those countries, take our wives someplace new. We got along all right. I had the sense that, wherever we went, we'd have a fine time, together."

The tunnel curved to the left. Marissa wondered how far down the pit—or beneath it—their ride had taken them. She did not look behind her.

"I'm sorry," Barry said. "'A fine time together' sounds like something out of bloody F. Scott Fitzgerald, doesn't it? Chin chin, old boy, jolly good. Or maybe Wodehouse. The fact is, we weren't especially close. After he died—disappeared, but who is anyone kidding?—afterward, I was waiting for one of Wally's other friends, the fellows I considered his close friends, Skip Arden or Randy Freeman, to step forward, keep up with the police investigation, ensure that everything that could be done was being done to locate whoever was responsible and bring them to account. No one took that step—Skip and Randy seemed to have fallen off the face of the earth—so eventually, I did. I picked up the phone and dialed the police because I could, because it was necessary that someone should do so and I was available. You could call it loyalty, I suppose. It's difficult to speak about without sounding ridiculous to yourself."

"It's okay," Marissa said, "I understand loyalty."

In front of her, the tunnel dead-ended in a concrete wall in which a flat, grey metal door was centered. Marissa said, "Through here?"

"I assume so."

She pulled off her right mitten and reached inside her coat for the pistol. She withdrew it from its holster, and let it hang muzzle-down in her hand as she approached the door.

"What is it?" Barry said.

"Just being cautious."

A simple doorknob swung the door in. A wave of warm, humid air spilled over her. A rough, unlit corridor stretched maybe fifty feet to a doorway full of soft, yellow light.

"Well?" Barry said.

Before she could answer, the silhouette of an enormous man occulted the doorway. Marissa raised the .38. Mouth dry, she called, "Hello?"

The voice that answered made her want to scream. "Is that Barret Langan?" it called.

"It is," Barry said. "Is that Tyler Choate?"

"The very same," the voice said. "And you brought a little friend."

"Ms. Osterhoudt sees to my well-being," Barry said. "I'm sure you have employees who do the same for you."

"Not employees, no," Tyler Choate said. "I prefer to think of them as associates, fellow-travelers who have not progressed as far along the particular road we walk. Nonetheless, your point is taken. I would consider it a favor, though, if she would lower her pistol. Good manners, you know."

"Go ahead," Barry said, "but keep it handy."

Whatever rock the corridor had been carved from was full of tiny crystals that caught the lights shining at either end of the passageway and glowed like stars. Some peculiarity of the walls' contours lent the crystals the impression of depth, so that, in walking the passageway, Marissa had the impression of crossing a bridge spanning the stars. The sensation received a boost when she noticed that certain groupings of the lights seemed to align into patterns, constellations; albeit, none of them familiar. She could not hear her boots scraping the floor. She glanced down, and saw a ball of light streak from left to right, apparently far below her. *Shooting star*, she thought, then, *That's ridiculous.* All the same, the relief that suffused her on reaching the other end of the corridor—from which Tyler Choate had withdrawn—was palpable.

She stepped out onto a white marble floor. Directly in front of her, plush leather seats ringed the base of a sizable marble column. A newspaper lay folded on one of them. A mural whose brightly costumed figures suggested Renaissance Italy decorated the walls before and to either side of her. On her right, a rectangle of black marble, set lengthwise, formed a counter atop which sat a gold pen in a polished wood holder and a small crystal bowl full of candies in gold wrappers. The entire space was suffused with the buttery glow of the sun descending the sky, which appeared to originate from the wall in which the doorway was set. Marissa leaned forward, and saw rows of tall windows bracketing the entrance, each one brimming with daylight. "What the fuck?" Barry had followed her into the room. "Why," he said, "this is the Broadsword. What are we doing here?"

"This is the Broadsword," Tyler Choate said. He was standing to the right of the marble column. How, Marissa thought, could she possibly have missed him? The man was a giant, easily eight feet tall, five hundred pounds at minimum. A sleeveless white robe draped him to the tops of his thighs; the garment looked to be a sheet in whose center a hole had been cut for Choate's outsized head. An assortment of astronomical symbols—stylized suns, moons, stars, planets, comets—had been written on the material in what appeared to be black magic marker. The body under the robe was exaggerated, swollen with muscles traversed by rigid veins. Nor was the face any better, the almost-delicate features situated in an expanse of flesh bordered by glossy black hair that draped Choate's shoulders. What Marissa took to be a white dunce cap rose from his head—a wizard's hat, she realized, to match the robe. A single symbol was inscribed on its front, a circle, its circumference broken at about the three o'clock mark.

There was no way for Marissa to have missed him, and yet, she had. It was as if he'd stepped out from behind the creamy light. His voice something with too many legs skittering over her, he said, "To be precise, this is Olympia's famous hotel as it was mid-afternoon on March 5, 1927."

"It's an excellent reproduction," Barry said. "I could almost believe I'm standing in the Broadsword at that exact moment."

"You are," Choate said, "although, the moment has been sliced from its context and slotted here."

Wonderful, Marissa thought, *guy thinks he's a supervillain. Must be all the steroids he took to get this big.*

"Why?" Barry said.

"My father was very fond of the Broadsword," Choate said. "His father took him to dine at it when he was a boy, and he retained a lifelong affection for the establishment. Call this an act of filial piety."

"All right," Barry said. "Why are we meeting you here? What does this location have to do with what happened to Wallace and Helen Smith?"

"Truthfully, not much," Choate said, "although, given its association with my father, it is not completely inappropriate."

"Wallace ran afoul of your father?" Barry said.

"Father developed an unusually... *intimate* relationship with Helen Smith," Choate said. "In the end it tore her—and her husband—apart." He grinned at the obvious pun.

"I was hoping for a more detailed explanation," Barry said.

"He split her head open," Choate said. "He crushed her husband between his teeth. Is that detailed enough for you?"

"Where is he, now?"

Choate waved his enormous hands to take in the surrounding luxury. "Father was much further along in his development than either me or my brother, Joshua. While he could still appreciate the immediate pleasures of your friend and his wife, his form had become more subtle in nature. It was an ideal substance for the process I described to you in our chat. You remember: the sublime trepanation."

"Drilling a hole in the skull of a dead god," Barry said.

"It's a metaphor, of course; except, it's also true. You can imagine, an enterprise of this magnitude requires unprecedented tools. Together, my brother and I were able to fashion such a device from our sire's form."

Great, Marissa thought. *We're in the underground lair of a crazy, giant sex-offender who, from the sound of it, is also a patricide. And who knows? He's probably a cannibal, too.*

As if reading her mind, Barry said, "You killed him? Your father?"

A look of almost comic frustration twisted Choate's features. "Come in," he said, beckoning them toward him. "Come in, and have a look out the windows."

Marissa glanced back at Barry. He nodded. She advanced three steps across the floor, and half-turned to view the wall in which the door opened. There were seven to eight windows to either side of the entrance. Tall, wide, arched at the top, they shone as if their very glass had been ground from light. It was a good trick, but not nearly as good as what she saw through the shining panes. A cratered plane of black sand stretched away to blackness. The sky was black, too, with the exception of a scattering of stars, several of them much larger and brighter than any she knew from the night sky. While she watched, one of the stars swelled, two, three times its diameter, more, before contracting to half its original size, then bursting in a phosphorous-flare that jerked her hand in front of her eyes. "Jesus!" she shouted. Behind and to her left, she heard Barry murmur, "Fuck!" Vision bleached, lids fluttering, she pivoted toward Choate. If he wanted to make a move, now was the time. She raised the .38 in his general direction.

Someone was standing next to him, equally tall, wearing a plain robe whose hood had been raised. *This must be the brother*, she thought, *Joshua*. When he lifted his hands and drew back the hood, she saw that she was right; although this sibling seemed much thinner, the skin shrunken around the contours of his enlarged skull. "Can you see anything?" Barry said. She could. She could see Joshua Choate reach his right hand into the left sleeve of his robe and withdraw a knife that was more a machete, a sinister bit of slight-of-hand. He exchanged a nod with his brother, and started toward her and Barry.

Marissa shot him five times, centering on his chest and tracking up to his head. The first two shots cracked the air and puckered the tops of Joshua's robe. The third shot rung in Marissa's ears like a hammer striking an actual bell; she didn't hear the fourth and fifth shots, only felt the revolver buck in her hand. Holes opened in Joshua's throat, his right cheek, his forehead. His knife bounced on the marble floor where he dropped it; he collapsed next to it and did not move. Marissa swung the gun at Tyler Choate, who had not strayed from his position. His lips were moving, but whatever words were leaving them were kept from her by the ringing in her ears. She shook her head. "I can't hear you."

Tyler nodded, held up one paw with all five fingers extended.

"That leaves me one," she said, "and I'm betting I can put it someplace that will hurt."

A hand pressed her shoulder: Barry, his cell-phone out in his other hand. She did not need to hear what he was saying to know the threat in it.

Choate, however, grinned and gestured at the windows with their special-effects scene. Marissa looked at Barry, who was frowning at his phone. Were they too deep underground? Speaking in the too-loud voice of someone whose hearing was still stunned, Barry uttered a retort that was on the verge of being audible. Marissa thought he was accusing Choate and his brother of luring him here to murder him, to put an end to his investigation into Wallace and Helen Smith's deaths.

That she could see, Choate did nothing. But the roof, the walls, the furniture of the room in which they were standing flew off in different directions, as if yanked away on enormous strings. Now nothing separated them from the desolate plane she had viewed through the windows. In the blackness overhead, a trio of stars flashed one-two-three, strobing the black sand with silent light. Joshua Choate lay where he had fallen; though his knife had been swept away in the disassembling of the room. Tyler Choate also remained in place. Marissa had the impression of something vast looming in the dark landscape behind him, a great, tumorous mass to which he was tethered by a fine thread that floated up from the back of his head and corkscrewed over what she judged a considerable distance.

This time, when Choate spoke, it was as if he was whispering in her ear. "You?" he said. "Barry, my friend, you're incidental. Your companion is the reason you're here."

It was perhaps more shocking than anything Marissa had witnessed. "Me?"

"I required someone to kill my brother." He tilted his head at Joshua's remains.

His words still half-shouted, Barry said, "What?"

"This was a hit?" Marissa said. The notion was laughable, completely out-of-keeping with the madness surrounding them.

"A sacrifice," Choate said, "of himself to himself. Like Odin on Yggdrasil's branch. The only way out of this festering cosmos, this heaving meatwheel. My brother underwent a *kenosis*, an emptying; he divested himself of all he had become. He learned, you understand. From the vantage point we established, here, my brother taught himself to decipher Ymir's dying thoughts. Spelled out in a language of dying suns, he found the key that unlocked the exit to this cadaver universe. That key was nothing, the place that is not a place, the state that is not a state. There, where all things are equally non-existent, he would have parity with Ymir, and might discover what the ancients called the *Ginnungagap*, the breach that birthed the giant.

"Funny," Choate said, "it all sounds rather Eastern, doesn't it? The renunciation of everything and all that. I had always dismissed such notions as so much hippie nonsense. According to my brother, though, those fellows were onto something.

"I helped him to expunge the more . . . developed aspects of his self. But when it came to helping him out of that most fundamental encumbrance, his life, I could not bring myself to offer him that assistance." Choate smiled tightly. "I will admit, of the multitude of vices I might have numbered amongst my practice, sentimentality, family-feeling, would not have been one of them. Well. I could not take my brother's life; any more, I suspect, than Joshua could have taken mine. I searched for a suitable vehicle to deliver my brother's death to him. You may imagine, I have a substantial list of potential names. By this time, however, Barret's interest in me and mine had drawn my attention, and after I conducted an inquiry into him, I discovered Ms. Osterhoudt in his employ. Further research into the particulars of her history convinced me that she was the person for the job. It seems I was correct."

"All right," Barry said, "all right." The words quivered with strain. "We've done what you brought us here for. It's time for us to go."

The great, dark shape behind Tyler Choate rushed forward, as if the distance between it and him had collapsed. His body rippled, the skin tearing up and down his arms and legs. His mouth split at the corners, widening across his considerable face. Curved teeth that would have been at home in a tiger's jaws burst from his gums. A hellish light ignited within his eyes. "Go?" he said, and the single syllable contained a brief monologue's worth of sinister statements. *My brother may have believed in renunciation, but as far as I'm concerned, the jury's still out. He may have wanted it, but you killed my brother. We haven't had anything to eat, and I'm starving.* Blood streamed from his body, steaming with whatever energy was burning through it. He stepped toward them.

Would the single bullet remaining in her pistol be any use against whatever vision of raw appetite Tyler Choate was becoming? Even allowing for a miraculous shot to the eye or forehead, she doubted it. She raised the pistol, turned, and shot Barry in the head. His expression blank, he fell dead. She tossed the gun down beside him.

Choate's face was mostly a gaping maw; the look on what was visible of the rest of it was unreadable. Marissa said, "Loyalty."

He gave a wet, barking cough she realized was a laugh.

"Fuck you," she said.

And he was gone. In his place was the child, the one who had traveled with her in the elevator, the one who had been standing on the ice in front of the Hummer, the one whose death she had felt tremble the steering wheel of her truck. Its mouth was open, alight with unearthly fire.

"You," she said. "Okay. I'm ready for this. Okay. Let's go. I'm ready."

As it turned out, she was not.

For Fiona, and for Laird, amigo

PLINK

KURT DINAN

Nodder.

It was written in black Sharpie on the index card Derrick passed me while I stood behind the circulation desk during fifth period.

"This is you," he said. "We start tomorrow."

Thinking I'd missed something, I re-read the card.

Nodder.

In his arms, Derrick carried the stack of psychology books I'd helped him find a week earlier. They were all there—Freud, Watson, Skinner, and others. He'd been reading and scribbling notes ever since. On top of the pile was *About Behaviorism* with its picture of a rat inside a Skinner box.

Nodder.

My mouth went dry at the realization. Derrick's grey eyes watched as I slipped the white 3X5 into my back pocket. I nodded like I was practicing.

"It's sad, isn't it? Seeing him now?" I said. "He isn't half of what he used to be."

"I never said it was sad," Derrick said, turning to leave. "It's actually rather fascinating when you think about it."

Plink.

⟜○⟝

The tragedy had led the local news for days. Anchors spoke solemnly over footage of Merritt's house taken at a respectful distance, followed by neighbors remarking in interviews how heartbreaking it all was. Always included were shots of Merritt with students building a house for Habitat for Humanity. Or Merritt leading the cheers at the homecoming game. Or Merritt receiving yet another Teacher of the Year commendation from the school board. But with nothing further to report once the fire chief repeated the dangers of carbon monoxide poisoning, and maybe one final image of Merritt's wife and nineteen-year-old daughter, the story's lifecycle ended, leaving Merritt alone to his inevitable breakdown.

⟜○⟝

On the first day, I counted three nodders, five smilers, and two leaners. The majority of the class made up the questioners who raised their hands high when required. The rest comprised the miscellaneous, people like Tori in the front row crossing and re-crossing her bare legs, or Josh near the door with his theatrical coughing fits whenever Merritt strayed. AP American History soon shifted from sixty-two minutes of furious note taking to a full-scaled aerobic workout where we nodded and leaned and smiled and questioned as if it was part of our final grade. All the while, Derrick took notes on his clipboard like a scientist in the field.

"Today went well, don't you think? It sets a solid foundation," Derrick said to me later in the library.

It was strange talking to him. Derrick mostly kept to himself, eyeing everyone in a way that let us know we were inferior. In four years of high school, he'd never said a word to me, but his excitement over the project must have been too much.

"I've estimated it should take eight weeks. We might only need seven if we didn't have the weekends to contend with. Under ideal circumstances, the reinforcement schedule should be continuous."

I knew better than to tell him none of us believed it would work. Derrick had spent his education probing for weaknesses in his teachers' knowledge, then lying in wait. During Merritt's six-week absence, Derrick had kept his head on his desk, only raising it occasionally to ask the substitute teacher questions like why Adolf Hitler and Osama bin Laden weren't pictured with Mother Theresa, Martin Luther King, Jr., and the others on the "One Person Can Change the World" poster over the door.

"He still looks the same," Derrick said, talking more to himself than to me. "The white shirt and khaki pants, those stupid joke ties and black Converse High Tops. The breakdown's sewn into his face, though. Have you noticed that dazed look he gets or how his mouth sags like he's had a stroke?"

"Yeah," I said, honored he'd chosen me to confide in. "And the way it's straight lecture bell to bell. He used to be so friendly. Now, he doesn't ask about our weekends or college or anything. It's like he's on autopilot until he can retire."

"The really interesting part is how he's never mentioned what happened," Derrick said. "Denial is common, it's in all the books. But his family died two months ago. Think of how that's building inside of him. Imagine what'll happen when it boils over."

⊸

The first *plink* sounded two days after Merritt had returned from bereavement leave. He spent class lecturing on the Tea Pot Dome Scandal from behind his podium with its "Question Authority" sticker prominently displayed. Derrick, ranked first in our graduating class despite never seeming to pay attention, rolled a pencil from one knuckle to the next while staring out the window. When Shane's book slammed to the floor, everyone jumped. Nervous laughter filled the room, then—

Plink.

It sounded like a window crack spidering out or a penny dropping into a piggy bank, but really, it was its own noise—a *plink.*

Merritt's hands moved from beneath the podium back to his notes. He said, "At this point, Robert La Follette, a Republican Senator from Wisconsin, arranged a committee . . ." and continued on as if there had been no *plink.*

But we had all heard it. We looked at one another wishing someone would ask the question. Beside me, Derrick leaned forward, his head slightly cocked, staring at Merritt as if the man had changed color.

The next day in the hall, following a class filled with countless *plinks* from underneath the podium, Derrick said to no one in particular, "He's releasing stress. Just watch. Whenever anything sudden happens—any sort of interruption—his face tightens. He must have learned it in the hospital, some sort of symbolic action to alleviate tension."

The following day, I kept a secret tally of plinks. When Courtney walked into class late—*plink*. When the nurse interrupted over the intercom as Merritt discussed the Immigration Act of 1924—*plink*. After each one, Merritt's eyes seemed to press farther back into his head. Then in the middle of a pop quiz, Derrick's cell phone blasted "Ride of the Valkyries." He continued working, letting the piece play.

"Derrick, would you please?" Merritt finally said.

"Sorry, sir."

Derrick shut off the alarm, Merritt's hand slipped down, and—

Plink.

It was later that day that Derrick brought the list of psychology books to me in the library. Soon after, my nodding began.

⤚o⤙

Plink.

⤚o⤙

Our goal—a 5X7 color photo—hung thumb tacked on the bulletin board among a collection of news articles on world events. In the picture, Merritt's wife wears a black, sleeveless dress with her hair pinned up and a pendant necklace glinting in the flash. His daughter, probably sixteen at the time, is in a red top and black skirt. She wears an identical pendant, and the two stand with their arms around one another, smiling as if sharing a joke only mothers and daughters could understand.

Everyone in class executed our roles as if we'd practiced for months. Whenever Merritt made any movement toward the picture, the nodders would nod and the smilers would smile and the questioners would question. But the moment Merritt stepped away, we'd stifle all interest. Some put heads down or tapped pencils or whispered to a neighbor. Others pulled out phones or began homework from another class.

Our reinforcements were likely too exaggerated to work on someone with a clear mind, but in his medicinal haze, Merritt didn't recognize what was happening. From the outset, he responded to the rewards, occasionally reverting back to his smiling and joking self, but always with that ever-present vacancy underneath. And then slowly, agonizingly, after two weeks, the reinforcements took hold and Merritt ventured from his usual station behind the podium, and began teaching closer and closer to the picture.

⊸

Plink.

⊸

My grades soon suffered. In the beginning, Derrick's assignment was a simple distraction for the final months of our senior year. However, as I witnessed Merritt's steady decline, I began daydreaming through classes. Bell by bell, I would sit in different desks and make silent promises that as soon as the period ended, I would sneak into the principal's office to admit everything. And when released back into the halls, I'd weather the dirty looks and whispers of "snitch" by taking solace in how I'd done what was right, ending the secret torture of a man who'd been beaten down enough by life.

But loitering in the principal's hallway was the closest I ever got to confessing the ongoing destruction in Merritt's room. Whatever feelings of guilt accompanied seeing Merritt slowing each day—his body moving like it was underwater, his voice displaced and distant as if he was talking in his sleep—curiosity overpowered it all. I simply had to know if Derrick's plan would work. So with Merritt now lecturing within reaching distance of the picture of his dead wife and daughter, I followed orders and nodded, a part of me secretly hoping we'd be caught, but wishing against it all the same.

⊸

Maybe Derrick sensed my uncertainty or had noticed the half-hearted nods I'd been giving, but one morning before school he caught me at my locker. He held up the front page of the *Kansas City Star*: *Forty Dead in Bridge Collapse.*

"You saw this, right?"

Everyone had. The accident had happened the previous evening during rush hour. The main bridge connecting the city to the surrounding suburbs had given way sending carloads of commuters plummeting into the river.

"Do you know what the engineers are saying?" he said. "They think the bridge weakened to the point where finally just one additional car collapsed the entire structure. One moment the bridge was standing, the next, it was gone. Think about that. All it took was one simple addition. What if the guy driving the final car hadn't brought his briefcase home with him? Or if he'd unloaded his golf clubs before heading in to work? Would it still have been his car that brought down the bridge? Or would it have been the car behind his?"

"What's your point?"

He pointed down the hall.

"We can be the final addition," Derrick said.

"Why would we want to do that?"

Derrick looked like the question confused him.

"Why wouldn't we?"

I shut my locker and walked away, only looking over my shoulder when certain it was safe. But Derrick continued observing me, his face emotionless, sending a chill through my body that lasted the rest of the day.

⊸o⊷

Why didn't Merritt stop us? Even after his hospital stay he certainly wasn't aloof. Didn't he recognize what we were doing? The in-depth questions about the effects gas chambers had on a body—

Plink.

Casually slipping in anecdotes about dead relatives during class discussions—

Plink.

Suzy requesting everyone call her Susan so Merritt would be forced to say his dead wife's name throughout the bell—

Plink.

If Merritt detected the betrayal, he never let on. He simply continued teaching as a living ghost, dropping pebbles into a glass jar with greater and greater frequency until an anger festered inside of me not only toward Merritt for his ignorance, but also to his wife and daughter for dying in the first place.

⊸o⊷

Plink.

⟜

In week six the project stalled. Class would begin and Merritt, positioned inches from the picture, would start lecturing. We'd smile and nod and lean, but despite our best efforts, Merritt wouldn't reach. His hand might move toward the photograph inadvertently, but there was no unconscious motivation to keep it there. On the fourth day of the stalemate, Merritt stepped out for a drink of water. Derrick smacked the desktop in frustration.

"We're running out of time. You've got a chance to do something great here, and you're squandering it. Every one of you needs to be better, damn it."

When Merritt re-entered the room, fear of Derrick's wrath fueled our enthusiasm. Each time Merritt's arm made the slightest motion toward the photograph, the room filled with broad smiles, hands reaching for the ceiling, and the complicated questions Merritt loved. And of course, there was me nodding more eagerly than ever.

Nothing worked.

Afterward in the library, Derrick sat with his head in his hands.

"Did you know he doesn't live in that house anymore?" Derrick said. "He moved into a little apartment and sold their car. Remember how he used to go on and on about his family? Now, there's nothing, not even a hint they existed. He's gone so deep into denial he's eliminating all memories of them. He must've forgotten about the picture. It would be gone if he knew it was there. If we could get him to . . . " He trailed off, then added, "We can't quit with him this close. He's right there."

Maybe it was my own frustration, or maybe Derrick's moment of weakness stoked the remaining ember of guilt in me, but I gathered the courage to say, "You know, this just might be an equation you can't solve, Derrick. You can't force him into thinking of his wife and daughter."

"Of course I can. Why couldn't I?"

"Because you're assuming you know what's going on in his head. Jesus, their ghosts are probably everywhere to him."

Derrick lifted his head from the table and stared over my shoulder like he'd spied something on the wall behind me. He was so still that I thought I'd finally reached him. Then, leaving his books behind and without saying goodbye, he left.

Years passed before I would admit to myself that despite my best intentions, I was the one who'd inadvertently given Derrick the additional weight needed to collapse Merritt's bridge.

⊸

Plink.

⊸

Derrick wasn't in class the day following our talk. I'd seen him in Anatomy earlier, and assumed he was hiding in the library stacks, turning over the Merritt problem in his head. I didn't realize it then, but also missing from the room were the twins, Courtney and Kayla. Now I know they were busy preparing.

Merritt was ten minutes into a lesson on the My Lai Massacre. Derrick entered. He'd changed clothes since third period, and now wore khaki pants, a white button down with a Snoopy tie, and black Chuck Taylors. He walked to his seat carrying a black briefcase with a "Question Authority" sticker plastered across the front.

If he recognized the impersonation, Merritt didn't acknowledge it. He simply continued to stand by the bulletin board, hands at his sides, mechanically reciting the events of the notorious incident from the Vietnam War. The rest of us, however, had our eyes on Derrick. He opened the briefcase, then withdrew an empty baby food jar and a sandwich bag filled with pebbles.

Plink.

Merritt never stopped talking. Instead, he crossed the room saying, "At the edge of the village, Lieutenant William Calley gave the order to open fire." When he reached the podium he slid his hands underneath.

Plink.

Derrick—*Plink.*

Merritt—*Plink.*

Derrick—*Plink.*

With Merritt away from the picture, we all responded accordingly. Adrenaline flooding through me, I forced my head on my desk. Some drowned out Merritt's teaching with loud conversations while others exaggerated yawns or texted friends.

Merritt—*Plink.*

Derrick—*Plink.*

Merritt moved from the podium back to the bulletin board. In his hands, he carried an empty jelly jar and bag of stones. Once back at his post, we resumed nodding and leaning and smiling and questioning.

"Over four hundred unarmed villagers were murdered, including women and children—"

The classroom door opened again. Standing in the doorway with their arms around each other were Courtney and Kayla, dressed in the identical outfits Merritt's wife and daughter wore in the picture. The girls had even found the matching pendants.

Merritt—*Plink. Plink.*

Derrick—*Plink. Plink.*

Merritt's eyes followed the twins as they crossed in front of him. When the girls reached Derrick, he joined them, the happy family reunited.

Merritt's hand slowly began to rise.

"Calley regretted his actions the rest of his life," Merritt whispered, his eyes not leaving his family.

Arm outstretched.

"He said he was only following orders."

Fingers on the picture.

"Mr. Merritt?"

The lecture ended. Merritt continued staring at the three, his mouth frozen mid-word. Derrick pointed to the bulletin board.

"Mr. Merritt," Derrick said. "What are you doing?"

Merritt looked at his fingers tracing the glossy faces of his wife and daughter like he was whispering goodnight.

I couldn't stop nodding.

When Merritt turned back, he'd aged twenty years. His mouth twitched, and for a second I thought he might resume teaching. Instead, he softly shook his head, and walked slumped-shouldered from the room for the final time. The door clicked shut behind him in a sad farewell.

We all rocketed from our seats. Our high-fives and desk pounding shook the windows. Courtney and Kayla grasped their throats in over-exaggeration of Merritt's wife and daughter, collapsing to the floor while we cheered them on. My smile was so wide my cheeks hurt.

Through the chaos, I spotted Derrick sitting calmly at his desk writing on his clipboard. He behaved as if he was alone in the room. I peered over his shoulder:

As theorized, subjects' reaction is jubilant. No regret or apprehension evident.

Derrick marked the time and placed the clipboard back in his briefcase. As he headed down the aisle past our celebrating classmates, he turned to me.

"Like I said, fascinating, right?"

Then Derrick walked out leaving behind his jar of pebbles, and me feeling like I'd just taken part in an execution.

⊸

Plink.

⊸

With Merritt gone, Derrick no longer visited the library or stopped by my locker. He spent the rest of the year in class with his head on his desk, ignoring everyone, not even acknowledging the substitute when she called roll. When the picture went missing from the bulletin board, I thought it would either find its way onto the wall of Derrick's future dorm room or be stuffed into a drawer somewhere, an artifact he'd rediscover in two decades and recall with an indifferent shrug. Neither would surprise me.

All this time later, there are nights once my wife and daughter are in bed that the house goes quiet and Merritt visits. He stands planted against the wall, his eyes empty, his pale fingers caressing an invisible picture. There he lectures silently about grief, about regret, and about how everything we have can be taken from us in the time it takes to nod your head. Underneath it all, I hear the echoes of my classmates rejoicing, my voice loud in the celebration.

That's when I begin nodding in the darkness.

And that's when I reach for my jar and bag of stones.

Plink.

NIGREDO

CODY GOODFELLOW

Few cult deprogrammers these days would even try to take someone from Ex Libris. Hardly any even call themselves deprogrammers, anymore. "Exit counselor" is the warmer, fuzzier new title. A human brain must be more than just Descartes's materialist cognitive model, or its feelings wouldn't get so hurt by the truth.

My methods were not popular, but they worked. Most of my business was by referral. My clients had exhausted every other hope. When I could not convince them to accept that perhaps their loved one was better off, in their new lifestyle, then I had them sign my waiver and went to work.

Ex Libris was a hard target. They didn't greet at airports or convention centers or lurk outside euthanasia booths. They didn't panhandle or turn tricks. Mostly, they meditated to the Master's audiobooks while toiling in digital sweatshops up and down the coast.

Their leader was a creative writing professor. Dr. Preston Marble used the classics—"guided" meditation, hypnosis, sleep deprivation, protein starvation, mild hallucinogens, and traumatic writing assignments. Ex Libris grew out of Marble's intensive writing seminars and his "Awakened Editions" series of classic books annotated for neurotics desperately yearning to become psychopaths, harvesting the most hopeless wanna-bes, fans, and impressionable victims into a militant bibliomancy cult.

Marble's guide to story structure translated more easily into a practical bible than the Bible, complete with interactive commandments. Every devotee had to compose an "antibiography" of everything they were not and never would be. On average, they ran to five hundred thousand words composed on no sleep and amphetamine-laced oatmeal. When your Editor finally approved your antibiography, you had to burn it and throw the ashes in the ocean or eat it.

If they used Allah, Buddha, or Jesus, they'd be on FBI watch-lists, but to the outside world, they're just a fucking book club.

Sometimes, I can dress up as a senior cult official and pull them out with no headaches. This outfit had no such slack to exploit. Four surfers in each one-bedroom unit at all times. A van came every other day to rotate them out. Eight more places like this, just in this part of town.

I cut their DSL line, then knocked on their door. Cable guy uniform. Tool belt. Wig and mustache, cotton plugs in my cheeks, lifts in my shoes. I chloroformed the geek who answered the door, caught him, threw the deadbolt, and dragged him into the living room.

No furniture except for four workstations and a couple futons in the corner. Lysol, incense, and macrobiotic farts. Two were awake and pecking at their boards. Another lay on a futon with headphones on. The one I wanted.

She wore a biofeedback harness and a Cranio-Electrical Stimulation cap. She listens to his heartbeat and EEG mixed with his endless lectures while she works. The more her brain activity conforms to Marble's template, the more mildly pleasurable zaps she gets from the cap.

And all while copy-editing or revising the mass media equivalent of lead-painted, asbestos infant's teething rings. If you've ever watched a slab of direct-to-video dreck or mind-numbing scripted reality show patter and wondered how sane human beings can create such empty noise, well… sane people don't.

The system also tracks bodily functions and location for the home office. Anyone unplugging their unit or wandering out of range triggers an alarm and the Editors come running.

I unplugged her and took off her headphones—Marble's sleepy bullroarer voice reading something about an anarchist exploding himself at Greenwich Observatory. She was semi-catatonic, dead on her feet. I didn't even need the chloroform. I stood her up and escorted her to the balcony.

Someone knocked on the front door, then tried the knob.

Out on the balcony overlooking the alley. My assistant Carl waited on the roof of our parked van, ready to catch the product. I bagged her and lowered her over the railing.

Carl caught the bag and gave me a hand down onto the van, then jumped down and caught the product again, dropping her in the back. In and out in less than two minutes.

We took her out to Imperial County, to the Olde Desert Inn. It was abandoned long before I set up shop, and no one ever happened by. Two miles off the Interstate, at a dead place that never quite became a town. You can see anyone coming from five minutes away, watch satellites pass overhead at night.

As soon as we got the product strapped down in the honeymoon suite, Carl went home to his family and I got busy. My client had paid a big premium for a rush job. He wanted his wife back. I had to open up the product and find her.

She had the kind of bright, nervous beauty that you feel sparking at you just before you look her way. Smart, fine features; good bones showing too starkly through her pale, jaundiced skin. Avid, hungry eyes.

Real deprogrammers, the old school guys, kept their techniques under wraps like stage magicians, but it's almost always some variation on the old interrogation, aversion therapy model. I didn't have any tricks, training, dirty little secrets.

I didn't interrogate them or break them down the way the burnout FBI agents and MK-ULTRA stooges who started our game did it. I didn't have to. I was more of an assassin. The product died and the person was reborn, saved by the Elixir.

I liked to measure out dosages not just to body size, age, and health, but to degree of indoctrination. I usually interviewed the product before, but this one was unresponsive. Semi-catatonic. She'd get up and go where you pushed her, but there was nobody home.

A quick physical turned up scalp scabs from constant electrical shocks and bruises from recent IV abuse. Her pupils were responsive and pulse fine, but someone had already worked her.

I wanted to wait, but I gave her the shot. Her pulse spiked, then flattened out. I checked her restraints. If she didn't come around in an hour, I'd give her the second dose.

It wasn't therapy. I studied psychology, but I'm no doctor. Nobody can teach you how to raise the dead. To join any cult, from the Masons to Aum Shinrikyo, you have to die. The old You dies and is buried inside you to fertilize the budding of the new You. To resurrect them, I just had to go digging. The Elixir was my shovel. It's just easy enough, the results miraculous enough, that you'd kid yourself you know what you're doing.

Under the Elixir, you are outwardly conscious. You speak when spoken to. You obey. You don't ask questions. You know nothing but what you are told. You are utterly suggestible. I could make you blow me, hijack a bus, and drive it into a nuclear power plant. It's not like hypnosis, where the idiot on stage *wants* to act like a chicken. What the product wanted, who they were, what they would or wouldn't do... all of it erased and gone away. In its place... whatever I put into them.

But she was doing it wrong.

She took me so completely by surprise that I almost didn't see that I'd found what I'd always been looking for. Someone who could show me what it was like to be nothing.

She babbled in French, faster than I could understand. Then, "*See the stars beneath the sea*... Do you remember before you were born? You remember what it was like...? I'd give anything if you could send me back..."

Usually, the product has to be coaxed out of the clouds. Sometimes it helps to guide them out with imagery; childhood snapshots as stepping-stones, recreating history with a big red editorial pen.

She didn't need me to set the scene. I couldn't stop it. The walls of the motel room turned to stained canvas flats in the wings of a musty black cathedral.

The ceiling vanished in a jumble of scenery dangling from cables. Some I recognized—the apartment, the Ex Libris Chapterhouse, the beach at night, a Hillcrest townhouse—but there were hundreds of others, an armory of scenes. Flakes of corroded varnish fluttered down to settle on her hair like golden snow.

"Before your script was written? Before the Plot had sharpened and bent and broken you to its ends." She winced, trying to smile. "If you're here, you must be an actor..."

"Then you're an actress?"

Her laughter shivered flurries of paintflakes from above. "If you're alive, you must act. Are you so sure you're alive?" She tossed her head and fussed with the ash-roses embroidered in the sleeves of her gray gown. The fabric was dull yet subtly iridescent, like a shed snakeskin. "I like this one ever so much more than the last play..."

"What play was that? What was your role?"

"I was a mirror for a man to admire his own mask. So few real roles for women, now as ever... I loved my Lord the King more than my husband. I had forsaken all others to become a thought in my Lord's mind. But then he revealed to me my particular purpose..."

"And what purpose is that?"

She knelt before the pool that had been only a square chalk outline on the floor of the stage. "To murder him," she said. The buckled, warped boards were now pitted umber flagstones, the corsages of stained paper extravagantly sexual lilies on still, emerald water.

"Do you want to be free of him? Of... all this?"

"Oh, he's no burden. His sinister hand stopped my dagger as if it were a feather. By his fear and by his blood, I knew he was but a pretender. No, the one I want to be free of, no one can escape."

"Who's that?"

She leaned in close and whispered, "The Plot."

Looking up into the gallery, she hunched closer to me. I could feel my warmth leeching away into her. "I like this one ever so much better. So many places to hide... Do you not know the French Play?"

I shuddered and told her no.

"No matter, the lines read *you*, as it were. But we must enter! The call! Here, you must don your mask!"

The theater throbbed with the tolling of a vast, leaden bell. She shoved the cold, dry thing into my hands. Before I could look at it, I had pressed it to my face. Shadowy hands came out of the dark to guide us up twisting stairs and through a velvet miasma of rotting curtains into a cold white light...

We lay side by side upon the bed. Her pulse was steady. Her eyes were empty.

I thought better of giving her the second shot, decided instead on a serious sedative. But when I turned around, the syringe was gone.

It was in her hand. Then it was in my neck.

⊸

Before 9/11, the airport was much more than a place to wait in line and get searched. It was also really easy to steal people's luggage.

I did it to pick up quick cash after I dropped out of college. It beat waiting to be expelled once my misuse of the clinical psychology department's resources was uncovered, or the new law requiring piss tests for financial aid went into effect.

At LAX, the passengers would crowd up to the belt even if their luggage was nowhere in sight, so if something went 'round the loop more than twice, it was probably unclaimed. Missed passenger connection, misrouted baggage, or maybe just a protracted restroom visit. Regardless, within ten seconds of spotting my quarry, I could have it out the turnstile door and into my friend's waiting car.

My friend. Naomi was philosophy on a pre-law track and still doing swimmingly. We had little in common except she enjoyed drugs even more than me, which pretty much guaranteed her at least some sort of regional title. Strikingly homely, smarter than me, and a fry-guide *non pareil.* Any time you wanted to drop acid and go walkabout up the coast, she was down, if she didn't have a term paper due. I told myself she hung out with me because she was writing a paper about me.

So this one time, I cased the claim corrals in the international terminal, which was always sketchy and seldom worth it. Flights from Hong Kong, South America, or the Middle East, where customs or immigration might hold them up for me, were also searched the most often. Even back then, they had cameras everywhere, and sometimes someone was watching them. I did a paper on recognition cues that guide our treatment of people we see as young/old, rich/poor, ugly/pretty, hostile/friendly, threatening/helpless, etc. The grabs started as part of those experiments. Everyone is a bigot, but a memorable prop or stereotypical mannerisms were cues that one noticed even above gender or race. I got a C+ and a journeyman's degree in spycraft.

We kept a suitcase full of Iranian currency—fifteen hundred dollars after exchange—and two pounds of hash. We pursued the experiments elsewhere—shoplifting, dining and dashing, pharmaceutical burglary, etc. Much was learned.

But this last one... it was everything we hoped for and deserved.

I saw this oddly long, odd-shaped, expensive-looking case on a played-out Cathay Pacific from Bangkok and figured it for something fun. Maybe a musical instrument. I wasn't looking for money, though I was broke and hungry. I wanted secrets.

I was dressed in a distressed linen suit, perfect for humid tropical climes, and a Panama hat with a snakeskin band. The dissolute young sex tourist, bringing back only viral contraband incubating where no customs agent dare search, or the callow expatriate, returning to liquidate a deceased parent's estate before returning to kick the gong around with the ladyboys of Patpong.

Already a scrum of vultures from the next flight were converging around the belt from the next flight, providing plenty of cover from airport security.

I was on the far side of the belt with a clear shot for the doors. Naomi waited at the curb in her ketchup-red Sentra with a bungee-cord holding the trunk shut. I passed "security" when I noticed I'd grabbed the wrong bag. This one was beat up, dull matte-black brushed steel with three key locks on it. It was too late to turn back, so I ran with it.

Three guesses what was inside.

Naomi and I went to a Shakey's Pizza in Culver City. Her dad was a retired cop upstate, but she learned how to pick locks to steal her classmates' Ritalin and weed in middle school. She got it open before our pie arrived and I lost my last ball on the ancient Zardoz pinball machine.

Neither of us knew French, so we couldn't read the greasy, piss-stinking diary. We got disgusted by the pictures of naked or near-naked Thai boys posed in rice paddies, in muddy alleys, in brothels, coatrooms, and riverbanks. Everywhere this guy went, he must have paid boys to drop trou for a photograph, prologue to fuck-knows-what. Maybe he paid them in something other than money, for all of them had the same dreamy, vacant expression, eyes drooping shut or fixedly staring up at the contents of their own skulls. I was never so fucking glad I couldn't read French.

I wanted to go back to LAX and play our other favorite game, Spot the Pervert, but he wouldn't make it easy by going to security. He'd run straightaway he suspected they were onto him, and anyway, I got to the bottom of the suitcase and found the big bottles of weird yellow-gray powder.

Naomi wanted to snort it. I wanted to consult the diary first. Only the thought that it could be cremains, deadly insecticide, or uranium, dissuaded us from a trial bump.

And the rest, as they say, is history... When they don't want to talk anymore about how the chance discovery became destiny, or whom they ran over on the way.

In less than six weeks, I had learned enough French to know what I had, and what kind of monster I took it from. Don't believe that I tried to turn evil to good, to redeem it or myself, by going underground and turning the Elixir to a cult deprogramming tool. I could've become the greatest pornographer in history or a revolutionary therapist, a salesman, anything...But I only wanted to learn what people were made of.

Another experiment.

In the interest of science, Naomi and I tried an intramuscular injection of fifty micrograms in solution of the Elixir. That was his name for it.

I don't remember anything after that. Naomi was gone when I came down. I never saw her again. I freaked out and took off and I hid out here and there and everywhere, shedding myself on the road until I was only the Deprogrammer. I believed that the euphoric migraines that overtook me almost like menstrual clockwork every few months were flashbacks, withdrawal symptoms, but I never tried it again.

Using the powdered Elixir, I delivered fifty-two prisoners of cults and successfully converted all but two of them into reasonable facsimiles of their old selves, minus a traumatic scar or an empty hole that made a cult seem like a good idea. I fixed them.

After four years, my supply of the Elixir was nearly used up. I had a sample tested once and learned it was a fungal derivative, but I'd never get spores to grow from it. Nowhere near close to having learned anything real, I was looking at retirement.

⊸○⊷

Carl came within seconds of my paging him. This was because he and his family lived in the motel...and also because his "family" didn't really exist, except as an elaborate skein of posthypnotic suggestions. (Carl was my first product. Mistakes were made.)

Nothing like this, though.

Carl let me get it out of my system. Just apologized and said he didn't see her leave.

Nobody ever escaped from the motel before. An unrehabilitated product would go running back to the cult, which might go to the police. I would have to call the client to let him know his wife was missing with a head full of nameless psychogenic drugs.

Richard Resley, PhD, was a professor of nothing so mundane as one discipline, a postmodern *enfant terrible* who could never be contained on one campus, let alone one bed. The first article pulled up by a Google search called him the Deacon of Deconstruction. I had to get into the double digits to find things I wished I'd known before I agreed to abduct his wife.

I deployed Carl to look for the product and drove into the city to meet with Resley.

He was being interviewed at the local public radio affiliate, but agreed to give me a few minutes between demolishing patriarchal dialectics and delineating game-changing paradigms for a chubby ash-blond postgrad who looked ready to jump his boring bones.

He took it well.

"So, she is no longer your responsibility then." He nodded to me, turned to go. "She is very headstrong. I trust you did your best."

I took his arm, sure he wouldn't want his pet coed to hear what I had to say. "I won't try to complicate the situation any further, if you'll just tell me why you'd pay good money to have your wife deprogrammed from a cult that *you* still belong to."

His face tightened. "I suppose there's no point equivocating. My interests and Preston's are still deeply entangled, though I was never as devoted to his philosophy as my wife." Air-quoted *philosophy*, the prick.

Resley coauthored three major studies of "psychocultural engineering" with Marble two decades ago, just before the guru left UCSD and started his sewing circle. Never publicly connected to the cult, but the pattern was there, if you were paranoid enough to see it. "So, you get all the benefits and none of the starvation . . ."

"My antibiography wasn't all that long. Preston is doing some extraordinary things with expanding human potential, and I've been privileged to witness some of it. Listen, this is beginning to sound like some sort of blackmail attempt . . ."

"It's not. Your wife disappeared in the middle of a session. She's extremely suggestible . . ."

"I could've told you that," he said. "Listen, if you're so concerned, why not go to the police? I'm sure they'd be very thorough in locating her, once they sorted *you* out." Impatiently, he sped up and crossed the street just ahead of a truck loaded with liquid CO2.

I gave up chasing after him. Just stopped and shouted in the street, "Was it you or Marble who turned her onto the French Play?"

"Jesus fucking *Christ*!" Resley whirled and came back up to me where I waited on the curb.

I couldn't resist. "She dreams she's acting in it. Says she was in another play, too, where somebody tried to get her to kill somebody—"

He hit pretty hard for a middle-aged college professor. The punch folded me into his shoulder, which shoved me back onto the curb.

His face was frozen milk. I smelled urine, and it wasn't mine. "Stay the hell away from me or I'll call *my* police. Would you like that?"

I watched him walk away. The postgrad skipped after him, looking sideways at me as she followed him to his office.

⸺

I could've left it alone. Nobody was paying me to press further. I didn't like being used, but if Ex Libris wanted to play games, they would have been subtler about it. The easiest explanation, that Mrs. Resley had been a plant to spy on my methods, would explain it all, if anyone had ever gotten up and walked away in the middle of an Elixir session.

But one person had, and I never saw her again.

No one under the Elixir had ever successfully dragged me into their head. And I had heard only once before of the French Play, in the journal I found with the Elixir.

"And the games! Such delightful entertainments our pretty toys gave us . . . Never has the French Play been performed with such abandon, as my little troupe put on for the Khmer Jaune Festival. Every performance consumed a raft of Cassildas, a platoon of Thales, and taxed my art to its core. Such ecstasies, such wondrous pitiful pain! My dolls laid so bare the veiled face of power and desire that the Pallid Mask wept tears of priceless ichor and the Hidden City beckoned beyond the rotten red moons . . . We all saw it, and beheld the colorless, cold corona of the Crown of No Nation . . . "

The King in Yellow was only one more bullet point in an inventory of depravity that yawned at pedophilia and cannibalism. I tracked down and attempted to read it back when I was still trying to find out what I had, but I couldn't tell you what the big deal was. My memory of it was like a hole in a pocket. I ran down a copy at a Xian Science Reading Room where the curator owed me a big favor.

I put out an underground APB on my car with some contacts in the repo and private security industries. I prowled the Ex Libris chapterhouses in Ocean Beach and Encinitas. I got nothing and nowhere, and hoped for better news from Carl when we met at a taco shop on PCH. He had ignored my calls all day, so I assumed he was either busy or had lost it. He was always losing things when I forgot to remind him.

He looked like he'd lost a lot more than his phone. He sat down next to me on a picnic bench out front. The surfers and landscaping grunts had all gone and the shop was deserted. On the wall, they had that mural in every taco shop, of the dead Indian prince on the woman's lap, an Aztec Pieta...

"I found her," he said.

I lit up. I asked him where, how, why didn't he tell me on the phone...?

He rubbed his eye, looked absently at the smear of blood on his fingertip. He took out a picture. It was creased and faded. He stared at it, cupped in his big, shaky hands. "Why didn't you tell me...?"

Where was she? I asked him.

"She's everywhere," he said, and dropped the picture on the scarred wood table. It wasn't Regina Resley. It was a picture of an emaciated, bald effigy that it took me several seconds to recognize.

Naomi—

It was hard to make out just what he was saying. Words didn't come easy, but he wanted to know what I did to him, to his daughter. Why did he have false memories of another family in the desert, and what was his real fucking name, please?

Before I could think of an answer, he let out a desolate sob and lunged at me, hands around my throat.

⊸⊷

Did I leave that part out?

Carl. I didn't let myself think too much about who he was or where he came from. It was so upsetting, I resented him if I even thought about it, because it never bothered him, and if I could fix myself so I didn't remember Naomi either, then I would have. I was jealous of Carl, because he had someone to fix him.

Carl came looking for his daughter about a month after the Incident. I had split town and was hiding, but he was a retired cop and a widower with nothing else to do. He wanted to know where his daughter was, and since nobody else knew and I was her good friend and had fled right when she went missing, I had a lot of explaining to do.

Instead, I stabbed him in the neck with a syringe of Elixir. I was still haphazardly translating the journal with a big Larousse French dictionary, and I was seriously considering throwing all of it in the ocean and starting over.

But then I had an ideal subject. It was easy to erase memories, but putting something in its place... that took nuance. Starting with Carl, I had gone from something resembling a sleepwalker to someone who believed quite firmly in the fantasy of a normal daily life I had given him, who enjoyed the love of a family in his head every night while he lay alone in a motel room. He was probably happier with my lies than when his real wife and daughter were alive.

But try to tell a man that when he's strangling you.

None of my safewords worked. Not even the nuclear one, the name of his daughter. Breathless, I gasped them in his ear, but he was a me-killing machine. More in sorrow than in panic, I took out the injector pen I'd mixed for Mrs. Resley and stuck it in his left armpit.

He went limp, crushing me on the table. I rolled out from under him and sat down, composing my thoughts. The taco shop workers watched me through the window. Cars passed on the street.

All my work ruined. Her name should have shut him down, but he had found it, and come back for me. I couldn't accept that my programming had simply come undone.

To rebuild Carl would be impossible... his identity was a patchwork stitched together over the last four years. I could leave him blank, but someone would come looking. A man with no memory is interesting, while a man with sad memories can't be buried fast enough. Far easier to restore him to where he was when I found him, with a few hasty updates to account for the missing time.

You've been drinking and drifting ever since you found out your daughter Naomi had died of a drug overdose. But now, it's time to go home, to pick up the pieces and live your life.

I gave him a little more off the top of my head, then put some cash in his wallet. I asked him who did this to him. Who gave him this picture of Naomi, digitally dated four years ago.

Even under the Elixir, he could not, or would not, say. The words he seemed to mouth but could not speak aloud, I could only guess that they were, *Your Master.*

⊸○⊷

I spent the next several hours hiding out from the Plot, trying to figure out what to do next. Waiting to see who tried to fuck me up next.

Reading the French Play.

Like naked celebrity photos or instructions for making a nuclear weapon, you can find no end of fakes and fragments of the French Play on the Internet. But all the versions out there are counterfeits, malware, or worse. Even the most scandalous English translations omitted much, and if an editor only suffered a stroke or a nervous breakdown in the process, he was lucky.

I felt something for Regina Resley that I had not for any of my other products. She was beautiful and smarter than me and she stood at the heart of everything I had thrown away my life to discover. How could I not fall for her?

That's what I told myself, but I loved her as I loved mystery, and because chasing after her lost me in a story less pathetic than my own.

There's just the stories, and people who weave them to trap a bit of reality and tame it, and people get trapped in them and think they're taming the world and playing it like a game to get what they want, like shaking a gourd and doing a dance to make it rain. Sympathetic magic. Spill blood, so it'll rain blood.

Stories do all that for us, and what do they ask in return?

I didn't own a copy. But I figured I for sure knew who did. The condo in Hillcrest had three pet grad students in it. None of them were wired Ex Libris drones, just the new crop of coeds from which Resley had once picked Regina. No wonder he didn't miss her.

I didn't have to search Resley's office. It was on the desk in plain sight, nicely annotated with Post-it tongues sticking out of the crumbling, acid-etched pages. He was nowhere to be found, so I sat behind his desk, donned a pair of rubber gloves, and started to read. I don't think I got through the dramatis personae before I blacked out again.

⊸○⊷

I sat upon a threadbare throne hidden behind a moth-eaten screen as the curtain fell. A river of parchment skin and brittle bones rattled applause out of the void beyond the footlights.

"You were marvelous," she said. She took the gold-trimmed tails of my cloak and slit them with a straight razor.

My hands went to my face and touched the mask. It wouldn't come off. Her hand on mine was colder than the razor. "It's a short intermission. Do you want them to see your naked face?"

I had to search for my own voice. The Lines hung in the air like the promise of plague. "In the . . . in the last play . . . your husband hired me to turn you against your master . . . "

Her hands went to her face. The razor sheared away a wing of her bangs. "Oh, look what you've made me do . . . You're gnawing at my motivation again."

"I'm sorry, Regina. I only wanted to know . . . "

Her eyes went blank and blind. "We're here now, and that's all that matters. We don't ever have to leave . . . *so long as we play*."

She returned to tattering my wardrobe, hysteria whickering in her throat so I didn't dare press. "All of this to be gotten through . . . all these scenes . . . As if any of it matters . . . But our reward . . . "

"What do we get? What comes at the end?"

She looked up from her work and kissed my frigid mask. "Why . . . *you* do!"

"In the next act . . . I can't recall the lines . . . but you . . . you're going to murder someone . . . ?"

"Imagine that! I couldn't murder my own shadow . . . Even when She almost . . . but no . . . No, you won't . . . "

Agitated, she cast about with the razor. "He's not going to find me here. You won't tell, will you? If he doesn't, if we get to the end, then we can go and live where everything has already happened, but we'll remember, won't we? The black starshine won't erase us . . . The sun beneath the sea . . . It won't forget us, because we'll stop it, we'll never have to be born again and we'll stop them, the stopping stoppers . . . stop . . . " The words seemed to come apart in her mind. She looked at me in alarm, the razor clenched in a white, birdlike fist, her soft white wrists cobwebbed with hesitation scars. "Oh my Lord, I'm undone . . . I have forgotten my lines! He's coming to correct us . . . "

The screen around us was hoisted into the gallery. The throne withdrew on whimpering casters with me on it, leaving her trembling alone on the boards when the curtain lifted. She threw up her hands and told me to run just before she dissolved in the pale yellow light.

⤙o⤚

I looked up from the book, my thumb jammed into the last act. He must've come while I was… reading? Sleeping? He sat on the leather couch under the picture window overlooking the ocean. He was wearing the same plum worsted wool suit he had on at school, which was fortunate. It hid the stains.

Resley had no face. Everything from ear to ear, from hairline to chin, was stripped away in a frenzy of slashing, flaying strokes that left only ribbons of gristle dangling from his naked skull. The worst of the mess lay strewn across transcripts of phone conversations with me that lay in his lap.

Two grad students were waiting in the hall. "We've called the police. You really should wait here." They didn't stop me leaving. They shot me with their phones as I fled the scene covering my face with the French Play.

Marble was slated to speak to a few thousand at the Extensions Festival, a massive New Age, human-potential snake oil block party on the Prado. I left my car in the zoo lot and cut through eucalyptus groves and twisting canyons to the backside of Balboa Park.

Yellow-gray clouds draped over the park, clammy fever sheets gravid with rain that couldn't fall. Shadows seeped up out of the decaying Spanish colonnades, alcoves choked with morbid satyrs and defaced saints, faces gouged off and bearded in graffiti and guano. Hotter in the shady arcades than under the stricken sun.

I heard the watery echoes of Marble's voice lapping at the walls everywhere in the park, but it took me a long time to locate him. A cohort of grad students surrounded the Spreckels Organ Pavilion and Ex Libris had bussed their dupes in, so the crowd overflowed the pavilion and swamped the Prado and forked around the goldfish pond to back up against the botanical gardens. Everywhere among them, you could see the earbuds of the ones already listening to his voice, his brainwaves, telling them how to be not just the heroes, but the authors of the story of their lives.

They followed me into the Model Railroad Museum. One of them shot me in the hand. The projectile was the size of a pub dart. My hand went rubbery and spasmed out from under me as I climbed up onto the tabletop model. I tripped over Cajon Pass, kicked a hole in Mt. Palomar, and wrecked the Santa Fe Super Chief. Ancient volunteer engineers in blue caps tried to pull me down, but I staggered toward the HO-scale downtown, intent on stomping Balboa Park, crushing the shoebox-sized replica of the Organ Pavilion and its tiny plastic Preston Marble before Regina could find him. I only made it as far as Fashion Valley. I collapsed on my face and had to be dragged out, numbly clutching many broken boxcars.

Tranquilizer darts. Seriously. It's heartbreaking to devote your life to abducting people efficiently and safely, and then to be taken by sadistic amateurs.

"D'you know how you can tell you're trapped in an inferior writer's universe?" someone said. "Nobody can speak for more than three sentences without sounding exactly like the narrator."

I woke up in a tiny, dusty tea room. The only window was covered up by a faded French, maybe Belgian, flag. I was a prisoner in one of the Houses of Hospitality.

Two big men with thick glasses blocked the door. A stocky man with doleful eyes and no hair of any kind on his head except for a full white handlebar mustache that hid his mouth, so his deep, overly familiar voice could have been coming from anywhere. His left hand rested on his lap like a dead pet, bandaged and splinted as it would be for a deep wound. Say stopping a knife—

"Do you know why cultures die, Mr. ———?" He took a cup of tea from a bodyguard with his right hand. Nobody offered me one. "The Native Americans saw their narrative arc demolished by the more dynamic European colonial dialectic. Their myth, their story-way, was gone, and they soon followed it. They were dead inside, long before we put them on reservations.

"Same with modern America. All our myths gone to rust and reality TV. Fantasies of quick fame and fortune, of swift retribution on the lazy, the stupid, the poor. There's no mythic resonance to daily life. That's why everyone dreams of writing a book or a screenplay. Everyone feels one in them, that never gets out. That story they can't tell is *themselves*!"

A bodyguard handed him a napkin to blot the spilled tea. "More powerful than drugs, than God or death or fear itself, are stories. With less instinct than any flatworm, we look for them to tell us what to do, how to behave, how we're going to end up. There're plenty of atheists in foxholes, but none without a personal mythology that gives them meaning. When life seems long and meaningless, stories make it short and exciting, make every accident into a test, into enemy action, into a *Plot*."

My head throbbed from the tranquilizer. I still couldn't feel my hand. Trying not to stare too fixedly at the teacup, I said, "I'm falling asleep again, you dick. Bullet points, please."

He smiled. "Exposition is death," he admitted. He tossed his empty teacup into the cold fireplace.

"Would it kill you to give me something to drink?"

The bodyguards looked at each other. One went to a tea service in the corner and graced me with lukewarm bottled water that wasn't French. It tasted like a kiss from someone with worse breath than mine.

"People call what I do a cult, and that hurts. I help people tell their stories. I teach them to see the mythic resonance in their daily lives. I tell them the world is full of shit, and I'm right. The disciple pays for wisdom with submission. But this isn't a cult. Nobody here worships me. I don't tell anyone what's going to happen to them when they die.

"Everyone who comes to me, I help them articulate their One Story, their narrative arc, and I don't just help them create a marketable masterpiece. I help them tell their story compellingly, because *that* is where they will go when they die."

My sleepy hand wouldn't cooperate with the clapping. "You should say that up front, more people would join up. What's this got to do with the Resleys? You know he hired me to deprogram Regina so he could try to get her to kill you."

He looked delighted. "Of course. He was only following my outline. Do you know the difference between a fringe cult and a legitimate religion?" He anticipated my obligatory smartass answer. "One dead messiah."

"It's hard to believe you're having a hard time getting someone to kill you."

"With respect, you're not a storyteller. Regina was addicted to escapism and had no real story of her own to tell, so she naturally insinuated herself into mine. Easier to be the villain in your own story, than trying to be something you can't imagine. At least you know where the end is."

Pointing at his mangled hand with mine, I asked, "Why didn't you let her finish you off when you had the chance?"

"Timing is everything. Our lives are like coal. Shaped for eons in darkness to be used up in an instant. Stories are the fire in which they burn."

"If we're lucky. So... your... *arc* comes to a dramatic end, cut down by a traitorous disciple... I think I've seen it before."

"Then you know how it ends. Preston Marble the Man dies, but Marble's Word lives on in *every* man. She'll play her part."

"She's playing it now. She killed her husband, less than an hour's walk from here."

"Nobody seems to have seen her there." He held up his phone to tab through a slew of amateur paparazzi snaps of yours truly fleeing the condo with a gray blur like a struggling dove trapped in my hand. "Just you."

"You don't know where she is."

"We thought you had her, but wherever her body's gone to ground, we're confident she'll rise to the occasion when the curtain goes up."

"Why *The King*—"

Shaking his head vehemently, "Don't." He gathered his thoughts, fetishism warring with fear. He told his bodyguards to wait outside.

"Few can bear to read it at all, and most give up or are thwarted, and everyone who claims to have read it has described a different ending, with variations large and small, but no two alike... because no reader or actor has ever *truly* finished it... "

"But that's not possible. It's just a play, for fuck's sake. How hard can it be to get to the end of a goddamn book... ?"

"Every reader must enter the text alone. None emerge unchanged. Some never return at all. Regina is that most *rara avis*: a *pure* reader. Only the most extreme spheres of abstraction satisfied her, but once dug in, she was impossible to shake out again.

"To reach her... to break her out of her fugue and quicken her to her purpose, we needed some radical outside element to catalyze the last act. You'll continue to serve our plot until your arc is complete."

"And your arc will end with her killing you... to try to make Ex Libris a mainstream religion... ?" He shrugged, all false modesty. A bodyguard watched us through the porthole window in the cottage door. I tossed my water at him.

The door flew open and they were on me before it hit him. My head hit the wall, but I saw how he caught it with his bandaged left hand. It seemed to hurt him a lot less than if someone had just stabbed him there.

"You're not Marble," I said, feeling brilliant.

"Well, of course not... But I've played him for many years, and I've only ever quoted the Master. Professor Marble retired from public life three years ago, and communicates only through bibliomancy and doubles."

Quotations selected at random from his own books on writing. "You're willingly going to die just so he can go to his own funeral?"

It was pure hell finding something that didn't make him smile. "He will be alive and yet mythologically dead. He will be, in point of phenomenological fact, a living god."

"And did *you* have any say in how this would... will...?"

"*The Secret Agent*, by Joseph Conrad. It's one of my favorites. Have you ever...?"

I shook my head. I lie a lot. "You're so tight with the, ah, Master... What's he really like?"

"Could you ever hope to attain mastery so complete that when you close your eyes, your disciple opens them, not merely believing in, but *being*, you? That's what he's like. I pray to him: TEACH ME TO BE YOU. And silently, wisely, he has."

Outside, the pipe organ was crushing the exultant final movement of Saint-Saëns's 3rd Symphony. A timid knock at the low, rounded door lifted Marble's double out of his chair. He shuffled through ankle-deep dust, looking over his shoulder at me from the open doorway. "I imagine you're about to be overwhelmed with remorse when you find out what your last patient has done. You're going to become very emotional over the undoing of your perverse amateur brainwashing operation, and with the police at your door and so many ruined lives in your wake, you'll be doing the world a favor. A real one, not like the sick games you played with helpless, vulnerable people's minds."

I couldn't help but nod along. "That does sound like me. Did you write it all out?"

Slapping his forehead, he produced his trademark overstuffed spiral-bound journal and shook out a slip of paper from my motel. Someone had surely meditated very deeply upon my choppy block-capital handwriting. "How much do I owe you for this?"

Chuckling, he nodded and walked out into a monsoon of applause. Three bodyguards came into the cottage once he was clear and escorted me to a limousine. The bitter tang of mildewed paper and incense. I got in without making a scene.

The book was gone, but I didn't need it. A bodyguard got in with me as the limo pulled away from the curb. He crushed me against the passenger seat. I hit and kicked to no effect. Try as I might, I couldn't even bruise myself against him. I wasn't there at all by the time he hooded me in a two-ply plastic yard waste bag and wrapped his arm around my neck in a truly professional sleeper hold.

⤙⤚

I was back in the gallery. I wore a soldier's uniform. Regina wore a tattered ochre cloak made from an asbestos fire curtain.

She pulled back a drape hiding an alcove and a tarnished brazen bell cover. She lifted the cover and showered us in verdigris-hued light that seemed to rot all that it illuminated.

Underneath it, her husband's severed, faceless head. Upon his brow, cruelly piercing it, the source of the dismal glow—a plain golden circlet transfixed with barbarous, spiky coronal flares.

"A cabal of Spanish conquistadors who sought the seven cities of gold from California to Patagonia made it with all the gold they found. In their bitter madness, they dedicated the crown to Cibola, a kingdom that never was.

"A crown must be ritually consecrated by blood and soil to bind the land and the people to the ruler's bloodline. It was drowned in blood, but never has it touched earth. Outside, it's only a curiosity, but because it's here, the play has outrun the Plot. Whoever claims it becomes King of Hastur. They shall don it and declare a state of war and lay siege to Carcosa...And bring the curtain down upon us all. If he is not stopped...Take it."

I knew it would burn and mutilate my hand. It hurt to touch it, until I realized *I* was hurting me. My fear of it turned to raw, phantom agony, an almost magnetic repulsion.

"Now, I must play my role." The slip of paper clutched in her hand bore a strangely unfinished, yet overripe symbol, a kind of three-headed question mark rendered in saffron ink upon ivory foolscap.

I took her hand. I had no idea of how it ended, but I would do anything to stop it.

I pulled her close and kissed her. Her lips trembled and she clung to me until her passion dissolved into hysterical laughter. "He's coming! If you don't let me go and perform the scene, then we'll all go into the void . . . "

"No, let's go." And we ran.

Somewhere, a pipe organ swung deliriously into Saint-Saëns's *Danse Macabre*, with the slap of whips on flesh for percussion.

I leapt into the nearest canvas flat, but instead of ripping through painted fabric, I pancaked against immovable stone.

The chamber at our backs was crowded with broken statuary, headless kings and armless nymphs, clothed in drifts of crematory dust. The flagstones were gray-veined yellow marble, pitted with tiny marine fossils and worn down with centuries of pacing. Fumbling along the wall in the dark, I clung to her arm. I nearly lost her when a long butcher knife slashed through the *trompe l'oeil* scenery on brittle canvas.

Cassilda cried out and ripped her hand free, so I followed her.

We raced down a flight of stairs and through a courtyard of leafless trees; a cavernous library of books that disintegrated in a whirlwind of debris at our passage; a feasting hall with a bowed table buried to the rafters with uneaten, rotten meals; and a ballroom where the blindfolded organist attacked the crescendo of the delirious, reeling tune in a spastic frenzy. And behind us, just as we escaped each monumental, empty chamber, the butcher knife pierced the canvas and shredded it and our hooded pursuer staggered into fleeting, panicky view.

Breathless, at last we broke through the tall glass doors of the ballroom to end up on a wide balcony overlooking a lake still as stone under two moons. Almost annihilated by the discordant shower of moonlight, on the far shore of the lake and yet somehow farther away than the moons, I could see the spires of a city.

Cassilda threw off her robes and cast the Yellow Sign onto the water with a shiver of bravado. "Can you swim, my darling?"

I looked down, shaking my head. "It's not even water . . . "

She looked at my hand. Only then noticing the crown cutting into my fingers, I threw it after the Yellow Sign.

The ripples from our offerings passed like the quivers of sleeping meat. Deep within it, I could see sepulchral gray lights of unborn ghosts.

The now-familiar purr and crack of steel ripping through canvas and petrified wooden struts echoed through the ballroom. We had been lost, but now were found.

She climbed onto the railing, fingers dug into the eyeless mask of a caryatid. "Come, darling, if we are true, then we shall prevail and gain the far shore . . ."

She kissed me and took my hand. "Quickly, before the sun rises beneath . . ." I climbed up onto the rail alongside her, looking down into the depths of Hali and seeing those imprisoned souls whose dull light bored up through the queasy sheen of doubled moonlight on the skin of the water like the moans of the damned from an orchestra pit.

I kissed her one last time, and pushed her.

She did not grab me, but fell gracefully into the water like a knife.

I watched her dissolve in the darksome gray deeps and heard the chemical scream of her undone body and defiant soul, a pure peal of doomed beauty like an echo of the emptiness of Heaven. She would have to do it all over again, when next the curtain rose.

⊸

I jolted awake to find the trashbag slashed open around my neck, sodden with vomit. The man who'd been killing me only a minute ago now sat with his hands in his lap, looking out the window, pointedly oblivious to our other passengers.

A shrunken, careworn version of the man who'd dictated my suicide note sat across from me. He wore burgundy pajamas and a baggy cardigan with leather elbow patches, oddly stretched out like he had a bulletproof vest underneath. Resley's copy of *The King in Yellow* lay on his trembling knees, open to the beginning of the last act. His bandaged left hand upon it looked like a chicken's claw. His eyes were closed, his head bobbing in time with the whispers of the man who sat next to him, who had no face at all.

It wasn't that I can't recall it now, so much as that I simply could not perceive it, except as a colorless glass mask. He talked to Marble, whispering in his ear. Sheepishly, Marble nodded. The bodyguard on his other side looked right through me when I mouthed his name.

The limousine stopped and Carl got out to open the door. Marble shuffled out in corduroy slippers, out of the crosswalk and up the ramp to the Prado.

"It was you," was all I could say, "in the . . . in the play . . ."

"We've never really been apart," said the faceless man, "from the day you took what was mine."

I stared at him, really *tried* to see him. He smiled. I looked away. For just a moment, he had a face, but it was mine.

"If you knew where I was and what I was doing," I said, "then you could have stopped me... Why didn't you?"

"I could ask you the same question." He turned and rapped on the partition, whispered briefly to Carl. "You could have brought me to the attention of the authorities. We kept each other's secrets admirably. But now..."

I was unable to speak. Was there ever a time when I had not been someone's puppet?

He pointed at Carl. The bodyguard slid across the suede acreage of seat to mix a drink.

"When you stole what was mine, I was beside myself, but then it occurred to me that I might learn more from making a gift of it. And how you have taught me."

"I never used it the way you did."

"I know! You attempted to redeem my Elixir! A dismal failure as an alchemist, but what a failure! The raw material, you refined away all the wrong properties. In my own experiments, I called them my angels, because they lacked free will, and were innocent of desire. Your first instinct was to use it to discover, to learn, to interrogate your angels, but you deluded yourself, you set them free.

"Your choice of career was, of course, my suggestion. But you deserve the credit for the basic decency that gave me the idea to let you... help people with it."

Help people. Learn things. Lies within lies. He didn't even have to erase my true motivation, I did it myself. I wanted what we all want, love and revenge. A cult orphan, nobody's child in a generic post-acid hippie personality cult where children were assigned to adults as punishments. With a different broken, grudging parent every few months, you get to learn ulterior motives like the Eskimos know snow.

"Well, you're too late," I said. "It's all gone. I couldn't figure out how to make more."

Now, I could see his smile, but without eyes, it wasn't much comfort. "The Elixir's potency comes from the ease with which it penetrates the brain, and that is the secret of its rarity. It only propagates in human cerebrospinal fluid and brain matter, and its progress is exquisitely slow. In my home country, we would keep 'cows,' angels too used up to give pleasure, and milk them, but only a few milligrams can be had every year, unless it is allowed to ripen. This takes—"

About four years, I thought, touching my forehead. The headaches weren't withdrawal. The drug I had come to crave was already in my brain.

"It's not working inside your head, of course; there's a lengthy process to activate it, but you've given me a sizable start on a plantation in this country."

Fifty-two clients. Maybe the last few were just starting to have the headaches. Nobody had come to my door to complain yet—

"You know," he said, finishing the drink, "the most remarkable thing about the process . . . is that, as the fungi gradually digests it, the cow experiences some diminished function, to be sure, but remains a dutiful farm animal long after the brain is little more than a stem.

"The Elixir is far more potent, however, from a patient who enjoys at least the illusion of free will. Your associate Carl has no forelobe to speak of at all, and yet . . . " He took his drink from Carl, who'd been waiting to deliver it. "How is the family, Carl?"

"Doing real good, thank you, sir!" Carl, smiling.

"So you see, the Elixir makes its own use of the brain, and yet the mind goes on, like a ghost in a haunted house. So long after you have grown weary of your own purpose in life, you may still serve."

He held up a grotesquely long syringe. Carl took hold of my head and pressed it firmly against the opaque black window. "Hold still," he said. I was unable to move it at all even as the needle slid into the soft tissue beside my tear duct up behind my eyeball and into my skull.

It hurt like being sucked down a black hole, crushed and stretched into a monofilial string. I felt myself surging into the needle's fat reservoir, leaving behind the hapless amateur brainwasher I'd been. I could see the straw-colored fluid dribbling into the syringe. I was being drained out of myself.

When he let me go, I sagged onto a bus stop bench on Park Avenue, across from the zoo. People were running past me and police cars and fire engines surrounded the park. I lay there for a while until a bus came, and I got on and tried to get on with my life.

I spent two weeks in a motel, hiding out and listening. The news made much of Preston Marble's death at the hands of his fanatical understudy. We all saw the video of the disheveled maniac emerging from the crowd to embrace the terrified, charismatic spiritual leader. The black rubber bulb in one hand looks enough like a grenade that two bodyguards move to pry them apart, but somehow, their actions are confused until both men are engulfed in a blanket of white fire.

The vest stuffed with thermite cremated both men on their feet and badly burned thirteen bystanders. The resulting mess was spun to hide Marble's conspiracy, but the narcissistic murder-suicide turned him into another punchline, another hammily plotted fable that only proved some people will believe anything.

I never saw Regina again, not even in my dreams of the French Play. I hope she reached the city on the far side of the lake. Nobody who's been through what she endured should have to come back.

The alchemist was merciful. He told me that he would come to harvest from me only when he had to. So long as I cooperate, I can go about my business for as long as my brain function holds out. He would leave no memory of his visits, just as he would protect my old patients. He gave me a single dose of the Elixir and told me that if I regretted the way things turned out, I could fix it.

I have recorded a new cover story, a new antibiography, and secured the necessary fake IDs to make it stick.

When I wake up, I will tell myself who I am. But I could not resist giving myself an escape hatch. Next to the tape recorder, Resley's annotated copy of *Le Roi en Jaune.*

Whatever the newborn tenant of this motel room chooses, he will deny you the neat, poignant denouement you seek. He will burn this manuscript and go into the world and write his own ending.

HONORABLE MENTIONS

Bailey, Dale "The End of the End of Everything," *Tor.com*, April 23.

Ballingrud, Nathan "Skullpocket" *Nightmare Carnival.*

Barron, Laird "Screaming Elk, Mt.," *Nightmare Carnival.*

Bossert, Gregory Norman "Spinning the Thread," *Kaleidotrope*, Autumn.

Cadigan, Pat "Will the Real Psycho in This Story Please Stand Up?" *Fearful Symmetries.*

Carroll, Siobhan "Wendigo Nights," *Fearful Symmetries.*

Castro, Adam-Troy "The Totals," *Nightmare*, February #17.

Cataneo, Emily B. "The Rondelium Girl of Rue Marseilles," *Qualia Nous.*

Cheney, Matthew "Patrimony," *Black Static* #42, September/October.

Cowen, David "Seven Hauntings in Seven Storms,"(poem) *The Madness of Empty Spaces.*

Crighton, Katherine "The Inside and the Outside," *Women Destroy Horror.*

Emrys, Ruthanna "The Litany of Earth," *Tor.com*, May 15.

Evenson, Brian "Cult," Conjunctions: 62, *Exile.*

Files, Gemma "A Wish from a Bone," *Fearful Symmetries.*

Ford, Jeffrey "Mount Chary Galore," *Fearful Symmetries.*

Fowler, Karen Joy "Nanny Anne and the Christmas Story," *Subterranean*, Winter.

Halsall, Rachel "The Conch," *Hauntings.*

Hirshberg, Glen "A Small Part in the Pantomime," *Nightmare Carnival.*

Johnstone, Carole "Catching Flies," *Fearful Symmetries.*

Jones, Stephen Graham "The Darkest Part," *Nightmare Carnival.*

Jones, Stephen Graham "The Elvis Room," (novella) *This Is Horror.*

Kiernan, Caitlín R. "The Beginning of a Year without Summer," *Sirenia Digest* 99.

Kiernan, Caitlín R. "Far from Any Shore," *Sirenia Digest* 101.

Langan, John "Children of the Fang," (novella) *Lovecraft's Monsters.*

Larson, Rich "The Air We Breathe Is Stormy, Stormy," *Strange Horizons*, August.

Link, Kelly "I Can See Right through You," *McSweeney's Quarterly* 48.

Llewellyn, Livia "It Feels Better Biting Down," *Women Destroy Horror.*

Llewellyn, Livia "The Last, Clean, Bright Summer," *Primeval* #2.

Machado, Carmen Maria "The Husband Stitch," *Granta 129: Fate.*

MacLeod, Catherine "The Attic," *Fearful Symmetries.*

Malik, Usman T. "Resurrection Points," *Strange Horizons*, August.

Manzetti, Alessandro "Nature's Oddities," *The Shaman and Other Shadows.*

McCammon, Robert "White," RobertMcCammon.com.

McMahon, Gary "Dull Fire," *The Spectral Book of Horror Stories.*

Moore, Alison "Eastmouth," *The Spectral Book of Horror Stories.*

Morris, Mark "They Walk as Men," *Terror Tales of Yorkshire.*

Ogawa, Yukimi "In Her Head, in Her Eyes," *The Book Smugglers*, October.

SanGiovanni, Mary "The Mime," *LampLight*, March.

Shearman, Robert "Suffer Little Children," *Fearful Symmetries.*

Slatter, Angela "Home and Hearth," Spectral Press chapbook.

Strantzas, Simon "On Ice," *Burnt Black Suns.*

Tobler, E. Catherine "Migratory Patterns of Underground Birds," *Clarkesworld* 9.

Tobler, E. Catherine "We as One, Trailing Embers," *Beneath Ceaseless Skies* #147.

Valentine, Genevieve "Dream Houses," (novella) WSFA Press.

Wehunt, Michael "Onanon," *Shadows & Tall Trees* 2014.

Wilson, Kai Ashante "The Devil in America," *Tor.com*, April 2.

Wise, A. C. "And the Carnival Leaves Town," *Nightmare Carnival.*

ABOUT THE AUTHORS

Dale Bailey lives in North Carolina with his family, and has published three novels, *The Fallen, House of Bones,* and *Sleeping Policemen* (with Jack Slay, Jr.). His short fiction, collected in *The Resurrection Man's Legacy and Other Stories,* has been a three-time finalist for the International Horror Guild Award, a two-time finalist for the Nebula Award, and a finalist for the Shirley Jackson Award and the Bram Stoker Award.

His International Horror Guild Award-winning novelette "Death and Suffrage" was adapted by director Joe Dante as part of Showtime Television's anthology series, *Masters of Horror*. His collection, *The End of the End of Everything: Stories,* came out in the spring. A novel, *The Subterranean Season*, will be out this fall.

"The Culvert" was originally published in *The Magazine of Fantasy & Science Fiction*, September/October.

⊸o⊷

Nathan Ballingrud is the author of *North American Lake Monsters: Stories*, from Small Beer Press; and *The Visible Filth*, a novella from *This Is Horror*. His work has appeared in numerous Year's Best anthologies, and he has twice won the Shirley Jackson Award. He lives with his daughter in Asheville, North Carolina.

"The Atlas of Hell" was originally published in *Fearful Symmetries*, edited by Ellen Datlow.

⊸o⊷

Laird Barron is the author of several books, including *The Croning, Occultation,* and *The Beautiful Thing That Awaits Us All.* His work has also appeared in many magazines and anthologies. An expatriate Alaskan, Barron currently resides in upstate New York.

"the worms crawl in" was originally published in *Fearful Symmetries*, edited by Ellen Datlow.

⊸

Rhoads Brazos has written stories across the entire spectrum of speculative fiction, from light fantasy to the most decrepit tales of horror to quirky sci-fi. His works can be found in *Apex Magazine*, Pantheon Magazine's *Gaia: Shadow and Breath Anthologies, vols. 1 & 2, Death's Realm Anthology* by Grey Matter Press, and a dozen other magazines and collections. He currently lives in Colorado with his wife and son.

"Tread Upon the Brittle Shell" was originally published in *SQ Mag* edition 14, May.

⊸

Kurt Dinan teaches high school English in Cincinnati where he lives with his wife and four children. His debut novel, *The Water Tower 5,* is scheduled for publication in April of 2016.

"Plink" was originally published in *Far Voyager PS 32/33,* edited by Nick Gevers.

⊸

Brian Evenson is the author of over a dozen books of fiction, most recently the story collection *Windeye* (Coffee House Press 2012) and the novel *Immobility* (Tor 2012), both of which were finalists for a Shirley Jackson Award.

His novel *Last Days* won the American Library Association's award for Best Horror Novel of 2009. His novel *The Open Curtain* (Coffee House Press) was a finalist for an Edgar Award and an International Horror Guild Award.

A new collection, *A Collapse of Horses,* is forthcoming in 2016. He is the recipient of three O. Henry Prizes as well as an NEA fellowship. He lives in Providence, Rhode Island, and works at Brown University.

"Past Reno" was originally published in *Letters to Lovecraft*, edited by Jesse Bullington.

⤚○⤙

Former film critic and teacher-turned-horror-author **Gemma Files** is best known for her Weird Western Hexslinger series: *A Book of Tongues*, *A Rope of Thorns*, and *A Tree of Bones*, all from ChiZine Publications.

She has also published two collections of short fiction, *Kissing Carrion* and *The Worm in Every Heart*, two chapbooks of speculative poetry, and a linked story-cycle, *We Will All Go Down Together: Stories of the Five-Family Coven.*

In 1999, she won the International Horror Guild Best Short Fiction Award for her story "The Emperor's Old Bones." Her next novel, *Experimental Film*, will be available from CZP by the end of 2015.

"This Is Not for You" was originally published in the Ellen Datlow-edited *Women Destroy Horror* issue of *Nightmare* Magazine.

⤚○⤙

Cody Goodfellow has written five novels—his latest is *Repo Shark* (Broken River Books)—co-written three others with John Skipp, and three collections—*Silent Weapons for Quiet Wars*, *All-Monster Action,* and *Strategies against Nature.*

He wrote, co-produced, and scored the short Lovecraftian hygiene film *Stay at Home Dad*, which can be viewed on YouTube. He is also a director of the H. P. Lovecraft Film Festival-Los Angeles and co-founder of Perilous Press, a micropublisher of modern cosmic horror. He lives in Burbank, California, and is currently working very hard on building a perfect bowling team.

"Nigredo" was originally published in the anthology *In the Court of the Yellow King*, edited by Glynn Owen Barrass.

⤚○⤙

Orrin Grey is a writer, editor, amateur film scholar, and monster expert who was born on the night before Halloween. He's the author of *Never Bet the Devil & Other Warnings* and *Painted Monsters & Other Strange Beasts*, as well as the co-editor of *Fungi*, an anthology of weird fungus-themed stories. You can find him online at orringrey.com.

"Persistence of Vision" was originally published in *Fractured: Tales of the Canadian Post-Apocalypse*, edited by Silvia Moreno-Garcia.

Carole Johnstone's fiction has appeared in numerous magazines and anthologies, published by ChiZine, PS Publishing, Night Shade Books, TTA Press, and Apex Book Company, among many others. In 2014, she won the British Fantasy Award for Best Short Story. Her work has been reprinted in various Best of anthologies, including a previous *Best Horror of the Year* and Salt Publishing's Best British Fantasy series.

Her 2014 novella, *Cold Turkey*, was published by TTA Press. She is presently at work on her second novel, while seeking fame and fortune with the first—but just can't seem to kick the short story habit.

More information on the author can be found at carolejohnstone.com.

"Departures," inspired by a not inconsiderable hatred of airport departure lounges (and was, in fact, begun in one), was originally published in her debut short story collection, *The Bright Day Is Done*.

Stephen Graham Jones is the author of fifteen novels and six short story collections. The most recent are *Not for Nothing*, *After the People Lights Have Gone Off*, and, with Paul Tremblay, *Floating Boy and the Girl Who Couldn't Fly*.

Jones has more than two hundred stories published, many reprinted in Best of the Year annuals. He's won the Texas Institute of Letters Award for fiction, the Independent Publishers Award for Multicultural Fiction, and an NEA fellowship in fiction. He teaches in the MFA programs at CU Boulder and UCR–Palm Desert.

He lives in Boulder, Colorado, with his wife and kids. For more information: demontheory.net or you can find him on Twitter: @SGJ72.

"Chapter Six" was originally published on *Tor.com*, June 11.

Caitlín R. Kiernan was recently hailed by the *New York Times* as "one of our essential authors of dark fiction." A two-time winner of both the World Fantasy and Bram Stoker Awards, she's published ten novels, including *The Red Tree* and *The Drowning Girl: A Memoir*. She is also the recipient of the

Locus and the James Tiptree, Jr. Awards. Her short fiction has been collected in thirteen volumes, including *Tales of Pain and Wonder*, *The Ammonite Violin & Others*, *A is for Alien*, and *The Ape's Wife and Other Stories.*

Subterranean Press has released a two-volume set collecting the "best" of her short fiction, *Two Worlds and In Between* and *Beneath an Oil-Dark Sea.* She is currently working on a screenplay and her next novel, *Interstate Love Song: Murder Ballads.*

"Interstate Love Song (Murder Ballad No. 8)" was originally published in *Sirenia Digest* 100.

⟜

John Langan is the author of two collections, *The Wide, Carnivorous Sky and Other Monstrous Geographies* (Hippocampus 2013) and *Mr. Gaunt and Other Uneasy Encounters* (Prime 2008), and a novel, *House of Windows* (Night Shade 2009). With Paul Tremblay, he co-edited *Creatures: Thirty Years of Monsters* (Prime 2011). One of the founders of the Shirley Jackson Award, he lives in upstate New York with his wife, younger son, and a houseful of animals.

"Ymir" was originally published in *The Children of Old Leech*, edited by Ross E. Lockhart and Justin Steele.

⟜

Alison Littlewood is the author of *A Cold Season*, published by Jo Fletcher Books. The novel was selected for the Richard and Judy Book Club, where it was described as "perfect reading for a dark winter's night." Her second novel, *Path of Needles*—a dark blend of fairy tales and crime fiction—was recently short-listed for a British Fantasy Award. Her third, *The Unquiet House*, is a ghost story set in the Yorkshire countryside. Alison's short stories have been picked for *The Best Horror of the Year Volume Four, Best British Horror*, and *The Mammoth Book of Best New Horror* anthologies, as well as *The Best British Fantasy 2013* and *The Mammoth Book of Best British Crime 10.* She lives in Yorkshire with her partner Fergus, in a house of creaking doors and crooked walls. Visit her at www.alisonlittlewood.co.uk.

"The Dog's Home" was originally published in *The Spectral Book of Horror Stories*, edited by Mark Morris.

⟜

Livia Llewellyn is a writer of horror, dark fantasy, and erotica, whose fiction has appeared in ChiZine, Subterranean, *Apex Magazine*, *Postscripts*, *Nightmare* Magazine, as well as numerous anthologies. Her first collection, *Engines of Desire: Tales of Love & Other Horrors*, was published in 2011 by Lethe Press, and received two Shirley Jackson Award nominations, for Best Collection, and Best Novelette (for "Omphalos"). Her story "Furnace" received a 2013 SJA nomination for Best Short Fiction. Her second collection will be published by Word Horde Press in 2016. You can find her online at liviallewellyn.com.

"Allochton" was originally published in *Letters to Lovecraft*, edited by Jesse Bullington.

⊸

Keris McDonald turned to horror writing during a miserable year as a library assistant in the south of England, but nowadays lives in a disappointingly pleasant part of North Yorkshire. Her short stories have appeared in three Ash Tree Press anthologies and the magazines *Weird Tales*, *Supernatural Tales*, and *All Hallows*, as well as the Hic Dragones collections *Impossible Spaces* and *Hauntings*.

Keris now spends most of her writing time under the name "Janine Ashbless," spinning stories of paranormal erotica and hot dark romance for publishers such as HarperCollins and Ebury/Random House. Her ninth novel, *Cover Him with Darkness*, an uncompromising tale of fallen angels and religious conspiracy, was published in 2014 by Cleis Press.

"The Coat off His Back" was originally published in *Terror Tales of Yorkshire*, edited by Paul Finch.

⊸

Garth Nix was born in Melbourne, Australia. A full-time writer since 2001, he has worked as a literary agent, marketing consultant, book editor, book publicist, book sales representative, bookseller, and as a part-time soldier in the Australian Army Reserve.

Nix's books include the award-winning fantasy novels *Sabriel*, *Lirael*, and *Abhorsen* and the science fiction novels *Shade's Children* and *A Confusion of Princes*. His fantasy novels for children include *The Ragwitch*; the six books of *The Seventh Tower* sequence; *The Keys to the Kingdom* series; and the *Troubletwisters* books (with Sean Williams).

More than five million copies of Nix's books have been sold around the world, his books have appeared on the bestseller lists of *The New York Times*, *Publishers Weekly*, *The Guardian*, and *The Australian*, and his work has been translated into forty languages. He lives in Sydney, Australia.

⊸o⊷

Robert Shearman has written five short story collections, and collectively they have won the World Fantasy Award, the Shirley Jackson Award, the Edge Hill Readers' Prize, and three British Fantasy Awards. He began his career in theater, both as playwright and director, and his work has won the *Sunday Times* Playwriting Award, the Sophie Winter Memorial Trust Award, and the Guinness Award for Ingenuity in association with the Royal National Theatre. His interactive series for BBC Radio Four, *The Chain Gang*, ran for three seasons and won two Sony Awards.

However, he may be best known as a writer for *Doctor Who*, reintroducing the Daleks for its BAFTA-winning first series in an episode nominated for a Hugo Award.

"It Flows from the Mouth" was originally published in *Shadows & Tall Trees 2014*, edited by Michael Kelly.

⊸o⊷

Angela Slatter is the author of the Aurealis Award-winning *The Girl with No Hands and Other Tales*, World Fantasy Award finalist *Sourdough and Other Stories*, Aurealis finalist *Midnight and Moonshine* (with Lisa L. Hannett), *Black-Winged Angels*, *The Bitterwood Bible and Other Recountings*, and *The Female Factory* (again with Hannett).

She's the first Australian to win a British Fantasy Award, holds an MA and a PhD in Creative Writing, is a graduate of the Clarion South and Tin House Summer Writers Workshops, and was an inaugural Queensland Writers Fellow. She blogs at www.angelaslatter.com.

"Winter Children" was originally published in *Far Voyager PS 32/33*, edited by Nick Gevers.

⊸o⊷

Lucy Taylor is the author of seven novels, including the Stoker Award-winning *The Safety of Unknown Cities*. Her most recent work includes the collection *Fatal Journeys* and the novelette chapbook *A Respite for the Dead.* Her story "In the Cave of the Delicate Singers" will appear in the June issue of Tor.com. An illustrated edition of *The Safety of Unknown Cities* will be published in fall 2015 by Overlook Connection Press.

Taylor lives in the high desert outside Santa Fe, New Mexico, and is at work on a collection of New Mexico-themed horror.

"Wingless Beasts" was originally published in the signed, limited edition of Taylor's collection *Fatal Journeys.*

⟜

Genevieve Valentine's first novel, *Mechanique: A Tale of the Circus Tresaulti,* won the 2012 Crawford Award. Her second novel is speakeasy fairy tale *The Girls at the Kingfisher Club.* Her third, *Persona,* is due from Saga Press in 2015. Her short fiction has been nominated for the World Fantasy Award and the Shirley Jackson Award, and her stories have appeared in several Best of the Year anthologies. Her nonfiction and reviews have appeared at NPR.org, *The AV Club*, *Strange Horizons*, *The Toast*, *LA Review of Books,* and others. She's currently the writer of DC's Catwoman.

"A Dweller in Amenty" was originally published in *Nightmare* #18, March.

⟜

Rio Youers is the British Fantasy Award-nominated author of *End Times* and *Old Man Scratch.* His short fiction has appeared in many notable anthologies, and his previous novel, *Westlake Soul,* was nominated for Canada's prestigious Sunburst Award. Rio lives in southwestern Ontario with his wife, Emily, and their children, Lily and Charlie.

"Outside Heavenly" was originally published in *The Spectral Book of Horror Stories*, edited by Mark Morris.

ACKNOWLEDGMENT IS MADE FOR REPRINTING THE FOLLOWING MATERIAL

"The Atlas of Hell" by Nathan Ballingrud. Copyright © 2014 by Nathan Ballingrud. First published in *Fearful Symmetries* edited by Ellen Datlow, ChiZine Publications. Reprinted with permission of the author.

"Winter Children" by Angela Slatter. Copyright © 2014 by Angela Slatter. First published in Far Voyager, PS 32/33 edited by Nick Gevers. Reprinted with permission of the author.

"A Dweller in Amenty" by Genevieve Valentine. Copyright © 2014 by Genevieve Valentine. First published in *Nightmare* #18, March. Reprinted with permission of the author.

"Outside Heavenly" by Rio Youers. Copyright © 2014 by Rio Youers. First published in *The Spectral Book of Horror Stories* edited by Mark Morris, Spectral Press. Reprinted with permission of the author.

"Shay Corsham Worsted" by Garth Nix. Copyright © 2014 by Garth Nix. First published in *Fearful Symmetries* edited by Ellen Datlow, ChiZine Publications. Reprinted with permission of the author.

"Tread Upon the Brittle Shell" by Rhoads Brazos. Copyright © 2014 by Rhoads Brazos. First published in *SQ Mag* Edition 14, May. Reprinted with permission of the author.

"Persistence of Vision" by Orrin Grey. Copyright © 2014 by Orrin Grey. First published in *Fractured: Tales of the Canadian Post-Apocalypse* edited by Silvia Moreno-Garcia, Exile Editions. Reprinted with permission of the author.

"It Flows from the Mouth" by Robert Shearman. Copyright © 2014 by Robert Shearman. First published in *Shadows & Tall Trees 2014* edited by Michael Kelly, Undertow Books. Reprinted with permission of the author.

"Wingless Beasts" by Lucy Taylor. Copyright © 2014 by Lucy Taylor. First published in *Fatal Journeys*, signed limited edition, Overlook Connection Press. Reprinted with permission of the author.

"Departures" by Carole Johnstone. Copyright © 2014 by Carole Johnstone. First published in *The Bright Day Is Done*, Gray Friar Press. Reprinted with permission of the author.

"Ymir" by John Langan. Copyright © 2014 by John Langan. First published in *The Children of Old Leech* edited by Ross E. Lockhart and Justin Steele, Word Horde. Reprinted with permission of the author.

"Plink" by Kurt Dinan. Copyright © 2014 by Kurt Dinan. First published in *Far Voyager, PS 32/33* edited by Nick Gevers. Reprinted with permission of the author.

"Nigredo" by Cody Goodfellow. Copyright © 2014 by Cody Goodfellow. First published in *In the Court of the Yellow King* edited by Glynn Owen Barrass, Celaeno Press. Reprinted with permission of the author.

ABOUT THE EDITOR

Ellen Datlow has been editing science fiction, fantasy, and horror short fiction for over thirty years. She currently acquires short fiction for Tor.com. In addition, she has edited more than fifty science fiction, fantasy, and horror anthologies, including *Lovecraft's Monsters, Fearful Symmetries, Nightmare Carnival, The Cutting Room*, the *Women Destroy Horror* issue of *Nightmare* Magazine, and *The Doll Collection.*

She's won multiple World Fantasy Awards, Locus Awards, Hugo Awards, Stoker Awards, International Horror Guild Awards, Shirley Jackson Awards, and the 2012 Il Posto Nero Black Spot Award for Excellence as Best Foreign Editor. Datlow was named recipient of the 2007 Karl Edward Wagner Award, given at the British Fantasy Convention for "outstanding contribution to the genre," and was honored with the Life Achievement Award given by the Horror Writers Association, in acknowledgment of superior achievement over an entire career, and the Life Achievement Award by the World Fantasy Convention.

She lives in New York and co-hosts the monthly Fantastic Fiction Reading Series at KGB Bar. More information can be found at www.datlow.com, on Facebook, and on Twitter as @EllenDatlow.